# Eden's Gate

## Book I: The Reborn

A LitRPG Adventure

Edward Brody

Looking for perfect heroes on a quest to destroy evil?
That isn't this story.

Looking for an overpowered character or social butterfly
who always makes righteous decisions?
You won't find him here.

*Eden's Gate: The Reborn* is a story of a flawed, average
guy and his growth in a new, mysterious world. He'll
make some bad choices along the way, and he'll fail a lot
of the time. But in the end, he'll change and grow as a
person just as much as he grows in power.

There are unique game rules he must follow, leveling,
quests, loot and consequences for every action.

Thanks for reading, and I hope you enjoy ride.

# CONTENTS

*"Humans are inherently flawed creatures. They assume things to be true that aren't there. They project their own life experience over new situations without giving much thought to the idea that maybe they could be wrong.*

*Maybe they could be completely wrong."*

*-Sword & Scale*

# Chapter 1

*Release Day (Earth)*

"You're on in 5 minutes," a petite woman dressed in a sleek black skirt suit said.

"Thanks, Kendra," Dr. Rupert Winston replied. He waved a dismissive hand, and she disappeared behind his dressing room door.

He let out an audible sigh as he savored the last few minutes that he would enjoy inside the tiny room—one of the last few minutes that he'd enjoy on this world even—if everything went to plan.

He stood from his dressing room chair and combed back what was left of his thinning, gray hair. He straightened his black turtleneck and made sure that it was neatly tucked deep inside his matching black slacks.

If Steve Jobs could see him now, he wondered. If the Bitcoin inventors, smartphone giants, and VR pioneers had any idea how far things would come in a few short decades.

He swallowed hard as he stared at himself in the mirror, and for a brief moment, he wrestled with the decision he was about to make. He could still turn back. A part of him told him that it was wrong, immoral, maybe even sinister to do what he was about to do, but another part of him danced with joy at the gift that he was about to unleash.

He shook his head from side to side and smiled, brushing away his fleeting doubts. It was a gift, indeed. *A world.* A new world that was far superior to the one that he was standing in. No one would understand it now, but eventually, they'd come around and see why he had to do things this way.

His watch beeped a high-pitched sound a few times, signaling that his time was up, and he reached for the door and stepped outside. Production staff lined the hallway leading to the stage, all staring hard at him, waiting for any last-minute instructions.

None came as he passed them without saying a word.

His assistant VP, Aaron, a small man wearing a white dress shirt and glasses was already standing at the center of his stage with his hands behind his back. "Please welcome the CEO and founder of Nexicon Inc., Dr. Rupert Winston!"

Dr. Winston raised his hand high in the air as he stepped onto the brightly lit stage, and the crowd of thousands stood from their seats and cheered. The spotlights followed Rupert's every move as he crossed to take the other man's position, and behind him was a large glass monitor that covered the entire wall. In the center of the display was the Nexicon logo—a pear with a cute worm dangling out of its side.

"Thank you. Thank you," he said as he waved his hand in a downward motion, trying to get everyone to settle down and sit back in their chairs. He smiled and repeated it a few times until the room grew silent and everyone gave their full attention.

Rupert folded his hands together and pushed his knuckles up under his chin. He frowned and looked to the ground before asking, "What is life?" His words caught his hidden mic and echoed through the venue. He let go of his hands and pinched himself. "If you can feel pain, is that life? If you can love, hate, smell and taste, is that life? If you can see, hear, feel and even kill, is that life?" He tilted his head to the side, smirked, and nodded lightly. "I think so."

The crowd was wide-eyed and glued to his every word.

"Ladies and gentlemen, I give you life! I give you Eden's Gate!" Dr. Winston stepped sideways and motioned his hand toward the monitor.

The Nexicon logo disappeared, and adventurous music roared through the building. The screen flashed to the bird's-eye image of a lush land with dense foliage, tall hills, and a raging river. The camera panned forward then spun around, revealing a pale, human-like creature running out of the jungle and jumping off a cliff and into a pool of water below. The image flashed to a man standing in a dark room, pounding a hammer across the hot iron of a blade.

"Be anyone. Do anything," Rupert said, his voice deep, harsh.

The image switched to a barren desert view, then to an image of a large wooden ship lumbering through the ocean, then to a land frozen over by ice, burly wolves running through the snow. A creature flew by on what appeared to be a giant eagle.

"Go anywhere."

The screen went black, and the sound of steel piercing flesh rippled through the speakers. An image of a hand pulling a sword from a fallen body appeared. The hand twisted the sword as if the person holding it off-screen was inspecting the blood, but then there was rattling explosion, and the body of the hand flew forward and erupted in strange, blue-hued flames. And slowly so did the rest of the image. In the middle of the flames the words "Eden's Gate" appeared, and the music faded off into silence.

"Carve your destiny. Kick some ass. Live a new life however you see fit!"

The crowd practically leapt out of their chairs as they started clapping and cheering at the display.

Dr. Winston raised his fist and spoke loudly over the cheers. "Today we celebrate the launch of the first fully-immersive, full-world, virtual MMO! This is unlike anything you've ever experienced before." He walked across the stage and gestured with his hands as he spoke. "You will feel everything you touch, taste everything you eat. You'll grow in expertise, gather loot and experience magic like you've only dreamed. Your full consciousness will actually live inside of Eden's Gate!"

The cheering started to die down as people listened, many of them practically salivating at the mouth for more. Dr. Winston waved his hand back to the display, and the burning image was replaced with a large number 5,300,670 on a black background that was increasing each second—5,300,788—5,300,801.

"This is only day one, and already we have over 5 million people logged in, starting their journey in this new, incredible world." Rupert smirked. "I expect after today, that number will only increase."

*If they only knew.*

"How big is the game exactly?!" a reporter near the front yelled out at him.

Dr. Winston seemed startled by the sudden question but let the interruption slide, since he was about to begin the Q&A segment anyway.

"Eden's Gate is roughly 10 times the size of Earth. There's so much content that it would take multiple lifetimes to explore the entire…'game'." He was hesitant to call his creation a game. It was far, far more than that.

"This technology which… takes over your consciousness. How do we know it's safe?" another reporter asked.

"I guess you'll have to trust me on that one." He swallowed hard and smiled. Game? Safe? Maybe a Q&A segment wasn't the best idea. "I think we should just go ahead and get to the demonstration."

One of the production staff wheeled out a rolling bed, and resting on top of the bed was one of Nexicon's patented VR machines, designed to work exclusively with Eden's Gate. Dr. Winston's assistant VP came back on stage and started up a laptop that he placed on a nearby pedestal and sat down on a stool.

The doctor lifted the VR machine—a thick white and gold front visor with a black strap to wrap around the back of the head. "There are no screens inside our machine. When you place the Nexicon VR system on your head, a gentle laser is beamed into your retina, and pulse-neuro waves send and receive data from your brain. Once inside, you will be fully immersed. *Fully*," he stressed.

He took a deep breath and raised his finger to Aaron. He had trusted him with more knowledge about Nexicon's properties than anyone else, but not even he knew what was about to happen. Aaron had only been instructed to launch the demo mode of the game so everyone could watch Dr. Winston play his character in Eden's Gate, but he had no idea that Dr. Winston had programmed 'demo mode' to kill off everyone currently logged into the game, along with Dr. Winston himself.

It had been Dr. Winston's life work to create a true virtual reality, and after decades of laboring, he had finally realized his dream when he completed Eden's Gate. But Eden's Gate exceeded his expectations, turned out so lifelike, so much realer than he ever imagined—he couldn't just let it be a game. It should be *respected* as a real world, he thought—a place that people could go and truly live their lives. And the only way to keep the game as real as possible was to close any and all exit paths. If people could just log in and log out it would always be a simple escape fantasy.

The 5,000,000+ people who were already logged in weren't really dying, he thought. They were just coming over to another plane of existence—a better one even. Immortalized. And with that many people consciously living in Eden's Gate, who would ever dare to try turning it off? Essentially, it would go on forever. *He* would go on forever.

Dr. Winston climbed onto the bed and placed the machine on his head. "Now I'm going to login," he said loudly to the crowd. His heart was racing. He was sure that he would be safe once his consciousness was transported to Eden's Gate, but his body hadn't ever died before—at least not on Earth. The idea that something could go wrong was a bit frightening even to him. There was always the possibility he'd made a miscalculation. He lowered his head on the pillow, took a deep breath and swallowed his worries before powering the VR headset on.

A red light flashed across the top of the visor, and the laser shot into Dr. Winston's eye. Immediately, he felt disconnected from his frame of existence.

His body lay immobile.

Aaron glanced over to the bed, and when the red light flashing across the top of Dr. Winston's visor turned green, he looked up at the crowd. "Looks like he's already in," he said stridently. "Since the Nexicon VR is designed solely to work with Eden's gate, the transfer into the virtual world is extremely quick!"

He looked back down at his computer and keyed in the sequence to launch demo mode.

There was a loud "Zrrrrrrp!" noise that buzzed out of the doctor's visor, and his body flinched violently. Suddenly, the visor powered down, and Dr. Winston's body lay there with his arm dangling like a wet noodle.

"Whoa, Whoa, Whoa!" Aaron said and his stool tipped over as he shot to his feet. His face twisted in confusion as he looked back to the monitor behind him—It was completely black. And despite the visor being off, Dr. Winston wasn't moving at all.

Two of the production assistants rushed out on the stage while Aaron pulled the visor off and started testing Dr. Winston's vitals. The crowd was standing wide-eyed, whispering, some grabbing their chest in panic.

"Medic! We need a medic!" Aaron yelled.

Before anything else could happen, the panel on the wall suddenly lit up, and standing there on the screen was Dr. Winston himself. He wasn't wearing a turtleneck anymore but instead wore a long, brown robe. He was standing on the balcony of what may have been a castle, and behind him were two large double doors and a room filled with a desk and bookshelves filled with hundreds, if not thousands of books. His face was practically the same, but he looked a little younger and his hair was thicker and had lost most of its gray.

The whole venue immediately went silent and stared at the inconceivable visage.

"Well, there you have it," Dr. Winston said. "I suppose today marks me as the biggest mass murderer in Earth's history." He sighed nonchalantly. "To cut a long story short, everyone who was plugged into Eden's Gate is now, or should be dead—at least in the traditional sense, they're dead. Their consciousness lives on in Eden's Gate, and in many ways, I have made them immortal."

There was a pause of a few seconds in which the venue erupted in chatter, some chuckling, assuming it was a silly launch day gimmick and some audibly holding their breath, but everyone quieted again when the doctor spoke.

"More than 5 million people didn't have a choice, but now you do. Throw on a Nexicon VR, and you too can live your life in Eden's Gate—No more 9 to 5s and overpriced mortgages. No more Democrats and Republicans. No more bullshit. A new, magical world where your life has an unlimited number of paths. A world larger and more exciting than Earth could ever be. But just be aware that you can't turn back." The doctor smiled one last time. "Good luck."

The screen went blank, and Dr. Rupert Winston's body still lay there on the bed, unmoving.

"Is this some sort of publicity stunt?" one of the reporters yelled out.

Aaron just shook his head in confusion and turned back towards his computer, trying to figure out what was going on.

One of the production staffers dialed 911 while Kendra, second only to Aaron at Nexicon, rushed to Aaron's side. "What the fuck is this? Millions of people around the world are watching this keynote."

"I… I don't know?" he replied.

Kendra looked up to the guests. People had their phones out and were making calls. Some were taking videos of the scene. The chatter was growing almost deafening.

"Well, can you fix it? Whatever this is… I mean… He's not really in there, right?"

Aaron shook his head as he pulled up the Eden's Gate code. A dizzying string of letters, numbers, and symbols fell across his screen. "It looks like he's encrypted all the source code without telling anyone. I can't do anything. I wouldn't even know what to do if I could."

"You're telling me you can't do *anything*?"

Aaron launched the administration terminal and was prompted for a passcode. "No one can do anything without Dr. Winston's password." Aaron swallowed and pulled up the server stats. 5,312,372 people were shown as logged in, and that number wasn't changing anymore.

"Oh my god…" Kendra muttered and stared at the number with a slack jaw. "What in the hell has he done?"

# Chapter 2

*Release Day (Earth)*

"Oh my god!" I screamed. "Are you fucking kidding me?!" I tore my headphones off and rubbed my fingers through my short, tangled brown hair as I looked at the giant "DEFEAT" staring back at me on my computer screen. I had been playing *Battle League*, a multiplayer online battle arena, and finished the game with 20 kills and 2 deaths, yet my team of 5 other random people still managed to make me lose.

*GG*, one of my teammates wrote in the after-battle chat.

I leaned over towards my mic. "Yeah, good fucking game, deadweights. I couldn't carry you if I tried."

I heard the scuffle of someone else's mic. "Fuck you, asshole! We lost because you were too busy trying to solo the whole fucking match."

*Knock, knock, knock.*

I shook my head and quickly closed out of Battle League. Idiots. I had enough of dealing with the toxic players in that game for a day even if someone hadn't just knocked on my door. "Just a minute!" I yelled.

I grabbed the crutch leaning against my computer desk and snugged it up under my left armpit as I stood from my chair. It had been about a week since Matt Finley, my co-worker at BestFoods decided that it would be a good idea to drop a tall pallet of canned food on my foot while I was stocking the end of an aisle. He claimed he didn't see me, of course.

An entire 5'10" and 155-pound human being gone unseen in a brightly lit supermarket.

I don't know how that could happen, but then again, I was used to going unnoticed. My dad bounced when I was young—who knows where that asshole went—and my mom was in and out of drug rehab, leaving me to be raised by my widowed grandma. Grans was already in the early stages of dementia when I moved in with her, and shortly after my 18th birthday, she had to be moved into a caretaking facility and couldn't even recognize me anymore.

School—same story. I had a pretty decent run right up until High School, but those last 4 years I could have been a ghost. I was never invited to parties, never asked to hang out after class, and when there was a group assignment, my anxiety ran high because I was most likely to be the one left without a group.

If invisibility were a skill, I was pretty damn good at it.

But hey, no big deal. I didn't spend my nights crying myself to sleep over the shitty hand I was dealt. After high school, I buckled down, got my own place and a job at the local food store where I had been working for the past 3 years. It paid the bills, and I made a few acquaintances who were good for a nice talk during our lunch break. I wouldn't consider them 'friends', but for the most part, I liked keeping to myself anyway. Gaming was my passion, and I would rather stay at home going on a dungeon crawl or working on my rank in arena-based games.

I reached for the doorknob of my tiny studio apartment, thinking that it was probably my annoying landlord stopping by as he did every week to 'check to make sure the fire detector was working,' when in reality, he just wanted to make sure I hadn't damaged anything inside his property.

As if his 100 square-foot box was worth anything.

"Hey babe!" A pair of shiny blue eyes and a bright smile beamed at me when I opened the door.

"Rachel?" I limped forward and pulled her into a hug with my one free arm. While we stood there, locked together in the doorway, I looked up and saw a tiny spider building a web right above the entryway which caused me to jerk back erratically and almost lose balance on my crutch.

"What is it?" Rachel asked with wide, worried eyes.

"A fucking spider behind you."

Rachel turned and looked up at the tiny creature. "It's just a fucking baby."

"Bleh," I spat and shook my body in disgust. I wasn't afraid of much of anything in the world, but spiders were my bane. I didn't want to see or have a spider of any size or shape anywhere near me. "Why didn't you call?"

"I wanted to surprise you," she said.

Did I say I liked keeping to myself? That was true, except when I was spending time with my girlfriend. I had met Rachel about 6 months earlier via an online gaming forum, and as we got to talking, I found out that she lived less than a 10-minute drive from me. I'm not sure what she saw in me—I wasn't exactly a lady's man, and if anything she was out of my league—but within a month we had met up and started dating.

So at least I had one good thing going for me.

I limped aside and eyed a large, heavy-looking brown bag she was carrying as she made her way inside my room. "What's in the bag?"

"I told you, it's a surprise." She pushed a piece of her long, sandy blonde hair back behind her ear and sat down on my bed. She had a nice frame—not too skinny, and not too thick—and her 5'4" stature was a perfect 'fit' for me—if you know what I mean… "How's your foot?"

"It still pretty achy," I said. I limped closer to her and used my crutch to point towards her bag. "Don't leave me hanging."

She rolled her eyes and lifted the bag. "Okay, well I thought this might cheer you up while you're recovering." As soon as she slid the first brown box out of the bag, I noticed the Nexicon logo immediately.

"You're kidding me, right?"

"One for me," she cooed and pulled out a second matching box. "And one for you."

I dropped my crutch and hopped as fast as I could to sit on the bed beside her. I picked up one of the Nexicon boxes and stared in awe at the pear/worm etching on the front. "You got *two* on launch day? These are over a grand a piece. How did you—?"

"I had a little bit of savings, and I knew your money was tight." She poked her index finger in my shoulder. "Plus you're always going on and on about how Eden's Gate is the next big step in gaming."

"You have no fucking idea…"

I had been following Eden's Gate since the hype broke online about 3 years earlier. The Nexicon CEO had written in a blog post that he was working on a Virtual MMO that would change our perception of gaming forever; a game in which the user's consciousness would somehow communicate with the game world and provide a lifelike experience. No screenshots or videos of the game were ever released, but no one had any right to doubt him. Hardware that Nexicon released was always cutting edge, and their software always blew away the competition. People would buy a shitmobile if it had the Nexicon logo on it.

Then there was a leaker who broke the Eden's Gate NDA (non-disclosure agreement), a beta tester who went by the name darkknight35. He wrote in a Reddit post about his experience during testing and claimed that he felt like he was *really* in the game, that NPCs (non-player characters) looked and acted like real people, that it was the best gaming experience he had ever had even though they wouldn't allow him past the tutorial section.

His post was deleted within hours, and the guy was never heard from again, but that was enough to fuel whole online communities of people speculating what the Nexicon VR could really do. The only official facts released by Nexicon VR were that it was preloaded with a fantasy MMO with a world much larger than Earth. And the name of course—Eden's Gate.

She shoved me hard in the shoulder and smirked. "I know just as much about it as you."

I smiled, sat the box down, and pulled her into a huge hug. "You're the best. This is too much."

She pulled away from the hug and pointed a finger at my nose. "We're doing this on one condition, okay?"

"Yeah?" I lifted an eyebrow.

"As soon as your foot is better, I want you to get out of your room. Go out and make some real friends. We can go together even."

I huffed and rolled my eyes. "This again? I told you that you're all I need. What do you want me to do? Be one of those guys who sits in a bar all day watching sports, scratching his nuts and talking about car parts with other nut scratchers? I'm not into all of that—"

"Gunnar, it's just not normal to stay in your room all day playing games. You're missing out on a lot of—"

"'Normal' is a subjective word. I have no interest in being like everyone else," I interrupted. "You knew who I was when you met me."

Rachel sighed. "Just try… All I'm asking is for you to give it a chance. People aren't so bad if you give them a chance."

I pursed my lips together and frowned, thinking of all the times when people let me down. I was perfectly happy doing things on my own and being a lone wolf.

"I just bought you a Nexicon VR, and you're brooding over me asking you a little favor?" She made a cute, kissy face and started talking to me in a baby voice. "Just one little favor?"

She had a point; it was one hell of a gift. I would've never been able to afford a Nexicon VR on my BestFoods salary. I owed her, big time. "Fine, fine," I said with a slight nod.

She threw an arm around my neck and kissed me on the cheek. "Thanks, babe. Now let's see what this Eden-thing is all about."

I could hardly contain my excitement as we started unboxing the Nexicon headsets. "You know, I read everyone spawns in a random place, right? Even if we both log in together, we could be thousands of miles apart."

Rachel threw a piece of Styrofoam from the box aside and shrugged. "I know, but we'll figure it out. When we log out, we'll compare notes and start working our way towards each other next time we login."

I lifted the thick, white visor from its box and turned it on each side, admiring the gold etching and high quality craftsmanship. On the edge were two buttons: Battery and Power. I clicked the Battery button and the visor lit up, showing a full bar of green. "This is awesome. I can't believe we get to play on launch day." Just holding such an incredible piece of technology in my hands made my heart race.

There was a small piece of paper inside of the box:

> **Warning:** *Place the visor over your head and power it on only when you are in a secure and safe area. Your body will be in an unresponsive state until you are completely logged out of the system. Use at your own risk.*

Rachel dropped her box and placed her headset over her head, working hard to make sure her strap was adjusted properly. "Come on," she said. "Let's get in! Let's get in!" She scooted to the far side of my bed and lay down as I placed my visor on my head and slid in beside her.

With the power off, there was nothing but dark inside the Nexicon VR. "I've got my visor on. You ready?"

Her hand reached over and grabbed on to mine. "I'm ready. 1…"

I placed my hand on the power button and waited for her to finish counting down.

"2…"

"Wait!" I shouted.

"Yeah?"

"How long should we play 'til we log out? I don't want you doing anything weird to me while I'm in game."

Rachel giggled. "Let's say about half an hour for our first run?"

"Alright." I squeezed her hand tighter.

"3!"

I pressed the power button and white light flashed in front of my eyes, then black. Within a second, I could no longer feel Rachel's hand.

# Chapter 3

*01/01/0001*                    ✴

*Welcome to your new life.*
*Welcome to Eden's Gate.*

I felt weightless as I watched the introduction screen flash before my eyes, and I sensed a prickly sensation as each part of my body slowly became tangible. The darkness slowly began to dissolve, and I blinked, and then again until I could see everything around me.

I was standing on a ground made of broken cobblestone and grass. Directly in front of me was a stone fence with an open, arched gate that appeared to lead off to a long dirt path and a forest far into the distance.

I looked down to my hands and squeezed them tightly then relaxed them. They looked exactly like my real hands—in fact, I couldn't tell the difference no matter how hard I tried. I was wearing a pair of plain black cotton pants that stopped at the knee, brown woven shoes, and a white cotton vest that was cut off at the shoulders. My crutch was missing, and my foot was no longer broken, but otherwise my body felt exactly the same. I looked like the fashion police was about to arrest me at any moment, but I felt healthier than I had my entire life.

I took a deep breath, and the air was light and pure. Birds were chirping in the distance. I really was in another world.

"Look lively!" a husky voice shouted from behind me.

I whipped myself around and watched as a tall man with thick gray hair and beard marched quickly down a tall set of cobblestone steps. He was wearing a chainmail vest and plate leggings, a long sword draped at his side. At the top of the steps was a temple of some sort with open walls and pillars on each of its four corners. Off to the side was a small, cobblestone building with a single brown door.

I took a couple steps back as he approached.

"Welcome to Eden's Gate, stranger. Have you a name?" the man asked when I reached the base of the steps.

A small semi-transparent window appeared in front of me.

*Please select your name by speaking it.*

I spent a moment to think about whether to use a pseudonym or not, but with the old man staring daggers at me, I figured I'd go with what I knew best. "Gunnar…" I said. "My name is Gunnar Long."

The window disappeared.

"A pleasure to meet you Gunnar Long."

"And you are?"

"Trainer." The man smiled. "The name's Trainer."

"Just Trainer?"

"I'm afraid that's the only name I was given."

"Okay, nice to meet you," I said, shrugging. I turned my head from side to side. "Where exactly am I?"

"You're in the instanced tutorial of Eden's Gate."

"Instanced? I thought there were no instances in this game?"

"Only the tutorial is instanced. Gotta make sure everyone knows basic functions before they begin their journey into the unknown. But don't worry, this shouldn't take long. Once you step through that gate," he said, indicating the front gate behind me, "you'll never step foot into this tutorial again."

"Okay." I nodded. "Got it."

"How old are you, Gunnar?"

*Please select your age by speaking it.*

"I'm 21," I replied.

"Very well. You're old enough to continue. Go ahead and check your status screen to confirm your details."

I lifted my hands and looked at my palms, not sure what I was looking for. "How do I do that?"

"Hmph," Trainer grunted. "Just think about your status screen appearing in front of you or you can say 'show status screen,' if that's easier for you."

I pressed my lips tight and imagined a status screen appearing before me. To my surprise, it materialized with very little effort.

## GUNNAR LONG

| | |
|---|---|
| Race: | Human |
| Level: | 1 (Progression 0%) |
| Title: | None |
| Health/Mana/Stamina: | 100/100/100 |
| Strength: | 10 |
| Dexterity: | 10 |
| Intelligence: | 10 |
| Vitality: | 10 |
| Wisdom: | 10 |
| Willpower: | 10 |
| Charisma: | 10 |
| AR Rating: | 0 |
| Resists: | |
| | None |
| Traits: | |
| | None |
| Primary Skills | |
| | None |
| Combat Skills: | |
| | None |
| Magic Skills: | |
| | None |

"I guess it all seems right," I said as the screen disappeared from my sight.

"Very well. For your first lesson…" The old man kicked out a plated boot and connected with me directly in my chest.

The blow was hard, unexpected, and I jolted backwards, tumbling roughly on the uneven cobblestones. Fire ripped through my chest as I struggled for air, and the uneven stones below me jutted against my skin. It was supposed to be a game, but the pain damn-well felt a little too much like real life. What the hell? I looked down at my palms and noticed that they were scraped and blistered from the fall.

I coughed hard, trying to catch my breath. "Why'd you do that?" I sputtered.

The man paced forward and offered his hand to which I accepted. "The first lesson is to know that while Eden's Gate may often seem beautiful and friendly, pain and death can come from unexpected places. Always be on your guard, Gunnar."

"Well, fuck," I spat. "You could've just said it."

I noticed that in the top left corner of my vision, three bars had appeared. The first was red, the center was blue, and the last one was green. The red bar was missing around 40% of its length, and I had played enough games to know that the bars signified my health, mana, and stamina. Another two kicks from the old man, and I'd be dead before I even started.

"Shall we try again?" Trainer asked. "Lesson number one is…" He kicked out his foot, but this time I was more aware of what was coming. As he reared back and his iron toe came lashing towards me, I sidestepped and shifted towards the right, not allowing any contact.

A system alert appeared at the bottom of my screen, and the sound of drums echoed around me.

> *Advancement! You have learned the skill:*
> **Dodge**. *Why mitigate damage when you can*
> *avoid it altogether? Dodge is linked to the*
> *base stat Dexterity. Increase your Dexterity*
> *to increase your chances to Dodge.*

"Excellent, Gunnar. You're catching on quickly." The man turned away from me and started walking up the stairs. "Follow along now."

I followed him up the flight of stairs and noticed that my health bar wasn't replenishing right away. "How do I heal myself from the damage I took from you?"

"There are several ways you can heal yourself, Gunnar. Magic based healing from a spell or a magical item, physical healing from potions, salves and bandages, or you can simply let your wounds heal over time. Sleeping, eating and meditating accelerate the natural healing process."

"Do you have anything I can use? My hands are killing me."

"Such is life," Trainer said. "One of the purposes of this tutorial is to teach you that Eden's Gate is not just game. It's a world filled with both pain and pleasure. But do not fret—you will be healed of your training wounds automatically when you're transferred to the main world."

"Not just a game? Yeah, okay," I replied. I had to admit that the world didn't feel at all like a game—aside from the prompts and screens. My hands were *really* throbbing, and Trainer's AI (artificial intelligence) seemed especially sophisticated. If I didn't know any better, I wouldn't be able to tell him from a real person. But I wasn't stupid. No matter how real everything felt, I was still logged into a game, and I'd eventually have to log back out to go on with my real life.

At the top of the stairs and inside the temple area was a large table with a small dagger resting on top and a large pile of crinkled up, white papers were sitting off to the side.

"I'm sure you've noticed by now that you're a level 1 with only the most basic stats. As you earn experience, you'll gain levels which will increase your health, mana, and stamina pools. You'll also receive 3 attribute points per level that you can allocate to any stats you choose. Skills can only be increased by exercising them throughout the world or through special circumstances, but you'll also receive one free increase of your choice each time you level. Any questions?"

I scratched my head and visualized my stats screen again, causing it to instantly appear in front of me. I had been gaming long enough that I had a good idea of how most of them worked... Strength, Intelligence, and Stamina were pretty standard. But the others always had different meanings depending on the game I played.

"What's vitality for?"

"Vitality increases your natural health and stamina regeneration and ability to recover from effects such as poisons and sickness among other things."

"Wisdom?"

"Increases your mana regeneration rate among other things."

"Willpower?"

"A high willpower is just that. How willing are you to fight through the pain? How stable will you be when you're on your last drop of health, mana or stamina? How willing are you—"

"I've got it..." I interrupted.

Trainer cleared his throat. "In most cases, you can focus on a particular statistic or skill to get more detailed information."

"What's the difference between traits and skills?"

"Traits are important characteristics you may acquire, whether they be positive or negative. Skills are your abilities. It's difficult to explain, but I'm sure you'll understand as you continue on your journey."

"Okay." I shrugged and let the status screen disappear.

"Go ahead and grab the dagger when you're ready to continue," Trainer said.

I did as he instructed, and another alert appeared in the bottom left of my screen.

> *You've received:* **Copper Training Dagger***.*
> *1-4 Attack Damage. Durability: 10/10.*
> *Quality: Average. Rarity: Common. Weight:*
> *0.2 kg*

I rubbed my finger against the blade. The edges were a bit dull, and altogether it looked pretty unremarkable, but it was sharp enough to hurt something and definitely felt real.

"Now let's give it a whirl," Trainer said. He closed his eyes and started mumbling something.

"Give it a whirl against what?"

Trainer opened his eyes and lifted his hand towards the pile of crumpled paper on the ground. "Against that."

I felt a light breeze as the small pieces quickly started stacking together, one on top of another. Crinkled paper legs were soon visible, and then a paper torso, and finally crinkled paper arms and legs. The thin, paper effigy that appeared tilted its head to the side and rattled as it treaded toward me.

"Wow! That's freaking awesome!" I blurted.

"Look lively!" Trainer said, his words a reminder of the pain I felt when I got a boot to my chest. I wasn't sure what his paper man was capable of, but I didn't want to find out.

I squeezed the hilt of the dagger with my right hand and squared off before the paper effigy was right on top of me. It swung its arm at my head surprisingly slow, and I easily dodged its attack. Again, it swung its other arm, and this time, I whipped the dagger upwards, connecting with the base what would have been its tricep.

The effigy looked down as the tiny papers of its arm tumbled to the ground, but it didn't make a sound. It just turned back to me and started swinging its one remaining arm, stepping towards me each time I backed away.

I felt a bit dizzy all of a sudden and paused to grab my head… It was if something important happened far, far away. I couldn't pinpoint what it was, but I figured that perhaps the VR headset was acting up. It was a brand-new system on launch day after all. I shook my head and the cobwebs subsided.

The effigy raised its fist as high as it could and slammed it down towards me, but I rolled out of the way and ran. I was faster than the effigy—much faster—and I easily found its back. I flipped the dagger in my hand, and thrust the point of the blade a few inches above the effigy's waist, and immediately all the paper tumbled quietly to the ground.

> *You've gained 10 XP!*
>
> *Advancement! You have learned the skill: Small Blades. A wise woman said, "It's not the size of the tool that matters. It's the… you know." Small Blades is linked the base stat Dexterity. Increase your Dexterity to increase your affinity with Small Blades.*
>
> *Advancement! You have learned the skill:* **Backstab**. *Strike swiftly and precisely. A well-placed tip can down even the largest of foes. Backstab is linked the base stat Dexterity. Increase your Dexterity to increase your damage with Backstab. 100% critical chance for surprise attacks.*

"Well done, Gunnar," Trainer said. "Well done."

I smirked and flipped the dagger in my hand. My confidence was already starting to grow, despite only defeating my first, very weak enemy. The game was already proving to be fun and it was so damn realistic. I couldn't get over how much I was loving it already.

"I think that just about wraps up—"

Whatever Trainer was telling me was cut off by an odd zipping sound, and everything seemed to pause around me. A large, semitransparent window jumped in front of my eyes.

*||System Wide Broadcast||*

The text faded, and in its place was the vivid image of a man I recognized immediately as the CEO of Nexicon Inc. He had been all over business and technology websites and television, so anyone would recognize him—even if he happened to be covered in a long, brown robe from the neck down and looked slightly younger than I remembered. In his holographic image, he was sitting in a large wooden desk with books lining the walls behind him.

"Greetings players… or should I rather say, Eden's Gate residents," he began. "Thank you so much for being early adopters of the Nexicon VR. Today you've been given a gift. You've been given the chance to live your life in a wonderful world filled with magic and adventure." He cleared his throat and his eyes darted to the desk and back up again. His voice turned flat. "Your bodies are dead, and you no longer exist outside of this world."

"What?" I voiced out loud and couldn't help but smirk. "What is this guy smokin'?"

"As of a few minutes ago, everyone plugged into the Nexicon VR has the chance to live forever. As you may already know, you can die in Eden's Gate, but if do, you'll respawn wherever you were bound with some penalties. Immortality may be scary to some of you and exciting to others, but rest assured that I did think ahead for every circumstance.

"While you can live a very long and fruitful life here on Eden's Gate, if you ever actually wish to truly die, simply open up your settings and toggle aging to 'on'. You'll grow old similar to the way you would on Earth and eventually die of natural causes. Alternatively, there is one area in Eden's Gate where permadeath has been enabled." The camera panned out and showed an area of land that was covered in dark soil, barren trees, and a castle dangling on the side of a large mountain cliff before panning back in to Rupert Winston's face. "If you ever wish to cease existing, a death in The Mastalands is final. I'd recommend everyone who wants to continue living, avoid coming here."

Rupert Winston sighed. "Part of me wants to apologize for bringing you here without your permission, but another part of me knows that no life on Earth could ever rival the experience you'll have here. I'm certain that many others will log in for the same chance that you already have." He stood from his desk and placed his hands flat as he leaned forward, a cocky smirk on his face. "Welcome to Eden's Gate. Welcome to your new life."

The image flashed away, and I was left standing there with my jaw slack. "What the fuck?" I whispered to myself.

"Gunnar?"

I turned around to see Trainer smiling at me. "That about wraps things up."

"What the hell did that message mean?!" I snapped.

Trainer creased his brow. "What message?"

"That freakin' system message that just popped up. The guy in the robe!"

"I didn't see anything." He looked clueless.

I snapped my lips together and gritted my teeth. I took a deep breath and focused on the idea of my settings window opening up, and just like my status page, a settings window appeared. I paid no attention to any of options other than 'Logoff' button listed at the bottom of the menu and the counter at the top that said "**Playtime: 00:32**". I had been in the game just a little more than thirty minutes and Rachel was probably logging out now if she hadn't already.

I tried to will myself to logoff and then tried to press the translucent button with my finger, but nothing happened either time.

"Logoff!" I said loudly. "Sign out! End game! Shutdown! Get me the fuck out of here!"

Nothing happened no matter what I said.

"What in the world are you yapping about, Gunnar?" Trainer asked.

"I'm trying to exit this damned game," I replied.

"Exit what?" Trainer looked genuinely confused. "I told you that Eden's Gate isn't just a game. Gunnar, this is your home now."

# Chapter 4

*01/01/0001*

"You can't just stay in the tutorial," Trainer said.

I had been sitting on the stairs of the temple trying to figure out a way to log out for the past 15 minutes. Nothing seemed to work. "Maybe if you'd just tell me how to get out of here…" I grumbled.

"The way forward is through the gate," Trainer repeated for probably the fifth time.

I sighed and leaned back as I let my settings menu close in front of me. I wasn't sure what to make of the situation. I mean, Rupert Winston's message was loud and clear—I was supposedly dead, or at least dead outside of the world of Eden's Gate, but my brain couldn't process how that was really possible. There was no way that I was dead outside but still walking around in-game. Maybe it was just some sort of twisted launch day joke for early adopters.

I wondered about Rachel. Was she also stuck in game or had she already started drawing obscene pictures on my skin with sharpies and filled my hand with shaving cream? I made a mental note to be very cautious after logging off.

But then I considered… What if what that system message wasn't a joke? What if I was really stuck in the game?

I shook my head violently. There was no fucking way…

No matter what the situation, there was no use in me sitting on the stairs in the tutorial and clicking a non-responsive logoff button over and over. If anything, the battery of the VR module would eventually drain, and I'd be dropped back into the real world.

I sighed loudly and stood from the stairs. "Alright, let's just keep moving."

"Back to your senses, I see." Trainer walked to the top of the temple and pulled a satchel out from under the table. "This will get you started," he said as he handed me the bag.

> You've received: **Basic Torch**. 0-1 Attack Damage. Durability: 10/10. Quality: Average. Rarity: Common. Weight: 0.3 kg. This item provides a basic light source when lit.

> You've received: **Basic Flint & Steel**. Durability: 20/20. Quality: Average. Rarity: Common. Weight: 0.1 kg. Combine with kindling or other flammables to start a campfire.

> You've received: **2 Small Bandages**. Durability: 5/5. Quality: Average. Rarity: Common. Weight: 0.1 kg. Useful for healing light wounds.

> You've received: **Small Food Ration**. Durability: 5/5. Quality: Average. Rarity: Common. Weight: 0.2 kg. Who knows what's in these tasteless things? All you know is that they keep you alive.

"Thanks," I said.

Trainer placed his hand on my shoulder and started leading me down the stairs of the temple. "You'll learn most skills naturally as you progress, but magic is generally gained via finding scrolls, books and learning them from other magic users."

"Do I select a class at some point? Wizard, thief, warrior?"

"Everyone in Eden's Gate is unique. As you progress you may earn titles based on your choices, achievements or renown, but you can't simply select a class or title."

I nodded and followed, only being able to halfway pay attention as I worried about what was going on back home.

When we arrived at the open gate outside of temple, Trainer looked at me and smiled. "When you gain a level, your stats are restored, but only if you're not cursed, diseased, or poisoned. If you die, you'll awaken where you spawn until you bind yourself to another location."

"And how do I bind? To what?"

Trainer smiled. "You'll know when the time comes."

I raised my eyebrows and shrugged. "Alright then. Is there anything else I should know?"

"I can only tell you a few basics. You're a baby fresh from the womb and must learn about the world through your own discovery."

"Hmm... Well, thanks."

"Good Luck, Gunnar."

Trainer turned and headed back to the temple, and I started past the gate that led to the distant forest. Just a few paces outside the gate, my vision started to a blur and a weightlessness took over my body. Everything soon went white and then that white faded into a complete and total darkness.

\*\*\*

*You have spawned and must learn to survive on your own from this point. Good luck!*

I no longer felt weightless, and the air around me was cold and musty. A high-pitched squeak echoed out above me.

*Great... a cave,* I thought. Out of all the places I could have spawned, I had to be spawned underground.

I felt something crawl over my ankle, and I kicked out instinctively, trying to rid myself of whatever it was. I lifted my foot and jerked to the side, bumping my head against something hard and rocky.

"Fuckkkkkkkk!" I grunted and grabbed my head. My voice echoed several times, and I heard several high-pitched squeaks answer my curse.

Bats. At least ten or more, I guessed.

I took a deep breath and gathered myself, then felt around in my satchel for the flint and torch. My hands were no longer hurting, but the fact that my health bar was at about 95% meant that I had taken some damage just by hitting my head.

I sat the torch on the ground and knocked my flint & steel together a few times over it until the sparks caught the tiny kindling that jutted crudely at the top. An ember appeared, and I blew hard until the ember puffed up into flames.

I lifted the lit torch and inspected my surroundings. The cave was wide and circular, and directly behind me, large stalactites hung down, blocking all but a small crawlspace that led to who-knows-where. There was only one other obvious passage which was a few meters in front of me. But most importantly, the place was crawling with maggots. Hundreds of them were squirming all over the ground.

"Gross!" I spat as I flicked my foot, trying to rid myself of the ones clinging to my shoes. Wherever I was, I wanted to get out as soon as possible.

I bagged my flint and steel, pulled out my dagger, and started forward, cringing every time I heard the squishy noise of the tiny maggots bursting under my shoes. I followed the path ahead and found myself coughing as a whisk of air carrying the smell of something rotten suddenly caught my nostrils.

What a wonderful place they decided to start me in… the toilet of Eden's Gate.

There was a low screech, and before I could even see where it was coming from, a maggot the size of a small dog slithered quickly towards me, its puckered, pink mouth opening and closing with each creep forward. I instinctively took a step back, but the maggot was surprisingly fast, and when it was right on top of me, I kicked it hard, sending it flying far back down the passage.

"Nasty!" I spat.

The sound of several low screeches cried out from the direction the maggot flew, and I immediately knew that I had made a mistake. Within seconds, 3 more giant maggots were slithering towards me even more aggressively than the first.

"I guess it's on then, bitches," I said as I gave both my dagger and torch a tighter grip. Even if I ran back, there was nowhere for me to go unless I were to jump in the crawlspace which was probably home to even more disgusting creatures.

When the first maggot closed in, I kicked it aside and swung the fire of my torch down towards the second. It screeched loudly and seemed stunned by the flames, but it was saved when the third giant maggot leapt up and sunk its teeth into my leg.

I screamed and almost lost my balance as pain burst through my calf. I dropped the torch and swung my dagger frantically at the maggot that was latched on to me, and a yellow puss-like substance spilled out of its body and dripped down my leg. It released its grip and fell to the ground curling and screeching.

The smell of the maggot juice would have made me vomit if it weren't for the pain and adrenaline pumping through me.

I noticed that my health had already been brought down to 80%, and I kneeled, reaching for my fallen torch while simultaneously driving my dagger as hard as I could into the maggot that had earlier been stunned. Yellow liquid surged out of its mouth, and it immediately went limp.

Before I could even stand, another giant maggot jumped on to my arm and sank its teeth into my shoulder. I dropped my torch again, and used my free hand to grab hold of the maggot, pulling as hard as I could, ripping it from my skin. I pinned it against the wall as I drove my dagger into its body repeatedly until it stopped moving.

The body of the gooey, mangled maggot fell to the cave floor, and I grabbed at my searing shoulder. Another low screech rang out, and I turned to see that the first maggot that I stabbed was still alive, crawling slowly towards me with liquid still seeping out of its body. I took a step forward, lifted my foot high, and slammed it down as hard as I physically could, causing yellow liquid to splat all over the cavern floor.

*You have gained 90 XP!*

A low, celebratory drumming sound echoed around me.

*Advancement! You have reached **level 2** and gained 3 attribute points. To assign your attribute points, open your status page. You can also increase any of your known skills by 1 level. Choose wisely, as your choices cannot be undone.*

*You have gained 10 HP!*

I should have been celebrating the increase, but the pain from the maggot bites was excruciating. I inspected the damage, and blood was dripping out of both my shoulder and my legs. My health bar was down to 50%, and below my status bars were two icons. One was like a dark red blood drop, and the other was a green skull and crossbones. I focused on their meaning and two alerts displayed at the bottom of my screen.

> *You are* **bleeding** *and require medical attention. Bleeding is a damage-over-time effect.*
>
> *You have been* **poisoned** *and require medical attention. Poison is a weakening and damage-over-time effect.*

Pain shot out in my shoulder, and I watched as my health bar dropped to 45%.

"Shit!" I gritted my teeth and tried to ignore the pain as I began searching through my satchel for a bandage. I gripped on to a soft cloth, but before I even had time to take any action, I looked up and saw 3 more giant maggots approaching.

"You have got to be kidding me…"

Pain coursed through my body, and then another sharp pain pulsed in the wound of my leg. My health fell to 35%, and I was starting to feel dizzy. There was no way I would survive another battle against 3 more maggots in my current state. My only choice was to try to run.

I reached for my torch and bolted towards the maggots as fast as I could, kicking one out of the way and jumping over the other two. Each step of the way, my feet squished on the smaller maggots that littered the floor, soaking my feet in an icky mess. The pungent smell of death grew stronger as I continued.

Another shock of pain thudded through my body, and my health was down to 30%.

The thin passageway opened into another large room, and as soon as I stepped inside, I was almost choked by the heavy odor in the air. The source of the smell was apparent right away as against the far left wall, a huge dead body, maybe fifty times my size, lay dead on the ground. Its head was half missing and both small and large maggots were feasting on its decomposing, gray flesh.

When the light of my torch light bounced off the cave walls, I noticed a chest lying at the foot of the giant body and a sword leaning against the wall. But most importantly, I noticed one massive maggot the size of a bear that had been sucking at the body's neck. It turned to me and screeched in rage. All the other maggots turned in attention, and the screams from them all at once were like daggers in my ears.

Another thudding pain—health at 25%.

I swung my torch in panic, looking for an escape route, and I could see the faintest bit of light coming from one of two other passages that branched off from the room. I staggered towards the light as fast as my weakened body would let me with bloodthirsty maggots right on my trail.

I had to kick several maggots out of the way before I reached the dimly lit passage, but when I finally got out of the main room, there seemed to be nothing but a few smaller maggots and vines growing out of the ceiling the rest of the way.

I didn't stop running from the screeches behind me until the path reached such an incline that running wasn't possible and it was clear that there was an exit ahead of me. I had to drop my torch and grab on to rocks and hard roots to pull myself up and out, but finally, I reached the mouth of the cave.

The ground leveled out once I was above ground, and I found myself in some sort of a forest. It seemed to be right after dusk, and there was barely any light left in the sky. Birds and insects filled the air with sounds, and the coolness of the hard wind intensified the stinging of my wounds.

Health at 15%.

My status bar started blinking at that point, a clear indication that I was in very serious trouble.

I limped forward, scanning my surroundings, but all I could see were trees in every direction. I continued on, making sure to put a decent amount of distance between me and the cave, just in case something nasty were to crawl from inside. When I was a safe distance away, I plopped myself down hard at the base of a large stump.

My head swam as I reached for my bandages, and I sloppily tried to tie one around my bleeding shoulder. It seemed impossible to tie the cloth off at such an awkward angle, and the bandage quickly became saturated in blood. As I struggled with making a loose knot, the cloth slipped out of my fingers and fell into the dirt below.

*You have failed to bandage your wounds!*

"Yeah, no shit, Sherlock..." I muttered weakly from my drying mouth.

I grabbed my other bandage and wrapped it tightly around my ankle. While it went on a bit sloppily, I managed to get it tied off this time.

> *Advancement! You have learned the skill:*
> ***First Aid***. *Appointment at 10:00? I'll see you*
> *at 10:45! First Aid is linked the base stat*
> *Intelligence. Increase your Intelligence to*
> *increase your ability to perform First Aid.*

The bleeding around my ankle seemed to be nullified by the bandage, but there was still blood coming out of my shoulder, and I was still poisoned.

I groaned loudly as pain coursed through my body again and my health fell to 10%. At that point my vision was becoming blurry, and I knew that I was knocking on death's door. I reached for my satchel and pulled the food ration out with shaky hands. I remembered Trainer telling me that eating would increase my natural recovery rate, and by then, I was willing to try anything.

I pulled open the brown paper covering the rectangular food ration, and inside was something the same color as the paper that covered it. It certainly didn't look good. The smell was a bit like bread and cheese, but when I bit into it, it had the same consistency and taste as bologna. It was unpalatable, but I forced as many bites down my throat as I could.

My vision flashed as another streak of pain coursed through my body, and I fell sideways, dropping the rest of my food.

Health at 5%.

I sighed and gently rocked my head against the ground as my stomach churned and cramped, cursing my bad luck. Not only had I spawned in the worst location ever, but I'd have to run through that stinky maggot-filled place again after I respawned. I wasn't even sure if I'd still have my starting items after I died.

What a crazy, broken game, I thought. I had never felt so much pain in my life! Even having a few hundred cans of food dropped on my foot hadn't come close.

The idea of full-immersion virtual reality was great when you thought about the adventures, battles, and maybe even virtual sex you could possibly have. But when you added the pain, the gore and death… I wasn't sure how appealing it really was. Cool concept, but everything was a little too real.

Health at 2%.

My eyelids were heavy, and I could barely pull them open at that point. My entire body ached, and there was a loud ringing in my ears, drowning out the sound of everything around me. The pain was so intense that I pretty much blacked out.

The last thing I remembered was wondering if Rachel was okay.

# Chapter 5

*01/01/0001*

"There you go, buddy. Eat up…" a voice said.

I could hear the sound of jaws chomping down on something and burning wood crackling in the distance. It felt warm and safe.

*Safe?* I pulled open groggy eyes and groaned. I could see wooden panels above me and something smelled amazing. I tried to move my hands and legs, but they were stuck.

"Oh, so you're finally awake?"

I blinked a few times as my strength started to surface, and a tall man with an evening shadow and dark, long hair stood over me. Again, I tried to move, this time with a little more enthusiasm, but each pull was met with resistance. I was tied down by something.

"Where am I?" I questioned frantically. "Why am I tied up?"

The man sighed. "Sorry about that. I wasn't sure if you're a thief or not. It's better to be safe than sorry."

"I'm not a thief!"

"Yeah, and all the thieves admit to being thieves, right?" The man stood up straight and ripped a piece of bread off a loaf he was holding, tossing it in his mouth.

He swiftly rubbed his hand off against the front of his brown leather tunic, then swiped again against his leather pants. "But considering you only had a dagger and flint on you, you must be a pretty bad thief."

"I told you I'm not a thief!"

"Or a murderer…"

"I'm not a murderer!"

"Hmm…" the man said. "You are only level 2. I suppose the idea of you being a murderer is a bit far-fetched. But—"

"Come on. Let me out!" I interrupted, yanking at the rope that was bounding my hands to the bed.

The man chewed on his bread for a moment then threw in another bite. His mouth was full as he spoke. "How about we get to know each other first. What's your name and where do you come from?"

"My name is Gunnar," I said. "I'm from Los Angeles."

The man's head jolted back, and it looked like he was thinking hard. "Los Angeles? I don't think I've heard of there. What's it near?"

"You wouldn't know. It's not in Eden's Gate."

"What? I don't understand." He looked perplexed.

"Look, I just logged into this game."

"Game?"

I sighed. "Umm… I just turned level 2. I just got here."

"Ahh, yes. You're a newbie adventurer. That I can understand."

"And who are you?"

"I'm Jax." The man grinned wide and grabbed the fingers of one of my tied-up hands, shaking it comically. "It's a pleasure to meet you."

"Can you let me go now?"

Jax rubbed his chin with two fingers and thought a moment before he nodded gently. "Okay, I'll untie you. But if you try anything funny, you either get an arrow in your back or Fenris will eat your ass."

"Fenris?"

Jax quickly untied the ropes that were binding me to the bedpost, and I pushed myself up into a sitting position, rubbing at the soreness around my feet and ankles.

"That's Fenris." Jax pointed.

Directly in front of me was a massive gray and white wolf, thrice the size of the biggest dog I had ever seen, nearly thrice the size of Jax. It was busy chewing the meat off a large bone, but as soon as I made eye contact with him, he looked up, showed his razor-sharp teeth and growled.

I had already been eaten alive by maggots. There was no way that I'd stand a chance against that thing.

"How did I get here?" I asked. "The last thing I remember was dying at the base of a tree stump."

"Your skin was pale as white when I saw you. Poisoned and *almost* dead, but you still had a breath of life in you. I poured a cure potion down your throat and bandaged your shoulder before I brought you back here."

I looked to my shoulder and the bandage on it was tied far superior to the one on my leg. "Thank you," I said.

"Thank the gods. Another minute out there and you'd be a goner," Jax replied.

I was sitting in what seemed to be a small cabin. There was a burning fireplace right behind Fenris who was resting on a bearskin rug, and a hog was being spit roasted over the flames. Behind me was a small dining table and a cabinet desk that was covered in various flasks and bowls.

My stomach growled loudly.

"Hungry?" Jax asked.

"Very much so."

Jax prepared me a simple meal of ham, bread and wild berries. I could barely control myself as I rammed piece after piece down my throat. It was delicious, and I couldn't tell if it was because the game made it that way or if was just dying to eat something of sustenance after a near-death experience. Whatever the case, it beat the food ration 100 times over.

The small icon of an apple appeared below my stats bar, and I focused on its meaning.

> *You are **well-fed**! Stamina and Vitality increased by 15% while this effect is active.*

I took a large swig of water and sighed at the brisk, refreshing feeling. "Where is this place anyway?"

"This is the Addenfall Forest," Jax said, sitting in a wooden rocking chair near the fireplace. "I found you near Old Nambunga's cave."

"Old Nambunga?" I asked, squishing a piece of bread and throwing it in my mouth.

"He's an Ogre that used to roam these parts. Legend says that he fell down the slope of the cave years ago and couldn't get his fat ass out. He feeds on bats and whatever else wanders down there." Jax pounded his fist on his chest a couple times and his face winced in pain as he belched. "You don't want to go down there unless you want to end up as a splotch on the end of his club."

I picked a piece of ham off my plate and started chewing on it while thinking about what Jax said. "I think Old Nambunga is dead actually."

"What do you mean?"

"When I was in the cave near the tree stump, I saw a huge dead body. Had to have been dead a least a few days. Maggots were feasting on it, including one that was bigger than me."

Jax's brow creased, and his eyes pierced into me. "Are you sure?"

"I can't be positive, but something larger than this cabin is dead down there."

"Hmm…" Jax grunted. "I suppose he would be getting old by now." He looked at me closely. "But you didn't find anything while you were down there, did you?"

"I was too busy running for my life," I replied. "But I did see a chest and what I think was a sword."

"Ogres love treasure. I bet Nambunga has a nice little horde." Jax clicked his lips and stood from his chair. He walked over to the door and placed a thick wooden board in a slot across its front. "You should probably get some sleep."

"Sleep here?" I asked.

"Well, that is unless you want to sleep outside. But it's a whole lot safer in here." Jax smiled.

49

Through Jax's window, I could see that night had fallen. Several hours must have passed since the moment I blacked out at the stump. Why wasn't the battery of the Nexicon VR dead yet, and better yet, why hadn't Rachel just powered down my damn headset and taken it off me? The only explanation was that she was still in the game too. Or maybe I was really dead? Noo… no way.

I willed my settings screen to appear and again tried to click the logoff button and will myself out of the game. Nothing happened. "You wouldn't happen to know how to log out of this game, would you?"

Jax frowned. "What is 'log out'? And what game are you talking about?"

I swallowed my last piece of ham hard and suddenly didn't feel like eating anymore. "Yeah…" I moaned. "I guess I'll sleep here."

"That's what I figured." Jax walked over to the bearskin rug where Fenris was curled up in front of the fire. He lay down, legs stretched and leaned his head against the soft mane of Fenris's stomach. "You're welcome to the bed. I'll be fine down here with Fenris."

"Is there a toilet around here?" I asked.

"Toilet?" Jax asked.

"You know? Someplace to go if I need to take a piss or… do something else?"

Jax's lips curled, and his face twisted in disgust. "Where does anyone take a shit? You go deep in the forest, out of sight!" Jax sighed and shook his head as he closed his eyes.

Nice. I guess I'd have to wipe my ass with leaves too.

I left my scraps of food at the table and made my way over to the bed. My mind was still racing at the possibility that I was permanently stuck in Eden's Gate, but I was so exhausted after my first day in game that I could've probably slept standing up.

I glanced over to Jax who had wrapped his arm around Fenris' neck and gently caressed the beast's fur. I was surprised that the guy seemed just as real or even moreso than just about any real person I had ever met back on Earth.

He actually noticed me and seemed to care. And I was 100% certain that he had never heard of Bustin Snieber, *Creeping up on the Fartdashians*, or any of the other crap that people back home were obsessed with. I actually kind of liked the dude.

Shame he was just an AI.

# Chapter 6

*01/02/0001*

I woke up the next morning *still* in Eden's Gate. I immediately tried to logoff, but again nothing happened. If I had any doubts before that something had gone horribly wrong on launch day, now I was certain.

My next thought: *My browser history! Holy shit, I didn't delete my browser history!* What if Rachel went through the *ahem* on my computer?! Maybe *that's* why she didn't wake me. Embarrassment caused the hairs on the back of my neck to stand.

I scanned through my settings again, for about the 100th time, hoping to see a HELP option or something else I was overlooking, but there was literally no support option anywhere in the game.

Jax was mixing some fragrant liquids on the standing desk behind me as I rubbed my eyes and sat up from the bed.

"What is that?" I asked as he poured a thin, green substance into a vial.

"What? You've never heard of alchemy? I'm putting together a few things before I head out hunting. I wasted my last cure potion on you yesterday."

I stretched my limbs out and stood up, scanning the cabin for my shoes. "Thanks for the bed," I said. "I guess I should be going."

"Where are you headed?" Jax asked with a smile.

Truth was, I had no idea. I wanted to figure out a way to get out of the game, but if Rachel were stuck in Eden's Gate also, I needed to find her. And the only two places I had heard of so far were Addenfall—where I was—and The Mastalands. Knowing how driven Rachel was, she would probably head straight for that castle that Rupert Winston was standing in if she found herself stuck inside the game too.

"I'm going to go find my girlfriend," I replied.

"Ohh…" Jax cooed. "Looking for your love, yeah? Whereabouts is she?"

"I don't know…" I muttered. "I figure I'll start by heading towards The Mastalands."

"The Mastalands?" Jax leaned his head back and started laughing hysterically. He grabbed his stomach and cackled so hard that he almost dropped the vial of liquid he was holding. "The Mastalands? You're kidding me, right?"

"What?" I asked.

"Well first off," Jax said pushing a cork hard into the top of his vial, "The Mastalands is hundreds of thousands of kilometers away, and second, you're only level 2. The Mastalands is one of the highest-level zones in Eden's Gate. Even if you were some major badass— which you're not—you'd need a small army of additional badasses to survive there."

"So basically—"

"Do you even know what direction The Mastalands is?" he interrupted.

I shook my head and looked down at the wooden panels of the small cabin, feeling deflated about the situation.

"So settle down and get some levels under your belt. Learn some skills. You've got a long way to go if you even want to get anywhere near The Mastalands."

"But my girlfriend is probably looking for me."

"What level is your girlfriend?"

I shook my head. "I don't know. Probably about the same as me."

"So then she'll have to start somewhere too." Jax lifted a satchel over his shoulder and slid the flask he was holding inside. "Don't worry. I'm sure you find her eventually."

I sighed, but I had to accept that he was right. I was still holding on to hope that something in Eden's Gate was glitched or that the whole "dead" broadcast thing was a prank. Maybe I'd be logged off automatically at any moment. But either way, I wouldn't make it very far in the game without learning some skills. "Maybe you could teach me alchemy?"

Being able to conjure up health potions certainly wouldn't hurt.

Jax scanned me up and down. "So you want to become an alchemist, eh?"

"No, not really. But like you said, I've got to start somewhere."

"Hmph," Jax huffed. "I'm not much of an alchemist myself. I only know a few basics. But I'll tell you what… You said you saw a sword down in Old Nambunga's Cave? If you can go down there and fetch it for me, I'll teach you a thing or two about alchemy."

A window appeared in the center of my screen.

*You have been offered a quest: **Old
Nambunga's Cave***

*Retrieve the sword from Old Nambunga's
Cave and return it to Jax.*

*Reward: Alchemy Training, 300XP
Do you accept this quest? Accept/Decline*

"Why do you want me to get it?" I asked. "It'd be much easier if you just went down there and got it yourself. You're obviously a lot stronger than me."

Jax smiled. "You certainly are naïve, Gunnar. I just met you yesterday, and you came to me with the story that Old Nambunga's dead. How do I know he's not really dead and you're just trying to lure me into the cave to get my head smashed in?"

"You're pretty paranoid."

"There's a difference between paranoid and smart."

I huffed. "Fine. I'll get you the sword."

*You have accepted the quest: **Old
Nambunga's Cave!***

"Good." Jax smiled, and there was a twinkle in his eye. It made me wonder if there was something about the sword or cave he wasn't telling me.

I grabbed my satchel and checked that my dagger and flint were still inside. "It would help if you could spare a torch."

"What?" Jax chuckled. "Look at yourself. You can't go back down there with no gear." Jax kneeled down and slid a wooden crate from under his bed.

Inside, he pulled out a plain wooden longbow and slipped it onto his back along with a quiver of arrows. There was another quiver and a smaller bow which he handed to me. "It's not much but should get you started."

> *You've received:* **Wooden Shortbow**. *2-5 Attack Damage. Durability: 9/10. Quality: Average. Rarity: Common. Weight: 0.4 kg*

> *You've received:* **Basic Wooden Arrows**. *+1 Attack Damage. Durability: 10/10. Quality: Average. Rarity: Common. Weight: 0.5 kg*

"And take these," he said, sliding a pair of floppy, burnt-red leather boots in my direction. "The shoes you were wearing when I found you were soaked in something that stunk a mess."

> *You've received:* **Battered Leather Boots**. *+2 Armor. Durability: 4/10. Quality: Average. Rarity: Common. Weight: 0.4 kg*

"Thanks," I said as I slid the boots on my feet and fastened both the quiver and bow the same as Jax had. I must have looked like a cross between Ronald McDonald and Robin Hood, but it was still better than what I had before.

"Let's go see what we can find."

"I thought you didn't want to go in the cave?"

Jax sighed. "No… Save the cave for later. For now, just come with me."

I followed Jax outside the cabin, and I immediately noticed that Fenris was missing. "Where's your wolf?"

Jax shrugged. "I released him. He's a wild beast. I've got to let him have his freedom sometimes."

"And he just comes back whenever he feels like it?"

"Sometimes he shows up on his own," Jax replied. "But usually I summon him."

"You can summon Fenris?"

"*Summon Beast* is a skill you can learn with patience and care, but it's not something I can teach you directly. A master either has to dominate the mind of a beast or develop an unwavering bond in order for the beast to allow itself to be summoned. Fenris and I have that bond."

"That's amazing…" I said. "Now that's something that I'd like to learn."

"One thing at a time… One thing at a time."

Addenfall Forest was beautiful during the daytime. Large oak trees, roofed with green, rose out of the soil, and mosaic of red, yellow, and green leaves lay sprinkled on the grass-covered ground. Flowers of every color were speckled in every direction and the chirps of birds and other wildlife gave the place a magical feeling.

I followed Jax through the woods a good kilometer before he paused and placed a hand on my shoulder to stop me from moving. He lifted his finger to his lips and then pointed over a swathe of brush. A small squirrel, or something resembling a squirrel, was sniffing around at the ground.

"Do you know how to inspect your targets?" Jax whispered low.

I leaned my head to the side in a questioning manner then shook it from left to right.

"This is a good target for you to learn on. Focus in on that squirrel and try to feel its energy. Try to get an understanding of everything you can about the creature."

"Okay," I said, still unsure of exactly what he was trying to get me to do.

I focused in on the squirrel and watched as it continued to prance around sniffing. I concentrated on the animal, trying to get a deeper understanding of the creature, and surprisingly text appeared above the critter's head after a few seconds.

*Name: a small squirrel*
*Race: animal*
*Level: 1*
*Health/Mana/Stamina: 5/5/20*
*Status: neutral*

*Advancement! You have learned the skill: Inspect. If you know only yourself but not the enemy, for every victory gained you will also suffer a defeat. Inspect is linked to the base state Intelligence. Increase your Intelligence to increase your ability to Inspect.*

"Level 1, neutral, 5 HP..." I whispered.

"Good," Jax replied. "As you get higher in levels, you can learn more information about your targets. If a target is too high level for the inspect skill, you'll get partial information or nothing at all."

Jax pulled his longbow from his back and lifted an arrow out of his quiver. He made a show of nocking the arrow and gestured to me to do the same.

I followed his example and nocked an arrow into my bow, aiming at the creature.

"Go ahead when you're ready," he whispered.

I let the arrow fly, and it soared through the air towards the squirrel, missing it by an inch. The squirrel immediately darted behind a bush and then skirmished up and behind a tree to safety.

"Fuck," I spat under my breath. I had played archers in simulation-based games before, so I had a decent aim, but the difficulty curve here was on a whole different level. Just pulling back the tightly wound string of the bow had drained a little of my stamina.

Jax stuck a finger to his lips again and then tapped me on the shoulder, signaling to another squirrel that was to our left, resting on a nearby tree branch. He nodded towards me and I nocked another arrow.

This time I focused hard and took note of the distance I missed on the first shot, adjusting my aim to compensate. I pulled the string as hard as I could and let the arrow fly.

I cringed a little when the arrow made contact as I could hear the sound of the animal's tiny bones being split by the impact. It flew with the arrow off the tree and landed several feet away.

"Hit!" Jax said low but excitedly.

> *Advancement! You have learned the skill: **Archery**. Is there any more rewarding feeling than an arrow that hits its mark? Archery is linked the base stat Dexterity. Increase your Dexterity to increase your affinity with Archery.*
>
> *You have gained 25 XP!*

*You have gained 1 point of Dexterity!*

Nice, I thought to myself. I wasn't expecting that point of dexterity. That prompted me to take a look at my status screen.

## GUNNAR LONG

| | |
|---|---|
| Race: | Human |
| Level: | 2(Progress 15%) [3 AP, 1 LP] |
| Title: | None |
| Health/Mana/Stamina: | 110/100/100 |
| Strength: | 10 |
| Dexterity: | 11 |
| Intelligence: | 10 |
| Vitality: | 10 |
| Wisdom: | 10 |
| Willpower: | 10 |
| Charisma: | 10 |
| AR Rating: | 2 |
| Resists: | |
| | None |
| Traits: | |
| | None |
| Primary Skills: | |
| | First Aid Lvl 1: progress 10% |
| | Inspect Lvl 1: progress 10% |
| Combat Skills: | |
| | Dodge Lvl 1: progress 20% |
| | Small Blades Lvl 1: progress 75% |
| | Backstab Lvl 1: progress 5% |
| | Archery Lvl 1: progress 10% |
| Magic Skills: | |
| | None |

I had forgotten that I still had 3 attribute points and a free level up in a skill of my choice to allocate, which was indicated beside my currently level. I quickly focused on putting 2 of the attribute points into dexterity, since it seemed like just about everything I was using lately was linked to dexterity. I decided to save one AP (attribute point) and my LP (level point) for later since I still wasn't sure what kind of build I was going to go with yet. That left me with 1 AP and one 1 LP.

I followed Jax towards my kill, and he quickly pulled the arrow out of the squirrel and handed it back to me, bloody tip and all. He did a quick inspection of the dead carcass and then tied it to a string that was attached to his belt.

"Good kill," he said.

I wasn't sure what I thought about killing the squirrel. I had never killed a real animal before but had killed hundreds—if not thousands—of animals in other games over the years and never gave it a second thought. But seeing Jax handling my kill just felt way too real. I could even smell the gamey scent coming off the carcass.

"What are you going to do with it?" I asked.

"Trade the pelts for gold at the local village. If you can get me a few more, it should be enough to swing you some better gear as well." Jax looked up to the trees. "The forest is crawling with animals. Think you can get a few more on your own?"

*You have been offered a quest:* **Pelts for Jax**

*Collect 5 furry animal carcasses for Jax to make pelts.*

*Reward: unknown, 100xp*
*Do you accept this quest? Accept/Decline*

I nodded. "I think I can handle it."

*You have accepted the quest:* **Pelts for Jax!**

Jax reached in his bag and handed me a red flask.

*You've received:* **Minor Healing Potion.** *Durability: 10/10. Quality: Average. Rarity: Common. Weight: 0.1 kg. Drink to recover 50 HP over 5 seconds.*

"Just in case." Jax winked and patted me on the shoulder. "I'm going to scout out the surrounding area for larger game and any potential trouble. If you need me, just whistle. Otherwise, just stay around this area, and I'll find you in a bit."

"Sounds good."

I slid the flask in my satchel and continued forward as Jax swiftly slunk away. I marveled at the fact that I could barely hear anything coming from Jax as he made his exit, but nearly every step I took was causing leaves to crackle and branches to snap, no matter how hard I tried to be silent.

I spotted another squirrel off in the distance a few meters ahead, eating something akin to a round, brown chestnut, but as I took a step closer, I snapped a twig and startled it slightly. It ran forward a bit then stood tall, scanning the area around it.

I froze, careful not to scare it away.

After a few seconds, the squirrel diverted its attention back to the nut, and I crept forward again, trying to get in firing distance. This time, I moved as quietly and slowly as I physically could. It didn't seem disturbed.

> *Advancement! You have learned the skill:* **Sneak**. *The quietest man often strikes the loudest. Sneak is linked the base stat Dexterity. Increase your Dexterity to increase your ability to Sneak.*

I nocked an arrow and focused on the back of the squirrel. When I let the arrow fly, the squirrel was hit so hard that it was lifted off the ground from the impact of the arrow and then bounced, tumbling several meters in the dirt before being stopped by a tree.

The bottom of my screen read 'critical hit' but even without a notification, it was pretty obvious.

> *You have gained 25 XP!*

I walked up to the fallen squirrel and pulled my arrow out of its side. The body was warm and the fur was bloody where the arrow made impact and at its exit wound. My stomach turned as I looked at its frozen face, staring back at me with dead, open eyes. Death in Eden's Gate way too real.

I sighed and tossed the carcass on the ground. Jax hadn't given me anything to carry the dead bodies with, so I figured I'd just pile them all up in one spot rather than putting them in my satchel.

For the next 30 minutes, I snuck around the area nearby killing 2 more squirrels and 2 racoons. Another racoon took an arrow to its side but survived and scurried away somewhere, arrow and all.

> *You have completed all requirements for the quest:* **Pelts for Jax!** *Return the spoils to Jax to collect your reward.*

I carried the last couple of carcasses to the pile in front the tree and stretched my arms out as I scanned the forest for Jax. He was nowhere to be seen, but I did see something just as interesting. A chubby, brown animal a bit bigger than a pig was roughly 20 meters away chewing on some leaves.

I immediately readied my bow and nocked an arrow while at the same time performing my Inspect ability.

**Name:** *a small wild boar*
**Race:** *animal*
**Level:** *4*
**Health/Mana/Stamina:** *15/5/30*
**Status:** *aggressive*

I weighed my options after I saw the boar's information. It was 2 levels higher than me, and thus far, I had only focused on the lowest level creatures. But, it also only had 15 HP… If I could get a critical hit or a few arrows into it before I got to me, there was a chance that I could gain some nice XP and an impressive kill. Maybe a dead boar would even fetch a good penny at the village? If not, it would make another nice meal like the one from the night before.

My stomach growled. I was feeling hungry again.

I decided to take the chance and pulled the arrow back hard, ready to let it fly when I felt a slight tickle at my side. If I hadn't been so focused, I might have brushed it off as wind, but when I looked down to see what it was, I was shocked to see my satchel flap closing and a small, furry brown creature, roughly 2 and a half feet tall, running away with my potion in its tiny hands.

"Hey! What the fuck!?" I yelled.

I forgot about the boar and started running after the creature, which was surprisingly fast given the shortness of its legs. It dipped under foliage and jumped over branches expertly, and with each step it was gaining a little distance on me.

"Stop!" I shouted. "That's my potion!"

The creature didn't listen and just continued scurrying ahead.

I chased for a couple minutes before we came upon a small clearing, and I realized there was just no way I was going beat him in a foot race. I took a chance and stopped, nocked back an arrow and fired.

My arrow soared through the air and landed with a thud, right in the back of the creature's leg.

➤

*You have reached level 2 in **Archery**!*

The creature tumbled and screamed, its voice beady and sounding more like a kazoo than anything. The potion that it was carrying fell out of its hands and rolled on the ground in front of it.

"Yes!" I quietly cheered to myself as I ran towards the fallen, furry thing.

The creature crawled towards the fallen flask with its hands, seemingly more desperate to get the potion back rather than any worry about the injury in its leg. I quickly holstered the shortbow to my back and pulled out my dagger as I ran and jumped on top of it. It turned, and its large, brown eyes went wide as I latched my hand around its neck and raised my dagger high.

"Nooooo!" it wailed.

I hesitated to strike, maybe because the creature was just so damn cute. Its fur was thick and soft, and its flat facial features reminded me of anything but danger.

"Bad!" a beady voice shrieked, and I felt a sharp pain shoot out in my side.

My back arched instinctively and I turned to the pain just in time to see the tip of a small spear pulling out of me, dripping in blood, another of the small creatures at the other end of the stick. He jumped back and then jumped forward again as if threatening another strike, and that's when I noticed I was surrounded.

"Bad!" several of them wailed. "Bad!"

There must have been 30 or more of the 2 and a half foot furballs surrounding me. A few of them were holding half-sized bows with arrows pointing right at me, and the others were holding long spears that were three times their height.

I dropped my dagger and put my hands in the air. The one stab from the creature's spear had brought me down to 50% health, so I probably wouldn't survive another.

"Whoa!" I said. "Please don't kill me! I'm sorry. I just wanted to get my potion back."

"Bad!" Several of the creatures were jumping back and forth, waving their points at me. I wasn't sure if they understood what I was saying or not since they just kept saying the same thing over and over.

"Gunnar!" I heard Jax yell from somewhere nearby. I turned to see him press through a jumble of bushes and enter the clearing.

"Jax!" I huffed, careful not to put my hands down.

"Jaxxxxyzz!" Several of the fur-covered creatures seemed to completely lose interest in me and hobbled as fast as possible to Jax, thumping their bodies into his legs as they tried to hug him. A couple of them started climbing up his body and grabbing at his neck.

I tried to stand up, but when I did, the few of the creatures that stayed behind jumped forward and pointed their weapon tips at me again.

"Hey, fellas!" Jax said with a smile. "What's going on over here?"

"Bad!" Several shouted and pointed their stubby fingers or their weapons at me. "Bad man!"

"Bad man, huh?" Jax asked in a fatherly voice.

The creatures nodded.

The furry one that I was straddling shimmied out from under me, grabbing its leg and whimpering. "Heeza hurt me! Hurt! Heeza bad!" it cried.

"Oh no…" Jax muttered and rushed over to where the injured creature squirmed. He looked down at the arrow in its leg and then looked up at me. "What did you do, Gunnar?"

"It tried to steal the health potion you gave me! I was just trying to get it back!"

"Oh hell… Did you pay your tribute?"

"Tribute? What tribute?"

"Yesterday when you entered the forest, did you pay your tribute?"

"I don't know what you're talking about."

"You shot a keemu, Gunnar. These are the protectors of Addenfall. Anyone who enters has to pay tribute to the forest or the guardians will collect it on their own."

I shook my head. "Well, fuck. I didn't know."

Jax sighed. He looked down to the writhing creature and rubbed his hand over its furry temple. "Take a deep breath, buddy. This is going to hurt, okay?"

"Whatz!? Hurtz?!"

Jax swallowed and grabbed the arrow jutting out of the keemu's leg and pulled it out before it had the chance to respond.

"Ahhhhhhhhhhhhhhhhhhhhh!" the keemu wailed.

The keemu's surrounding us pointed their weapons and started jumping around as if they were ready to kill something.

"It's okay," Jax said, holding the bloody vice up for all to see. "I just needed to get the arrow out."

Jax reached into his satchel and pulled out another health potion. He popped the vial and poured a little of the liquid over the keemu's leg wound and then poured more of it into the keemu's mouth. The keemu almost instantly stopped its whining, but still looked like it was on the verge of tears.

Jax handed me the other half of the health potion and then scooped the fallen keemu up into his arms. "You're okay now," he said softly. He turned to me with a disapproving glare. "Drink it."

I lifted the vial to my lips and let the red liquid spill into my mouth and down my throat. It had a fruity flavor with a strong flowery aftertaste. Surprisingly tasty, I thought.

My health bar immediately started to fill up again, and I could feel the pain of the spear wound starting to decrease. It didn't bring me to full health, but I was at a comfortable 85%.

Jax leaned over, grabbed the stolen health potion and handed it to me. I started to place it in my satchel but he gripped me by the wrist and dipped his chin. "Pay tribute," he ordered.

I swallowed and looked at the keemus that were surrounding us. They didn't seem as alarmed as before, but were still very cautious. I held the potion out in my hands towards one of the keemus with a spear, but he just looked at me with curiosity.

"Lower your head and say 'Tribute for Addenfall,'" Jax instructed.

I looked down at the grassy ground. "Tribute for Addenfall," I repeated.

The keemus buzzed. They weren't talking—I don't think—they just buzzed at each other. But after a couple seconds, the potion was lifted out of my hand, and I heard a beady voice say, "Welcome."

When I raised my head up, the keemus lowered their spears and holstered their bows. The tension seemed go from 100 to 0 in a second, but I did notice the keemu that I shot give me menacing eyes over Jax's shoulder.

"Next time, be careful what you attack," Jax said as he sat the keemu down and stood to his feet. "I don't dare to think of what would've happened if you actually killed one of the guardians of the forest."

I stood up as well and watched as more of the keemus tugged on Jax's clothing and tried to play with him as if they were children. "They don't expect tribute from you?"

"I'm not a visitor," Jax explained. "I've lived in this forest for many years."

"And may you live in Addenfall for many years to come," a singsong voice said.

I turned to see a pale-skinned, lithe female walking into the clearing. Her eyes were the softest of greens and her hair long hair was the blondest of blondes. She was beautiful—perhaps the most beautiful girl I had ever seen, and her small leathery green top cut off above her waist, exposing a perfectly flat stomach and hips that fit snugly into a short leather skirt. Her clothes were etched in gold, and tall green boots rose up to her knees.

The keemus all kneeled in unison at the sight of her. Jax pressed my shoulder and spoke low, "Kneel."

Jax dropped to one knee and put his head down. I considered defiance for a moment. Who was I to kneel to someone? I didn't even know who the lady was. But at the same time, I had been through enough trouble for one day, and so far, Jax had steered me in the right direction. I dropped down and mimicked Jax's pose.

"You can rise," The woman spoke. "You know I don't care for formalities, Jax."

Both Jax and the keemus stood back up to their feet and I followed their actions.

"It's a pleasure to see you again, Adeelee. It's been too long." Jax smiled.

"A pleasure to see you as well, Jax." The woman turned and looked down to one of the keemus that was looking up at her in awe. That's when I noticed her elongated, pointed ears. I knew immediately that she was some sort of elf. "I heard a guardian cry, so I decided to have a look."

Jax smiled. "Just a misunderstanding. It's all taken care of now."

Adeelee looked at Jax as if reading his mind and then turned to me. "And your companion?"

"He's new to the forest," Jax explained. "Just out here helping me collect some goods for trade."

I scratched the top of my head and gave an embarrassed smile. The elf woman was gorgeous and there I was wearing battered, red boots, and a pair of capri pants that looked like they came out of the little girl section at K-Mart. Story of my life, I tell you. "The name's Gunnar. Nice to meet you."

"I see…" Adeelee said softly, making no effort to return an introduction.

"What brings you to this side of Addenfall?" Jax asked. "You're a long way from The Vale."

"The Scourge," Adeelee said.

"The Scourge?" Jax asked. "What does the Scourge have to do with Addenfall?"

"Word has traveled that some of the Scourge set up camps along the Crystal River, and mother sent me here to investigate."

"The Crystal River?" Jax questioned. "The Scourge has never gathered so close to here."

"It's true. I've seen it with my own eyes. It's not clear if they're planning something or just passing through, but they're there."

"The Scourge would never dare cross the river and enter the forest. War with the elves would be genocide."

Adeelee sighed. "Let's hope that's their thoughts as well. For now, we'll be on high alert until they leave." Adeelee kneeled down and rubbed her fingers through one of the keemus' hair. "Eden's Gate doesn't need any more bloodshed."

"The forest is strong, Princess."

Princess? I wondered. Good god. This gorgeous girl was a princess even? I tried my best to perform an *Inspect* on her, but the same message kept appearing over and over again.

*You have failed to inspect your target!*

*You have failed to inspect your target!*

If she only knew the things I'd like to inspect on her... I had a girlfriend sure, but I was still a man. You can't put something like that in front of a guy without his mind going wild.

Princess Adeelee stood. "I should get back to the Vale and warn mother of the news. Please let us know if you see anything that would be cause for concern."

"Of course, Adeelee," Jax said.

Adeelee turned to me. "And you... Gunnar. Will you be kind enough to alert the elves if you find anything suspicious?"

*You've been offered a quest:* **Scourge Activity**

*Princess Adeelee has requested that you alert the elves if you find anything that would be of concern.*

*Reward: unknown, 350xp*
*Do you accept this quest? Accept/Decline*

I scratched the back of my head again, feeling like a shy school kid talking to that one unattainable cheerleader babe. "Absolutely!"

*You have accepted the Quest:* **Scourge Activity!**

"Thank you Gunnar, and may we meet again." Adeelee turned to Jax and dipped her chin. "Jax."

Jax nodded, and Adeelee waved to the keemus as she ran off into the deep of the forest, making hardly a sound as she moved.

"Gunnar?" Jax asked.

I shook my head out of whatever trance I had found myself in as I watched Adeelee disappear between the trees. "I'm sorry. What?"

Jax cleared his voice and looked at me curiously. "You okay?"

"Yeah, I'm good."

"Then we should probably head back and retrieve the animals I saw you'd killed back there. The pelts?"

"Yeah…" I groaned. "The pelts."

Jax and I gathered up and started back toward where we began our hunting.

"You know, it's alright," Jax said as we pushed through some thick brush.

"What's alright?" I asked.

"I just about spoiled my pants too the first time I saw an elven princess."

Shit! Was I really that obvious?!

.

# Chapter 7

*01/02/0001*

*You have completed the quest: **Pelts for Jax!***

*You have gained 100 XP!*

*Advancement! You have reached **level 3** and have gained 3 attribute points. To assign your attribute points, open your status page. You can also increase any of your known skills by 1 level. Choose wisely, as your choice cannot be undone.*

*You have gained 10 HP!*

"Looks good," Jax said, inspecting one of the dead racoons. "Give me a few minutes and we can head south to Linden to sell these off."

As Jax was busy cutting out the innards of the dead animals, I wandered around nearby, trying to rack up a little more XP while I waited. I managed to score two more squirrels before he finished up, which he also made quick work of.

We gathered up all the pelts and headed off for Linden.

"So everyone kneels to The Princess?" I asked.

"You should kneel to any elf when in a forest, Princess or not. The Vale may be the home of the High-Elves, but they're considered the rulers of all forests,"

Jax explained. "Outside of the forest, they're considered no different than you or me."

"All elves?"

Jax huffed. "Maybe not dark elves. But I'll leave that one up to you."

"What about dark elves? Do they live underground?" I could only assume so, given the amount of fiction I'd read and video games I had played back when I was on Earth.

"What makes you think that?" Jax shook his head. "I suppose some do but not all. Dark elves are simply elves that have left the forest for too long. It's hard on an elf's soul to be away from their natural homes for extended periods, and that strain causes their skin to change. Many dark elves return to the forest, but they're often met with contempt and lack of respect from other elves."

Sort of like elf-on-elf racism, I thought. "So then they're not necessarily evil?"

"Not all of them… Some lose their mind from the trauma, but many still maintain a good heart and strong connection with nature."

"And the Scourge?"

"There's not much to say about the Scourge. Orcs mostly, goblins, and some other baddies who make their homes in the Wastelands. Savages. Their only goal seems to be to murder, pillage, and loot whatever they can. No one really knows what compels them to do what they do, but they seem hellbent on destroying Eden's Gate."

"If they destroy Eden's Gate, wouldn't that destroy them too?"

"Maybe I worded that the wrong. They want to destroy everyone and everything in Eden's Gate. Everything but The Scourge."

***

It was more than three hours of walking before we reached Linden Village, and the sun was just starting to go down.

There were several wooden buildings littered around the unpaved streets that surrounded a large well in the center of the village, and several smaller homes were sprinkled further out. Going by the insignia dangling in front of the doors of the larger buildings, I noticed an inn, a stable, an armorer, a general goods store, and—by the book etched in the wood of the sign—a library or magic shop of some kind.

There were a couple of children dressed in dirty clothes that were chasing each other around the well, and a couple of horses tied off near the Inn. A woman carrying a basket of fruit was on her way somewhere, and a man was busy looking at a bulletin board outside the inn, but otherwise there weren't many people outside.

Jax ducked his head inside the general goods store while I waited outside, and when he returned, he came out carrying two small bags filled with coins. "Here's your cut as promised," he said as he handed me one of the bags. "This should be enough for you to buy a bit of gear." He looked up and eyed the etching of a foamy mug that was dangling in front of the Inn. "I'm going to go have a beer and blow off some steam. I'll meet you inside the inn later."

*You've received:* **25 Gold Pieces**

"Thanks," I said.

I pocketed the gold and headed straight for the Armorer.

When I opened the creaky wooden door to the armorer, a balding man in a white cotton shirt and overalls stood up from his chair and leaned on the counter. He was the only person inside. "Well, hello there. Welcome."

"Hey…" I replied.

"Looks like someone needs an upgrade."

I just ignored his comment and started scanning the goods he had inside his store. There were breastplates hanging on the wall, gloves, bracers, leggings, and boots of all different types. There was plate, chainmail, ringmail, and a small amount of leather selection. Small paper tags hung from each of the different items indicating the prices, and a good percentage of it was way more than I could afford. As I focused on each item, their stats appeared at the bottom of my screen.

I figured I would start by finding a chestpiece— since that would likely be the most effective piece of armor—and narrowed the choice down to four pieces, mostly because they were the only ones I could afford:

> ***Battered Leather Chestpiece***. *+10 Armor. Durability: 4/10. Quality: Average. Rarity: Common. Weight: 1.5 kg* ***Price: 4 Gold***

*Leather Footpad's Vest. +11 Armor. Durability: 10/10. Quality: Average. Rarity: Common. Weight: 1.2 kg **Price: 5 Gold***

*Rugged Leather Tunic. +14 Armor. Durability: 9/10. Quality: Average. Rarity: Common. Weight: 1.6 kg **Price: 6 Gold***

"Will you negotiate?" I asked the vendor.

The vendor rolled his eyes. "What are you offering?"

"How about 3 for your Rugged Leather Tunic?" I asked.

"Get the hell out of here!" The guy yelled and waved his hand. "I don't need any of your lunacy in my shop."

I wasn't sure if he was being serious when he told me to get out, but I knew then that the only way to save the deal was to offer something a lot closer to the asking price.

"5 for the Rugged?"

The guy lifted his chin. "Alright, I can handle that."

I passed the required gold to the vendor.

*You have received: **Rugged Leather Tunic**. +14 Defense. Durability: 9/10. Quality: Average. Rarity: Common. Weight: 1.6 kg*

I equipped the item right away, and it fit right over my shirt. It felt loose at first, but then mysteriously shrank to fit my frame. I pounded a fist onto the tunic, and I could tell that the hard, thick leather would certainly take a lot of damage.

The leather selection in the store was kind of poor, but I narrowed the rest of my choices down to four other items:

> **Thick Hide Gloves**. *+3 Armor. Durability: 10/10. Quality: Average. Rarity: Common. Weight: 0.3 kg* **Price: 3 Gold**

> **Basic Leather Leggings**. *+7 Armor. Durability: 10/10. Quality: Average. Rarity: Common. Weight: 0.9 kg* **Price: 4 Gold**

> **Rough Leather Bracers**. *+4 Armor. Durability: 7/10. Quality: Below Average. Rarity: Common. Weight: 0.4 kg* **Price: 4 Gold**

> **Battered Leather Cowl**. *+2 Armor. Durability: 3/10. Quality: Poor. Rarity: Common. Weight: 0.3 kg* **Price: 3 Gold**

"I'll give you 13 Gold for the lot," I said.

The vendor started counting up the cost and then gave me a slight nod. "That's a fair deal."

After giving over the gold to the vendor, I equipped all the items and immediately felt like less of a noob. The items that didn't fit all adjusted to size and the leather felt like a second skin to me. Aside from the Leather Cowl—which I bought because there were no other leather helmet alternatives—all of it was in decent condition. All the items were a dark brown leather as well, so I looked a lot less like a drunken clown.

Except for the boots. The red stood out like a sore thumb.

I pulled the boots that Jax had given me off and sat them on the vendor's counter. "How much will you give me for these?" I asked.

The vendor picked up the boots and gave them a good look over. "I'll give you 1 gold for these."

"1 Gold!?" I shouted. I looked over to another pair of leather boots were sitting on a side counter.

> ***Rough Footpad's Boots***. *+4 Defense. Durability: 7/10. Quality: Average. Rarity: Common. Weight: 0.5 kg **Price: 4 Gold***

"You're asking 4 gold for these and they aren't *that* much better!"

"I'll give you 2 gold, but that's my final offer," the vendor said.

I shook my head and huffed. "Fine. Take the boots and 2 gold for the Footpad's Boots."

The vendor nodded.

I slid on the Footpad's Boots, and finally, I had a complete set of decent looking leather armor.

I walked out of the armorer feeling stronger and more confident than I had before, but with a much, much smaller wallet. I had only 5 gold pieces left, but I wanted to see if there was anything else useful that I could buy.

When I walked into the general goods store, I had a similar experience with the man behind the counter standing up and welcoming me. The sheer quantity of things that the man had in his shop was overwhelming. There were resources galore, crafting equipment, potions, oils, and even a few stray pieces of armor. I didn't know how many of the things were useful, but I didn't spend too much time in there since I was nearly broke anyway.

My next stop was the magic shop. When I walked in, I expected the same sort of greeting that I received when I went inside the armorer and general goods store, but instead I wasn't greeted at all.

There was a bookshelf inside with several books, and a few tables with scrolls sitting on top. Inside a glass case were several pieces of jewelry—some plain gold or silver, and some topped with emeralds, diamonds and other stones. There was a smell of incense burning in the air and a large white bird was perched on a wooden peg in the corner.

An old man with a scattered, gray beard and a scholar's robe was dusting off the bookshelf, and the minute I walked through the door, he turned and said, "Don't touch anything."

Not the best way to welcome your customers, I thought, but I shrugged it off and browsed the goods anyway. All the scrolls were out of my price range. For example:

> **Scroll: Arcane Missile.** *Unleash a targeted, arcane blast. Requires 10 Intelligence. Arcane Magic Level 1. Durability: 10/10. Quality: Average. Rarity: Uncommon. Weight: 0.1 kg.* **Price: 500 gold**

> **Scroll: Boost Strength.** *+5 Strength for 5 minutes. Requires 10 Intelligence. Divine Magic Lvl 1. Durability: 10/10. Quality: Average. Rarity: Uncommon. Weight: 0.1 kg* **Price: 450 gold**

> **Scroll: Conjure Food.** *Conjure a basic, edible food ration. Requires 10 Intelligence. Conjuring Lvl 1. Durability: 10/10. Quality: Average. Rarity: Uncommon. Weight: 0.1 kg*
> **Price: 350 gold**

My ears tingled as I looked at all the different scrolls. Archery was fun, and there was nothing like hand-to-hand combat, but magic? The idea of being a badass caster who rained chaos down on his enemies was just too exciting of a thought.

"What are you looking for?" The old man asked.

"Just browsing," I replied.

"Of course…" The old man huffed. "I sense no magic coming from you, so what else would you be doing? By the looks of it, you're probably poor as well."

"I'm only level 3."

"I know," the man said confidently. He must have inspected me already.

"I just started the game."

"Game?"

I shook my head. Again, I forgot that no one but me seemed to consider Eden's Gate a game. "Never mind."

"Are you looking to become a magic user?" the man asked.

"I like the idea but don't even know where to start." I pointed towards the scrolls. "I just read one of these, right?"

The man groaned. "You can learn spells through scrolls or spellbooks so long as you have the requirements. For example, you can learn *Arcane*

*Missile* so long as you have *Arcane Magic Level 1* skill and 10 intelligence."

"I have 10 intelligence. How do I learn Arcane Magic Level 1?"

"Someone with Arcane Magic Level 35 or higher has to teach you the basics." The man chuckled. "Someone who trusts you. Imagine if anyone could just read a scroll and learn magic. We'd have kids lobbing fireballs all over Eden's Gate."

"So if I buy one of these scrolls, it's useless?"

"If you haven't had someone to teach you the basics, I suppose they could make cute wall décor."

I sighed loudly. Learning magic was obviously going to be much harder than picking up archery or daggers. Not that I had the money to buy a scroll anyway. "Thanks," I said and turned for the door.

As soon as I my hand on the door handle, the man yelled in his raspy voice, "Wait!"

I turned my head, and the man had moved behind his counter and waved a hand to come closer. "Come here for a moment. I might have a proposition for you."

"Yeah?" I asked as I stepped in front of the counter.

"Are you a traveler? I've never see you in Linden before."

"I guess you could say that. I've been staying in Addenfall." He wouldn't understand if I told him I was from Earth.

"Have you ever committed a crime?"

I thought back to the time I had to appear in court to fight a speeding ticket. And I guess downloading copyrighted music and games was technically a crime.

But I was pretty sure those weren't the kind of crimes he was talking about. "Not really."

"Well, let me tell you about a crime. Gerard, the general goods vendor next door has started selling some of the same scrolls that I offer and undercutting prices, sometimes up to 50%!" The old man snarled his nose. "Obviously, his one-stop shop is causing a huge impact on my business and others. In fact, there was once an herbalist in town, and as soon as he started offering herbs at bottom-of-the-barrel prices, he damn well ran her out of town!"

I wasn't sure if I should tell him that competition was good for industry or if the Gerard guy was trying to be the Wal-Mart of Linden. Either way, I wasn't sure what he was getting at. "What does this have to do with me?"

"What is your name?" he asked.

"My name is Gunnar. And you are?"

"Eanos…" The man held out a hand which I shook. "Eanos Grey. I happen to be skilled in several branches of the magic, and I could give you a lesson and throw in a couple spells if you would be willing to help me put a stop to his bad business practices."

"What is it that you would have me to do exactly?"

"If you've been in Gerard's shop, I'm sure you've seen what a mess it is." He threw his arms up. "He has things scattered everywhere! No organization whatsoever. But he keeps his scrolls sitting in an open crate near the front counter."

Eanos turned and opened a cabinet door behind him, producing three thick, blank sheets of parchment and a feathered pen.

"If you could sabotage his stock by dropping a few phony scrolls in his inventory, word would eventually get around that he's selling fake scrolls, ruining his credibility for magic items." Eanos lifted the feathered pin and tapped it against his inkwell. "What do you say? A favor for me, a favor for you?"

*You have been offered a quest:* **Unfair Trade Practices**

*Eanos wants you to slip fake scrolls inside the Linden General Good's store's stock.*

*Reward: Spell Training, 100xp*
*Do you accept this quest? Accept/Decline*

I took a moment to weigh my options. Most RPGs had obvious perks that you could gain by doing certain quests, but there were also underlying consequences to completing many of them. If what Eanos said was true, then Gerard was selling scrolls at a much lower price, which would provide me with a nice touchpoint for buying more spells as I leveled up at a lower cost.

But then again, I really wanted to get some magic training under my belt and I wasn't sure when I would run into someone else could train me. I was willing to roll the dice on Eanos.

"I'll do it," I said.

*You have accepted the Quest:* **Unfair Trade Practices!**

Eanos cracked a devious smile and immediately started scribbling on the scrolls. Within a few minutes has had scribed 3 very convincing copies, and when I looked at them, I couldn't tell the difference between the fakes and the ones he had on display.

"If you get caught, I expect that you'll take full responsibility. As far as you know, this conversation never took place."

"My lips are sealed."

> *You've received:* **Fake Magic Scrolls.** *Attempting to cast these will create nothing but a nasty flatulence sound. Requires 0 Intelligence. Durability: 10/10. Quality: Above Average. Rarity: Rare. Weight: 0.1 kg*

I walked from Eanos' arcane shop feeling a bit nervous and a bit wicked about what I was about to do. How much would Gerard suffer, and what if I got caught?

Whatever the case, the thought of learning magic was more than enough to make me throw caution to the wind.

# Chapter 8

*01/02/0001*

"Welcome!" Gerard stood from behind his counter and smiled. "Oh… You're back so soon?"

I scratched the back my head and smiled back at him. "Yeah, there were a few things I wanted to have a look at!"

"Great! Great! Make yourself at home. I assure you that we have the lowest prices in town. If you find a lower price on something anywhere in Linden, just let me know and I'll match it."

I walked over to the counter and looked down at some plants that he had resting under the glass. "Pricing matching? You're an awfully competitive salesman."

Gerard snickered. "Well, I want to make sure that everyone in Linden can afford the things they need. Some people say that I'm forcing profits down for other businesses by offering such low prices, but I think I'm bringing more travelers in and preventing the other shops from price gouging!"

He was already making me feel a little bad about my Quest.

I pointed down to one of the random plants. "Are you the only one offering these kind of herbs in town?"

"Hmm," Gerard touched his cleanly shaven chin. "Sometimes the innkeeper has a few herbs stocked, but that's rare. There used to be a pretty little lady who also sold herbs at the end of town, but she got caught up with some swordsmith and they ran off and got married. Last I heard, they built a farm over near Shallow Marsh."

Hmmm, I thought. Either Eanos or Gerard were lying—and given how friendly Gerard was, it was probably Eanos—but I also remember how friendly Trainer was right before he kicked me in the chest when I entered the tutorial. Things weren't always as they seemed in Eden's Gate.

I spotted the crate that Eanos had told me about in the corner of my vision then looked up to an axe that Gerard had hanging on the wall behind him. "Do you mind if I have a look at that axe?"

Gerard turned. "Oh, of course. Let me just get my step-stool here." Gerard walked from behind the counter and grabbed a small wooden stool, which he moved to right in front of the axe. He stepped up on it and reached for the axe, and while his back was turned, I flipped open my satchel and tossed the fake scrolls into the crate with the rest, rolling my hand around to mix them up.

> *You have completed all requirements for the quest:* **Unfair Trade Practices!** *Return to Eanos to collect your reward.*

"Hey, what are you doing?!" Gerard asked and stepped off the stool holding the axe in both hands.

"Sorry, I just noticed that you had a few magic scrolls down here. I wanted to have a look."

Gerard placed the axe on the counter and smiled. "Oh? You're interested in magic. You don't seem like you'd be a magic user."

"Not yet. I'm still only level 3 but hopefully soon."

Gerard lifted the axe a little off the glass counter and leaned over. "I don't tell many people this, but I happen to know a little bit of magic myself." He raised his eyebrows comically a few times. "I love helping other people, so if you buy this wood axe, I'll give you some basic magic training for free. As a matter of fact, you've been so kind, I'll give you the axe for 50% off. Only 3 gold pieces."

My stomach turned. For the bargain price of 3 gold, I would've had a nice axe, and gotten the magic training I wanted without having to perform any dirty deeds. But the damage had been done already. There was no way I would be able to find the fake scrolls in the mess of others that he had. I'd have to live with the choice I had already made.

Apparently, the game knew that too. I didn't even get a prompt for another quest.

I walked up to the counter and touched the axe, making an effort to pretend that I was still making up my mind. I knocked my knuckle on the counter a couple times and snapped my lips together. "You know, I'm going to have to sleep on it. I'll come back later if it's still available."

Gerard beamed a kind smile and nodded. "I understand. If there's anything else you're interested in, just let me know."

I nodded back. "Thanks."

I turned around and pushed through the door of the shop hard, hoping that I hadn't just totally fucked Gerard's life up too much. He really seemed like a nice guy.

I spent a few moments gathering myself before I walked back in Eanos' arcane shop, a smug look on my face.

He was busy feeding his bird as I stepped through the door and turned to me as I entered. "I take it that you have some news?"

"It's done," I said.

> *You have completed the quest:* **Unfair Trade Practices***!*

> *You have gained 100 XP!*

Eanos rubbed his hands together and showed a wide smile. "Good job. Finally, that caveman will get what he deserves."

"You lied to me!" I spat.

"Lied?" Eanos tossed a piece of bread towards his bird. The bird caught the bread expertly and chomped it down as Eanos paced behind his counter. "I have every intention of holding up my end of the bargain."

"You made it sound like Gerard was a monster and said that he ran the herbalist out of town. He seemed like a good guy. And he told me the herbalist left for love."

"I never said that he was a monster. I said that he was a bad businessman. And the other stuff…" Eanos shrugged and smirked. "It's all just minor details."

"Maybe you're the monster."

Eanos rolled his eyes. "Oh please. I'm the monster? Did you sabotage Gerard because you thought he was suchhhhh a bad guy, or did you do it because you wanted to learn magic?"

I puffed up my chest and swallowed but I didn't reply. He was right, after all. Had he not offered me the chance to learn some magic, I wouldn't have had any interest in getting involved in their affairs.

"Right. Now quit being a little pansy, and let's get this over with. I'd rather not spend too long teaching some low level how to blow himself up."

I took a step forward as Eanos started shuffling through scrolls.

"I'm skilled in Arcane, Fire, and Water Magic. Which branch would you prefer to learn?"

If only I had access to a gaming guide. Had I been playing any other game I would have loaded up a wiki page or forum to plan a path towards the best possible build, but being stuck in Eden's gate offered me no such option. The game forced you to figure out just about everything on your own.

"What would you suggest?" I asked.

"Every branch of magic serves a purpose. You can't go wrong no matter what path you choose." Eanos tilted his head sideways and looked me up and down. "Might I suggest fire magic?" He turned around and opened his cabinet, withdrawing two scrolls from within. He slid one on top of the glass. "Judging by the fact that you're an archer, this should help you."

> **Scroll: Fire Arrow.** *Ignite a flying arrow with fire, causing additional fire damage upon impact. Requires 10 Intelligence. Requires Archery Level 1. Fire Magic Level 1. Durability: 10/10. Quality: Average. Rarity: Uncommon. Weight: 0.1 kg*

"And this," He slid another scroll on top of the glass, "is a nice complement."

> **Scroll: Fireblast.** *Release a blazing ball of fire. Requires 10 Intelligence. Fire Magic Level 1. Durability: 10/10. Quality: Average. Rarity: Uncommon. Weight: 0.1 kg*

"Is there any limit to how much magic I can learn?"

"Learning magic is only limited by your own personal mental capacity. Assuming you can remember all your spells, you could learn all the magic in existence. But even Master magic users usually only scratch the surface of what's available. I've never met someone who knows it all."

"Alright. I'll go with Fire." It seemed like a good place to start, and since I wasn't limited to learning anything, I could always try a different branch later on. Plus, releasing "a blazing ball of fire" sounded really fucking cool.

Eanos grinned. "Very well. Let's turn you into a firestarter." He flicked two of his fingers in a 'come hither' motion. "Lcan forward."

I leaned my head forward. "Just like this?" I asked.

Eanos ignored my question and simply placed his open palm on the top of my head. In my peripheral vision, I could see him close his eyes and raise his free hand. "With my Fire, I release your Fire! Become one with Fire!" his voice boomed.

Heat poured over my body, and it felt as if energy was coursing through my veins. My skin crawled with something that I could only describe as power, and then suddenly the feeling died away.

> *You've gained 10% resistance to fire!*
>
> *Advancement! You have learned the skill:* ***Fire Magic****. Let it burn! Let it burn! Let it burn! Fire Magic is linked the base stat Intelligence. Increase your Intelligence to increase your ability to perform Fire Magic.*

"I gained magic resistance?" I asked.

"Of course," Eanos said. "Anyone skilled in certain types of magic automatically gains a small amount of resistance or even additional characteristics when they learn them." He reached for the two scrolls and handed them to me. "Now all you have to do is read."

I looked at the first scroll, Fire Arrow, and the words seemed to shift around on the page as if they were floating in liquid. When I saw them on the counter, the writing had just looked a like a scribble of strange letters and symbols, but now that I had learned Fire Magic, it had changed, and I had a feeling deep inside my gut that I understood it somehow. As soon as I tried to read the first word, the letters floated off the page and a soft, unintelligible voice whispered something in my head.

The words disappeared into thin air, and the scroll vanished into a puff of red mist.

> *Advancement! You have learned the spell:* ***Fire Arrow****.*

I repeated the process with the second scroll.

*Advancement! You have learned the spell:*
**Fireblast.**

"That's it?" I asked. "Now I can cast spells?" I looked down at my hands, trying to figure out if anything had changed.

"Don't try to cast any fire magic in here!" Eanos snapped. "If you burn my scrolls, I'll have your head. Here…" Eanos stepped behind his counter and pushed open a backdoor. "Come outside."

I followed Eanos to behind his shop which was mostly an empty lot of grass. On each side was a wooden fence, and several meters in the distance was a sloping stone wall—the side of a rising path that led off to a hillside.

"Just will yourself to a cast Fireblast at the wall. And *please*," Eanos stressed. "Make sure your hand is pointed towards the wall."

I lifted my hand out and pointed my palm towards the center of the wall and concentrated on casting Fireblast. In an instant, I could feel heat surge around my wrist and slither towards my fingertips. In front of my palm, a golf ball sized globe of fire formed, then rocketed away from me almost as fast as one of my arrows.

Flames trailed the fireball as it flew through the air, and it landed against the wall with a low boom, searing the rock as the flames dissipated.

"Holy shit!" I said as I looked at my hands "Did you see that?! Oh my god."

Eanos rolled his eyes. "Yeah, I saw it, and we better hurry back inside just in case someone else saw it too."

"Wait! I want to do it again," I huffed. "And I still need to test my Fire Arrow spell!"

Eanos pushed on my shoulder and indicated the door. "You'll have plenty of time to practice your magic when you're out on your own. People don't take lightly to individuals casting damaging spells like Fireblast right in the middle of town."

I followed Eanos back into his shop, my breath still heavy with excitement over my new ability. I noticed in my stats bar that my mana had dropped about 20%, so at my current level, I'd be able to cast Fireblast about five times before my mana pool was empty, however the bar was slowly but surely filling back up.

"Well, thanks for your help," I said.

"Yeah, sure," Eanos said and flicked his fingers towards the door, shooing me away. "Be careful with your new magic, and if I find that you lied to me about Gerard, you'll need a lot more than Fireblast to save you."

I chuckled at how crabby the old man was as I exited his shop. He certainly wasn't a people person, that's for sure. And my Fireblast... *Fuck,* that was awesome. I couldn't wait to get out of the village so I could experiment with it more.

I marched towards the inn to find Jax and paused at the bulletin board that was posted outside. It was already dark outside, but the lantern hanging over the inn door gave off enough light that I could still make out the various parchments that were nailed the board's wood. Some of them said "HELP" with descriptions of various tasks or items that people were seeking. Others said "WANTED DEAD" with photos or descriptions of individuals. Bounties listed were between 10-300 gold, depending on the task.

A nice way to make money, I thought. I made a mental note to return to the board if I ever needed a straightforward way to make cash.

The sound of violins, tapping and people chattering bounced off the walls as I made my way into the brightly lit Inn. At the center of it all was a bald man with a beard and an apron standing behind a large wooden counter, wiping it down with a towel, kegs stacked tall behind him.

There were around fifteen people sitting around various tables, drinking ale, some eating, and in the far corner a couple of women in thick, cotton dresses were happily dancing to the sound of the cheery music that two nearby musicians were playing. It was like I had been transported into my favorite RPG tavern—but wait—*that's what really happened.*

I immediately noticed Jax sitting in a far corner across from a man half his size. The other man was stout, with a large, flat forehead and long, tangled red beard. Jax was laughing at something as they both knocked their mugs together and took a swig of ale. Several empty mugs were pushed off to the side of the table.

Jax noticed me out of the corner of his eye as I approached and turned with a large smile on his face. "Gunnar!" He scanned me up and down. "You look like a new man!"

"Not quite as noob, right?"

"If I didn't know any better, I'd guess you were at least level 10."

"And I learned a couple spells too."

Jax's head jerked back and he looked at his companion out of the corner of his eye. He gave a slight smile to his friend then patted the wooden bench beside him. "Have a seat and order yourself some ale. A mug is only 2 gold."

I sat down beside him and shook my head. "I'm down to my last 5 gold pieces. I should probably save it."

"Oh hell!" Jax huffed and leaned back, turning his head towards the innkeeper. "Can we get another round?!" he yelled and pointed to our table. "All three of us!"

The innkeeper smiled and nodded.

"I've got you covered. Next time save a little bit of your gold for food and drink. Gotta learn to have a little fun after a long day!" He leaned in close and whispered the rest in my ear. "And it's never a good idea to discuss your magic in a place like this. You don't want to attract the wrong kind of attention."

I wasn't sure what he meant by that but I just nodded in understanding.

"Kronos, this is Gunnar," Jax said. "He's pretty good with a bow. Helped with a few kills today."

"Oy!" the dwarf said and raised his mug to his lips. After a large swig, he clicked his lips and exhaled. "Not like you to hang 'round folks much. Is he your kin?"

"No, just someone helping me out with a few tasks." Jax turned to me and winked.

"Well, look at these three fellas!" A group of 3 women seemed to appear out of nowhere and shimmied over to our table.

"If I never seen a more handsome lot!" one of the woman cooed and shook her shoulders.

The three girls were quite attractive and the tight, ruffled tops they were wearing seemed intended to show off the fact that they were all well-endowed.

"How about some company?!" one of the ladies said as she plopped herself in Jax's lap, not waiting for a response. Another squatted down and rubbed her finger down Kronos' beard.

"Careful now!" Jax said as he balanced his mug in his hand, trying to avoid spilling it on the frisky lady.

The innkeeper slammed a mug of ale in front of me and slid another two in front of Kronos and Jax as I felt a soft hand reach between my lowered cowl and tunic, squeezing on my flesh. "Relax and enjoy yourself, handsome."

I swallowed and grinned shyly as I picked the ale up and brought it to my lips.

Jax turned and raised his ale in the air. "Relax!"

I spent the next 3 hours drinking and listening to Kronos and Jax share stories of their adventures. Kronos did most of the talking, telling tales that seemed exaggerated out of proportion—slaying giant monsters solo, sailing across oceans and finding caverns filled with magical treasure. It all seemed fabricated beyond belief, but Jax and the ladies ate it up. The pair continued to buy rounds, and by the end of the night, we were all drunk—especially me.

Yesterday, I would've been shocked to think it were possible to get drunk in a game, but thus far, nothing seemed impossible in Eden's Gate.

"So these three ghouls are chasing me down Shadowrock Mountain, and I've got maybe 10% of my health left and my stamina is just about spent," Kronos gloated, waving his hands around as he told his story. "I was halfway near pissing my pants until—"

*Thunk!*

My head smacked hard against the wooden table, waking me right up from my about-to-pass-out moment.

The girl beside me stroked my hair. "Oh, poor baby! Drunk as a skunk!"

I grabbed my head and moaned. The room was spinning. "I guess I had a little too much ale."

"You should go ahead and sleep it off in one of the rooms," Jax said. "We'll head out first thing in the morning."

"How much is a room?" I asked.

"Probably more than you have, but I'll cover you for tonight." Jax turned towards the innkeep and yelled, "Got a room for this one?"

"Room number ten is open," The innkeeper replied.

"Go on," Jax motioned his head towards the stairs as he got up to pay the innkeeper.

I stood slowly, and the girl who had been fawning over me all night rose up with me, making sure I didn't fall.

"Safe journey," Kronos said as he raised a half-empty mug, dumping it down his throat. His stomach seemed to have an endless hole designed specifically for beer.

"Nice to meet you," I slurred.

I struggled up the stairs with the girl hanging onto me each step of the way, and on the second level of the

Inn was a long, straight hall with several doors on either side. Thankfully, we didn't have to walk far before we were in front of a wooden door with the number 10 nailed to the front. I pushed open the door and inside was a low bed, a table, a cabinet and a chest. Simple but effective.

"Thanks," I said to the girl as I waited for her to turn and leave.

"What?" The drunken girl look perplexed. "You don't want any company, sweetheart?" She rubbed her fingers down her neck and across her bosom. "Sleeping alone is never fun."

I was tempted. I really was. The way her breasts were spilling out of her shirt was even more titillating in my drunken state, and I wasn't used to attractive girls throwing themselves at me the way she was. But I knew whatever price she had for a night of fun was way more than I had. And given how real Eden's Gate was, I wouldn't have been surprised if they programmed STDs into the game as well. I didn't want to wake up with an icon that said '***You have been diseased***' and find myself on a quest to find the great wizard of wart removal.

Nah.

And if Rachel found out I was sleeping with NPCs that probably wouldn't go over well either.

"Sorry, but I think I'll spend the night alone."

The girl pouted and crossed her arms as I closed and locked the door. I could hear her feet pounding on the steps as she went back downstairs.

I lay down on the soft mattress of the bed and rested my head on the pillow, my head still spinning. My mind shifted back towards Rachel. I wondered what she was doing or if she was even still in-game. Hell, I had been having so much fun all day that I had practically forgotten about my dilemma. I had gone on a bit of an adventure, learned magic, and had a great time drinking with friends.

Friends…? If I had been out in the real world with a couple of guys, I'd feel out of place and like everyone was judging me—which they probably would be—but somehow I felt comfortable when I was downstairs with the hunter and the dwarf.

And magic? I rubbed my fingers together and replayed the moment I sent a fireball into the wall. The feeling of using magic was indescribable. I couldn't wait to get even more powerful, to cast more spells.

Did I even care anymore if I was stuck in game? Did I even want to go home? I wasn't sure anymore. Already, Eden's Gate was starting to feel like a place where I wanted to stay. But maybe that was the alcohol talking.

The party downstairs continued on, and the music they were playing easily pierced through the uninsulated walls of the Inn. In fact, I could still hear the faint sound of muffled voices traveling through the air.

"Let's talk business," I thought I heard. In fact, it sounded a lot like Jax's voice.

"Let's," another voice said. That was definitely Kronos.

I sat up in my bed, head still spinning, and navigated toward the floor. At the very edge of the bed was a small hole where light and sound was passing through unobstructed. I peeked through the hole and could see the top of Jax and Kronos' heads. I had been placed in a room directly above the table where I was sitting earlier.

I placed my ear up to the hole and listened.

"Are you sure you can get it?" Kronos asked.

"I can't be sure, but there's a very good chance. I'm convinced that the sword is still in Nambunga's Cave."

"How are you going to do it? That's all I want to know."

"I can't reveal all my secrets, Kronos."

"Having my brother's sword would mean a lot to me and my family."

"How much does it mean to you exactly?"

"1500 gold," Kronos said.

"2000," Jax counters.

"1700," Kronos bantered back.

"1800."

"Alight," Kronos said. "If you can get me the sword, then I'll get you 1800 gold. But I suspect that if you're going down into the cave with that ogre, I won't be seeing you again."

"Don't worry," Jax assured him. "I'll either get the sword or I won't. Either way, I won't die. I assure you that."

"We'll see about that," Kronos said.

I stood from the floor, and my ears were burning. What the fuck? Jax had commissioned me to go into the cave to get the sword, but in exchange he only planned to teach me alchemy. He never mentioned that the sword was worth a small fortune, nor had he offered me any of the money if he sold it.

I had just decked myself in a few decent starting items for a little less than 20 gold. 1800 gold would change everything for me. I could buy new weapons, scrolls and who knows what else?

Maybe that's why Jax was being so friendly towards me? He was just using me to go into the cave and collect the sword. At first, I thought I was getting a good deal with him offering to teach me alchemy, but now I was second guessing the offer.

My head swam as I lay back down on the bed, and I was having trouble processing the newfound information in my drunken state. I still planned go back down into the cave, but now I had some serious thinking to do.

# Chapter 9

*01/03/0001*

I raised my hand towards the squirrel and sent a blazing Fireblast in its direction. The impact of the spell sent it hurling back and the carcass made a sizzling noise as the creature died.

*You have gained 25 XP!*

"Nice," Jax said. "But it's a bit pointless to use that on a squirrel. The pelt is ruined and the meat is charred."

"Just practice," I explained. "I want to make sure I'm comfortable with the spell when I use it in a real situation. And I get XP."

Jax shrugged. "Alright."

As we continued through the forest, heading back towards Jax's cabin, I had been looking at anything and everything for target practice. I had to be careful using Fireblast—I didn't want to cause a forest fire, but anytime I saw a squirrel or a large rock in a relatively clear position, I'd send a Fireblast its way.

When we came to a clearing with a stump surrounded by a circle of barren dirt, I nocked an arrow and focused on my other magic spell, Fire Arrow. The arrow burst into flames the moment I tried to light it, and I just about caught my bow on fire before it crumbled into ash fell to the ground.

"What the hell?" I asked.

"So you have Fire Arrow too?"

"Yeah," I replied.

"I've seen Scourge archers use the spell before. You have to cast it on the arrow as it's flying through the air."

I nocked another arrow, aimed for the stump, and let the arrow fly. As the arrow, soared, I tried casting Fire Arrow, but the arrow just landed in the stump and burst into flames a second later.

"Your timing is off. If you want to get the full effect of the spell, you'll need it to light while it's still in the air."

I made a mental note of that, and we moved on. I definitely needed to practice Fire Arrow, but unlike shooting normal arrows, I obviously couldn't just recover the arrows that I burned to ash. I'd have to use the spell sparingly or I'd run out of arrows.

"How'd you afford your armor *and* two spells when we were in Linden?" Jax asked. "I imagine a magic user would charge you at least a few hundred gold just to teach you the basics of Fire Magic. That's if they'd even be willing to teach you."

I shrugged. "It's a long story, but I found someone who offered me a one-time deal." Being vague was better than telling him that I sabotaged the nicest guy in town to help a crabby magician.

The journey through Addenfall Forest seemed to go quicker on our way back, probably because I had been practicing Fireblast every chance I got, and by the time we arrived at the mouth of Nambunga's Cave, I had already progressed 20% through the first level of Fire Magic.

"Are you sure you want to go down there?" Jax asked. "If you'd like to take some time to rest up at the cabin first, we can do so."

I looked at the cave, its deep-dark staring back at me. I had almost died the last time I was down there, but before I had nothing but my starting dagger. Now, I had gained a few levels, had armor, a bow, and Fire Magic even.

"I think I'll go now," I said confidently.

Jax smiled and fetched a few items out of his bag for me:

> *You've received:* **Basic Torch**. *0-1 Attack Damage. Durability: 10/10. Quality: Average. Rarity: Common. Weight: 0.3 kg. This item provides a basic light source when lit.*

> *You've received:* **Minor Healing Potion.** *Durability: 10/10. Quality: Average. Rarity: Common. Weight: 0.1 kg. Drink to recover 50 HP over 5 seconds.*

> *You've received:* **Minor Cure Potion.** *Durability: 10/10. Quality: Average. Rarity: Common. Weight: 0.1 kg. Drink to cure minor poison effects.*

> *You've received:* **Small Bandage**. *Durability: 5/5. Quality: Average. Rarity: Common. Weight: 0.1 kg. Useful for healing light wounds.*

"I'll be nearby hunting for food. If you haven't come back out for too long, then I'll assume you've died."

"I'll be back," I said with a smile. *Maybe*. I had kept the information that I learned at the inn in the back of my mind the whole trip through Addenfall and had considered confronting Jax about it. But to be fair, I wasn't even sure if the sword was still there or if I'd be able to recover it. I needed to have the item in my hands before I made any decisions.

Jax nodded and his words seemed sincere. "Be careful down there."

I stopped at the mouth of the cave as Jax disappeared through the trees and took a moment to pull up my stats screen. I still had 4 attribute points and 2 level points to allocate, and now seemed as good of a time as any to allocate them. I placed 1 AP in Dexterity and 3 AP in Intelligence. I still wasn't sure how much I would focus on my dexterity-based skills as I progressed, but after casting my first Fireblast, I was certain that I would put a heavy emphasis on magic.

I used one 1 LP in my Archery Skill and 1 LP in my Fire Magic. I noticed that leveling my skills via level points reset my progress to 0% in each skill, so I lost all the progress I made in the previous level. I would have to consider that as I continued to level. It was probably a better idea to save LP for a skill that I just finished leveling up for the most effectiveness.

## GUNNAR LONG

| | |
|---|---|
| Race: | Human |
| Level: | 3 (Progress 49%) |
| Title: | None |
| Health/Mana/Stamina: | 120/100/100 |
| Strength: | 10 |
| Dexterity: | 14 |
| Intelligence: | 13 |
| Vitality: | 10 |
| Wisdom: | 10 |
| Willpower: | 10 |
| Charisma: | 10 |
| AR Rating: | 34 |
| Resists: | |
| | 10% Fire Resistance |
| Traits: | |
| | None |
| Primary Skills: | |
| | First Aid Lvl 1: progress 10% |
| | Inspect Lvl 1: progress 20% |
| | Sneak Lvl 1: progress 75% |
| Combat Skills: | |
| | Dodge Lvl 1: progress 20% |
| | Small Blades Lvl 1: progress 75% |
| | Backstab Lvl 1: progress 5% |
| | Archery Lvl 3: progress 0% |
| Magic Skills: | |
| | Fire Magic Lvl 2: progress 0% |

I closed my status screen and started my descent into the mouth of the cave. I grabbed at roots and vines as I climbed down the slippery dirt, and I was only halfway down the passage when the familiar smell of death hit my nostrils. The smell was even worse than I remembered—if that were possible—and I took short, shallow breaths to avoid inhaling a big whiff of the pungent air. Halfway down is when I started noticing tiny maggots clinging on to the ground and surrounding walls.

As the slope of the passage leveled out and I reached the area where the last drop of light shined from above, I quickly pulled out my torch and lit it with my flint and steel. The light from the torch lit up the dark cavern, and as expected, maggots were everywhere, feasting on the giant, rotten carcass. The dead ogre had since had much more of its flesh and entrails whittled away and a pool of foul liquid surrounded the area around the body. The sword was still there, catching the light of the torch as it leaned passively against the cavern wall.

I immediately saw the enormous maggot from before, which appeared to have doubled in size and changed from its previous pale white color to a dark brown hue. The horde of giant maggots that had been feasting away on the rot turned when they sensed the light and screeched loudly, bringing back the terrible memory of my first moments in the world. The massive brown maggot was a little bit slower to turn around, but when it did, its bubbling cry made the hair on the back of my neck stand on end.

All but the largest maggot rushed towards me at an alarming speed, leaving me little time to think. I reached my arm out and cast Fireblast towards the thick of the group, the impact causing the closest to the blast to explode and be tossed aside, while several of the maggots nearby curled when their bodies made contact with the residual flames.

Three more times I cast Fireblast at the giant maggots, whittling their numbers down substantially each time. By that point, my mana was down to 20%, so I dropped my torch, unsheathed my bow and started nocking arrow after arrow at the maggots who were still squirming their way towards me.

I started with whatever maggot was closest, and each time my arrow landed against their squishy flesh, they were easily punctured and pinned to the ground while a nasty liquid gushed out their wounds.

The smell of the tiniest maggots sizzling where I had unleashed my fire coupled with the smell of maggot guts and rotting flesh made breathing practically unbearable, and with only a couple of giant maggots still alive, I ran back towards the tunnel in which I came from so I could catch my breath.

After scrambling five or six meters up the passage, I turned and took a long, deep huff of air. The air there was still rank, but it was nowhere near as bad as the odor on the cave the cave floor.

It was only then that I noticed that I had spent all but 20 of my stamina in my flurry of arrows and quick scramble to retreat, but the bar was filling back up fast. My mana, however, was still only at 35% and recovering slowly. If I was going to pursue a path of magic, I would definitely need to toss a few points in wisdom to help with that.

I looked down the passage and could see the two remaining giant maggots trying their best to climb the slope of the passage. They would jump and try to latch on, but each time they tried, the weight of their fattened bodies caused them to lose their grip and fall back down the floor screaming.

I braced myself, readied my bow, and lobbed a couple arrows down at the easy targets, finishing off the last of the giant maggots.

> *Advancement! You have reached **level 4** and gained 3 attribute points. To assign your attribute points, open your status page. You can also increase any of your known skills by 1 level. Choose wisely, as your choices cannot be undone.*
>
> *You have gained 10 HP!*

Hell yeah! I thought. The boom of the drums every time I leveled was always exciting, and that was the first time that I noticed that both my stamina and mana jumped to 100% the moment that I reached a level. Awesome.

I immediately opened my status page and assigned two of my AP to wisdom and one to intelligence, but since my encounter with maggots had given me a substantial bump in Archery and Fire Magic, I decided to save my LP for later.

I closed the status page and considered the fact that the one massive maggot hadn't attacked. It chased after me on my first day in Eden's gate when I was running for the cave exit, but this time it didn't move other than turning around and screaming at me. And why was it suddenly brown? I suppose sitting around in a pool of rotten mess might change its color but all the other maggots were still a pale white.

Whatever the case, it was very weird and I needed to get back down there and kill that thing if I were going to scavenge the cave in safety.

I headed back to the cave floor and fetched my torch, which was still lying on the ground burning, and recovered a few of my arrows from the closest maggots that were lying nearby. The large mutant maggot was back to eating the flesh of the ogre and seemingly had forgot that I was down there, even after killing all of its friends—it was a dumb being, whatever it was.

I crouched down and slowly crept a little closer to the monstrosity, trying hard to use my Inspect skill on it.

*You have failed to inspect your target!*

*You have failed to inspect your target!*

After a few more tries, some details of the monster finally appeared.

**Name:** *Maggot Queen Pupa* ₊
**Race:** *insect*
**Level:** *9*
**Health/Mana/Stamina:** *160/80/80*
**Status:** *aggressive*

Pupa? I remembered something about those from my High School science class. Something regarding the stage that insects went through right before they transformed into whatever being they were destined to be. That would explain the change in its skin color.

The Maggot Queen was level 9, which would make it the strongest creature that I had encountered since I had been in Eden's Gate, but if the thing was going to transform into something else soon, I didn't have time to go back out of the cave and level up. I needed to kill it now before it got stronger.

I held out my hand and cast Fireblast at the Maggot Queen, and it reared its head back and screeched. The spot where my blast made impact with the Pupa sizzled a bit and left a black mark, but other than royally pissing off the maggot, it didn't seem to do a whole lot of damage.

The maggot flailed its body back and forth against the ground, it's heavy weight causing the walls of the cavern to rattle and tiny pebbles of dirt to fall from the ceiling. Although it didn't seem like the Pupa was mobile, it had enough power that it could crush me if I got too close.

I readied my bow and nocked an arrow, aiming directly for its fang-filled, puckered mouth, but with it moving around so much, my arrow missed its mouth and struck its body instead. But rather than penetrating the maggot's flesh the arrow simply ricocheted off and tumbled to the ground without doing any real damage.

The maggot screeched again, reared its head back and then towards me. Its puckered mouth opened wide, and a thick yellow substance rocketed out of its mouth like a pressured water hose. I tried to dodge the blast, but the spray of liquid was too wide, and I got a face full of the nasty goop.

My skin burned when the Maggot's acid hit me, and the smell was so overwhelming that I dropped to my knees and evacuated the sausage and eggs breakfast that Jax and I had eaten at the Linden Inn early in the morning.

I coughed hard and wiped my mouth of vomit then rubbed my hands across my face, trying to clear any acid away from my eyes and scurried backwards, desperate to get out of range of another blast.

"Fuck!" I cursed. That one hit knocked out 25% of my health and my stamina was dropped to 50% instantly. I also had that dreaded green skull and crossbones hovering below my stat bars.

> *You have been **poisoned** and require medical attention. Poison is a weakening and damage-over-time effect.*

My stomach turned inside me like the writhing maggots that I had just killed, and the pain coursed up and down my spine. My health bar dropped to 70%

I watched as the Maggot Queen pounded its body from side to side and tried to formulate a plan. I was down to roughly 10 arrows and still had most of my mana, but both my Archery and Fireblast seemed ineffective. I had a cure potion, but if I drank it right away, I might get sprayed again by another blast and another poisoning would probably kill me even if I managed to kill the Queen first.

The problem was the damn thing's hard skin seemed to absorb my Fireblast and my arrow strikes. The only weak spot that it seemed to have was its mouth, but the chances of me getting a solid shot into its trap with it flopping around the way it was slim. There was a possibility that my dagger would be more effective, but I ran the risk of getting crushed under the weight of the monster if I got too close and couldn't avoid its slams.

*Fire Arrow...* I wasn't sure if it would work or even if I could get the timing down right, but it seemed like the last logical step to try, otherwise I'd have to call it a day and come back again after a couple levels, hoping it hadn't mutated any further.

I stood to my feet, fighting off the weakness from the poisoning and gripped my bow tightly. I stepped forward into the Maggot Queen's range of attack and braced myself for another spew. The Pupa screeched just as it had before, reared its head back then forward, shooting another load of vile liquid from its mouth.

I ducked and rolled this time, narrowly missing the projectile's path and ran as fast as I could towards the Maggot Queen's flank. Another pulse of pain was felt and my health dropped 5% more as I dropped to one knee and pulled back a single arrow as hard as I could. I released the bowstring, and in the short time it was in the air, I concentrated on my Fire Arrow spell, and this time it had the desired effect.

The was a slight "woosh" sound as the arrow tip changed to a glowing hot red, and flames trailed the shaft of the arrow. The scalding arrow tip pierced the Queen's shell as it made contact and a flash of fire exploded out of the point of impact.

The Pupa screeched even louder as its hard casing near the area impacted fell charred to the ground, and a green gooey liquid poured out of its side. Inside the shell, I could see a long, stringy black leg kick out, and a mess of other jumbled appendages jumping around randomly as the Pupa floundered about.

Whatever was inside of that thing was about to come out.

I ran forward as the sound of the Pupa's shell cracking caught my ears and fired another Fire Arrow which seemed to rock the Maggot Queen, then followed it up with another two Fireblasts to the exposed portion of the insect body underneath.

My mana was almost spent.

The mangled creature writhed on the ground, but I could still see the inner insect kicking out a leg against the ground. I sheathed my bow and grabbed my dagger from my satchel, jumping on top of the Pupa just as two giant eyes stretched open the Queen Maggot's mouth and made its first contact with the cavern's air.

I aimed the dagger for the crevice right between the insect's two giant globes and thrust it down as hard as I could. More green liquid gushed from where I penetrated its head, and the creature kicked out its leg hard enough that I fell off the slippery Pupa shell.

*You have reached level 2 in **Small Blades**!*

The impact of the fall knocked 10% of my health off, and then a surge of poison pain depleted another 5%, but the dagger attack proved worth it. The Maggot Queen kicked its leg again, softer, and then softer again before it wasn't moving at all.

*You have gained 350 XP!*

"Fuck you, maggot bitch!" I panted and chuckled to myself as I tried to catch my breath. "Hell yes!"

I reached inside my satchel as another poison pain gripped my body and pulled out the cure potion, pouring it down my throat as fast as I could. The taste was a mix of mint and pine with the slightest hint of cucumber. Immediately the green skull and crossbones disappeared, and I felt a little stronger. I followed it up by drinking the health potion. I figured that I could probably survive on the health I still had left, since there were no more baddies around, but I didn't want to risk killing myself if there were any traps or dangers that I had yet to see.

I sat there on the ground as my stamina recovered and the heal potion took care of the acid damage; the scalded areas of my skin seemed to regenerate into healthy skin right before my eyes.

"I guess it's time to see if this was all worth it," I said out loud. I stood to my feet and walked across the cavern to pick up my fallen torch. Then, I immediately headed for the sword.

> *You've received:* **unidentified magic sword.** *Requires 17 Strength. Durability: 8/10. Quality: Exceptional. Rarity: Epic. Weight: 4.0 kg*

> *You have completed all requirements for the quest:* **Old Nambunga's Cave!** *Return the sword to Jax to collect your reward.*

As I lifted the sword in my hands, I was immediately impressed by the craftsmanship. The blade was thick in the center and sloped down to an ultra-sharp tip. I grabbed it with both hands by the jagged golden hilt and tried to swing it around, but each attempted swing drained 50% of my stamina, and my movement with it was really, really slow.

"Too damn heavy," I muttered. There was no way I was going to be able to use a sword that required 17 strength when I only had 10.

The hilt had two oval impressions carved out on either side, and above them was the carving of a bear. I didn't know what any of it meant, but the sword definitely looked expensive. The few other swords that I had seen in game so far were quite basic in comparison.

Did Jax really think that I wouldn't notice that this was an extraordinary item? Did he really think that I would go into the cave, retrieve the sword and just hand it to him in exchange for simple Alchemy training? I mean, he thought I might be coming here to steal the sword away from a living Ogre, but even fighting the Maggot Queen was damn exhausting.

Jax hadn't done anything at all. While I was down in a smelly ass cavern risking my life, he was out hunting for food. Why would he deserve to claim the 1800 gold? I deserved at least half, probably all. In fact, what was stopping me from marching the sword down to Linden and selling it to Kronos or one of the vendors?

Or what was stopping me from keeping the sword? It would a massive upgrade from my training dagger, and I just needed to level a few times and invest all my points into Strength before I could wield it properly.

*Critical Choice Detected*

*You have reached a critical choice. In Eden's Gate, you will reach critical moments in which you will face complicated choices that will affect you and the world around you substantially. There is no right or wrong way to approach these critical choices, but be aware that your decisions could result in major rewards or grave consequences and may also shape the world around you in unexpected ways. Choose carefully.*
*This is a one-time message that you will not see again as you reach future critical points.*

Interesting... Even the game seemed to recognize that I could easily abandon my quest and keep the sword or sell it if I wanted to. And the more I thought about it, selling it seemed like the best option for me. 1800 gold would be *huge* for a low level like me and would give me a substantial advantage towards leveling and getting better gear.

Lying on the ground near the sword was a dirty sheath that obviously belonged to the weapon. I slid the sword inside and attached it to my armor as I continued to look around the cave.

There was a large wooden chest near the ogre's body which I found was unlocked as I lifted the lid. Inside were several dead bats and a number of weapons that were rusted beyond recognition. But there were a few salvageable items and many gold coins scattered along the bottom.

*You've received:* **Corroded Short Sword.** *7-12 Attack Damage. Durability: 6/10. Quality: Poor. Rarity: Common. Weight: 2.9*

*You've received:* **Ringmail Gauntlets.** *+10 Armor. Durability: 8/10. Quality: Average. Rarity: Common. Weight: 1.4 kg*

*You've received:* **Minor Healing Potion.** *Durability: 10/10. Quality: Average. Rarity: Common. Weight: 0.1 kg. Drink to recover 50 HP over 5 seconds.*

*You've received:* **133 Gold Pieces**

I smiled as I scooped the coins into my satchel. 133 coins was a nice payload for me and a good start for saving up for my next set of gear. I wouldn't have to rely on Jax the next time I headed over to Linden Inn either. Maybe I would be the one buying rounds next time.

I stepped through the pool of rot, purposely breathing through my mouth rather than my nose as I inspected the dead Ogre. I found nothing in its pockets other than a couple of rotten bat wings, but I noticed a piece of wet, black cloth poking out beneath its body. But it didn't seem like just any cloth as it had golden letters etched at the hem.

A magic cloak? I wondered.

I held my breath and pushed hard against the weight of the heavy, rotten body. My hands sank into the nasty flesh as I pushed, and my feet were slipping on the goop on the floor, but I finally managed to get the rot to flop over enough that I could see what was underneath.

An orc—or what I could only assume was an orc—was lying lifeless on the ground, its body flattened like a pancake. It was wearing a black hooded robe with gold letters etched across the bottom, and in its hand was a straight black staff with a skull resting on the top. Right above it was another crushed creature with emaciated, wrinkled skin, floppy, flat ears and pair of torn leather shorts. A broken longbow lay beside it along with a quiver of crushed arrows.

> *You have completed all requirements for the quest:* **Scourge Activity!** *The information you discovered may have of value to Princess Adeelee. Return to her to collect your reward.*

Damn, I was on a roll! I wasn't sure exactly why, but I guess the fact that I had found the orc and the other mangled humanoid was the type of information that the princess wanted. Whatever, I thought. More rewards for me!

I grabbed the staff and pulled the robe off the dead orc. Thankfully it was wearing underwear. But judging by the bulge in the monster's pants, orcs put humans to shame in that department.

> *You've received:* **unidentified magic robe***. Requires 28 Intelligence. Durability: 9/10. Quality: Exceptional. Rarity: Epic. Weight: 1.0 kg*

> *You've received:* **unidentified magic staff***. Requires 30 Intelligence. Durability: 9/10. Quality: Exceptional. Rarity: Epic. Weight: 1.1 kg*

I didn't need the system prompt to know that I was dealing with magic items. The staff, in particular, made my blood turn cold the moment I picked it up, and I could practically feel the energy pouring out of the robe. It was... tingly!

I tried to use my Inspect ability on the items, but nothing happened. Not even a system prompt. I could only assume that Inspect would only work on living on beings, not items. I had no idea how to identify magic items, so I'd have to do some asking around once I got back to the surface.

I found nothing of use on the other creature—which by that point, I assumed was a goblin, but right when I was about to turn to pack up, I noticed a ring on the orc's fingers.

> *You've received:* **unidentified magic ring**.
> *Requires 15 Intelligence. Durability: 9/10.*
> *Quality: Exceptional. Rarity: Epic. Weight:*
> *0.1 kg*

I pulled the golden ring off the orc and had a good look at it before slipping it over my finger. Everything seemed okay. I had no idea what magic properties the ring had, but the 15 intelligence requirement didn't seem to be an issue, despite me only having 14. It wasn't until I was gathering up all my loot and walking around the perimeter of the cave to collect my still-intact arrows that I noticed that my hand was trembling.

It wasn't a violent shake, but it certainly was uncomfortable. There was no way I'd be able to walk around shaking like I was on the verge of a drug overdose. Needless to say, I took the ring off and threw it in my satchel. Stat requirements mattered.

I saw nothing else in the cave that looked interesting, but there was still another unexplored passage that led off somewhere. I considered having a look, but decided against it as the weight of the two swords, the staff and the other items was already going to be a lot to lug up the cave exit.

I was exhausted when I reached the mouth of the cave, but I was relieved to finally get a breath of much needed fresh air. I didn't want to see the bottom of that cave again for a long, long time, if ever.

Jax wasn't anywhere in sight when I emerged, and I was kind of glad. I was carrying a ton of loot, and the most notable item was the magic sword that I heard him negotiating for 1800 gold. I looked in the direction of his cabin and really considered hiking back there to give him the sword with a demand for at least half of the gold. The other items would probably be worth enough to get me by.

But why? Eden's Gate was huge, and I had no intention of staying with him any longer than I had to. Why not go to Linden and get the whole 1800 gold myself? That would be enough for me to afford a room for a while and have enough money for upgrades. Surely, someone in Linden knew how to find Princess Adeelee in order to complete my other quest, and I could take up some of the bounties that were posted on the bulletin board.

A perfect plan!

I headed straight for Linden, following the same trajectory that I took when I went there with Jax. I was exhausted after the hike back to Addenfall and the fighting in the cave, but I knew that a few more hours of walking was going to pay off for me big time. My mouth was salivating with the idea of all the things I could buy. More fire spells! Or maybe I'd try to talk Eanos in teaching me another branch of magic for a nice sum of gold? The possibilities seemed endless.

I had only been walking for about 30 minutes when I noticed a bush filled with wild blackberries. Just the sight of the juicy morsels dangling there made my stomach growl. I hadn't eaten since I left Linden, and I left a lot of that meal on the bottom of the cave floor.

I stopped at the bush and started picking the berries one by one, shoving them in my mouth. I leaned my head back and let out a slight moan, enjoying the burst of fruity flavor, when I heard the slightest sound of what I thought were voices. I immediately went on guard and started sneaking as slowly as I could towards the noise.

The closer I got, the louder the voices became, and I started to hear the crackles of burning wood. Eventually, I reached the edge of a small clearing and ducked behind a bush, watching as a group of four men were throwing branches on a freshly lit fire.

*You have reached level 2 in **Sneak**!*

Nice, I thought. Now was a great time for me to gain more sneaking skills.

The four men were dressed in a mix of leather and cloth clothing, and they had their stash cast off to the side. A couple of dead birds were laying near the fire, and they were all well-armed. Each one of them had a dagger or sword dangling from their belt and two of them had bows.

I attempted to use my Inspect skill on one of them.

*Name:* Forest Bandit
*Race:* Human
*Level:* 7
*Health/Mana/Stamina:* 110/10/60
*Status:* Unknown

*You have reached level 2 in* **Inspect***!*

I wasn't sure if the group of men were friendly or not, but judging by the fact that they garnered the label "Bandit," I figured the chances were pretty high that they weren't.

I slowly backed away from the bush that I was hiding behind and quietly sneaked away from the bandit camp. I wanted to get as far away from there as possible to avoid any potential problems. If I was right and they ended up being aggressive, I wasn't sure how long I'd last against four level 7s. I'd have no choice but to run.

When I was a safe distance from the bandits, I stood back up and started my way back towards Linden, wondering if the bandits had paid their tribute to the forest. The thought of the keemus showing up and stealing all their shit brought a smile to my face.

I gasped hard.

Pain rippled through my body, and my smile disappeared when I heard the sound of cold steel piercing through the center of my back. I could no longer feel my legs and involuntarily dropped to my knees as I watched 90% of my health bar wipe away instantly.

I struggled to breathe—the pain was so great—and I reached around right as someone was pulling the dagger that they just stabbed me with out of my spine.

I cried out in agony and felt the warm blood gushing out the wound, down my back and into my leather leggings. It was shocking—the most intense pain I had ever felt, even worse than my first day in Eden's gate when I had almost died.

All I could think was "*Why? Who would want to kill me?*"

A strong boot kicked out, knocking me to the ground face-first, and I screamed again at the pain, ignoring the dirt and grass that was working its way into my mouth.

My shoulder was yanked hard, turning me until I was looking up at my attacker. Dark thin eyes squinted at me, and I could only assume that he was smiling under the red bandana that was covering his mouth and nose. Was he one of the bandits? I wasn't sure. But I knew I didn't have much longer to fight for my life.

I blocked out the indescribable pain and started to cast my Fireblast, but the moment the fire started streaming out of my fingertips, the guised man stepped hard on my hand, breaking several bones in the process.

Again, I screamed in anguish.

"None of that now," he whispered under his cloth.

He leaned down and placed his hand over my mouth to muffle my cries and raised the bloody dagger in front of my face.

"Nighty night," he mused.

The last thing I remember seeing was a black necklace strung from his neck with the emblem of a sparrow dangling at the end.

Blood spewed out and onto his covered face when he rubbed the sharp edge of his blade across my throat, and although I tried to scream again, all I got was a mouth full of salty blood.

My heath bar dropped to 0, and all I could hear was the sound of my heartbeat slowing and a low ringing in my ears. My strength faded so fast that I could no longer hold open my eyes, and as my lids closed and my heart thumped its last couple times, my entirety fell into darkness.

*YOU HAVE DIED*

*All of your current level's progression has been reset to 0% and any unused attribute and level points have been lost.*

*You will respawn at your last bound location in approximately 2:00:00*

*Take this time to reflect on your choices.*

# Chapter 10

*Day 3 (Earth)*

The television was tuned to popular show, *Real Events*. On one side of the screen was a window was the blonde host, Kimberly, her face set in a strong frown. On the other side of the screen was her guest, Robert Murray, a geeky looking fellow with glasses hugging tightly against curly brown hair.

"It's only been a few days since the mass murder of millions of people around the world via a piece of technology known as the Nexicon VR—something that very few people have experienced and lived to tell the tale," Kimberly spoke firmly. "Today, we have someone who has been inside this VR world, ironically named "Eden's Gate", and is sitting with us here today—Mr. Robert Murray."

Robert nodded and smiled.

"Welcome to the show, Mr. Murray. Can you tell us a little bit about yourself?"

"Thanks for having me, Kim. I'm 24 years old and I'm an accountant here in Lubbock, Texas. I'm also a professional gamer."

Kimberly looked down at her script. "And from what I've been told, you've actually been inside of Eden's Gate and somehow didn't die. Can you tell us a little bit about how that happened?"

Robert shuffled in his chair and cleared his throat. "Well, I logged into Eden's Gate the moment I got my VR headset in the mail. I imagine that was around 11 in the morning… so I got in almost 3 hours of playtime in before I logged out."

Kimberly dropped her chin. "You were able to just log out?"

"I'm a huge Nexicon fan, so I only logged out so that I didn't miss the keynote. It was before everything went down. I was just as shocked as anyone when I watched what happened on my TV."

Kimberly looked down at her script again. "And what's more shocking about your experience is that you've claimed online and on internet forums that you would actually like to go *back* inside of Eden's gate?"

"Yeah, I've really been considering it. I've got very little holding me back."

"So you would commit suicide?"

Robert's eyes shuffled to the side. "Well, if what people are saying is true, then it's not really suicide. I mean, if people are actually living inside of Eden's Gate."

Kimberly rocked her head from side to side and blinked her eyes. "So you're telling me you would give up your life on Earth for a chance to—" Kimberly raised her fingers and bent them at the center knuckle. "—'*live*' inside of Eden's Gate?"

Robert shrugged. "Well, I guess if it—"

"Yes or no, Mr. Murray."

Robert took a deep breath. "Yes, I guess that's what I'm saying."

Kimberly chuckled, rolled her eyes and slapped her script against her desk. "This is unbelievable." She looked straight at the screen. "And get this, people. Mr. Murray isn't the only one claiming that they're willing to die to transfer their consciousness inside of this so-called *'game'*. There have already been reports of multiple *intentional suicides* where people have put on the VR headset, with full knowledge of the repercussions. You support this kind of behavior, Mr. Murray?"

"If that's what they want to do..."

Kimberly rolled her eyes again and shook her head. "Can you tell me exactly what you experienced in Eden's Gate that makes you feel the way you do?"

Robert smiled and shook his head slowly as if he were reminiscing something special. "I experienced life in Eden's Gate. A different life. It wasn't just a game. It was real."

"And it says here you... *ahem*...'spawned on an ice-covered area of the map and leveled up your fencing and fishing skills before making friends with a helpful non-player character'."

"Yes, it was an ice village known as Tillos. The whole place was beautiful and I had time to run a quest before I—"

"Stop, Mr. Murray." Kimberly held up one of her palms. "You know that you sound like a delusional madman, right?"

Robert sighed. "It might sound crazy, but being inside of Eden's Gate was one of the most enjoyable moments of my life. If I could have that forever, I think I probably would."

# Chapter 11

## *01/03/0001*

> *You have failed to complete the quest:* **Old Nambunga's Cave!** *Failure to complete quests may result in deteriorated relationships with quest givers and their companions.*
>
> '

I clawed at my neck and coughed the moment I respawned. *Holy-fucking-shit!* Dying in Eden's Gate was easily the worst experience of my life. The pain, the terror, the feeling of going black. Even after existing in what I can only describe as "nothingness" for two hours, I still had to sit down and pull myself together after all that. Over and over again, the shock of the dagger going into my spine and the blade slashing against my throat played out in my head.

When my heart slowed to a normal pace and I could finally think straight, I realized that I was once again sitting inside the first chamber of the cave that I started in. The next thought came hard and fast:

*My gear!*

I felt at my sides, and my satchel was missing. In fact, the only thing that I spawned with was a pair of cotton boxers. *Everything* that I had was gone!

My body was trembling when I stood up in the pitch black of the cave—from the cold or the fear of going through another death like I just had, I didn't know—and I held my arms out, trying to feel around for the wall. There was a chance that I could have felt my way back towards the area where the dead ogre was and make my way out of the passage, but I had an idea.

I cast a Fireblast out into the center of the room which lit the place up, and the residual flames gave off a fair amount of light for a few seconds after impact. I knew that I could only cast Fireblast a few times without expending my mana, so I ran desperately through the cave before the light of the fire burned out.

I cast Fireblast three more times before I was in the chamber with the ogre and had to cast once more to find the exit passage. It was already dark outside so no natural light was shining down to guide me.

"Fuck this!" I cursed as I climbed out of the mouth of the cave.

It was then that I realized just how much I had took light for granted my whole life. I was born and raised in the city, and there wasn't anywhere you could go without a street light or bulb hanging from a home or business to guide your way. There in Addenfall, a distant moon—a near clone to the moon on Earth—gave off the tiniest bit of lunar light, but otherwise I had almost 0 visibility in the forest that night.

I waited nervously for my mana to refill, jumping each time I heard the crackling of a branch of the howl of an animal. I didn't want to die again… No fucking way! I never wanted to go through that again.

I opened my stats to see the damage that had been done.

## GUNNAR LONG

| | |
|---|---|
| Race: | Human |
| Level: | 4 (Progress 0%) |
| Title: | None |
| Health/Mana/Stamina: | 130/100/100 |
| Strength: | 10 |
| Dexterity: | 14 |
| Intelligence: | 15 |
| Vitality: | 10 |
| Wisdom: | 12 |
| Willpower: | 10 |
| Charisma: | 10 |
| AR Rating: | 0 |
| Resists: | |
| | 10% Fire Resistance |
| Traits: | |
| | None |
| Primary Skills: | |
| | First Aid Lvl 1: progress 0% |
| | Inspect Lvl 2: progress 0% |
| | Sneak Lvl 2: progress 0% |
| Combat Skills: | |
| | Dodge Lvl 1: progress 0% |
| | Small Blades Lvl 2: progress 0% |
| | Backstab Lvl 1: progress 0% |
| | Archery Lvl 3: progress 0% |
| Magic Skills: | |
| | Fire Magic Lvl 2: progress 0% |

I still maintained my levels, but all progress towards the next levels had been lost. The biggest ding to my stats was the fact that I had lost two level points that I hadn't invested. Thankfully, I hadn't left any attribute points on the table, but the loss of the two LP still hurt. Now I knew that there was major risk for not spending your points right away and substantial consequences for dying—the worst being the experience of death altogether. Even if there was no stat loss, no one would want to experience that kind of pain.

When my mana had replenished itself, I cast Fireblast nearby a few times and used the short life of the light to run around and collect small, fallen tree branches, dry leaves and scrape some bark from a tree. I tied three branches together with a few thin pieces of stringy tree bark and stuffed the dry leaves inside. Then, I cast Fireblast at the ground and stuck the end of my creation over the residual fire.

Thankfully, it worked.

> *You have gained 1 point of Intelligence!*
>
> *You've received:* **Makeshift Torch**. *0-1 Attack Damage. Durability: 10/10. Quality: Poor. Rarity: Common. Weight: 0.6 kg. This item provides a basic light source when lit.*
>
> *Advancement! You have learned the skill:* **Tinkering**. *If you never try, you never know! Tinkering is linked to the base stat Intelligence. Increase your Intelligence to increase your ability to Tinker.*

Fire magic sure was coming in handy…

I didn't have time to celebrate my gains as being barefoot, shirtless and without any sort of weapons or armor in a weird-ass forest in the middle of the night was definitely not safe. And after my death, safety was my number one priority.

I sat around just long enough to gain half of my mana back and figure out what I was going to do. Walking towards where I died with a torch in my hands would likely be suicide. If the guy who ki!led me or the forest bandits were still nearby, I'd probably get noticed and murdered again. Or kidnapped. Or tortured. Or worse. Having my throat slit was really wigging me out. I wanted to see if they had left any of my items at my death site, but it was just too risky to try.

The only logical choice was to go to Jax's cabin to see if he was around. Maybe he'd let me stay there again 'til I could get back on my feet.

I tiptoed through the forest, holding in my curses each time the soft flat of my foot stepped on a sharp branch or rock. I held my torch high in front of me, certain that every few minutes I had seen eyes staring back at me from somewhere, certain that I was hearing footsteps that weren't my own. Basically, I was paranoid as a motherfucker.

I eventually made it to Jax's cabin without incident, but there were no lights shining through the single window at the front of his home. Either he wasn't there or he was sleeping.

I knocked on the door, and within seconds, I heard footsteps coming from inside. A lantern was lit and I could see a shadow peek through the window.

Thank god! I thought.

I waited a minute or more without anyone coming to the door before I knocked again. I couldn't figure out why he wasn't answering. "Jax! It's me, Gunnar!"

The door flung open and rather than a friendly greeting, Jax jumped on top of me, knocking my torch out of my hand and pinning me to the ground with a heavy knee on my abdomen. He held the tip of a sharp sword right up against my jugular.

"Show your true self now!" Jax spat. His eyes were wide and manic, and I had no doubt that he wouldn't hesitate to kill me at any moment.

I felt the muscles in my bowels constrict, and I was pretty sure if I hadn't just died and had any liquid in my bladder, I would've pissed my pants.

*Was it Jax who killed me?* I wondered. I hadn't paid much attention to my killer's hair, but from my vague memory it was long and stringy just the same. And both men had roughly the same build. Maybe he saw that I tried to run off with the sword that I promised him in the quest, and killing me was the fastest way for him to get the item back. There was a real possibility that Jax had been behind that red bandana.

"Don't kill me!" I begged.

"I said show yourself!" he insisted louder.

"What do you mean?"

"Don't fuck with me, shapeshifter! I will cut your throat right now." He pressed the tip right up against my skin and even the slightest additional pressure would have drawn blood.

"Shapeshifter?" I tried to shake my head but every movement tormented the spot where the blade threatened my neck. "It's Gunnar, Jax. I'm not a shapeshifter... please."

"Gunnar is dead," he hissed. "Now show yourself or die!"

*So it was Jax who killed me!* I thought. I was shocked. Trainer had told me, "Pain and death can come from unexpected places." Today was proving that his words were 100% true.

"Yes, I died but I respawned." I swallowed hard. "Just let me go… please. I'll leave."

"Respawned?" Jax leaned his head back and smirked, but there was a bit of curiosity in his eyes. "What do you mean 'respawned'?"

"My spawn point. After I died, I woke up back there."

"Spawn point?"

"The day you found me outside Nambunga's Cave… I had just spawned inside of there. When I die, that's where I ultimately start again."

Jax shifted his weight back and released some of the pressure from his knee and sword. "Impossible."

"It's true."

Jax pushed the sword tip back up against my neck hard and his lips turned to a vicious smile. "If it's true then I can just kill you now and you'll wake up back in the cave, right?"

"No! No! Please!" I pleaded. "I don't want to die again."

Jax took a took deep breath and sat back once more. "If you're really not a shapeshifter, if you really are Gunnar Long, then show me your fire magic."

I nodded slightly then looked up to one of my trembling hands. It was hard to focus in my frantic state, but energy began seeping out of my fingertips as I started casting Fireblast. I aimed for a young shrub, and the blast sparked out of my hand and instantly lit it up in flames.

Jax's eyes went wide in disbelief. "So then it's true…" he muttered. "The Reborns have arrived."

# Chapter 12

*01/03/0001*

Jax stood up and offered me his hand to help me to my feet.

"What's do you mean by 'Reborns have arrived'?" I asked as I brushed the dirt of my body.

"A stone tablet in the center of Highcastle speaks of a day when a group of people will arrive, who are reborn after their death. It says they would start as nothing and know little about the world... level ones and twos, just like you when I found you. But they would grow to shape the landscape of Eden's Gate."

Yeah, okay. So that made sense. Any real people who logged into Eden's Gate were considered 'The Reborn'. It was a good way to distinguish real people who could respawn versus the NPCS that couldn't and it fit players in with the lore of the game. Smart.

But I didn't have time for lore. I was standing in my boxers in front of a murderer.

"Why'd you kill me, Jax?" I asked. "Was it just because of that stupid sword?"

"Kill you?" Jax scoffed. "I didn't kill you." Jax turned his head to each side and looked into the trees as if he was looking out for something. "Quash your torch and come inside."

I extinguished my makeshift torch and left the remnants on the ground as I stepped inside of Jax's cabin. It was warm inside, but I was still shaking off the cold and anxiousness of being half-naked outside in the forest. "Do you have anything I can put on?" I asked. "And I'm really sorry about the sword... I lost it after I—"

"You mean this sword?" Jax interrupted as he kneeled and yanked the magic sword from Nambunga's Cave out from under his bed. "He lifted it up in front of his face and turned the blade from side to side as he eyed its beauty.

"Wha...?" I stuttered and took a step back. "How did you get that? You said you didn't kill me."

"Screams can travel pretty far in this forest. When I heard you yelping, I summoned Fenris and he followed your scent. I arrived while whoever killed you was still counting the coins in your bag."

"Fuck," I cursed. "I lost everything. I had so much on me when I died."

Jax pursed his lips and looked down at me with disapproving eyes before he kneeled again and pulled out an open wooden crate. The wood grunted as it slid against the floor. "It's all in there... aside from the gold that was taken."

"What?" I asked. I bent over and checked the crate's contents. Sure enough, all my loot and gear was inside. "How did you get all of this?"

"A couple warning shots got the guy's attention, and when he saw Fenris running towards him, he fled. He was too far away for me to inspect him, but he must have realized that he couldn't take me and the graywolf

146

alone. That's when I saw you lying there dead. I wanted the sword, of course, but I looted everything else to make sure the killer wasn't privy."

"And you're just giving it all back to me?"

Jax eyes burned daggers into me. "Why'd you try to run off with the sword?"

I let out a deep breath as I slid the leather garb over my frame. "I overheard you and Kronos talking in the Inn. He was offering you 1800 for the sword and—"

"And you thought you could profit by selling the sword yourself?" Jax finished for me.

"Yeah..." I muttered and lowered my head in shame.

"Dick move," Jax said pointedly. "We had an agreement."

"It was stupid... I just wanted to try to get ahead."

Jax huffed. "Well, I did end up getting the sword after all, which is all I wanted in the first place." Jax rubbed his hand against the blade. "I would've never gone down there myself, so I suppose I wouldn't have lost anything had you survived. And obviously, you weren't lying when you told me that Nambunga's dead."

"He's certainly dead..." I huffed. I lifted up my satchel and started organizing my loot inside.

"The magic staff and the strange robe. The ogre was hoarding those?"

"No, there was a dead orc and some other creature inside the cave, smashed under the ogre's body. I took the robe from the orc's body and the staff was in its hand."

"An orc?" Jax asked. "Are you sure it was an orc?"

I had experienced enough orcs in video games over the years to know when I saw one. "I'm certain. And the other thing may have been a goblin."

"So the Scourge is moving…" Jax whispered to himself, so low that I almost didn't hear.

"I should inform Adeelee," I said.

Jax nodded his head, his face a twist of worry. "Tomorrow I'll accompany you to The Vale to alert the elves, not only about the orc but about you. If you're really a Reborn…" Jax trailed like he was having trouble processing his thoughts. "Are there others like you?"

"Yeah," I replied. "I mean… I assume so. I haven't met any yet, but my girlfriend logged in with me, and many other people should've been logged in too."

"Logged in?" Jax asked.

"Ughh…." How could I explain it to him? "It just means she came into the world with me. There's probably others."

Jax picked up the lantern and sat it near the bed. "You should get some sleep. We'll move out first thing in the morning."

My stomach growled as I nodded. "Do you have anything that I can eat?"

Jax groaned, walked across the room and pulled something out of a cabinet. He turned around and tossed it at me.

> *You've received:* **Small Food Ration**. *Durability: 5/5. Quality: Average. Rarity: Common. Weight: 0.2 kg. Who knows what's in these tasteless things? All you know is that they keep you alive.*

So much for the delicious meal I had the first night I was in his home.

He walked back across the room and stretched himself across the bed. He gripped the hilt of his sword and held it across his chest as he pointed towards the spot that Fenris usually occupied. "Tonight you sleep on the floor," he said. "And in case you were wondering, you won't be learning any alchemy... at least not from me."

"I figured that much."

I shuffled my way over to the rug, pulled open the bland food ration and started eating as I watched Jax close his eyes. I wasn't sure if I was imagining things, but it seemed like one of his lids was partially cracked, almost like he was waiting for me to do something to him in his sleep.

It was a terrible feeling, really. Him allowing me to sleep on his floor and eat his food ration was more than I deserved, given that I had tried to cross him. He didn't have to give me back all my gear either.

But what really bothered me was the feeling of losing a friend. I hadn't known Jax that long, but it still felt like I had lost someone who had been kind to me and offered me some form of friendship.

I learned a lot of hard lessons that day. One of them being that you shouldn't cross good people just so you can make a few extra bucks.

It generally doesn't end well.

# Chapter 13

*01/04/0001*

Jax locked up his cabin as we headed out for our journey to The Vale the next day.

"How far is the walk?" I asked.

Jax pushed and pulled on his door to make sure the lock was sturdy before turning around. "Oh, we won't be walking. Without a haste spell of some sort, The Vale would be much too far to travel on foot."

"Not walking? What do you mean?" I didn't see any horses or other transportation around.

I watched as Jax stepped on the grass and closed his eyes. He held his hands out in front of him, one of them held sideways while he pressed his other fist into the palm. He looked like he was in a moment of intense concentration for a good five seconds before his eyes jolted open and he slammed his fist into the ground.

"Fenris!" Jax shouted.

A circle of fast, green energy pulsed out from around his fist and grew wider as it travelled away. Only a second later, a heavy pounding of feet could be heard nearby, and Fenris jumped into the clearing, almost knocking me down as it passed by to stop at its master's feet.

"Hey boy," Jax said as he kneeled down and rubbed at the giant wolf's ears. "How you feeling?"

The wolf tilted its head up and clapped its jaws a couple times. To me, it seemed like nothing but random animal behavior, but Jax's interaction with the wolf almost seemed like he knew what the wolf was trying to say.

"I know how much you hate being ridden, but today—"

Fenris pulled away and yelped a couple times, tossing its head.

"Come on, buddy. I've got important matters."

Fenris yelped again and tilted its snout down as it moved back into its master's reach.

"Good boy," Jax praised. "I'll need you to carry both me and Gunnar this time."

The wolf pulled the side of its lips back and showed a little bit of teeth. One of its eyes stared at me as it snarled.

"I think he likes me," I joked.

Jax patted Fenris on the head, and the wolf lowered itself to its belly so that Jax could hop on its back. Once Jax was on, he raised his chin and signaled for me to hop on behind him. "Try not to step on his mane. He hates that."

Fenris let out a low growl the whole time that I was approaching and throwing my leg over its massive back. The wolf radiated heat from its body which was only intensified by the thickness of its fur.

"Try to keep on by gripping with your knees and avoid pulling on his fur too much."

I immediately felt off balance as soon as Fenris stood to his feet, but after a few seconds I could feel the wolf's weight shifting under my body and was able to adjust myself to compensate for his movements.

"Hang on," Jax said to me and then turned his attention to the wolf. He gave Fenris a light pat on its side. "To Mist Vale!"

Riding a giant wolf through the forest was a bit like riding a horse on steroids. It felt like Fenris was flying at the speed he was going, and when he'd jump over logs and other obstacles, my stomach turned every time. The scene around me was mostly a blur, but I did catch sight of bears, snakes, wolves and even a couple keemus as we blazed by. There were a few random huts and houses that we passed as well as a cemetery, temples, ruins, streams, ponds and caves. I hadn't even touched the surface of all there was to explore in Addenfall!

It was a couple hours of Fenris running nonstop before we reached an area of the forest that grew thick with fog, and as we proceeded through the dense, cloudy white, I noticed that the greenery around us was slowly turning to a much darker green mixed with a hue of blue.

This thick fog began to thin as we continued, and eventually we found ourselves in an area of the forest where a thin mist hung in the air. It didn't seem to fall, like I would expect during a light rain. It just hoovered there and was so light that it made my skin feel moist and cool, but never so much that I really felt wet.

The foliage had changed more from a more traditional temperate forest like the area of Addenfall near Jax's hut to something more akin to a rainforest, with vines hanging down, and thick, leafy plants rising high out of the ground. Tall ceiba trees arced high in the sky and bamboo was growing in every direction.

Eventually, we reach an area where two round, wooden platforms had been built at the top of the large trees, and two male elves were standing at each one. The moment we came into sight, the elves pulled their bows off their backs and held them low in front of their body, prepared at any moment for an attack. On the ground, in between the two platforms, was a thin trail of flat stones that led deeper into the jungle.

Jax patted Fenris on his side and the wolf stopped a few meters ahead of the path. The hunter looked up to the two stations and shouted. "We're here to see the Queen Mother and Princess Adeelee."

"Stow the wolf, Jax Horn of Addenfall!" one of the elves yelled down.

Jax patted Fenris and Fenris dropped to his belly. Jax hopped off and I followed suit, right before Jax turned back to the wolf and gave him a nod and smile. "Thank you, my friend. Go for now."

Fenris stepped forward and nudged the top of his head against Jax's chest and Jax gave him a couple of good rubs. He reared his head, turned and bolted off in the direction from which we came.

Jax immediately kneeled to the elves, and I matched his actions.

"Who's your companion?" one of the elves said as he climbed down from a rope ladder attached to the platform.

"He's a newcomer to the forest. He holds news that the high elves would find valuable."

"You may rise."

"Please allow us passage," Jax said while we stood up.

"We trust you, Jax," the elf said, squinting his eyes tightly as if warning him at the same time. "You will be held responsible for his actions while in Mist Vale."

Jax nodded.

"Come," the elf said and started down the stone path.

We followed the elf another 15 minutes or so down winding paths that branched in several directions, until we finally came to a clearing where a large, stone building dangled seamlessly off the side of steep cliff. A balcony jutted off the side of the white-colored building and out of the center of the balcony a stream of water rushed out and fell into a large pool below.

All around were other immaculate, smaller buildings. Some resting on the grounds and others built into and in between the trees. Some were rounded and some were square, but they all had the same concave curved roofs with a sharp point jutting out of the top.

Elves walked about in every direction, all wearing green of the forest, but without the golden etching that Princess Adeelee's garb had. There were women, men and children, and all but the smallest amongst the group were armed with a sword or bow.

As we followed our escort towards the main building that hung off the face of the cliff, all heads turned towards Jax and I as we passed. Similarly, my own head turned every time I saw an elven female. They were blessed with good looks, that's for sure! And in the pool at the base of the waterfall were several nude elves, both men and women—and let me tell yah… The elven men had it made in the lady department. Holy shit!

We reached the beginning of a trail that led up the side of the cliff and two elves were standing at either side, sitting on top of large tigers, holding long pointy spears in their hands. They eyed us suspiciously, but when our escort gave the nod, they nodded back and let us pass.

My stomach did somersaults every time I looked over the edge as we climbed the steep cliff, but we made it to the top without incident, and when we walked through the entrance of the elven castle, there were another two guards on either side, standing beside tigers the same as the ones at the bottom of the cliff.

The inside of the castle was surreal, having a large stream rushing directly down the center. On each side of the stream were tall pillars rising to the roof and doors leading off to other rooms at the walls. Paths had been built at several spots along the stream to allow people cross, and at the far end of the stream, right before the balcony where the water fell off the edge, was a large platform built directly over the stream with steps leading up to it on either side.

At the top of the platform were two golden thrones. On one sat an elven female with a thin crown lined with emeralds resting atop her head, a long, white sleeveless dress draped down her frame, while on the other throne sat another elven man with a plain golden crown and dark leather armor. Their faces looked to be in their late 30s but their silver-gray hair indicated a much older age. A massive, white tiger lay by the Queen's side.

Our escort spoke as soon as we entered the room. "Queen Faranni and King Ryvvik, Jax Horn and his companion bring news from Addenfall."

We continued following the escort until he brought us up to the stream a few meters in front of the Queen and King's platform. Small stepping stones led to a large flat stone in the center of stream in which we stopped and kneeled before the royals.

"Rise," The Queen ordered.

As we stood up, I heard a familiar voice yell out from behind us "Jax!" Adeelee yelled. "You've come to the Vale, and I see you've brought your friend."

Jax grinned and nodded as he watched Adeelee pass us and climb the platform to join the King and Queen. Adeelee smiled while the Queen's lips were set in a hard line. The King just sat there and looked on, his head tilted to the side, resting on his knuckle. He seemed totally disinterested in the fact that we were there or anything we had to say.

"Why have you come to Mist Vale?" the Queen asked firmly.

"Did you bring news of the Scourge?" Adeelee questioned.

Jax nodded. "We bring news of the Scourge and much more than that."

"Go on," the Queen ordered.

Jax turned to me and spoke low. "Show them what you found in Nambunga's cave."

I reached in my satchel, pulled out the magic robe and sat it on the ground. Then, I unhooked the staff from my belt and held it up with both hands. "I found these on an orc inside Nambunga's cave," I said. "He was with another creature, perhaps a goblin of some sort."

*You have completed the quest:* **Scourge Activity!**

*You have gained 350 XP!*

There was a little bit of gasping from the Queen, Princess and the guards by the door. The King actually jerked his head up at the news and looked on with a little more attention.

"An orc so deep in Addenfall?" Adeelee asked. "There's no way an orc could make it that far into the forest without the guardians noticing."

The Queen sighed. "That's a warlock's staff. It's possible he could have cast a cloaking spell to get into the forest undetected."

"That type of spell drains your mana when it's in effect. He could have never made it in so far."

"Unless…" the King spoke up, his voice cracking. "He was a fairly high level Warlock traveling with a scout who might have had a haste spell."

"I suppose it's possible," the Queen agreed.

"But why would they go in the cave?" Adeelee asked.

"For exactly that fact," the Queen said. "They were running out of mana and needed a place to recharge without being detected."

There was a brief moment of silence while everyone took in all of the hypotheticals.

"You said that you found these on an orc?" the Queen asked. "I find it improbable that a low level such as yourself could stand your ground against both a warlock and a goblin scout."

"They were already dead," I explained. "Crushed under a dead ogre's... umm... Old Nambunga's dead body."

The Queen turned to her daughter. "That would be consistent with the theory."

"They went into the cave to rest, having no idea that they were walking into the home of a giant ogre," the King said. "The warlock was low on mana, having only enough time to throw off a couple curses, poisons or other damage over time effects. It was enough to kill the ogre, but not before the ogre killed them first."

"Sounds far-fetched," the Princess said low.

"Far-fetched or not,"the Queen spoke, "an orc traveled far past the Crystal River. The Scourge is growing bold."

The Princess turned to the Queen. "We should rally the elven army and march on the Wastelands. If we could get the support of the King at Highcastle, we may be able to exterminate the Scourge."

"Eliminating the Scourge would be a challenge even if Highcastle were to agree, and I wish not to march my children out of their home and into a war," the Queen said.

"Your Highness," Jax spoke. "There is more news that we bring."

"I'm listening," the Queen replied.

"I have reason to believe that my companion is a Reborn."

The King's posture grew very straight at that point, and the Princess looked shocked.

The Queen's eyes narrowed. "A Reborn? What makes you think that this man is a Reborn?"

"Gunnar was murdered in the forest, throat slit. I saw his dead body myself. Later on, he showed up on my doorstep without a scratch on his skin."

The Queen raised her hand and thick vines shot out of the water, encircling the stone we were standing on. They snaked forward, wrapping around my body like a tight vice. I was rendered immobile as the vines lifted me off the ground and brought me closer to the platform that the Queen was sitting on. The white tiger stood to its feet and roared in my direction.

"So your name is Gunnar?" The Queen asked.

"Yes," I muttered through tight lungs. "Gunnar Long."

"And are Jax's words true? You can return to life after death?"

"Yes."

"And there are others?"

"I think so. Yes."

The Queen chuckled, and after a moment the King joined in, chuckling as well. Princess Adeelee just looked on as if she were concerned with what was about to happen.

Suddenly, the Queen's laughter stopped and another vine shot out of the water. This one had a thorny tip, and it stopped right in front of my face.

"If you're a Reborn, then I can kill you now and it wouldn't matter, right? You can just..." The Queen smirked and shrugged, "...come back after you've been reborn."

"No! Please!" I begged.

"And why not?" she asked. "If you're a Reborn then you should not fear death."

"Reborn or not, death is painful. It was the worst experience of my life." I struggled hard to free my arms from the vines. "Please don't kill me."

The Queen considered my words for a moment before the King leaned over and whispered something in the Queen's ear. After hearing what the King had to say, her smirk turned to a straight line, and the vines that she was controlling lowered and sat me back down on the stone, releasing me from their grip.

"If the Reborns have really arrived and the tablet at Highcastle is true, then the High Elves have much to consider. Will the Reborns side with the elves?"

I shook my arms and tilted my neck, trying to regain my circulation after the tight squeeze. I shrugged. "I have no idea... uh... your highness. Everyone like me is independent to make their own choices. I'm sure there will be good people along with the bad."

The Queen looked displeased with the answer, but after a few seconds of silence she asked again, "Will *you*, Gunnar, side with The High Elves?"

*You've received an alliance invitation from the faction:* **The High Elves of Mist Vale**

*Aligning with a faction can give faction specific perks and open hidden quests that are unavailable to non-faction members. Once you are a member of a faction, negative action against that faction can result in harsh consequences.*

*You can side with as many factions as you want, but be careful of who you align with. If you align with two separate factions that*

*enter a war or have conflicting goals, you
may find yourself in a difficult situation!*

*Do you wish to align with this faction?*
*Accept/Decline*

That was one thing I both loved and hated about Eden's Gate. Every choice came with an air of uncertainty. I still knew little about the elves or any other factions that might be out there, but I couldn't just ask "Hey, will I get a chance to join later if I don't answer you now?"

But Jax was friendly with the elves, Princess Adeelee was amazing eye candy, and the Queen was perhaps the most powerful character that I had encountered in the game. Plus, Mist Vale was pretty fucking cool.

"I'll side with the elves," I said with a nod.

*You are now aligned with the faction: **The High Elves of Mist Vale!***

*You now have freedom of passage through: **Mist Vale!***

"Then we welcome you to the Vale," The Queen said.

The King leaned into the Queen's ear and whispered something again.

The Queen cleared her voice. "As I mentioned earlier, marching an army of elves against the Scourge could cause an all-out war which I'm unwilling to risk at this point. But I'd like to send a reminder to them that crossing the Crystal River and entering the forests will not be tolerated. If a small squad crossed the river and eliminated their camps, it may be enough to send them back to the Wastelands and think twice about crossing into Addenfall again.

"A small task for a Reborn, I'd think?"

*You have been offered a quest: **Push Them Back!***

*Queen Faranni has asked you to destroy the Scourge's camps along the Crystal River.*

*Reward: Unknown, 2000XP*

*Do you accept this quest? Accept/Decline*

Holy shit! I thought. 2000 XP for just one quest? That was more than five times any as much as I had been offered for any other quests. Hell yeah, I was game.

"I'll take out the camps."

*You have accepted the quest: **Push Them Back!***

"Good," The Queen said. "I'm glad to know that you're anxious to protect the forest."

The Queen had said "a small squad" in her description, so it didn't seem like a solo mission. I turned to Jax. "Will you join me, friend?"

Jax's face was blank. Obviously, he still held a little bit of resentment towards me about the sword. "Sorry, I can't." He turned to the Queen and bowed. "I have matters to attend to in Linden, your highness. If I may be excused?"

"You're excused," the Queen said.

I watched as Jax turned and walked out of the palace, and Adeelee stepped forward. "I will accompany you, Reborn."

"Adeelee…" the Queen muttered.

"I wish to make sure the task is completed, mother. The forest is just as important to me as my life."

The Queen stared at her daughter a moment before she gave a brief nod and turned back towards me. "Adeelee will accompany you."

I nodded. "Thank you, Princess Adeelee."

*Princess time? Thank you. Thank you. Thank you.*

"In the meantime, you should be rewarded for bringing us information about the orc. Is there anything that you require?"

I thought hard for a moment about what I could ask for—some new armor or a cool weapon maybe—but I was already sitting on a new sword and several unidentified magic items. Carrying them off to my next mission would be a chore. "If you could tell me how I can identify magic items and give me a place to store them, that would be great."

The Queen smiled. "Magic items are usually identified via spell or wand, and you do look like you're carrying quite a bit of weight on you…"

The Queen raised her hand, and again vines shot out of the water in front of the platform, but this time they slowly arranged to form a stairwell from the stone I was standing on up to the area right in front of the Queen.

"Step forward Gunnar," she ordered.

164

I swallowed and stepped on the vine stairwell, amazed at how well they held me up despite how squishy they felt under my boots. When I arrived in front of the Queen, she used two fingers to direct me closer.

"Kneel," she said.

I kneeled down until my face was mere inches from the Queen's knee.

"So long as you are friends with the High Elves, may you accept my gift to you." Queen Faranni leaned over and kissed me gently on the forehead. I felt tingles of magic shimmer all up and down my body and for a couple seconds, a flood of numbers and symbols flashed before my eyes. When it went away, I immediately felt different.

> *You have gained the **Elven Touch** trait and are now able to identify any magic items you encounter. You will retain this trait so long as you remain friendly with the High Elves.*

*Hell yes!* I thought. "Thank you, your highness."

"Adeelee, give him a more suitable bag and assign him a room on the ground floor where he can rest and store his belongings for now."

"Okay, Mother." Adeelee smiled and turned my way. "Follow me, Gunnar."

I followed Adeelee away from the Queen and King's platform, walking parallel to the stream. Our shoes clattered against the marble floors, and I awed at the stone carvings of elves that were carved into the walls every few meters of the way.

"Over here," Adeelee said as she dipped inside an open, arched door.

Inside of the room was an armory with hundreds of swords, daggers, and other powerful looking weapons hanging on the wall. Leather, plate, and mail armor was stacked on shelves and several chests lined the edges of the walls.

Adeelee pulled a key from her purse and opened one of the chests, fetching a brown, floppy looking bag from inside. "Here take this."

At first, I almost refused the bag, thinking that it was smaller and less durable than the satchel I already had, but the moment I touched it, I knew that I had found gold.

> *You've received:* **Elven Bag of Unburdening**. *Capacity 15. Durability: 1000/1000. Quality: Exceptional. Rarity: Legendary. Weight: 1.5 kg. This item opens to another plane of existence and can hold 15 items of any size (so long as they will fit in the mouth of the bag). [Spirit Item: Cannot be lost or stolen]*

Whoa… I had just been given Eden Gate's version of "Bag of Holding" like in other games I'd played in the past. Without a doubt, it was the most useful item I had come across so far. Strapping loot that didn't fit in my satchel to my belt was pretty uncomfortable. It wasn't clear if "Spirit Item" meant that I wouldn't lose the item if I died again or just that it couldn't be lost or stolen when alive, but if I woke up after death with anything more than a pair of boxers, then I was way further ahead than I was the day before.

I pulled open the bag, looked inside and all I could see was black. When I stuck my hand in, I couldn't feel the bottom or the edges.

"Whenever you're fetching an item from the bag, just think of it and you will feel it when you reach inside," Adeelee explained. "If you try to load it with more than 15 items, you will feel overburdened, but small consumables like potions and bandages can be stacked to occupy one space."

"Wow, this is awesome. Thanks!"

Adeelee smiled and indicated for me to follow her again.

We walked out of the palace and back down the long path towards the ground level of Mist Vale.

"When I inspect you, I see that you're a fire magic user. How far is your progression?" Adeelee asked.

I double checked my stats.

## GUNNAR LONG

| | |
|---|---|
| Race: | Human |
| Level: | 4 (Progress 25%) |
| Title: | None |
| Health/Mana/Stamina: | 130/100/100 |
| Strength: | 10 |
| Dexterity: | 14 |
| Intelligence: | 15 |
| Vitality: | 10 |
| Wisdom: | 12 |
| Willpower: | 10 |
| Charisma: | 10 |
| AR Rating: | 34 |
| Resists: | |
| | 10% Fire Resistance |
| Traits: | |
| | Elven Touch |
| Primary Skills: | |
| | First Aid Lvl 1: progress 0% |
| | Inspect Lvl 2: progress 0% |
| | Sneak Lvl 2: progress 0% |
| | Tinkering Lvl 1 progress 0% |
| Combat Skills: | |
| | Dodge Lvl 1: progress 0% |
| | Small Blades Lvl 2: progress 0% |
| | Backstab Lvl 1: progress 0% |
| | Archery Lvl 3: progress 0% |
| Magic Skills: | |
| | Fire Magic Lvl 2: progress 0% |

"Level 2. I can only cast Fireblast and Fire Arrow so far."

"Hmmm…" she said. "I don't know much about fire magic myself, but perhaps I can find something for you in the library. We'll need all the help we can get if we're to infiltrate the Scourge camps."

"When will we go?" I asked as we made it to the ground level and followed Adeelee around a stony path.

"Let's plan to push out tomorrow, but you should try to gain some experience before we go. You can hone your skills in the surrounding forest." We reached a small, square home, the size of a walk-in closet, just large enough for a bed and a small chest. "You can sleep here and use it for storage of items while you're in the Vale."

"Toilet?" I asked.

"Toilet?" Adeelee looked at me curiously.

My eyes scanned up and down Adeelee's healthy bosom and fit frame. I shook my head. "Ehhh... never mind." I wasn't prepared to push that question any further on an elven princess. *Leaves it is!*

# Chapter 14

*Day 4 (Earth)*

An old, grayhaired man in a fine business suit leaned over and spoke into his mic. "Mr. Sizemore, can you please tell us your involvement with the creation of Eden's Gate and the Nexicon VR system?"

Aaron looked over to Kendra who was sitting beside him and then back out to the hundreds of Congress members who were sitting in stands at the Congressional hearing. "As Assistant VP at Nexicon, I was closest to Dr. Winston in the creation of the product development."

"By 'Assistant VP' you mean that you were the assistant of the Vice President, correct?"

"No, that's incorrect. Technically, there was no Vice President of the company. While I was 2nd in command to Dr. Winston, he maintained such strict control over the product that I was never given a title greater than 'assistant'. VP just sounded cool, really."

The old man raised his eyebrows in surprise. "So on the day in which you launched the code in order to send Eden's Gate into 'demo mode', you had no idea the consequences of your actions. Is that correct, Mr. Sizemore?"

Aaron gulped and leaned forward into his mic. "That's correct."

The old man turned and looked to the audience of other Congress members and tilted his eyes to the side before turning back towards the stage in which the two Nexicon employees were sitting. "So you're telling me that as second in command and as one of the lead programmers of Eden's Gate, you had no idea that the demo mode launch had been tampered with, that the source code had been encoded, and that the administration process had been password protected?"

"That is correct."

"With all due respect, Mr. Sizemore, how is that possible?"

Aaron cleared his voice. "I helped code a small portion of the world and the base for the artificial intelligence, but Rupert... ahem... Dr. Winston was responsible for nearly everything. He was a genius, to say the least, and he wanted full control of pretty much everything."

The old man sighed. "Do you concur with Mr. Sizemore's statements, Mrs. Ramos?"

Kendra leaned forward into the mic and swallowed before speaking. Her brow was already building a visible layer of sweat. "I do."

The old man tapped his fingers on the thick, oak wood counter in front of him and silence hung in the air for several seconds.

"Let's get real for a moment, Mr. Sizemore," the old man spat. "Five million people." The old man allowed his words to resonate before he spoke again. "More than five million people have lost their lives, including my niece, and every day more people are killing themselves for the opportunity to be immortalized in this fictional world that *you* helped create." The man sucked on his lips and looked hard at

Aaron. "I want to know why you can't put a stop to this!"

Aaron grabbed his mic with his hand, causing reverberation to echo through the chamber. "Even if I wanted to stop it, Eden's gate uses 16,386-bit encryption which would never be cracked in our lifetime. Further, the system is running on a CPU blockchain. There is no power down button."

"CPU blockchain?" the old man asked. "Explain that for those of us who are less technically inclined."

"Basically, anyone who has ever installed Nexicon software—over 3 billion people—also installed our patented CPU blockchain. That means that more than 3 billion devices around the world are powering both Eden Gate's processing and CPU. Even if you shut down one device, the other devices will pick up the slack and validate the data so it cannot be tampered with."

"And how do these devices communicate? We could simply turn off the internet to cause your blockchain to fail."

"This isn't 2017 anymore, Senator Gates. Our blockchain was developed to use the internet, intranet, direct wi-fi, Bluetooth, satellite and Nexicon's 'Alt-Fi' technology... basically it will failsafe to any communication method. Every personal computer, cell phone, and gaming system in the world with Nexicon software is powering Eden's Gate."

Senator Gates sat down in his chair and leaned his body on a loose elbow. "So let's just say... there was a global shutdown? A complete blackout... For a day we shut down all processing devices, all data connections around the world. Would that be enough to put an end to this?"

"That's impossible," Kendra suddenly said into the mic.

"We're talking about lives here, Mrs. Ramos," Senator Gates said firmly. "If that kind of action is what it takes, we will make it happen." His eyes moved back over to Aaron. "Would that be enough to shut this thing down?"

Aaron sucked in a deep breath of air and thought for a moment. "If you could shut down enough equipment that there was not enough power for the CPU blockchain to run, then yeah, I guess it's theoretically possible. But even if there's an island in the South Pacific with 100 PCs that have the blockchain running, that would be enough to power Eden's Gate. And even if you could…" Aaron's eyes darted from left to right. "You wouldn't want to do that. There's millions of people conscious in there right now."

A low rumble of chuckles bounced off the chamber walls.

"We're talking about a video game, right?" Senator Gates asked.

"Yes, it's a video game, but—"

"Then it's not real!" the Senator blurted. "Do you agree that this game is merely a sequence of 1s and 0s running on a computer platform?"

Aaron sighed. "Of course. But if you break down human consciousness to the most basic level, we're just a sequence of complicated 1s and 0s as well. People are really living inside of the game."

Another rumble of laughter rang out.

"There's no evidence that people are *alive* in the game, right?" the Senator asked. "You can't see what they're doing. We can't communicate with them. As far as we know, the number of people that your system shows as logged in is just a number. It could mean anything."

Aaron held up his palm. "I understand the way you feel, but if you haven't been inside of Eden's Gate, then I don't think you'd understand. Eden's Gate is the pinnacle of virtual technology. It is basically like another world like we have here on Earth. When you're inside, you experience everything like you would in the real—"

"Real world," Senator Gates interrupted. "This—" He pointed his finger to the ground. "—is the real world. What you're talking about is a game. I think we all understand the difference between a real world created by God and a *game* created by a psychopathic programmer."

"You can simply recall the existing Nexicon VR units and let the system run," Aaron said dismissively. "It won't hurt anything to keep it running."

"You shipped 8 million units. There's no guarantee that we'd get them all or that someone wouldn't replicate the technology. It must be a full-scale shutdown."

"I don't know how else to explain it to you, but the people who transferred their consciousness to the game are alive, even if their bodies are dead."

There was a moan from the onlookers, and Senator Gates rolled his eyes as he turned around to face the committee. "We've lost millions already and every day people around the world are dying due to this ridiculous promise of living out the rest of their lives in Eden's Gate. What I'm proposing is a worldwide shutdown. A recall of all Nexicon VR units, a shutdown of the internet, power, and a clean sweep of all devices that have or may have Nexicon software installed. This is a huge undertaking, but we must protect the lives of this and future generations." Senator Gates paused and panned his hand all around the room. "All in favor say 'Aye'."

A near unanimous 'Aye' roared through the room.

Aaron swallowed hard and looked over to Kendra. He knew that nothing he could say could change the Congressmen's minds. They weren't gamers and would never understand gamers or virtual technology. Only someone who had experienced Eden's Gate would understand that the world was as real—on a perception level—as the world he was sitting in now and that people's consciousnesses were really living inside of that world.

"Very well," Senator Gates said. "We'll contact the President and start the recalls of the Nexicon VR as soon as possible. We'll connect with every government around the world to arrange for a global shutdown of the grid—whether data networks or power. We will get this shut down."

Aaron turned to Kendra, a worried look on his face. Only they and some gamers around the world would ever understand just how real Eden's Gate was. Only they would understand that by shutting down the system, they'd essentially be taking the lives of 5 million people… and counting.

# Chapter 15

*01/04/0001*

"There's a few vendors on the ground level of the Vale if you wish to buy or sell anything," Adeelee said. "There's also a tall runestone on the hill just above the palace. If you wish to pray to any God, you may do so there."

They had praying in the world as well? I couldn't imagine how that tied into the game, but surely it meant something. I recalled getting special power and bonuses through use of "faith" in other games. I'd need to check that out.

"Thanks."

"I'll be seeing you," Adeelee said and walked away.

I closed the door to my room and started moving things over to my new bag. Since I now had the 'Elven Touch' trait, I was also anxious to see what kind of magic items I had looted in Nambunga's Cave.

*You've received: **Warlock's Robe of Apathy**. +3 Armor. Requires 28 Intelligence. Durability: 9/10. Quality: Exceptional. Rarity: Epic. Weight: 1.0 kg. +20% Magic Resistance. +20% Magic Damage. -25% Health.*

*You've received: **Staff of Depravity**. 10-20 Attack Damage. Requires 30 Intelligence. Durability: 9/10. Quality: Exceptional. Rarity: Epic. Weight: 1.1 kg. +20% Magic Damage. -10 Health. On Cast: **Blight**: 17 Charges Left.*

*You've received: **Band of Divine Concentration**. Requires 15 Intelligence. Durability: 9/10. Quality: Exceptional. Rarity: Epic. Weight: 0.1 kg. Mana Regens 20% Faster. Spells That Require Channeling Cast 25% Faster.*

The massive boost of magic damage that the staff and robe gave were interesting, but they wouldn't do me any good for a long time coming. It seemed like a good idea to just sell them. The ring's 20% mana regen would be helpful however, and I had completely forgotten that I had reached 15 intelligence right after getting out of the cave.

I slid the ring over my finger and there was no more trembling. In fact, I could feel a soothing energy flowing out of it and all through my body. The ring also had a channeling reduction, but since I had no channeling spells or even knew what those were, it gave me no benefit. A nice find, in any event.

I decided to go for a walk around the Elven village, and the moment I stepped outside my new room, I already felt a little weird. I was literally the only human anywhere to be seen, and you would think that some of the elves had never seen a human the way that they looked at me. They were friendly though, and although they all stared a little too long, most of them made an effort to smile and talk.

"Welcome to the Vale," a young, elven girl said as I passed by her on my way to who-knows-where.

"Thank you," I replied.

"Welcome to the Vale," an elven man said 5 seconds later.

Figuring things out in Mist Vale was quite a bit more difficult than they were in Linden. None of the buildings had signs, so the only way to find specific places was to walk around until you stumbled across the right spot or ask around.

"Somewhere to sell weapons or armor?" I asked a passing elf.

The elf pointed to a circular home that looked just like any other. "Rhys lives in that building there. He usually buys arms at a fair price."

I immediately went into the shop to sell my spoils to Rhys, a tall, young elf, and while he was alarmed when he first saw a human walk through the door, once he realized I was there to do business, he quickly calmed. By the time I left his shop, I had sold the robe, the staff, and the ringmail gauntlets for a total of 494 gold.

Not bad, I thought.

I left Rhys' shop and continued my walk around until I noticed a wooden stall that was selling food and water. Thankfully, the game didn't seem programmed to cause too much harm if you went a day without food, but after a good 12 hours or so without eating or drinking, a severe thirst and hunger started to kick in.

I bought a flask of water, a loaf of bread, and an 'elven pie' for the bargain price of 5 gold. I have no idea what was in the elven pie, but it was perhaps the most delicious thing that I had ever eaten in my life.

*You are **well-fed**! Stamina and Vitality increased by 15% while this effect is active*

With a tummy full of food, I started up the hill above the palace, hoping to find the runestone that Adeelee told me about. It only took me about 10 minutes or so to get there, but once I was at the top of the hill, I saw a large, rectangular stone jutting out of the ground and several symbols etched on its front, a soft white glow, almost invisible throbbing around its entirety.

On the ground near the stone, were two elves, a male and a female, kneeling down in prayer position, their eyes closed and their palms pressed together. They spoke quietly to themselves in such whispers that I couldn't understand what they were saying.

As I walked closer to the runestone, I felt an energy drawing me towards it, and when I was only a meter or so from the stone, it almost felt like a physical hook was pulling me in.

Something compelled me—I can't explain what—but it was like I was being told to either kneel down and pray or touch the runestone. I chose to do both and leaned down directly in front of the runestone and placed my hand on the side.

> *Do you wish to **bind** yourself to **this** location?*

Aha! So that's what the purpose of the runestone was!

I concentrated on binding myself to the stone and tiny sparkles of nothingness began shimmering on my skin and rising into the sky, vanishing when they were a few inches into the air.

> *You have **bound** to to **this location**. Using a Recall Home spell or death will return you to this position.*

There was a recall spell in the game too? Add that to the list of things I wanted to get my hands on.

As I walked away from the runestone, the two elves were still praying seeming to not have even noticed me or me binding to the stone.

I started for the jungle surrounding Mist Vale as I needed to try to level up my skills in preparation for the attack on the Scourge camps. I started north, and walked for several minutes before I encountered anything other than tiny insects and a few creatures who I knew were hanging out in the foliage above me, but moved too fast for me to see what they were.

I eventually came across a small pool of muddy water and surrounding it was a large group of Frisbee-sized mosquitoes.

**Name:** *Jungle Mosquito*
**Race:** *Insect*
**Level:** *4*
**Health/Mana/Stamina:** *20/0/30*
**Status:** *aggressive*

They filled the air with an annoying buzzing sound, but they were flying fairly slow and spaced in a way that they seemed like they would be easy to pick off.

I shot the closest one with a Fireblast which knocked it to the ground floor. It buzzed around as it wings burned to a crisp and eventually stopped moving.

*You have gained 40 XP!*

I inspected the fallen mosquito and didn't find anything of use in its charred remains, but 40 XP seemed like a decent pull on such an easy kill. I Fireblasted a few more mosquitoes and they all went down just like the first, netting me 40 XP each in the process, and I took note that my mana was recharging notably faster since I got my new *Band of Divine Concentration.*

While I waited for my mana to recharge, I used arrows to shoot the mosquitoes, but shooting the flying mosquitoes was difficult and generally took at least two shots to take one down. There must been 15 or so mosquitoes I found around the stagnant water and I Fireblasted or shot them all, netting me significant XP. When the last one was down, I was already 60% towards my next level.

That's what you call powerleveling!

There was a small chest sticking out of the stagnant water, but it was locked, and a Fireblast, a Fire Arrow, and good old fashioned kick wouldn't open it up. I made a mental note to check back if I ever found a key or figured a way to open locks and moved on.

I continued further north until I heard the buzzy sound of mumbling or talking. I wasn't sure what it was that I was hearing, but it definitely didn't sound like an animal. As I grew closer, it was clear that it was a voice that I was hearing, so I sank into sneak mode and approached cautiously.

A small pink creature, no more the size of a house cat with no clothes and just a puff of white hair growing out of the top of its head, sat on a log, waving its hand around and talking to itself. It had beady eyes and two small gray horns were growing out of its hair. It smiled as it spoke and looked friendly enough.

**Name:** *Forest Imp*
**Race:** *demon*
**Level:** *11*
**Health/Mana/Stamina:** *150/150/50*
**Status:** *unknown*

At level 11, I knew there was little chance that I could kill the thing, but even if it had been a few levels lower, I'm not sure if I would have attacked. It was too damn cute, and maybe it could speak something other than the scrambled gibberish that it was saying to itself, but given its stats, I wasn't about to find out.

The creature laughed as if it had just told itself a funny joke and then started slapping its hand against the log.

What the fuck? I thought. Apparently the imp was insane. I turned and sneaked away, leaving the crazy imp to banter alone.

I turned back the way that I came, careful not to venture too far from the Mist Vale village and when I was almost at the area where I killed the mosquitoes, I started East to look for more things to kill. I walked for roughly 15 minutes in which all I managed to kill were a couple of level 1 frogs, granting me the smallest amount of XP, until I stumbled across a dilapidated house in a small clearing.

The two-story wooden house was overgrown with weeds and plants, the windows were busted out, and there was a massive hole in its slanted roof. The chances that someone was still living in a place like that was unlikely, but I hunkered down into Sneak mode, readied my bow and approached with caution anyway.

I did a quick check in the small garden nearby the home and found nothing. I looked behind the house where there were two large barrels, and when I checked inside I found that one of them contained a small vial with a sparkling red powder inside.

> *You've received:* **Red Inscription Powder.** *Durability: 5/5. Quality: Average. Rarity: Uncommon. Weight: 0.1 kg. Used for Inscription.*

Used for inscription? That wasn't helpful at all. I tried to focus more on the powder and then on the word 'Inscription', but no additional information was provided. I just bagged the item and moved on.

I nocked an arrow and took a deep breath before I kicked open the door to the house, and stepped inside like I was some sort of bow-wielding police officer looking for the dealer who was selling drug-infused food rations to children. As I scanned the room, I lowered my bow as everything looked okay.

There was a skeleton inside that was impaled in the center of its chest by a beautifully crafted sword. He still had on his clothes—a pair of nice slacks and white frilly dress shirt and a tricorne with gold etching on his head. It looked like he was going somewhere special but never made it—obviously.

I could almost feel the energy emanating from the sword, and I went to grab it to see what kind of loot I had come across. But right before my hand reached the sword's hilt, the skeleton became animated.

I immediately stepped back and was readying my bow as the skeleton stood to its feet, but it was too fast. The skeleton yanked the sword from its chest, narrowly missing my neck, but instead connecting with my bow, breaking it in two and sending pieces of broken wood and string flying across the room.

"Fuck!" I yelled as I ducked below another fast swipe of its sword.

"*Help meeeeeee,*" a slow, raspy voice rang out from somewhere. Was it the skeleton talking? I couldn't tell.

I rolled to my side, dodging another swing of the skeleton's sword and lashed out casting Fireblast on the skeleton. The impact was strong enough to send the skeleton flying backwards and to the ground, but just as soon as it hit the ground, it started standing up again.

**Name:** *Tormented Lover*
**Race:** *Undead*
**Level:** *7*
**Health/Mana/Stamina:** *80/0/80*
**Status:** *aggressive*

Tormented Lover? What the fuck? How about Skeletal Warrior or something a little more accurate?

I shot the skeleton with several more Fireblasts until my mana ran out, and while I managed to char its bones, it seemed like it was resisting a lot of the damage. I reached for my corroded sword, knowing that attacking or blocking it with my training dagger would probably not work out so well, considering the size of his sword and the amount of power he was putting behind each strike.

The skeleton swung again, and this time I held up my blade to block his strike. Sparks shot out from our blades colliding, and I could feel the force of the blow reverberate down the hilt and into the bones of my wrists and arms. I managed to block the strike, but even blocking such a hard blow hurt. My health dropped by 2%.

> *Advancement! You have learned the skill:* **Block***. Oops! Did I just mitigate all your damage? Block is linked to Strength and Dexterity. Increase your Strength and Dexterity to increase your ability to Block.*

I glanced at the message about block and figured I was still taking minimal damage because my strength was too low. Damnit, why did every stat have to be useful?!

The skeleton swung again, and I blocked, but this time I lashed back out with a swing of my own, connecting with one of its arms. The frail bone of its arm splintered off, leaving it nothing but a useless, bony stump. The skeleton seemed unaffected by this though, and still stomped forward swinging its sword with its remaining arm.

> *Advancement! You have learned the skill:*
> ***Swords***. *The pen is mightier than the sword?*
> *Says he who has never wielded a sword.*
> *Swords is linked to Strength and Dexterity.*
> *Increase your Strength and Dexterity to*
> *increase your ability with Swords.*

The skeleton raised its sword high and slammed it down hard at my head. I sidestepped slightly and again blocked the blow, but that block was incredibly painful.

Our blades were locked together as the 1-armed skeleton leaned in and looked at me with emptied pits for eyes. "*Help meeeeeee,*" again the raspy voice said from somewhere. Was it the skeleton's spirit or someone else?

Metal screeched against metal as I slid the blade of the corroded sword out from the weight of the skeleton's, and I ducked down, swinging my sword at the skeleton's kneecaps, taking both of its legs out at the same time.

The skeleton fell, more of its bones shattering as it hit the ground, but it still swung out, trying to connect with anything in its immobile state.

I parried the skeleton's erratic, last ditch effort to kill me, and swung at the skeleton's neck, severing its head from its body and causing it to roll a couple feet on the floor. Finally, the skeleton stopped moving.

*You have gained 150 XP!*

"That should help youuuuuuu," I mocked cockily as I sheathed my sword and caught my breath.

I bent down to pick up the nice looking sword that the skeleton was holding but the as soon as my hand was within a centimeter of touching the hilt, a thick, dark cloud swirled around my arm and froze it from moving any closer.

I pulled away and tried to grab the sword, but again, nothing but dark, swirly clouds and a hissing sound.

"What the hell?!" I spat. Maybe the sword was cursed or something or maybe it had a level requirement that was so far beyond me that I couldn't pick it up. I wasn't sure, but I apparently wasn't getting that piece of loot anytime soon.

I checked the skeleton's pockets and the only thing that I found was a tiny, worn box with a golden ring inside.

*You've received:* **Gold Wedding Band.** *Durability: 100/100. Quality: Exceptional. Rarity: Uncommon. Weight: 0.1 kg.*

"Jackpot!" I said. The ring was immaculate, despite its worn box, and better yet it looked real... Not that I could imagine them putting fake gold rings in the game—but hey, you never know! Whatever the case, a gold ring would most likely fetch a good deal at any vendor.

I pocketed the ring and started to search the house further. On the bottom level of the house, just about all the furniture and decorations were ruined. Nothing of value. There was however a wooden writing desk with a small drawer in the front, and when I pulled it open several unsealed letters were inside:

*Dear Aelynthi,*

*Oh, how deeply I miss thee. It's been only a few months that I've been gone, but my heart aches every moment that I'm away from you. Do you remember the night that we snuck off to the runestone and made sweet love under the moonlight in the sky?*

*Hopefully, this war will end soon. I long to be back in the Vale. I long to be back with you. Stay safe my sweetheart.*

*Forever yours,*
*Mythanthar*

*Dear Aelynthi,*

*The war rages on, and I'm afraid it only grows in intensity. Can you believe this? The war with the dwarves is unnecessary. We want no part of their land and they want no part of their forests! Why can't the two sides simply live in peace?*

.

*Hopefully, this chaos will end soon. All I want is to return to the Vale and share an elven pie with you like we did when we first met.*

*Forget me not,*
*Mythanthar*

*Dear Aelynthi,*

*I met a dark elf today. Or rather, one of our comrades became a dark elf. He has been fighting the war far longer than me, and this morning he woke up with his skin a tinge of gray. It's terrible! I fear that if this war doesn't end, I too will become a dark elf.*

*Would you still love me if that were to happen? If I were a dark elf? Nothing would break my heart more than to lose you.*

*I'm sending you all of my wages to commission a house be built near the center of the Vale, but far away enough that we won't be disturbed. I figure it will better for us to have a little privacy. When I get home I want to <u>ravage</u> you with my love, and I loathe to think of what the neighbors will think from all the noise that we'll be making.*

*Love eternally,*
*Mythanthar*

Cold steel connected with my back, causing me to drop the letter and scream out in pain. Again, someone had caught me from behind!

I glance at my health bar and 70% of my health was missing and a bloody teardrop was sitting right below.

> *You are **bleeding** and require medical attention. Bleeding is a damage-over-time effect.*

I had no time to think and rolled to the ground as I unsheathed my sword. Although the pain was searing in my back, I didn't want to die again.

It was the skeleton. He had somehow pulled himself back together, and now a burning fire was literally pouring out of his eye sockets. It had also gained 3 levels?! What the hell?!

**Name:** *Enraged Lover*
**Race:** *Undead*
**Level:** *10*
**Health/Mana/Stamina:** *130/0/100*
**Status:** *unknown*

"*Help meeeeeee!*" the raspy voice bellowed overhead as the skeleton stepped forward, swinging its sword faster and with more intensity than before.

I dodged and ducked, trying my best to avoid the blade, but his movements were much swifter than mine. He swung his blade towards my chest with a sweeping motion, and when I tried to block, the intensity was so hard it knocked my sword out of my hand.

> *You have reached level 2 in **Dodge**!*

I stuck out my palm and sent a Fireblast to its chest as a last-ditch effort, which pushed it away and knocked it down. I shot another Fireblast which connected with its shoulder, knocking off an arm, and then one more Fireblast towards the center of its flaming eyes.

The skeleton tremored for a second, and then then a black swirl of smoke surrounded its broken arm and then it reattached itself to the skeleton's body. The skeleton got back to its feet like it was completely unaffected.

My mana was spent, and I knew there was no way I was going to beat a level 10 in a swordfight. It was also blocking my escape route, and the likelihood of me dodging all its blows and making it out the front door were slim. The only option seemed to be to run for the stairs behind me.

I took each stair up the house as fast as I could, the skeleton just a few meters behind me. When I reached the top, there was a short hall and only one room at the end with a closed door.

"Please be open. Please be open," I muttered to myself as I took the last few paces to the door.

It was! I swung open the door, stepped inside and slammed it shut right as the skeleton smashed its sword into the wood.

There was a small wooden latch that I used to lock the door behind me, and I pressed my hands on the door as the skeleton pounded its fists against it hard.

"What the fuck?" I said, breathing heavily.

I could feel the blood running down my back, and I saw that I was at only 15% health. I reached inside my bag and pulled out my one and only health potion, drinking it to avoid an imminent death.

I knew that I needed bandaging, but with the skeleton banging on the door, I didn't have time to do it now.

Inside of the tiny room was a dirty bed with two skeletons lying on top. One of the skeletons had an arrow in its skull and the other had a dagger lying near its throat. I could only hope those skeletons wouldn't come alive as well.

There was a window inside the room, but when I looked down at the fall, I wasn't sure if I would survive. If I didn't die from the landing, I'd probably take enough damage that my bleeding would kill me before I could bandage myself.

I turned around looking for a weapon or anything that would allow me to fend off the Skeleton and slip past him down the hall. There was a chest inside the room, but it was empty and other than that there was a lantern and men and women's clothing scattered about the room. I got into a prone position and looked under the bed and discovered that there was a flat metal crate underneath, big enough for weapons storage, but when I pulled it out, there was a thick padlock attached to its front.

"*Help meeeeeee!*" the voice roared as the skeleton continued banging hard on the door.

By that time, I was sweating bullets. I remembered what it was like to die, and that was not a feeling I wanted to experience again. And *that* skeleton didn't seem like it would play nice. In all likelihood, it would decapitate me and sever all of my limbs before I passed over to the dark side.

I started searching through the clothes strung around the room frantically hoping that one of them had a key, and after searching a woman's dress and a man's dress shirt, finally I found a keyring with two identical sized keys—keys that looked like they would fit the padlock.

My hands trembled as I fumbled with the keys and stuck them in the padlock, and there was a resounding 'click' when I turned.

"Thank god!" I said, feeling certain that there must be a weapon, a rope, a bomb or something that could save me inside. But when I opened it up, my eyes went wide. "No… No!"

Letters… Nothing but unopened envelopes with a red wax seal still intact. Mail that someone had tossed in the box and forgotten.

The skeleton banged against the door and I could hear the hinges beginning to crack.

Pain seared through the wound in my back, and I moaned.

"Fuck it!" I thought. I ripped open one of the letters and started reading. Maybe there could be something inside. Maybe one of them would give me directions to a secret ability or magic weapon when I respawned. If I was going to die, I would make the best of it.

*Dear Aelynthi,*

*Have you been receiving my letters my love? It's been a week since I've gotten anything back from you and I grow more and more concerned as each day passes. Have you fallen ill? Please let me know that you're okay.*

*The war still rages on and has grown even more gruesome than ever. Some dark magic has been introduced, but I'll spare you the details lest your heart worry for me.*

*I'm happy to let you know that I have yet to turn into a dark elf. My hair still shines and my skin still glows a porcelain white, but alas my heart is blue. I miss you my love, and every moment away from you aches a pain that I could never fill into words.*

> *Forever yours,*
> *Mythanthar*

What the fuck!? I thought. Are these all love letters?!

*Dear Aelynthi,*

*Why haven't I heard from you, my love? I'm certain now that our mail must be getting lost somewhere in the post.*

*But I have news! The war is ending, Aelynthi! It's really going to end soon!*

*Yesterday we scored a striking victory against the other side, and our commanders see no way that the opposition can win.*

*There may be one or two more months that elves will be deployed to battle, but since the enemy's numbers have dwindled, some of us will be leaving soon. I have requested that my commander send me home as quickly as possible. It may be days, Aelynthi! Days! Only days and I can be in your loving arms again.*

*This war has made me realize something... I never want to be away from you again. I'm going to buy a ring the moment that I make it to the Vale, and I want to make you my wife. My heart will never rest until the symbol of my love rests comfortably on your finger.*

> *Forever yours,*
> *Mythanthar*

> *You've found a hidden quest:* **Tormented**
> **Lovers**
>
> *The skeleton of Mythanthar can never rest until his wedding ring reaches his lover's finger. You must take the wedding band from Mythanthar pocket and place it on the finger of Aelynthi's remains in the upstairs bedroom.*
>
> *Reward: Unknown, 350xp*
> *Do you accept this quest? Accept/Decline*

"YES!" I yelled. "Fucking yes, I accept!"

> *You have accepted the quest:* **Tormented**
> **Lovers!**

I jumped to my feet, and my heart was beating out of my chest as the skeleton pounded hard at the door. A hinge on the door came undone from the wood and tumbled to the floor.

I reached in my bag and fumbled around for the wedding ring just as the skeleton flung itself at the door a final time, breaking the door down completely and falling inside the room with it.

My mana had filled up just enough that I was able to send off another Fireblast in its direction, pushing it back and stunning it briefly.

I dove onto the bed, across the male skeleton, reaching for the more petite frame of bones, grabbing its hand as the raging skeleton was picking itself back up.

"*Help meeeeeee!*" the voice roared out again.

I lifted the skeleton's fingers and gently slid the wedding ring on its left hand, right as my attacker was stomping forward, raising its sword to strike me down.

The enraged skeleton paused in its tracks, and the fire pouring out of its sockets suddenly vanished. A large, transparent window popped in front of my eyes, and inside, I had a bird's eye view of a tall, muscular young elf with a bow on his back and a sword and dagger draped at his side, standing outside of the house that I was sitting in. But the house was not dilapidated in the image—it was pristine, and the garden outside was filled with flowers of every different color.

The elf knocked on the door to the house, holding a small box in his hands, and then knocked again before pushing open the front door. He looked around the main floor and smiled as he ran his fingers across the top of the writing desk. He was happy, excited.

His mouth opened as if he were calling for someone, but there was no sound. Rather, he just continued up the stairs until he came to the bedroom door. He casually pushed the door open, and when he did, his jaw dropped. On the bed was a woman, breasts exposed and sleeping. Beside her was another elf, shirtless, who seemed to be lost in slumber as well.

"Aelynthi," his lips muttered. I couldn't hear the words, but the pattern in his lip muscles spoke volumes.

The elf stood there for a second before he lowered his head and slid the ring into his pocket. Tears slowly fell down the elf's porcelain cheeks and within seconds he looked up with anger in his eyes. He pulled the bow off his back and notched an arrow before his lips spoke louder. "Aelynthi!"

The eyes of the female shot open, and she sat up in bed, pulling the blanket quickly over her naked body. The man shot up as well.

The woman said something and her face looked frantic, but the male elf looked scared and confused.

I have no idea what they were saying, but it only took a couple seconds before Mythanthar released his arrow and it shot directly into the man's skull, causing him to fall backward and immediately die.

Aelynthi face was a look of horror as she looked to her lover and said something else, but it didn't matter. The elf standing over her simply threw his bow to the side and pulled his dagger off his belt.

Mythanthar jumped forward on to the bed and stabbed Aelynthi in the chest, and then in the neck several times, causing blood to splash everywhere. Tears rolled down his face with each strike and when he finished, he left the dagger protruding from her neck and smeared the blood and tears on his face with the back of his hand.

He looked defeated as he stared down at his two victims, and then he slowly walked downstairs. When he reached the bottom room, he unsheathed his sword and said something towards the sky before he grabbed his sword by the hilt with both hands and shoved it deep in his chest cavity.

Blood seeped from the elf's mouth, and he fell forward, the impact causing the sword to lodge further into his body, and then he rolled to his side and against the wall.

The window in front of me eyes disappeared, and a translucent apparition of a tall, muscular young elf—Mythanthar—seemed to simply step outside the body of the skeleton and looked at its hands as another apparition rose out of the body of Aelynthi.

Mythanthar stared at Aelynthi as she rose from the bed, and after a moment he simply asked, "Why? How could you?"

Aelynthi's eyes looked watery, at least as watery as a translucent apparition could be as she looked up to Mythanthar. "Where did you go?"

"Where did I go?" Mythanthar asked. "I went to war, and then I came back for you."

"But he said you were dead."

"Dead?"

"After you sent the money to build this home, Alinar told me you were dead."

"Alinar?"

"The messenger." Aelynthi turned to the other skeleton on the bed. "He said you were killed in the war."

"I wasn't killed. I wrote you every day. I sent you money. You were everything to me!"

"I didn't receive your letters," Aelynthi claimed. "After the house money, you went silent."

Mythanthar turned and noticed the box that I opened on the floor. He kneeled over to them and shook his head from side to side. "My letters... The messenger must have kept them. He lied to you! He lied about everything!"

"I'm sorry!" Aelynthi cried.

Mythanthar stood up and turned back to his lady. "But why would he be in your bed... I mean, why would he be in *our* bed? Why him?"

Aelynthi's head dropped low. "I was alone. I thought you were gone and that I'd never see you again. I swear I waited. A year or more after he told me you were dead, I rejected his advances, but finally I caved to him. I was lonely, Mythanthar. I was in so much pain."

Mythanthar clenched his teeth and bored a hole in the other skeleton that was sitting on the bed. "Alinar, rise!" he bellowed.

A third apparition rose out of the male skeleton, and as soon as it formed, it looked shocked to be there.

"You were tasked with delivering my gold and my messages, but you betrayed both me and Aelynthi," Mythanthar condemned.

Alinar's apparition looked defeated. His head sank and for a moment, I thought he wouldn't say anything at all. Finally, he murmured, "I wanted her. The moment I saw her, I wanted her and would've done anything to get her."

"May you rot in hell!" Mythanthar spoke loudly, and almost instantly, the apparition of Alinar seemed to twist in to knots and then turn to jelly as it was visually pulled away to somewhere else.

"I'm sorry." Aelynthi started. "I'm sorry. I had no right—"

"It's okay," Mythanthar interrupted. "All I wanted was to be with you, and now we're together."

Aelynthi's apparition grabbed onto Mythanthar's apparition and squeezed.

Mythanthar turned to me and with and somber face, he said, "Thank you. I am finally free. Take my blade for your troubles."

Mythanthar raised a hand, and a dark cloud swirled around the tormented skeleton, causing it to drop to the ground in a heap of bones. Then the swirl of darkness swirled around the sword before dissipating into the air.

> *You have completed the quest:* **Tormented Lovers!**
>
> *You have gained 350 XP!*
>
> *You have gained 10 MP!*
>
> *Advancement! You have reached* **level 5** *and have gained 3 attribute points. To assign your attribute points, open your status page. You can also increase any of your known skills by 1 level. Choose wisely, as your choice cannot be undone.*

Since I wasn't poisoned, my bleeding stopped and I was brought to full health.

The two remaining apparitions embraced each other in a hug, and Mythanthar leaned down to kiss Aelynthi as they both faded from sight.

I let out a loud sigh and laid myself on the bed, trying to regain my composure. Leveling up had instantly restored all my health and cleared my bleeding, but I had still been on the brink of death. And that story… fuck! That crazy elf was obsessed with his girl!

I made me think of Rachel, actually. I had been so caught up in the game, that I hadn't been thinking about her as much since the first couple of days since I had been sucked in. I still wanted to find her, of course, but I was beginning to have doubts.

What if she wasn't looking for me? What if she met someone else?

I shook my head of those thoughts and got up out of the bed, reaching for the skeleton's sword.

> You've received: **Mythanthar's Blade**. 12-25 Attack Damage. Durability: 9/10. Exceptional: Average. Rarity: Legendary. Weight: 2.7. +5 Strength. 5% chance to apply Torment.

Torment? I focused, trying to will more information about the stat and an informational appeared:

> *Torment will cause enemies to cease fighting while they deal with an inner struggle within their head. Does not*

202

*work on beings with a very low intelligence or very high intelligence.*

The sword was almost two feet long and had a slightly red tinge running through the blade. It seemed the color was embedded in the metal somehow, and on the thick, black hilt were two shallow, oval cavities, similar to the magic sword that I had recovered from Nambunga's cave.

I quickly swapped out the corroded sword for Mythanthar's Blade. There was no comparison... The legendary sword was way better than my old sword, even if it didn't have the torment and a +5 strength bonus! I equipped the sword and could feel a massive surge of power pulse through my muscles as I pulled up my stats. The strength bonus was showing tacked on... nice. I unequipped the sword and re-equipped it, noticing that my stats changed, and each time it was equipped there was a "+" next to my strength. Apparently, that meant that the stat was being influence by an outside item or effect.

## GUNNAR LONG

| | |
|---|---|
| Race: | Human |
| Level: | 5 (Progress 0%) [3 AP, 1 LF] |
| Title: | None |
| Health/Mana/Stamina: | 130/110/100 |
| Strength: | 15+ |
| Dexterity: | 14 |
| Intelligence: | 15 |
| Vitality: | 10 |
| Wisdom: | 12 |
| Willpower: | 10 |
| Charisma: | 10 |
| AR Rating: | 34 |
| Resists: | |
| | 10% Fire Resistance |
| Traits: | |
| | Elven Touch |
| Primary Skills: | |
| | First Aid Lvl 1: progress 0% |
| | Inspect Lvl 2: progress 15% |
| | Sneak Lvl 2: progress 10% |
| | Tinkering Lvl 1: progress 0% |
| Combat Skills: | |
| | Dodge Lvl 2: progress 0% |
| | Small Blades Lvl 2: progress 0% |
| | Backstab Lvl 1: progress 0% |
| | Archery Lvl 3: progress 15% |
| | Block Lvl 1: progress 35% |
| | Swords Lvl 1: progress 30% |
| Magic Skills: | |
| | Fire Magic Lvl 2: progress 60% |

I thought then that I would probably stick to learning swords for close combat. Daggers were nice for sneak attacks and assassinations, but the ability to block attacks with swords meant that they would be a better bread and butter weapon as I continued to build up my character.

I immediately assigned my LP to Swords and put one AP point in Wisdom, Intelligence, and Dexterity each. I had gotten a big enough boost from strength from the sword stats already to worry about raising strength, and I didn't want to risk dying and unnecessarily losing any stats.

I was progressing nicely, I thought. I needed a new bow, but otherwise I was gaining skills and gear at a fast-enough rate. I did one last round of the house to make sure there wasn't anything valuable—there wasn't—and then I headed back out into the wild.

# Chapter 16

### *01/04/0001*

I started back in the direction of Mist Vale village in a sort of half circle, trying to cover new ground but also trying to get back to my room before it got too late. The sun was starting to set, and I had no idea what sort of dangers lurked in the jungle at night. The Amazon rainforest-like region was much denser in vegetation and seemed to have many more odd creatures crawling around than Addenfall.

I heard a bunch of monkey sounds and started in its direction, but stopped and turned tail when I heard the roar of something that sounded like a massive gorilla. I had already used my only health potion, so I didn't want to move into anything that was too risky.

Since I wasn't finding anything interesting, I used my sword to cut down small level 1 insects, and threw Fireblasts at birds and bugs that only granted me 20-25 XP with each kill. I must have killed 30 or so pointless critters and managed to gain another level in Swords before I heard a low growl and the sound of strange yelping not too far in the distance.

I approached cautiously and quietly as I recognized one of growls as some sort of large cat, and if it weren't for the whelps of pain that accompanied the growls, I probably wouldn't have had the courage to get any closer.

The growls—growls of multiple animals—turned to a roar and then more yelps and the sound of chaos. I eventually decided it wouldn't be safe to move any closer on the ground, but I was still curious to what was going on.

Beside me was a tall tree with a few low hanging branches and very little green. I grabbed onto the lowest branch and started my climb to the top.

I was ten feet in the air before I finally had a good enough look at my surroundings. Visibility was limited by other trees and foliage in the distance, but I could see that only about 20 meters from where I sat, the group of animals that were making noise were scuffling.

A big black cat—a panther of some sort but even bigger than a panther—more like the size of Fenris was backed up against a large tree. Surrounding it were five smaller creatures, the size of the average dog, hairless with skin like a dinosaur. They looked almost like dinosaurs actually, with their thick pointed tails, but I saw no arms or front legs, and their mouths were more like a flat beak.

**Name:** *wild skinner*
**Race:** *monster*
**Level:** *15*
**Health/Mana/Stamina:** *160/0/150*
**Status:** *unknown*

I attempted to inspect the large cat as well, but it must have been a much higher level as every attempt failed.

*You have failed to inspect your target!*

*You have failed to inspect your target!*

The giant panther backed its ass up against the tree and roared at the skinners surrounding it, but the skinners seemed unperturbed. They just bounced backwards and forward towards the panther, each one fighting for the panther's attention.

A portion of the panther's skin had been torn at the belly, and bloody flesh dangled near the ground, blood dripping with its every movement. There were other wet, matted areas of the panther's fur, which I could only assume were bloody wounds as well, but I couldn't be sure due to its jet-black color.

One of the skinners rushed forward as if about to attack, and the panther jumped towards it, swiping a paw. The blow from the panther was strong enough to knock the skinner down, but the claws of the panther couldn't penetrate the skinner's leathery skin.

As soon as the other skinners saw that the panther was distracted, the one behind the panther leapt towards the panther's back and opened its flat leathery beak, revealing a surprising set of several razor sharp teeth. Its fangs plunged into the panther's soft skin, and the panther cried and then roared as it turned its head trying to fend off its attacker. As soon as it turned, another skinner jumped at the panther and sunk its teeth in near the panther's neck, latching on as the panther swiped and flung itself around madly.

Eventually, the panther pried one of the attackers off, but the other only came from the pressure of the panther's swings and hard rolls against the ground, tearing another chunk of flesh off in the process.

This continued for several minutes, the skinners attacking, adding additional wounds to the panther's body and the panther doing everything possible to get them off. It was clear that the skinners were trying to wear down the panther and bit by bit cause the animal to bleed out.

Why was the panther putting up with it? I wondered. There was a huge tree right behind it, and cats know how to climb trees. Was it because the skinners could also climb trees? Whatever the case was, the panther needed to tuck its tail and run because it was clearly losing the battle.

The panther licked its bloody nose and shook its head in confusion, right before it briefly fell to its stomach. Several of the skinners jumped on it all at once, but the panther snapped back into its senses and started swatting at the various areas it had been attacked and rolling on the ground, desperate to get them off.

It was only then that I saw what the panther was fighting for. At the base of the towering tree it was guarding, was a small hole, and a pair of glistening green eyes pieced through the hole's darkness—a baby panther looking on as its mother's skin was ripped to shreds. The tiny cat peeked its head out with concern, but retracted into its hole when one of the skinners jumped in its direction.

Without a moment's hesitation, the mother panther roared and ignored the skinners clamping onto its body to jump towards the hole and block any chance that a skinner would get its child.

I never imagined myself as any sort of hero, and attacking those level 15 dinosaur-looking beasts was probably a bad idea, but I knew I'd have trouble sleeping at night if I continued watching the panther get chewed up followed by the consumption of the baby cat. And if I just walked away, I wasn't sure how I'd feel about myself in the morning.

I climbed down from the tree and ran as quickly as I could towards the ensuing battle and when I was firing range, I climbed up another tree and with one hand holding myself steady, I stuck out my other hand and unleashed a Fireblast at one of the skinners.

The impact knocked the skinner down, and its skin sizzled as the flames from the blast dissipated. The blast shocked the other skinners and they all started looking around for the source of the attack, ignoring the wounded panther behind it.

*You have reached level 3 in **Fire Magic**!*

I shot another Fireblast at one of the other skinners, knocking it down like the one before, and with that attack, even the panther looked startled. The panther's eyes quickly found me as I charged up another attack, and when I scalded yet another skinner's hide, the skinner yelped like an injured dog and ran off through the woods. The other skinners raised their beaks and yelped just like the one who ran and then scurried off behind it.

I could see the foliage shaking as the strange monsters ran further and further away, and the exhausted panther finally relaxed and laid its weary head on the ground, closing its eyes.

The baby panther crawled out of its hole and gave its best growl, which was really more of a meow as it approached its fallen mother. The small cat looked confused and meowed again as it started to lick at its mother's wounds.

For a moment, I only watched, hoping that the mother panther would rise and stroll away. I had mixed feelings about the situation. Eden's Gate was supposed to be a game, a programmed world, and the dying panther was supposed to be a NPC. But how could it seem so lifelike? Everything from wounds on it the panther's body to the muddled behavior of the baby cast a dark shade of gray over fiction versus reality.

I didn't want the baby panther to die.

Hell, I didn't want the mother panther to die either. And still, I didn't understand why because they were technically just code written in a computer system.

But… if I only existed in that world as well, didn't that make me the same as the panther? Just code being processed in a computer system? I couldn't get my mind around it, and just shook my head, ordering myself to quit thinking so much.

I quickly climbed down from the tree and cautiously approached the scene of the fight. My senses were on high alert, ready to bolt in the other direction if the skinners came back, and the moment I stepped into view of the baby panther, its eyes went wide and scurried off back into the tree hole.

The baby panther meowed loudly, increasing in frequency the closer I got to its mother.

When I was in reaching distance of the larger panther, one of its eyes shot opened and it roared furiously and swung a weak paw towards me, trying to get enough energy to attack, but it was helpless, really. It was on its last legs. Still, the power of its roar was enough to make me jump back and tense up.

"It's alright…" I said softly, holding a hand up. "I'm not going to hurt you."

The fallen panther stared at me with tired eyes and roared again as I moved in closer and crouched near it's body, but it didn't make an effort to attack this time.

I inspected the panther's wounds, and several of them were deeper than they appeared from further away, probably going deep enough puncture its organs.

If I only had a health potion! I thought. Then maybe I would have had the chance to save it.

I reached in my bag and found my bandages, hoping that maybe I could negate enough of the panther's damage that it could survive. I could bandage her up and maybe she would survive long enough for me to go back to the Mist Vale to buy a potion and return in time to fix her up.

I reached for the panther's worst wound near its neck, where it was bleeding profusely, and the moment I made contact, the panther roared and made a sad effort to lift its head.

"Relax… I'm just trying to fix you up."

Just as soon as I tried tying the bandage around the panther's neck, the white fabric became soaked with the panther's blood and slipped right out of my hands. It was no use.

> *You have failed to bandage your target's wounds!*

Figures, I thought. I looked down at the large beast and whispered, "I'm sorry..."

The baby panther came crawling out of the tree and walked up to me cautiously. It sniffed at me and then sniffed its mother before climbing on to the top of my thigh. It meowed and looked up at me then looked down to its mother and meowed again.

"I'm sorry," I repeated. "There's nothing more I can do."

The mother panther stared at me with glazed-over eyes and watched as the baby panther sat down on my lap, looking like it was unsure about the situation, but then it lifted a large, weak paw and gently rested it on my leg.

The baby panther reached out and patted its mother's paw twice, right before the mother growled one final time and closed its eyes, passing to wherever things in Eden's Gate passed to.

I took a deep breath and exhaled as I spat, "Fuck," saddened that I couldn't save the mother. I looked down at the baby cat, and it looked up at me with its big green eyes and then nuzzled the top of its head against my abdomen.

*Name:* a great panther
*Race:* animal
*Level:* 1
*Health/Mana/Stamina:* 10/10/20
*Status:* friendly

I wasn't sure what to do with the tiny thing. I thought about walking a few hundred meters away from its mother, releasing it, and letting it fend for itself, but I knew that it'd probably find its way back and end up getting killed or eaten.

But whatever selfish ideas I was cooking up in my head were thrown aside when I heard the foliage rustling not far away and the unusual barking noise coming from the skinners in the distance. I stood to my feet and gripped the baby panther in my arms as I ran.

# Chapter 17

### *Day 5 (Earth)*

Aaron pushed open the door to Nexicon Inc's head office and walked down the hall past hundreds of empty cubicles and work stations. In the days following the launch of the Nexicon VR and the death of millions of people around the world, the company's stock had plummeted and the multi-billion-dollar empire crumbled amidst the threat of multiple civil and criminal lawsuits.

Kendra was sitting in her corner office that overlooked downtown Los Angeles when Aaron tapped on the wall twice and walked inside. She turned her attention away from the television hanging from the wall and raised her chin at Aaron.

"What's the latest?" Aaron asked, his voice more serious than his usual fun-loving self.

"Have a look," she said.

On the television was an image of a SWAT team busting down the door of a small house. The police waved their assault rifles to several people whose eyes went big and raised their hands in the air. In the center of it all was a man in a wheelchair with a Nexicon VR on his head. His body was limp and he was slightly slumped over. On the floor nearby were several other lifeless bodies, young and old.

"They're calling them 'Transfer Houses' online, but the news is referring to them as 'Suicide Houses'," Kendra said.

The image on the screen flipped to a male newscaster sitting behind a desk. "Despite the nationwide order for all Nexicon VR units to be handed over to the authorities for disposal, reports are showing that only 65% of the machines have been recovered. After the government announcement of a Federal ban on possession of these machines, the amount of voluntary suicides using Nexicon VR actually increased by over 500%, and people who are desperate to 'get inside the game' are offering up large sums of cash in exchange for visor usage."

The image flipped to the President of the United States, standing behind a podium, American flags draped in the background.

"The people of America and around the world are facing tumultuous times, but with the swift help of Congress, we've managed to get permission from nearly every leader around the globe to move forward with our plan to combat this crisis." The President paused and looked from side to side, creating tension in his speech. "We're dealing with a technology that, quite frankly, very few people understand. But what we do know is that we'll need the help of everyone to put a stop to it. Over the next three days, our goal is to remove as many devices as possible from the Nexicon CPU blockchain. That means a complete shutdown of both power, internet and satellite communications, beginning with the most outward regions today and ending with a blackout here in the United States. During this time, only medical or structurally required technology will be allowed to run.

"Our goal is to weaken this 'CPU blockchain'— they're calling it—to the point that it does not have the processing power to run Eden's Gate. We're now asking—demanding—for everyone to dispose of any Nexicon hardware you have and delete any Nexicon software that you may have installed on your phones, gaming systems, or personal computers. Once the grid is brought back online, we will closely monitor that no system running the Nexicon blockchain can come online and act accordingly if anything slips by."

The image flipped back to the newscaster in the suit, who started talking about the scale of the undertaking right before Kendra flipped it off.

"You think they can really pull it off?" Kendra asked.

Aaron pulled out a chair beside Kendra's desk and crossed his arms as he sat down, a somber expression on his face. "Maybe," he said with a sigh. "Nexicon is global, but 95% of our technology is used here in the United States, so it's definitely a possibility."

"Even if there was a single server room running the blockchain somewhere off the coast of Africa, it would still be enough to power Eden's Gate."

"And that's exactly why their plan might work. If they really manage a global blackout everywhere outside of the United States first, that will increase their chances of containing the blockchain here. But 3 days is really pushing it to get other countries involved. Could be bullshit."

Kendra pulled her phone out and flipped it to her social media account. "I'm not so sure about that," she said. She handed the phone to Aaron.

*@PresidentOfPhillipines- 3 Day blackout in effect beginning tonight at 10pm. For your safety, please make sure home is stocked with flashlights, supplies, and stay indoors during this time. #StopEdensGate*

Below the post were several other similar messages from other leaders of small countries, along with a bunch of bickering from a few gamers and geeks talking about their rights and freedom of choice. *#RightToChooseRightToPlay*

Aaron handed the phone back to Kendra and shook his head. "This isn't the way they should be handling things," he said. "They're basically going to nuke everyone inside the game."

"That's what happens when 5 million bodies show up on the White House's lawn. How do you expect a non-gamer to believe people are really living inside the game when they have no way of communicating with them? There's never been technology like this before."

There was a long silence as Aaron stared straight into the far wall and tapped his fingers slowly on Kendra's desk.

"The communication port to Eden's Gate still works, right?" he finally spoke. "After I put Eden's Gate into Demo mode, Dr. Winston was still able to beam his image onto the screen at the keynote."

Kendra rattled her head and shrugged. "Yeah, I guess it still works, but Rupert is the one who activated it at the keynote. Without his password, only he is able to open communication, and he's inside—"

"I'll go inside," Aaron suddenly said.

Kendra darted her head back. "What?"

"I'll go inside Eden's Gate. We still have a VR unit somewhere in here, don't we?"

"What are you talking about, Aaron?" Kendra shook her head, her face twisted in confusion.

Aaron jammed his finger on the desk. "Who cares if they confiscate all the Nexicon VRs? If they stop people from going into Eden's Gate, then okay, great. But we can't let them just wipe out the blockchain with more than 5 million people inside."

"They're dead Aaron!"

"Their bodies are dead!" Aaron countered. "You of all people should know that. You spent time inside the game world."

"Oh, I just walked around picking herbs," she said. "I didn't even get past level 1. You know I'm not a gamer."

"And neither am I," Aaron explained. "At least I've never been much of a MMO gamer. But I've been inside, and I know how real that world is. It's more than an MMO. Hell, I was planning on playing the game too before all this shit went down."

Kendra took a deep breath. "Okay, so you'll go inside and do what? Go on a fucking quest?"

"I'll find Rupert and tell him what's going on. If he can open a communication channel with Earth and show that people are really alive inside, I think the government will put an end to this crazy plan."

Kendra snorted. "You think you can find Rupert in just 3 days? The game world is massive."

Aaron nodded. "It's definitely a risk, but I know the game mechanics better than anyone other than Dr.

Winston. If I could get some NPCs or players on my side, there's a chance that I could get to his castle."

Kendra sighed. "That's such a ridiculous idea…"

"Do you have a better alternative?" Aaron asked. "Or do you just want to let all those people die?"

"You'll die with them, Aaron," Kendra stressed. "You want to give up your life here on Earth?"

"It's not really dying; I'd just be transferring over. And I'm not married nor am I close to my family like you. I'm just a single, loner tech guy. Plus, if I don't go, I'll just be sitting in courtrooms for the next 5-10 years being scrutinized for my involvement with Eden's Gate. What kind of life will I have? Fuck that."

"I can't argue with the scrutiny part…" Kendra muttered.

"So I'll go into Eden's Gate, and I'll need to you to get a computer turned on and listening to the communication port. If I can find Rupert and get him to open the signal, then it's up for you to get the broadcast in the right hands."

"3 days is not enough—"

"2 and a half depending on the time they shut things down. I need you to do this, Kendra."

Kendra breathed heavily and thought in silence for a moment. "If we're doing this, it's got to be staged like you acted on your own. I don't want to go to jail for helping you into the VR."

Aaron nodded. "Let's go get a unit and quit wasting time." The two of them headed for the door, and when they stepped out into the hall, Aaron pulled his keys out of his pocket and handed them to her. "The small key is to my condo and the digital key is for the BMW… Take what you want, but um…" he twisted his face and scratched the back of his neck. "There's this 'Virtual Doll' inside my closet. Can you do me a favor and—"

"I'll burn it."

"Thanks…"

# Chapter 18

## *01/05/0001*

I woke up to the feeling of something wet in my ear. I groaned and slapped at my lobe, only to make contact with a thick, soft fur.

*Meow.*

I shot out of bed and clenched the side of my head in agony at the high-pitched sound of the baby panther crying directly in my ear canal. Ever heard a baby panther meow or roar or whatever the hell their noise is? Well, it's ridiculously cute, but it's also absurdly LOUD. My eardrum was throbbing.

"Oh come on," I moaned. "I'm not ready to wake up yet."

The panther jumped into my lap and started purring as it nuzzled its head against my body. It was hard to be angry at something so adorable.

After running from the skinners the previous night, I carried the cat back to my room in the Mist Vale village, throwing off random Fireblasts at level 1 creatures on the way. Thankfully, there were no other major incidents that happened, but it was pretty late when I returned. Most of the Elves, other than the guards, had locked up in their homes for the night, so I figured I'd call it a night as well and crashed after playing with the baby panther for a couple hours.

The light of morning shined through the tiny circular window of my miniature room, and I figured that the panther was probably feeling hungry by now. I knew I was. I stood up and started putting on my armor when there was a knock at the door.

"Just a minute!" I shouted as I slipped my leather chestpiece over my head. When I turned around and opened the door, there was the gorgeous bombshell herself.

Adeelee looked serious, but even with her lips set in a straight line, I swear it was almost like sparkles fluttered from her eyes as she spoke. "How was your first night in the Vale? Did everything go well?"

"Umm, yeah…" I said nodding my head. Being around a princess made me a little timid. "Everything's going well…"

*Meow.* The baby panther leapt up, digging its claws into my armor as it climbed my body and rested on my shoulder.

Adeelee looked startled. "Oh… You have a panther?"

"Well, no… I don't *have* a panther. I *found* a panther. I was hoping you could help me figure out what to do with him."

The panther lifted its paws and started grabbing at my neck and nibbling at my hair.

"It seems like she's fond of you."

"She's?" I asked.

"You didn't notice that she doesn't have any balls?"

I cleared my throat and held back my embarrassment. "I guess I didn't look…"

"Well, it's definitely a female panther, and if you don't want her, then you should probably return her to her family."

"Gone… killed by skinners," I said.

"Well, then you can kill her and sell her pelt, I suppose. That wouldn't be very noble of you, but you wouldn't be the first heartless human I've met."

"I don't want to kill her! I brought her here to save her!"

"Then why don't you bond with her? Most humans get eaten alive when they try to tame great beasts, but you have one here who is already quite affectionate towards you."

"What do you mean exactly?"

"You've seen how the elves have bonded with animals in the village… but we're naturally quite close to nature. It's usually quite difficult for humans to connect with large forest animals. Jax is quite the exception with Fenris."

"Large? This is just a baby!"

Adeelee laughed. "By my guess, that panther could grow to be twice the size of Fenris. Certainly just as powerful. Why don't you try to bond yourself with her?"

"How?" I asked.

"Give her a name. If she accepts your name, then you'll be bonded. But once you're bonded, then she's with you until death."

I turned my head towards the baby panther and it swatted the soft pad of its paws at my cheeks. I wasn't so much into the idea of taking care of a kitten, but she had already sucked me in with her cute eyes and tiny nose. "What would be a good name for you?" I asked the cat.

*Meow.*

"Sonya… Meadow… Shadow… Som?" I muttered. "Hmmm… How about Sora?" I raised my hand up and rubbed my palm over the panther's fur. "How do you feel about Sora?"

The panther looked at me curiously and then tilted its head to the side.

> You are now bound with **Sora**! Your beast companion is bound to you for life and cannot be transferred to any other characters.
>
> Advancement! You have learned the skill: **Summon Beast**. Summon Beast is a unique skill that is linked only to your bond with certain creatures. This skill cannot be improved or changed.

The panther jumped on the top of my head and started pawing at my forehead. I could almost feel its excitement as it played.

"Sora is nice name," Adeelee said.

I chuckled. "So what do I feed her? Cat food?"

"Cat food?" Adeelee asked, crossing her brow. "Bonded Beasts usually enjoy eating food rations or other animals, but when you release them to the Otherworld, they will feed and grow on their own."

"Otherworld?"

"The bag I gave you," Adeelee said. "You know it sends your items to another plane, correct?"

"Yeah…"

"It's the same place that bonded beasts go when you dismiss them. The astral plane—or The

Otherworld—is a magical place, and that magic will allow your beast to grow rapidly and to a much higher degree than if you were to just keep her here. It's something that sets bonded beasts apart from other animals."

"How do I release her?" I asked.

"Just look at her and tell her that she's free to go. It's pretty simple."

"And I summon her back how?"

"Summon Beast doesn't require mana, but it's a channeling ability. Focus on Sora coming back and call her name as you exert your energy somehow. So long as Sora is still alive and isn't involved in something pressing, she should come to you."

"That's all?"

"Just remember to let her roam free sometimes and treat her well. If you keep her in one place too long, she may lose sentiment towards you. Remain her master, but allow her to be wild, all the same."

I turned to Sora and tested my instructions. "Dismissed!... Ermm... You can go!"

Sora looked at me and purred a couple times, before she jumped off my shoulder and started running for the corner of the room. When she reached the corner wall, she jumped, and her body suddenly faded into translucent speckles of light then vanished altogether.

"And I call her like this?" I asked. I slammed a fist into my palm and started making the same motions that Jax did when he summoned Fenris.

"No, don't do that!" Adeelee held her hand out to stop me. "You don't want to summon a beast immediately after you release them. How would you feel if you were called to work immediately after you were granted time off? Give her time."

*Work? Pawing at my head was work?* "Okay, okay," I said. "But she's okay, right?"

"She'll be fine in the Otherworld." She glanced about my room as if she were looking for any other random creatures that may jump out. "If you're ready, we can start for the Crystal River to scout out the camp."

"I still need to buy some supplies. I broke my bow in battle yesterday." I reached into my bag and began to holster my Mythanthar's Blade.

"That's an elven blade," Adeelee said.

"Yeah, I looted it yesterday in the forest."

"May I see it?" Adeelee asked.

I shrugged and unsheathed the sword before handing it to Adeelee.

She rubbed her palm across the blade. "This a very powerful sword for your level. It should help you greatly in battle." She looked closer at the hilt, particularly the shallow impressions on either side. "And two empty slots as well. If you add runestones you'll get even more power out of this item."

"Runestones?" I asked.

Adeelee sighed and handed me back the sword. "I keep forgetting that you know so little about this world, Reborn," she said as she reached into her bag, pulling out an oval shaped stone with a flat surface. "This is a blank runestone that you can find by mining. So long as you know the rune pattern for a particular power and have the correct inscription powder, you can imbue these stones and attach them to items."

"Powder like this?" I asked. I pulled out the red inscription powder that I looted the prior day and handed it Adeelee.

"Powder like this, indeed. Where did you find this?"

"Looted it yesterday as well."

"Quite the find," Adeelee said. "Inscription powder is quite rare and can usually only be made by dismantling magic items. Of course, if you don't want to bother with inscription, you can always buy runestones from a vendor... but very costly."

"I see."

Adeelee reached into her bag and pulled out a second blank runestone and a metal chisel with blunt tip at the end. She handed me one of the runestones.

> *You've received:* ***Blank Runestone****.
> Durability: 10/10. Quality: Average. Rarity:
> Rare. Weight: 0.1 kg. A mysterious stone with
> lots of potential.*

"Watch…" She held the runestone in her hand and started carving a symbol that looked something like a distorted upside down Y. Once she carved the pattern, she blew the speckles of dust out of the crevice and held it up to me. "Can you copy this?"

I shrugged. "Maybe… I can try."

I took the chisel from her hand and forcefully grinded it against the face of the stone, making my best effort to copy her pattern. By the time I was finished, I ended up with something that was close to what she had made, but quite a bit more amateurish.

"Not great," Adeelee said, "but it should work." She gave me back the inscription powder and indicated that I could keep the chisel. "Now pour the powder inside the pattern to finish the inscription."

I popped the top of the small vial and started sprinkling the dust over the pattern as instructed. As the particles made contact with the stone, the inscription began glowing and the stone felt warm in my hand. When the last bit of the dust was poured, the powder seemed to shift inside the crevice, evening itself out. There was a slight, alien-like buzzing sound coming from the stone, and then all of a sudden there was a click. The powder solidified inside the crevice, and looked like it was part of the stone—just now a stone with a bright red, oddly shaped upside down Y.

> *You've received:* **Runestone of Minor Damage**. *+1 damage. Durability: 10/10. Quality: Poor. Rarity: Rare. Weight: 0.1 kg*

> *Advancement! You have learned the skill:* **Inscription**. *Write today's adventures in ink. Write tomorrow's victories in stone! Inscription is linked the base stat Intelligence. Increases your Intelligence to increase your Inscription ability.*

> *You have gained 1 point of Intelligence!*

"You'll do better as you progress," Adeelee said. "These smaller runestones are for weapons and armor, but a runestone master can build the large runestones like the one I told you about above the palace."

I started to move the runestone near the hilt of my blade to see if it would fit, but once they were in a few meters of touching each other, the stone was drawn into the sword like a magnet and sat flush inside the hilt. "Hey, I didn't want to put it in there yet!" I said as I tried to pry the stone back out.

Adeelee laughed. "Be careful next time. Runestones are permanent, and there's only a chance you'll get the powder back by dismantling the item."

"Well, fuck." At least the 1 damage was showing on the sword.

"Don't worry... You've still got another slot, and the minor bonus you're getting from that rune is better than nothing."

I shrugged and sheathed the sword.

Adeelee shifted her weight and sniffed in my direction, seemingly forgetting our topic of discussion. "Have you had a bath?" she asked.

"A bath? There's a bath around here?"

"Of course there's a bath, and quite frankly, you smell like a dirty panther."

I groaned. Maybe I needed to put a few points in charisma...? "Where are the shower rooms?" I asked.

"What are shower rooms?" She looked confused. "You'll bathe under the waterfall like everyone else."

"Under the waterfall?" I should have known *that* was the bath she was talking about.

"Yes, of course. I'm sure you'll find it quite relaxing."

Bathing in the presence of a bunch of naked elves didn't sound relaxing at all. More like *arousing* if any of girls I saw the day before were there. "Um yeah. I'll put that on my list of things to do before we leave."

"I'll meet you by the guards at the base of the palace in 2 hours. Make sure you have plenty of supplies, and you might want to have a bite to eat before we leave. Adventuring is never fun on an empty stomach."

# Chapter 19

*01/05/0001*

During my bath with the elves, I found myself trying to focus on goblins, skinners, baseball, dirty socks… anything to keep everything… ya know… *down*. The elves were totally comfortable with their nudity, just splashing about and cleaning off their bodies in full view of everyone, and the elven men seemed totally unphased at all the boobage on display or the fact that the girls could see their meat and veg.

But when in Rome, do as the Romans, they say, and I manned-up and put on my birthday suit when I jumped in the water. It was actually quite nice, the freedom of it all. I was surrounded by a beautiful landscape, dark green vegetation everywhere, large tigers walking along in the distance and a whole town of people who seemed liked they belonged together.

I thought back to my life on Earth—my stressful job at BestFoods, my studio apartment, the repetition of doing the same thing every day—and I felt scared. But it wasn't for the same reason that I had felt scared the first day that I was in the game. I was actually scared of what it would be like to go back to my old life.

Five days in Eden's Gate, and nothing felt the same. Every day had been an adventure, and it didn't hurt that I could cast magic, carried a sword and had crafting abilities. Hell, I even had a cute pet! I had no idea where my life would take me since I entered the game, but I felt so at home in my new world. The only thing I had back on Earth was Rachel.

Rachel.

Rachel...

I opened up my settings menu and tried the log out button again. It had been a while since I checked. Nothing happened, as I expected.

The reality that I was dead on Earth was really setting in. The likelihood of me surviving five days without food and water, laying in one position was slim, so how could I be alive? Maybe I was on life support? Maybe... Possibly. But that seemed unlikely. The only other alternative explanation was that it was all a dream.

It sure as hell seemed like a dream when I was standing under a waterfall surrounded by beautiful, naked elves.

And although my acceptance was growing that the Nexicon CEO's broadcast on my first day in game was true, I still needed to find Rachel. I had no way of knowing if she had made it out of the game or not, but if she was inside of Eden's Gate, I had to search for her. She was my girlfriend after all, and she was the one who had given me the damn headset in the first place.

After my bath, I headed to Rhys' shop in the village and bought a new bow and a new quiver of arrows.

*You've received: **Elven Shortbow**. 6-10 Attack Damage. Durability: 10/10. Quality: Average. Rarity: Uncommon. Weight: 0.5 kg*

*You've received: **Elven Arrows of Penetration**. +2 Attack Damage. Durability: 10/10. Quality: Average. Rarity: Uncommon. Weight: 0.5 kg*

I also picked up 2 minor health potions, 2 bandages, 1 cure potion, and 2 food rations. Total damage to my purse was 244 gold after trading my old quiver, leaving me only 245 gold left. It was more than I was expecting to spend, but the bow was a huge step up from what I had before.

After a quick stop at the food stand for another delicious elven pie and some water, I found Adeelee waiting for me by the rising path that led to the palace. A longbow was strapped to her back and a long, thin sword as draped at her side.

She leaned forward and sniffed. "You smell better."

"You're probably smelling the elven pie."

Adeelee smile. "The village favorite." Her eyes wandered toward the route out of the village. "Do you have everything ready?"

"Yeah, I'm all stocked up."

"Good," she said. "And I brought you this from the library as well."

*You've received: **Scroll: Fire Curtain.** Create a wall of fire at a target location. Requires 15 Intelligence. Fire Magic Level 2. Durability: 10/10. Quality: Average. Rarity: Uncommon. Weight: 0.1 kg*

"Really? You're just giving me this?"

"You may be a Reborn but you're still a low level. I want us to succeed in our mission."

Adeelee started walking towards the exit to the village, and I followed as I started reading this scroll.

> *Advancement! You have learned the spell:*
> **Fire Curtain.**

"Thank you!"

Adeelee didn't respond. She just kept walking straight head, leading us out of the village.

"So we're walking to the Crystal River?" I asked.

"We're not going to walk. We're going to run."

"Run?" I asked. "I've only got 100 stamina... I don't think we'll make it very far."

Adeelee snickered and kept walking.

"What's so funny?"

Once we reached the edge of the village, Adeelee held her hand in the air and leaves rose from the ground as a gust of wind started circling both of our bodies.

I took a step back and started swatting at the leaves. "What the?!"

The leaves tumbled back to the ground, and I suddenly felt like I had drunk a liter of Red Bull. My stamina bar was flashing, and below my stats was an icon of a twisting green leaf.

> **Spirit of the Forest**: *While traveling in forest regions, your draw energy from the nature around you, granting you unlimited stamina. Your run speed is increased by 300%. Spell duration: 20 minutes. Source: Adeelee*

"As I was saying, we'll be running," Adeelee cooed and smirked. "Don't underestimate the power of elves when they're in the forest."

I lifted my knees in the air and I felt light as a feather. "Whoa! This is awesome."

"Follow now," Adeelee said as she bolted away from the village. It was only a second or two before she was almost out of sight.

I started running after her, and I felt like a human greyhound. The green and the trees of the forest passed by in a blur of motion, and I could just as easily jump, duck and dodge over obstacles as if I were running at a normal speed.

I managed to catch Adeelee, and we ran together, side-by-side traversing the Vale nearly as fast as when I rode on the back of Fenris.

Adeelee had to recast the haste spell several times when it ran out, but after a couple hours we eventually reached Addenfall, and then a couple hours later we found ourselves breaking free of the forest boundaries and coming out to a wide bank with a long river that appeared to stretch for miles.

"The Crystal River," Adeelee said.

The river was only about 50 meters wide, and the surface of the water sparkled brightly, shimmering like crystals when the subdued waves caught sunlight. On the other side of the river, I saw a side of Eden's Gate I hadn't seen before. Rather than tall trees and thick foliage, there were plains with rolling hills. Several trees were present, but they were smaller and far less dense than Addenfall. Far in the horizon I could see mountains and homes scattered about. If it weren't for the fact that there was a massive tent with smoke near it by the river and creatures that were obviously not human walking near said tent, I would have thought I was in the American Midwest.

Adeelee pointed to an unoccupied hill that was nearby the camp. "We'll cross here and try to climb that hill undetected. Once we know what we're dealing with, we'll decide how we'll make our move."

I nodded.

Adeelee wasted no time stepping down into the water and immediately started swimming towards the other side like a nimble mermaid.

I was a little less graceful, and the moment my feet touched the water, I fell submerged, surprised at just how deep the river was. I pulled myself up and spat out water as I started swimming behind Adeelee. "Is there anything in the water I should worry about?"

"Yes, lots of things," Adeelee replied. "So swim fast. Fighting in the water isn't fun... especially if you're a fire magic user."

"Oh, fuck me!" I spat as I started swimming faster.

Adeelce stood out of the water and seemed generally unaffected by the fact that her clothes were wet, and other than the fact that her hair was soaked, she still looked like a million bucks. She might have even looked more alluring standing there dripping from head to toe. Maybe one day I'd catch her when she was bathing at the falls... That shower from earlier really got the gears in my head turning.

I felt miserable, however, when I exited the river. The water made the smell of my leather armor rise strong to my nostrils, and my feet squished as I climbed out to dry ground.

"We'll have to sneak the rest of the way," Adeelee warned.

"I know, I know," I replied as I poured water out of my boots.

"Hurry up then."

I gathered myself up and shook my head in an effort to dry my hair before I sank down and started sneaking behind Adeelee. We made a half circle around the camp, ducking behind trees and crouching behind tall grass, but eventually made it to the top of the hill without alerting anyone.

Below us was a huge piece of thin leather canvas draped over a few logs to form a rudimentary tent. At the entrance to the tent were two posts with human skulls sitting on top, and a few feet from the entrance was a campfire where around 10 creatures with wrinkled, sickly-looking skin, similar to the dead bow user I saw in Nambunga's cave.

A couple of the creatures wore loincloths and had bows across their backs, but the others had small swords and bucklers, and metal helmets on their head. I wondered whose idea it was to give them helmets but leave their chest and legs exposed? Goblin logic!

The goblins were talking to each other in something that sounded like gibberish, and one goblin had another goblin—I assume a female, based on its thin, saggy tits—laid out across its lap with its ass in the air, spanking it. It was a horrible—yet comical—sight, let me tell you, but several of the other goblins were watching the show wide-eyed. One rubbed his crotch with no shame while another chewed on a large bone with a piece of brown meat dangling on its end.

The smell stemming from the camp was intense, even from the top of the hill. Urine mixed with rot mixed with feces. And judging by the wet spots and brown circles of goo around the camp, that was probably exactly what I was smelling.

I focused in on one of the helmet wielders.

**Name:** *Goblin Fighter*
**Race:** *goblin*
**Level:** *5*
**Health/Mana/Stamina:** *40/0/30*
**Status:** *aggressive*

The scouts were the same level but had 10 less health and 10 more stamina.

In the distance, I could see two additional camps posted along the river, spaced a few hundred meters apart. They were far enough away that they probably couldn't hear anything going on in our location unless there was a loud commotion, but they were close enough that it wouldn't take long to run there or for reinforcements and maul us down.

"How are we going to take out this many without getting ourselves killed?"

> *You have been invited to join* **Adeelee's**
> **Party**.
> *Do you accept? Yes/No*

"So we can monitor each other's vitals," Adeelee whispered, ignoring my question.

I immediately willed myself to accept the invitation, and as soon I did, 3 smaller stat bars with Adeelee's name appeared below mine. I also noticed that if I tried to Inspect Adeelee, I got a screen with her basic stats, rather than the "failed inspection" message that I had gotten every other time.

| ADEELEE VOST | |
|---|---|
| Race: | High Elf |
| Level: | 16 |
| Title: | Princess |
| Health/Mana/Stamina: | 170/130/160 |
| Strength: | 18 |
| Dexterity: | 30 |
| Intelligence: | 20 |
| Vitality: | 20 |
| Wisdom: | 12 |
| Willpower: | 24 |
| Charisma: | 67 |

I wasn't shown her skills, armor or resist rating, but it still gave me enough about her that I knew what I was dealing with. "So basically, you're high enough level that you can just vaporize all these guys?"

"Level isn't everything, Gunnar. If I were to get surrounded, it's quite possible these level 5s could kill me. Unlikely, but possible." She pointed towards the tent. "And we don't know what's inside there."

"So then what's the plan?"

"The plan is to whittle their numbers down enough so that a close combat battle won't last long and so there's little chance that one runs off."

"Okay…" I said sarcastically. "How?"

Adeelee pulled her bow off her back. "What's your archery level?"

"Three."

"Good. This is a level 3 skill." Adeelee nocked one of her arrows, held it back and closed one of her eyes. Her breathing stopped, and she looked like solid stone. After several seconds, she let the arrow fly and it coursed silent as a ghost through the air and landed cleanly, quietly, in the back of the neck of a goblin who had walked away from the group and started for the back of the tent. The goblin fell forward in the grass, dying instantly, but the arrow didn't make a sound and none of the other goblins were the wiser.

"Nice shot," I said.

"You're up next."

I pulled my bow off my back along with one of my arrows. "Which one?" I asked.

"Wait for it."

Another one of the goblins eventually got up and strayed to the other end of the tent. It squatted and lifted its loincloth right before it started answering nature's call.

"That one," Adeelee said. "Pull your arrow back, close an eye and put all your focus into your aim. Concentrate on hitting a specific critical part of its body, and don't release until you're breathing has stopped and your hands are totally steady. What you're searching for is a completely silent, critical shot.

I did as she said and looked down the shaft of the arrow, concentrating on the spine of my defecating target. Like magic, my eyes felt like they were zooming in and the details of the spot I was aiming for appeared much closer than they actually were. My breathing stopped, and my body was completely still.

I released the arrow, and just like Adeelee's shot, my aim was silent and true, landing in the spine of my victim, causing him to lifelessly fall forward and shoot the last turd of his life up and into the air.

> *You have gained 90 XP!*

> *Advancement! You have learned the skill:* **Snipe Shot***. If they hear you, it means you missed. Snipe Shot is linked the base stat Dexterity. Increases your Dexterity to increase your ability to Snipe Shot.*

"A landed Snipe Shot has a 100% chance to critically hit if you land it from a location where you're undetected," Adeelee explained.

"Sick," I muttered, while noticing that only one Snipe Shot had drained my stamina by 30%. It wasn't something that I would be able to abuse.

"Sick?" Adeelee asked. "You don't appear to be diseased or poisoned."

I shook my head. "That's not what I meant. Where I come from, 'sick' means that something is really good."

"Being sick is good?" Adeelee's face twisted. "That sounds like something the Scourge would say."

I huffed. "Sorry, it's hard to explain."

Adeelee just rattled her head and turned back in the direction of the goblins. "No one else is wandering, so it looks like we're going to have to make our move now. If we can land two more Snipe Shots, that will bring us down to 6 goblins. I'll jump down, while you stay up here and keep firing."

"Got it," I replied.

Adeelee drew an arrow and nodded her chin towards me. We both nocked our arrows, and I could hear Adeelee counting down softly. "1… 2… 3…"

I focused in on another Snipe Shot, and the moment that Adeelee let her arrow fly, I let mine fly as well. Her arrow landed clean in the back of the head of the goblin spanker, and mine caught the side of the neck of the goblin who was still happily toying with his goblin jewels. They both keeled over dead, arrows sticking out of their bodies, and it took a second before the other goblins realized what was going on and started drawing their weapons.

By the time the goblins were alert, Adeelee was already scurrying down the hill with her sword drawn, and I had let another Snipe Shot fly, connecting with one of the scouts right in its mouth.

The goblins rattled off something in their native language, and started running towards Adeelee, but Adcclee raised her hand, causing green energy to encompass her fingertips and small vines to rise out of the ground, rooting all the remaining goblins in place.

I was careful not to drain any more stamina, so the rest of the arrows were just regular shots, chipping away at the goblins' health as Adeelee rushed forward to fight up close.

She made quick work of the goblins. As they grumbled and growled, pulling at their legs desperately to get back in motion, Adeelee drew her thin, slightly arced sword and spun the blade around like a graceful acrobat, severing the head of one, two, then tumbling on the ground to plunge the tip into the heart of a third.

I fired a couple of arrows into the female goblin who was basically lying on the ground, unarmed, trying to release her mangled body from the vines, and a third shot ended her life. By the time I looked up, all 10 goblins were dead, but stomping out of the tent were two larger goblins, at least 3 times the size of the ones who were outside.

> **Name:** *Goblin Brute*
> **Race:** *goblin*
> **Level:** *8*
> **Health/Mana/Stamina:** *135/0/75*
> **Status:** *aggressive*

The brutes had bulging muscles under their decrepit, gray skin, and both wore plated armor only across their shoulders, loincloths draped between their legs. In their hands, they both wielded large axes with thick wooden handles and blunt, stone blades.

The two large goblins took in the scene, at first shocked at the fact that their comrades were dead, and once they saw Adeelee standing there, grayish goblin blood dripping from her sword, they both charged in her direction and one of them roared.

Adeelee rolled out of the way as one of the Goblins swung its heavy axe down at her, kicking dirt up in the air as he missed. She rose to her feet, spun, and slashed her blade across the abdomen of the other, causing it to moan as it swung its axe in the air, missing her by a mile.

I let an arrow fly as the uninjured goblin started running back towards Adeelee, and it stuck him in knee, causing him to fall face forward with a thump and drop his axe. I fired two more shots towards the other goblin as Adeelee masterfully dodged its blows and struck it again and again, slicing its torso to pieces.

The goblin seemed to ignore my arrows as they plunged into its back, now swinging its axe wildly, desperate to hit anything. But its efforts were for nothing as Adeelee dodged an attack and closed in, driving her sword deep into its body.

Adeelee quickly pulled out her sword, knowing that the goblin was dead, and dashed for the other goblin that was clawing for its fallen axe and pulling itself to its feet. In a show of speed, she swung her sword at the axe, knocking it out of the way, and then drove the tip of her blade deep in the goblin's skull.

Granted, she was several levels higher than the goblins, but she still looked like a total badass out there.

Adeelee turned, motioned her hand towards me as she started sifting through one of the brute's pockets. I swiftly got up and ran down to the carnage, grabbing as many still-intact arrows and doing a brief sweep of each body to see if I could find anything.

I had limited slots in my bag, so I left all off the goblin's poor quality armor and weapons, but I managed to find 60 gold pieces amongst the corpses.

Inside the tent were three crates. Two of them were filled with nasty-looking uncooked animal meat—at least I think it was animal—and the other was filled with more crude weapons, another 50 gold, and a silver ring.

> *You've received:* **Ring of Sturdiness**.
> *Durability: 7/10. Quality: Average. Rarity:*
> *Rare. Weight: 0.1 kg. +15 HP*

I bagged the coins and slid the ring onto my finger, feeling its magic slip into my body.

"Over here," Adeelee called.

I turned and walked over to where the Princess was staring down at a paper that was sitting on a table. There was a crudely drawn map on the paper and at the top was something that looked like a black bird, and an arrow pointing in the direction of what looked to be Addenfall Forest. In thick letters was written, "KEEEL! SPAROW!"

"Keel Sparow?" I asked. "What the hell does that mean?"

"Kill Sparrow, I assume. Orcs and goblins aren't particularly good at Common Tongue."

"Who is Sparrow?"

Adeelee's eyes wandered. "Hmmm. I have my suspicions, but I can't be sure. Maybe we'll find out more as we move to the other camps. Let's head out before someone—"

"Rawwwwwwwwwwwwwr!"

I turned around to see a goblin, a bit smaller than the brutes, wielding two long, sharp swords—one in each hand. Two leather straps wrapped around his body and his legs were covered in thin cotton pants, but he was wearing no other armor. The muscles on his arms and legs were defined and his hulking chest heaved as he ran towards us.

*Name:* Goblin Berserker
*Race:* goblin
*Level:* 8
*Health/Mana/Stamina:* 120/0/100
*Status:* aggressive

The berserker was fast, and I only had time to pull out my sword and block his first sword as he closed in on me, his other sword lashing out and cutting me against my chest. My armor absorbed most of the blow, but he did break into my skin, causing me to jerk back at the pain.

Adeelee flung her sword out for the berserker's head, but the berserker ducked and roared "Shreddddaaa!"

The goblin spun on its feet with its arms wide, creating a deadly helicopter of blades. Again, I was struck by the attack, but Adeelee managed to jump back in time to avoid taking any damage. My health bar showed me at around 60%.

"Shredddaaa! Shredddaaa!" The goblin continued to shout as it spun, and I reached out and shot a Fireblast into the chaos, knocking him out of his move and causing him to almost lose his balance and fall.

Adeelee took advantage of the situation and sliced her sword hard at the Goblin's arm, severing it at the elbow, causing a sea of dark goblin blood to come spewing out. The goblin cried, and I sent another

Fireblast at the Goblin's other arm, knocking its second weapon out of its hand, just as Adeelee lashed her sword across its throat.

The berserker gurgled as blood surged out of its mouth and neck, and it fell slowly to its knees then face-first into the dirt below.

Adeelee checked the berserker for loot and slipped a few coins in her pocket before standing back up and raising a hand towards me.

Green energy pulsed off my body, and a flashing, dark green leaf appeared below my stats.

> ***Nature's Regrowth***: *You draw upon the power of nature to regenerate 3 health per second. Spell duration: 1 minute or until fully healed. Your run speed is increased by 300%. Source: Adeelee*

"Thanks," I said.

The berserker gurgled again, and there was a hint of movement that came from its body. Adeelee spun fast and drove her sword deep into its skull.

> *You have gained 185 XP!*

> *Advancement! You have reached **level 6** and gained 3 attribute points. To assign your attribute points, open your status page. You can also increase any of your known skills by 1 level. Choose wisely, as your choices cannot be undone.*

> *You have gained 10 SP!*

I pulled up my stats and assigned a couple points to my dexterity, and a point to my vitality. After seeing

Adeelee dodge so much damage and make goblin fillets, I realized just how much swift reflexes helped with swordplay. Vitality was one of my weak stats, and throwing an extra point in it would help round me out. The one LP went into my swords skill.

I rubbed my fingers across my chestpiece, and when I touched it, I noticed that the durability rating had dropped to 2/10 and was only granting me 12 armor rather than 14 that it usually granted. I'd need to replace it soon.

"Hurry… before another comes," Adeelee said, tilting her head towards the tent exit.

# Chapter 20

*01/05/0001*

Adeelee and I ran out of the tent and started for the 2nd camp, ducking behind various patches of grass. I wasn't sure if it was necessary though, as once we got in closer, it seemed like everyone at the 2nd location was too caught up with what was going on in their camp to care about what was happening around them.

There was a tent similar to the one at the other camp, and a fire just the same, but surrounding the fire was half circle of five orcs, all males around seven foot tall each. They all appeared to be grunts, wearing fur boots, fur loincloths, and generally one or two pieces of other mismatching armor.

*Name: Greenskin Grunt*
*Race: orc*
*Level: 8*
*Health/Mana/Stamina: 110/0/120*
*Status: aggressive*

Each had a single large, metal axe latched to their backs, and they all sat watching the only non-grunt of the lot. The other orc wore a large, plate helmet with two sharp horns jutting out of the top. He had a fur chestpiece, leather boots and a long, black whip in his hands.

*Name:* Greenskin Slaver
*Race:* orc
*Level:* 10
*Health/Mana/Stamina:* 140/0/140
*Status:* aggressive

A few meters away from the orc was a cage, and inside the cage was a skinny, pale human wearing only a pair of white boxer shorts.

"No goblins?" I whispered.

"Orcs and goblins work together, but even orcs have trouble sleeping in the filth that goblins make."

"Then they're smarter than they look…"

The cowering human clenched at the back of the metal cage and yelped, "Please just let me go!"

The onlooking orcs just laughed, and one of the grunts tried to mock the human in its deep, muffled voice. "Preaz jus ret me gro!" This caused another burst of laughter from all the other orcs.

"Okay! Just kill me! I won't come back, I swear!" the human said.

The slaver pulled his whip back and slung it at the cage, causing the human to slam backwards against the cage bars. The orcs burst into an even louder mirth.

"He wants to die?" I asked. "That's odd…"

"He said he won't return after they kill him," Adeelee muttered. "He could be a Reborn."

"I can't imagine that a Reborn would want to die… not after what I experienced."

"What other explanation would there be?"

"Maybe he meant that he won't haunt them? I don't know."

The slaver slung his whip at the cage again, and the tip slid through the cage bars, snapping against the chest of the human inside.

"Oh fuuuuuucck!" the human cried as he clenched at the shallow skin tear the whip created.

"Just kill him!" one of the orcs grunted as he stood up. "Whatever he is, he smells worse than the goblins!"

The slaver turned to the grunt and snarled. "You don't give the orders here!" he snapped, pointing his finger. "If he really is a Reborn, Ergoth must know!"

*So, he is a Reborn*, I thought. If it were true, that would make him the first real human that I'd encountered in the game. All the NPCs I had met seemed so real that it was easy to forget that there were others like me.

"Ergoth cares not for Reborns!" the grunt countered. "He only wants the Fellblade! And—"

"And what?" The slaver took a step towards the grunt and gripped his whip tightly.

"And there's no proof that he's a Reborn! It's goblin hearsay!"

The slaver slung his whip towards the grunt, cracking him against the arm, causing him to duck and flinch. "Dilug saw him return to the same spot where the goblin killed him. You question his word?"

The grunt flung his arm to the ground, defiantly ignoring the pain from the whip strike. He stood tall and puffed up his chest. "And what if I do?" He reached behind his back towards his axe.

257

The slaver smiled broadly and dropped his whip to the ground. "Axe, now!" he shouted. One of the other grunts pulled his axe off his back and tossed it in the slaver's hands.

"They're going to fight?" I asked.

"Deathmatch," Adeelee explained. "An orc can challenge any another orc to a battle 'til death if he feels disrespected. If it is a higher-ranking orc, he will assume that orc's position of power if he wins."

"Maybe we should attack while they're distracted," I suggested.

"The battle won't end 'til someone dies, so ready an arrow and wait for the deathblow. We may be able to take out two before they see us, and one of the orcs has given up his axe already, so that's another easy kill. That'll leave us at only two... one for you and one for me."

Adeelee and I crouched down in a patch of grass, and we both readied our Snipe Shot as we watched the orcs square off against each other.

The slaver coursed his feet against the ground and held his large metal axe in one hand, while the grunt gripped an identical axe with two, strafing sideways around the slaver as if he were about to swing it like a baseball bat.

The four orcs surrounding the two fighters stomped their feet and grunted, while the human sat with his head low to the ground, paying no attention to the fight.

The grunt rushed towards the slaver with a roar and started swinging his axe furiously in his direction, but the slaver easily dodged. The slaver countered with a one-handed swing of his own, which the grunt ducked away from, and then the grunt swung upwards, clipping the thick skin of the slaver, leaving a nasty cut across his chest.

The slaver took a step back and looked down at the blood dripping out of the incision in his pec. He rubbed his finger across the wound and tasted his own blood as the grunt smiled, looking proud at his accomplishment.

"Come on!" the grunt yelled, shaking his axe and taunting the slaver.

The slaver stormed forward angrily and when he was in distance of the grunt, the grunt swung out with his axe, which was parried by the slaver. The slaver kicked the grunt in the abdomen, causing him to jolt back, and then landed a clean, deep cleave, right to the grunt's ribs.

The grunt yelled in agony and swung its axe hard and wild, barely missing the slaver who rolled backwards and out of the way.

When the slaver stopped his roll, his eyes narrowed while the grunt looked down at his wound. The slaver pulled his axe back and threw it in a spinning, forward arch, landing with a bone cracking snap, deep in the center of the grunt's forehead.

"Now," Adeelee whispered, right as the orcs erupted into cheers.

Adeelee's arrow slammed right into the back of one of the sitting grunts, ending its life instantly, but while my arrow landed hard in the back of another grunt, it wasn't enough to end its life. The grunt fell, groaning and grabbing at the arrow protruding from its back.

The slaver immediately saw our hiding position and pointed towards us with rage in his eyes. "Kill them!" he bellowed.

The two uninjured grunts along with the slaver started running in our direction, while the grunt I hadn't managed to kill picked himself off the ground and started dislodging my arrow from its body.

I fired off another arrow that landed in the slaver's shoulder, but it didn't seem to have any effect on him.

"Get ready!" Adeelee yelled, drawing her sword and assuming a combat stance.

I holstered my bow and quickly drew my sword as I watched the 3 large orcs running towards us and the other unarmed orc searching for a weapon in the distance. It was frightening—the huge, green, beastly-looking men, clearly hungry for our blood.

When they were almost in striking distance, Adeelee raised her hands and cast her rooting spell, causing vines to grow out of the ground and stop the three orcs in their tracks. "Now! Use your Fire Curtain!"

While I had assumed that the Fire Curtain spell had been to block attacks, I could see what she was getting at. All three of the orcs were in a straight line, tugging at their feet, trying to break free.

I held my hand out and concentrated on casting Fire Curtain. It was the first time that I had used the spell, but after using Fireblast and Fire Arrow, I was pretty sure that the game would recognize exactly what I was trying to do.

A wall of flames suddenly surged up from the ground right across the three orcs, and they all screamed in agony as they were burned by the sudden flames.

Their loincloths ignited, and I could hear the sizzle of their skin. But the fire also ignited Adeelee's root, allowing the orcs to yank free from the wilting vines.

The orcs flopped forward on the ground rolling, extinguishing the flames, and Adeelee and I rushed in their direction. The orcs were resilient, and after only a couple seconds on the ground, they stood back up, clearly injured from the flames but angrier than they were before.

The Fire Curtain had claimed 30% of my mana, and I fired two Fireblasts at one of the grunts, leaving me with just about one-third of my pool.

"Good job!" Adeelee called out as the grunt I targeted died and she engaged in battle with another grunt.

That left the slaver for me. I'm not sure it was Adeelee's intention to leave me with the highest-level enemy in sight, but I leapt forward in a roll as the slaver swung his axe at me. He was surprisingly fast up close, but I could already tell that I had a little bit of a speed advantage.

I swung my sword at the slaver, but he blocked my blow, knocking my sword out of the way. He raised his axe for a death strike, but I quickly shot a Fireblast into his abs that knocked him back.

He clawed at the impact of the blast, and I could see in his desperate eyes that he was on the verge of death. The slice he took with the grunt, the Fire Curtain, and the Fireblast had put him on his last legs, and quick dive of my sword would probably take him out.

I raised my blade for the killing blow, but immeasurable pain caught me right below the side of my rib cage, a blow so hard that it knocked me to the side a couple feet and dropped me to the ground.

I looked down to see one of the orc's axes lodged into my body, and when the grunt orc yanked it out, I thought I was going to faint. 60% of my health was gone, and I was bleeding.

"Careful!" I heard Adeelee yell, and I looked up to see the slaver's axe coming towards me. I held my sword up and blocked it just in time, and right at that moment, I saw the green glow of Nature's Regrowth pulsing around me.

Another axe came swinging in my direction, and I rolled, barely avoiding another cleave, right as Adeelee slashed into the grunt's throat. Again, I rolled as the slaver made his last attempt to kill me, and I stuck my hand out, expending my last bit of mana to launch a Fireblast right in the slaver's face.

The slaver dropped his axe and screamed as it grabbed its eyes. It probably would have died from that, but I launched myself forward and dipped the tip of my blade in its throat to make sure he had no chance to survive.

*You have gained 755 XP!*

*You have gained 1 point of Willpower!*

*You are **bleeding** and require medical attention. Bleeding is a damage-over-time effect.*

"Fuck," I grunted, as I clenched onto my side. I used my free hand to pull out one of my bandages, and struggled to apply it to the cut.

*You have reached level 2 in **First Aid**!*

The bandage went on sloppily, but it worked to stop the bleeding icon that had been pulsing under my health bar, and the rest of my health was still rising from Adeelee's spell.

Adeelee walked over to me, offered me her hand and helped me to my feet. "Excellent," she said. "I can almost see you growing as a fighter. You took the level 10 on almost entirely alone."

I smirked a bit as I stood. "I got distracted when I got injured. I would've died if you weren't here."

"It'll be easier for you to continue fighting with those kind of wounds as your willpower increases," Adeelee explained.

"Hey!" a voice rang out. "Hey! Get me out of this fucking thing!"

We turned to see orcs' prisoner banging on his cage and waving his hand.

"I almost forgot about him..." Adeelee muttered.

"Oh god!" The man sighed as we approached. "Thank goodness you guys came here! Please get me out! I'm pretty sure the one with big helmet has the key."

I walked back to the slaver's corpse, fetched the key from his pocket and opened the captive's cave.

"Who are you?" I asked. "What are you doing in this cage?"

"Aaron. My name is Aaron," the guy huffed and quickly ran towards one of the dead grunts and started searching its pockets.

"Hey, that's our loot, you know?!" I yelled.

"Fuckkkk" the guy grunted as he picked up an axe. When he swung it, the weight of it almost made him fall over.

"Are you a Reborn?" Adeelee asked.

"Reborn?" The guy chuckled as he dropped the axe. "Yeah, I guess that's what we programmed you to call us." He ran to another grunt and started searching as fast as he could.

"Dude..." I said. "What's with you?"

"Dude?" The guy suddenly stopped what he was doing. He turned back towards Adeelee and I and paced furiously towards us. "Wait. Are you a player? I mean... are you a Reborn?"

"Yeah," I said and shrugged my shoulders. "You're the first human... I mean, Reborn that I've met since I've been in the world."

"You've got to fuckin' help me!" the guy said desperately. He reached out and gripped onto my leather shoulders. "There's not a lot of time!"

I pushed the guy off me. "Relax. What's wrong with you?" I looked him up and down. "And you've got to figure shit out yourself just the same as I did."

The guy's eyes darted to the ground, and he spoke breathlessly. "I was hunting rabbits and other bullshit near here, just trying to gain a couple levels before a goblin came out of nowhere. I ran but I still died, and

264

when I came back to get my stuff back, they captured me and started going on about me being a Reborn…" He looked up into my eyes. "But it doesn't matter now. I've got to move fast. You've got to help me."

They guy was seriously annoying and weird. He reminded me of people back on Earth—always thinking about themselves, always trying to get ahead without any consideration of other people—and I didn't like it one bit. Besides who would do a solo corpse run anywhere near these camps? He was obviously an idiot.

"Sorry, I'm more of a solo kind of guy."

"You're with her," the guy said looking towards Adeelee.

"Yeah, but she's…. different. She's not a Reborn." I held up my hand at the guy and turned towards the princess. "We should loot-up and move on to the next camp."

"Wait!" the guy shouted. "Just listen to me, please?"

I raised my eyebrows. "Alright, we're listening."

"I'm Aaron Sizemore, the VP assistant of Nexicon."

"What?" I pushed the guy hard and pulled my sword out of its sheath. "So you're responsible for me being stuck here?"

Aaron held up his hand. "Wait, no! I had nothing to do with it."

"Then what the hell is going on? Why the hell haven't I been able to logoff, and what was that broadcast that the Nexicon CEO sent about us all being dead?"

Aaron sighed and lowered his head. "It's true…"

I raised my sword at him. I'm not sure why... I knew I couldn't really "kill" him, but just the fact that someone had tampered with my life made me want to reign down some punishment.

"Wait!" Aaron said, holding his hands up again. "I swear, I had nothing to do with it. I only came here to save you!"

"Save me?" I asked, relaxing my sword a bit. Did he have a way for me to log out?

"Inside the tent," Adeelee interrupted. "There's still another camp. I don't want anyone to see us out here talking."

Aaron and I nodded, and we all moved inside the tent.

Aaron sat down on a chest that was inside and crossed his arms. "You know who Rupert Winston is, right?"

"Of course, I know. Everyone knows."

"I don't know," Adeelee added.

Aaron chuckled and dipped his chin at the elf. "As far as you're concerned, elf-girl, this is a Reborn-only conversation. You couldn't possibly understand." Aaron cleared his throat and turned back towards me. "Well, he's solely responsible for all of this, and back on Earth, people are going nuts."

"Earth?" Adeelee asked.

Aaron rolled his eyes. "I told you that you won't understand."

"Hey," I barked. "Be polite. If you were in the forest, you would kneel to her."

The guy rolled his eyes and shook his head. "Only five days and you already fully immersed, huh?" His eyes wandered. "I guess you should be, since it's the last world you'll ever know."

"Just get to the point. How the fuck do I log out?"

Aaron shook his head. "Did you miss the part where I just confirmed that you're dead? I mean, you're not dead, but your consciousness has been permanently transferred here. Your Earth body is dead."

"So then what the hell are you going on about saving me for?"

"Because back on Earth a lot of people—powerful people—the most powerful people—want Eden's Gate shut down."

"Why?"

"Because people are killing themselves to get in. That's why. Not many people understand this technology, because there's never been anything like it before."

There was a long moment of silence as I processed his words, and I turned to Adeelee, to see her brow wrinkled, trying hard to understand what we were talking about. She was clearly very confused.

But his words made me think hard about my situation. I had already considered the fact that I felt more comfortable in Eden's Gate as opposed to back on Earth, but hearing that other people were voluntarily killing themselves to get where I was confirmed that I wasn't a complete nut case.

"So people want it shut down, and?" I asked.

"And..." the guy said, nodding his head sarcastically. "If Eden's Gate shuts down, then that means you die." He pointed to me, and then pointed to Adeelee. "And all the NPCs too. Everything's gone."

Adeelee blinked and twisted her lips. "I don't understand. Someone wants to destroy Eden's Gate? Are you talking about the Scourge?"

"What the hell is the Scourge?" Aaron asked.

I pointed towards the corpses outside of the tent. "That's a part of the Scourge." I shook my head dismissively. "If you're a developer at Nexicon, you would know that."

"I helped design and develop the world, but it would be impossible to make something this big by hand in a lifetime. Many of the core elements and locations were hand-crafted, but the good majority of everything was procedurally generated."

"Okay, but what does this all have to do with me? If someone outside Eden's Gate wants the world shut down, how would I be able to do anything about it?"

"I need to get to Dr. Winston's castle. I can't do it alone."

"The same castle I saw in the launch day broadcast?" I asked. "In the Mastalands?"

Aaron's eyes widened. "Yeah, the same one. Help me get there and save everyone."

I rolled my eyes. "There's no way we can get there. I already know it's one of highest level zones in the game." I motioned my hand towards Adeelee. "Let's go finish our mission."

"Just listen!" the guy shouted. "There's a way we can get there. Remember, I helped design this game?"

I shook my head. "I don't know whether to believe you or not, but right now I'm more interested in leveling up."

"Level up for what?" Aaron asked. "So you can get some epic loot before everything goes dark?"

I turned and burned my eyes into him. "If you understood the game, you probably wouldn't need to ask why I want to gain experience, but even if I wasn't 'caught up in this world', my girlfriend is out there somewhere, and I have every intention of finding her."

"Your girlfriend?" Aaron asked. "From Earth?"

"Yeah…"

Aaron laughed loudly. "Do you realize how big the world is out there? There's no mini-map or pointer arrows in this game. Without being able to log out and compare notes, you expect to find her how?"

"Yeah, it's huge, but—"

"Where are you from?" Aaron asked.

"I'm from Los Angeles."

"Okay, so… City of Angels." Aaron rubbed his hands together. "So imagine walking on foot from Los Angeles to… I dunno, Zimbabwe. How long do you think that would take you?"

I pressed my lips together hard but didn't respond.

"Yeah, so multiply whatever you're thinking by 10, and that's most likely how long it'll would take you to travel to your sweetheart just by "leveling up," and that's if you could figure out where she is somehow. You'll likely be walking in circles, chasing your own tail. And are you certain she's even in the game?"

"I can't be certain she's didn't log out."

"So then you're an idiot."

"Fuck off," I spat and started walking towards the exit of the tent. I just wanted to loot the orcs and get the hell away from that guy.

269

"Wait!" Aaron shouted, but I just kept walking. "Look!"

I turned and spoke sharply. "Look at what?! You're wasting our time."

"I can help you."

"Help me how?"

"I helped Dr. Winston build this world, so I know more about the game mechanics than anyone else other than him." He drew his bottom lip into his mouth and moistened it with saliva. "And I placed a hidden portal to his castle in a dungeon. If we can get can get to that dungeon, we can reach the castle without going through all the high-level shit."

"And that helps me find my girlfriend how?" I scoffed.

"Dr. Winston controls this world now. If your girl is still in this game, he can tell you where she is."

I swallowed hard but I didn't speak. I just stared daggers into Aaron's eyes, trying to read him like a poker player.

"Look... Dr. Winston is the only hope that we have of keeping this world alive. I don't know if the people on Earth can actually shut this thing down, but even if they can't now, they won't stop until they figure out how." Aaron bent down and picked up a handful of dirt, then let it slowly fall from his hands. "No one other than gamers and the people inside here believe that this place is real, because he's shut the whole world off. We just need to get him to open communications with Earth one time so that he can show everyone that we're really alive inside. That's all. If they can see us—real people—inside, living our lives, they'll change."

"And then he'll tell me how to find my girl?"

Aaron shook his head and looked to the ground. "I can't promise you anything, but he's your best shot at finding your girl. He's the only one who has access to the game console."

"Rawwwr!" came a sound from behind us.

An arrow sailed in the direction of Adeelee, striking her in the shoulder. When the three of us turned around, there was an orc holding a longbow who immediately bolted away.

Adeelee looked down with flinching eyes to the arrow protruding from her shoulder and grabbed on to the wood just below the fletching. "Go!" she shouted. "Don't let him get away!"

I ran out of the tent after the orc scout, forgetting my conversation with Aaron. I could see the orc rushing across the field towards the last tent on the river. I held out my hand and focused a Fire Curtain right in front of his running path and nailed it; the orc ran right into the wall of fire.

As the orc whelped in pain and panicked, I dropped to one knee and pulled my bow from my back. I aimed at the orc, but didn't have time to focus a Snipe Shot. Instead, I just let the arrow fly, and as it soared through the air, I focused Fire Arrow on it.

The searing arrow met its mark, landing right above the hip of the groaning orc, causing it to cry and grab at its new wound. The orc mewed around on the ground but it didn't die, so I switched my bow out for my sword and ran towards it as fast as I could.

When I arrived to the orc, it seemed helpless, writhing on the ground. It had been affected by the fire more than the previous orcs. Its skin looked tortured, charred, rumpling in spots that prevented it from having full range of motion. It was definitely down to its last few HP.

I dove my blade into its blackened chest, and it stopped moving.

*You have gained 150 XP!*

I looked up towards the other camp, and didn't see anything really. No alarm bells were ringing, and I didn't spot any movement. The orc I killed must have just been a wanderer.

I turned back towards the tent where Aaron and Adeelee were waiting. Adeelee had already removed the arrow from her shoulder and the green of her healing spell was pulsing around her.

"It's all clear. We should head for the other camp," I said.

"We don't have time," Aaron said. "We've got 3 days, barely. I've already wasted most of the day."

I sighed. "You said that the portal is in a dungeon in the Mastalands. Even if Dr. Winston could help me find Rachel, there's no way we can get there anytime soon. Certainly, not in 3 days."

"Rachel is her name?" Adeelee asked. "Your girlfriend?"

I was surprised at her curiosity but I just nodded.

"The portal isn't in the Mastalands. There's a dungeon in a place called Gramora, several thousands of miles from the Mastalands. It's a mixed zone with all different levels of monsters."

"Why would he have a portal to his castle in a dungeon several thousands of miles away?"

"I told you, I placed it there." Aaron explained. "The Mastalands is one of the 'hand crafted' zones, and getting there or getting through there would be a pain in the ass. I'm not much of a RPG gamer; I had plans of playing as a crafter when the game launched, so I placed the hidden portal in a low-level dungeon, just in case I ever needed access to the castle. I never told Dr. Winston about it. He wouldn't have allowed it if he'd known."

"Gramora is across the Serpent Sea," Adeelee explained. "Just crossing the sea would take at least a week. And that's if you managed to survive."

"What we need is a mage. There's no real people…" Aaron cleared his voice and rose his eyebrows, "Ahem… There's no Reborns who would have high enough magic level to use teleportation yet, but if we could convince a NPC mage to transport us to Gramora, the three of us could probably clear the dungeon together."

Adeelee shook her head. "I'm sorry. I don't understand this 'RPG gamer' and 'NPC' jargon you're using, but I don't trust you enough to travel to some dungeon in Gramora. Even standing here in the Freelands, the forest calls for my return."

"I'm not sure I trust you either," I explained. I thought back to other MMORPGs that I played in the past, and there were always a few toxic sorts of players who just wanted to lure someone into a zone to get ganked and loot them.

"You're level what?" Aaron asked me.

"Level 6."

"So what do you have to lose? Six days of loot if you die? A waste of time? In three days, the government is going for a global blackout to shut down the Eden's Gate blockchain. I don't know how to get you to trust me, but if we don't make it to Dr. Winston, we're all dead, and there's no chance you'll see your girlfriend again."

I pinched my brow and swallowed his words. He looked like a total idiot standing there in his boxer shorts, but he didn't seem like he was being deceitful. If he was telling the truth, everything was on the line. "Adeelee, could your mother transport us to Gramora?"

"My mother isn't an arcane magic user, and the few elves I know who have arcane skills aren't practiced enough to cast a high-level teleportation spell."

"Do you know anyone else who could teleport us?" Aaron asked Adeelee.

Adeelee shook her head.

"Fuck," Aaron spat.

"There is one guy," I muttered. "I know he's skilled in Arcane, but I don't know how skilled. A shop owner in Linden. A real asshole, but…"

"Well, let's go!" Aaron said enthusiastically. "We've got to start somewhere."

"Wait a minute." I held up my hand. "I'm not going anywhere 'til I finish this quest. There's only one more camp left for us to take out."

"Come on man," Aaron whined. "Are you not listening?"

"We finish the quest, and I'll go. Take it or leave it. You said we have a couple days."

Aaron bit his bottom lip and sighed. "Alright, fine… but we've got to leave after this."

"Add him to the party?" I asked Addeelee. I scanned up and down his scrawny frame. "And you should probably scavenge some clothes from the dead orcs. You look ridiculous."

*Aaron Sizzle has joined your party!*

"Your last name is 'Sizzle'?"

"My real name is Aaron Sizemore, but I thought that if I was starting a new life here, I would spice things up… Be a little cooler, you know?"

"Sizzle?" I asked again, raising one of my eyebrows.

"For shizzle, my nizzle," Aaron said, raising his shoulders. "It's got a nice ring to it. If we manage to survive, maybe one day they'll know me as The Sizzler."

"For shizzle?" Adeelee asked.

"My nizzle…" Aaron replied. "It's slang for 'sure, my friend.'"

"Oh…" Adeelee replied.

Aaron ran outside and started going through the dead orcs, and I just sat there shaking my head. The guy was a total dork.

"Are you okay with this?" I asked Adeelee.

"For shizzle," she replied. "So long as he doesn't interfere with our mission, it should be fine."

"Umm…" I scratched the back of my head. "You probably want to avoid saying that. It doesn't really sound right coming from a High Elf."

"Okay, my nizzle."

*Ugh....*

I took a moment to pull up Aaron's stats. He was inexperienced alright.

| AARON SIZZLE | |
|---|---|
| Race: | Human |
| Level: | 2 |
| Title: | none |
| Health/Mana/Stamina: | 110/100/100 |
| Strength: | 10 |
| Dexterity: | 10 |
| Intelligence: | 12 |
| Vitality: | 11 |
| Wisdom: | 10 |
| Willpower: | 10 |
| Charisma: | 10 |

I opened the chest that Aaron had been sitting on in the Tent and inside found 100 gold, a food ration, and a pair of leather gloves.

> *You've received:* **Merciless Gladiator Gloves**. *+4 Armor. Durability: 10/10. Quality: Average. Rarity: Common. Weight: 0.3 kg. +2 Strength. +1 Vitality*

I immediately equipped the leather gloves and did a check of my stats.

## GUNNAR LONG

| | |
|---|---|
| Race: | Human |
| Level: | 6 (Progress 35%) |
| Title: | None |
| Health/Mana/Stamina: | 145+/110/110 |
| Strength: | 17+ |
| Dexterity: | 17 |
| Intelligence: | 17 |
| Vitality: | 12+ |
| Wisdom: | 13 |
| Willpower: | 11 |
| Charisma: | 10 |
| AR Rating: | 33 |
| Resists: | |
| | 10% Fire Resistance |
| Traits: | |
| | Elven Touch |
| Primary Skills: | |
| | First Aid Lvl 2: progress 0% |
| | Inspect Lvl 2: progress 70% |
| | Sneak Lvl 2: progress 90% |
| | Tinkering Lvl 1: progress 0% |
| | Summon Beast: Mastered |
| | Inscription Lvl 1: progress 0% |
| Combat Skills: | |
| | Dodge Lvl 2: progress 80% |
| | Small Blades Lvl 2: progress 0% |
| | Backstab Lvl 1: progress 0% |
| | Archery Lvl 3: progress 70% |
| | Block Lvl 1: progress 80% |
| | Swords Lvl 3: progress 20% |
| | Snipe Shot Lvl 1: progress 69% |
| Magic Skills: | |
| | Fire Magic Lvl 3: progress 75% |

I had come a long fucking way in 6 levels, that's for sure. When comparing myself to Aaron, I felt like a badass, but then again, he had this way of making himself look weak, regardless of his stats.

"I can't wield any of their axes," Aaron moaned. I looked up to see him walking towards me in a pair of fur boots, fur bracers, and a wacky looking metal shoulder pad. With his white boxer shorts on display, he looked like some sort of failed, Eskimo wrestler. "The strength requirement is 15. I practically break my back when I try to swing them."

"Here, you can have this," I said, reaching into my bag.

I handed him my copper training dagger. I hadn't been getting much use out of it since I found Mythanthar's Blade. I also gave him the leather gloves that I had just replaced and my flint and steel. I figured the flint was just taking up a slot in my bag since I could light things with my fire magic.

"What are your Sneak skills like?" Adeelee asked.

"Level 1, 10% progress," Aaron replied. "If I were sneaky, I probably wouldn't have gotten captured."

"You should probably stay far behind us then. This is an important mission to the elves."

"Yeah, I got it…" Aaron mumbled.

Adeelee led the way towards the third camp, sneaking behind trees and tall grass. Aaron was far behind us, making sure that we cleared an area before moving into our previous position.

We ducked behind a nearby rock that gave us a clear view into the camp. It was set up the same as the previous two, but the campfire wasn't lit and there were no orcs outside. A leather panel was draped over the tent's entrance.

"I sense magic…" Adeelee mumbled.

I nodded. I also felt something. It was as if the air was filled with thick, invisible soundwaves or something. It just felt weird…

"Come on now! Let's get on with it!"

Adeelee and I both flinched as Mr. Sizzle jumped behind us. Adeelee had her hand on her sword as if she were ready to counter an attack.

"What's wrong?" Aaron looked at us with innocent eyes. "The camp is clearly empty."

I shook my head at him. "Duck down, dumbass."

"I guess we're going to have to rush the tent," Adeelee explained. "Aaron, stay here behind this rock."

"Alright," Aaron said.

"If things get ugly, run for the Crystal River. Orcs are terrible swimmers, so let's just hope that there's just orcs in there…" Adeelee pointed to each side of the entrance and then tilted her chin.

We both dashed to either side of the tent and the heavy feeling of magic was even more intense there. The smell of herbs hung in the air, and I could hear a slight electrical buzz coming from inside.

*You have reached level 3 in **Sneak**!*

Adeelee used her fingers to count down to three, and then she rushed inside, me right behind her.

Both of us had our swords raised to strike, but the moment we entered, we both slowed and took in the sight ahead of us.

In the center of the tent was a boiling cauldron, and three orcs held their hands out towards the steam rising from it, their eyes glued shut. The orcs were covered in a mesh of loose leather armor and fur, and they all had wolf pelts draped from the top of their head and down their backs.

*Name:* Greenskin Shaman
*Race:* orc
*Level:* 10
*Health/Mana/Stamina:* 100/140/100
*Status:* aggressive

They didn't move, but whatever they were doing seemed to cause the steam above the cauldron to form an illusionary, first-person scene of someone running through a forest that was undoubtedly Addenfall.

At the back of the tent was another orc, sitting in a large, throne-like chair. He was covered in a thick black robe with long, curved thorns jutting out of his shoulders. Leaning beside him was a black staff with crystal skull at the top, and while he sat unmoving, his eyes were exploding with bright, white electricity.

*Name:* Commander Dilug
*Race:* orc
*Level:* 15
*Health/Mana/Stamina:* 200/160/100
*Status:* unknown

*You have reached level 3 in **Inspect**!*

None of them attacked.

"What is this?" I whispered.

"They're performing a ritual of some sort, it seems…"

We watched for a moment as the image over the cauldron continued rushing across Addenfall at a breakneck speed, turning at every corner, ignoring all obstructions in its way.

"It looks like they're searching for something," I said.

"Whatever it is, we need to end this," Adeelee said.

"What!? What the hell is this?" Aaron's voice spoke *loudly* behind us.

"Aaron!" I snapped.

There was loud roar, and a painful feeling swam through my body. My feet rose off the ground and I could barely move a muscle. I turned my head slowly and saw that Adeelee was rising as well, and dark bands of magic were pouring from the black-robed commander's hand.

"Run, Aaron!" Adeelee shouted.

I couldn't see Aaron, but I heard his feet scurry away from us. What I could see were the shamans in front of us who were slowly coming out of their trance.

"Why are you disrupting me, elf!?" Dilug roared.

Adeelee slowly raised her palm, and a flash of light erupted, dispelling whatever spell held us in place, and we both fell back onto our feet.

"Now!" Adeelee yelled, and drove her sword through the back of the Shaman closest to her. Blood erupted from the shaman's mouth, and he croaked as he fell, his head smashing against the rim of the cauldron and causing the contents of herbs and thick, gooey liquid to spill to the ground.

I drove my sword into the back of another shaman, and the shaman screamed in agony.

"I will kill you both!" Dilug shouted and raised his staff towards me. A ball of black energy shot out, knocking me back against the ground, leaving my sword sticking in the back of the shaman. My health fell to 60%.

Adeelee ran toward Dilug, but he repeated the motion, knocking Adeelee back with another ball of black energy from his staff.

As Adeelee crashed to the ground, she raised her hand to cast Nature's Regrowth on us both at the same time, and a green glow surrounded me.

I shot a Fireblast at Dilug which cause him to step back, but his robe didn't light on fire. Either the robe was magic—which it probably was—or he had a high enough resist to prevent it from happening.

Dilug smiled at me, raised his hand, and I suddenly felt a sense of dread wash over me. My vision went dark, and everything around me looked like strange, hard-to-make-out outlines.

> *You have been afflicted with **darkness**!*
> *Source: Commander Dilug*

Another splash of strange, magical pain splashed against my head, and I could only imagine that the commander had hit me with his staff's effect again.

My health dropped 30%.

"Cleanse!" Adeelee shouted, and my vision started to clear, right as the unharmed shaman's dagger was coming towards my face, slashing across my cheek and nose.

I panicked. I had no idea what to do without my weapon, so I shot a Fireblast at the Shaman, which knocked him back a little, and then I cast Fire Curtain in a diagonal pattern, trying to land my fire on all 3 of the orcs.

Adeelee slammed her sword down at Dilug, but he blocked her with his staff, and the moment my fire erupted from the ground, Adeelee jumped back to avoid taking damage.

The orcs roared at the pain, and the one with my sword in its back fell to the ground in death, but the one holding a dagger smashed his hands together and a hard gust of air flew out from him, dispelling all the fire. He raised his palm into an upward claw, and small globes of green light spewed from his hand, surrounded him and then flying over to Commander Dilug.

"He's healing!" Adeelee yelled. "The shaman has to die!" She jumped back towards Commander Dilug, swinging frantically for a disabling blow.

I dashed toward the shaman and fired another Fireblast to knock him back enough to have a clear shot at grabbing my sword. I yanked it out of the fallen orc's body as soon as it was in reach and turned, right before he raised his hand in the air and a mysterious lightning bolt crackled out of the sky and landed right on my head.

I gasped at the shocking pain, and if it weren't for Nature's Regrowth, it would've been enough to end my life. I was at 10% health, and starting to feel dizzy.

I gritted through the agony, charged for the shaman, and he held his hand out like he was about to cast another spell right before his eyes went wide and blood seeped from his mouth. I was confused at was happening at first, but still I raised my sword, and swung it hard across his neck, causing his head to lop off and roll to the floor.

As the body collapsed, there was Aaron, standing in his furry boots and boxer shorts, the bloody copper training dagger in his hands. He had the biggest shit-eating grin on his face. "Hell yeah motherfucker! I learned backstab just now!"

"You were supposed to stay back!" I yelled. "This is dangerous!"

Aaron ducked down behind the fallen cauldron as he shouted. "I saw your health bar dropping. I couldn't let you die! And you're welcome!"

"Well, thanks!" I yelled as I rushed towards the scene of Dilug and Adeelee fighting.

Adeelee slammed her sword swiftly at the warlock, landing a few shallow blows, but mostly getting blocked by Dilug's staff. After a solid block, Dilug lifted the base of his staff, connecting with Adeelee's abdomen, then shot another bolt of dark energy from the skull at its top, knocking her back hard.

Dilug slammed his staff hard into the ground and dark waves of magic pulsed out from it and dissipated as it travelled further away from him. I could hear a hissing sound behind me, but it didn't stop me from rushing at the warlock, slashing at him, and landing a solid blow against his shoulder. He cried out and dropped his staff, just as I lifted my foot and kicked him as hard as I could between the legs.

> *Advancement! You have learned the skill:*
> ***Dirty Fighting****. You might not feel great about your win, but hey, at least you won, right? Increase your Strength to increase your damage with Dirty Fighting.*

The warlock's eyes went wide and he was paralyzed as he held on to his crotch.

"Guyyyyys!" Aaron shouted.

When I turned, I saw the source of hissing sound. Right behind me was a large apparition about the size of a linebacker. It looked like a cloud of strange, black smoke—something like a dark genie—but it had hulking black arms and white flickering eyes. Apparently, Dilug had summoned it, and it was slowly floating towards Adeelee and I.

> ***Name:*** *Shadow Elemental*
> ***Race:*** *elemental*
> ***Level:*** *12*
> ***Health/Mana/Stamina:*** *100/100/100*
> ***Status:*** *aggressive*

"Tsarra!" Adeelee shouted and slammed the tip of her sword into the floor. A pulse of green energy traveled across the ground, and I could hear the strong patter of footsteps from outside the tent.

Through the entrance, a massive white tiger emerged, roared, and without even hesitating, it jumped at the elemental. The tiger clamped its teeth down on the side of the shadow and dug its paws deep, ripping shreds of black nothingness which faded away as they tumbled to the ground. The elemental howled something that sounded like a loud, whistling wind and raised its hulking arms, pounding on the back of the tiger, trying to get it off.

I turned back around right as Adeelee whipped her sword in an upwards motion, slashing the warlock from chest to face, and I shot another Fireblast out of my hand, knocking the warlock to the ground, then expended the last of my mana to shoot a blast in the other direction at the shadow elemental.

*You have reached level 4 in **Fire Magic**!*

Aaron stayed cowering behind the cauldron as Tsarra jumped up and tore a large piece of shadow from the elemental's neck, and a loud, whizzing wind sounded its demise, the rest of the shadow's body simply fading away.

Adeelee gracefully took two steps forward and looked down at the fallen warlock, pointing her sword directly at his face.

"Disgusting elf!" Dilug bellowed.

"Why does the Scourge enter the forest without permission and camp along the Crystal River?" Adeelee asked.

"We wish not to enter the forest. We simply want to find what belongs to us."

"A warlock and a goblin were found in Addenfall," Adeelee explained.

"Chasing a Sparrow."

"A Sparrow?"

"Prince Azhug is dead, murdered by The Sparrows. His Fellblade was stolen," he spat. "We chased him through the Freelands until he crossed the Crystal River, and we tasked only a warlock and a scout to continue. When they didn't return, my shamans and I began using magic to try to locate him. We camp here in case he crosses back over and because our location spell can only travel so far. But the King will not stop until the Fellblade is returned and Azhug is avenged."

Adeelee sighed before she said, "I'm sorry for your loss. May you join your prince on the other side."

"Nooo!" the warlock yelled as Adeelee pressed the tip of her sword through the Dilug's throat.

*You have gained 1415 XP!*

*Advancement! You have reached **level 7** and gained 3 attribute points. To assign your attribute points, open your status page. You can also increase any of your known skills by 1 level. Choose wisely, as your choices cannot be undone.*
*You have gained 10 MP!*

*You have completed all requirements for the quest: **Push Them Back!** Return to Queen Faranni to collect your reward.*

Adeelee sheathed her sword and cast Nature's Regrowth on herself. "It's done…" she said in a low, troubled voice. "We should destroy the camps and head back to the Vale to report to Mother."

"He said they were looking for a Sparrow?" I asked.

"The Sparrows… A surreptitious group of rogues. It's not unusual for them to harass traveling caravans or pick off easy targets in secret, but I'm surprised they would enter the Wastelands and assassinate a prince. It's quite bold of them."

I thought back to the day that I was murdered and remembered the insignia around my killer's neck. "Do they wear a necklace by chance?"

"Some of them—the ones with rank—wear a sparrow around their collar."

"Then they were definitely in the forest recently."

"If they really stole the Fellblade, that will mean trouble for the Freelands. King Ergoth will send more orcs from the Wastelands, I'm certain."

"So what should we do?"

"For now, let's finish up and return to the Vale. Mother will know how to proceed."

Tsarra strolled up to Adeelee and started rubbing her head against the princess's leg.

"Ummm... Hello?" Aaron said. I turned and he was waving and giving a phony smile. "I don't want to break up this celebratory discussion, but we kind of have bigger things to take care of. You know, saving everyone in Eden's Gate and all?"

Adeelee looked toward exit of the tent where the sun was starting to set. "Linden is too far to reach tonight, but I am happy to accompany you there tomorrow."

"No, we go tonight," Aaron insisted. "We have no time."

"It'll be night by the time we reach the Vale," I explained. "And without Adeelee's haste spell, it would take us forever to reach Linden from there. So just listen to her for now."

Aaron huffed and crossed his arms, but he seemed to accept the reality for what it was.

There were no chests to loot in the third camp, but I found another 120 gold on the orcs that were there. Aaron finally got a pair of fur pants from one of the shamans, a large, furry chestpiece, and he even draped one of the wolfskin pelts on the top of his head. He still looked like a failed Eskimo, but no longer a half-naked, wrestler, failed Eskimo.

Commander Dilug was carrying two interesting items:

> *Scroll: Siphon Spirit. You call upon dark powers to leech 50% of your target's mana and make it your own. Requires 20 Intelligence. Dark Magic Level 3. Durability: 10/10. Quality: Average. Rarity: Rare. Weight: 0.1 kg [10-minute cooldown]*

> *Water Repellant Choker. Requires 15 Intelligence. Durability: 7/10. Quality: Exceptional. Rarity: Rare. Weight: 0.2 kg. +15% Resist to Water Magic*

I equipped the choker and stuck the scroll in my bag. The 15% resist would surely be useful sometime down the road, and while the scroll was useless to me now, I could either sell it for a pretty penny or hold on it in case I ever decided to take up Dark Magic. It was the kind of spell that I could see being OP (overpowered) if used in conjunction with spells with low cooldowns, but it required level three ability, so I wouldn't be able to use it anytime soon, even if I found someone to teach me Dark Magic.

After looting all the orcs, Adeelee led us through the camps, and we pulled down the tents and stacked them in a big pile. I cast a few Fireblasts on them, and they went up in flames.

With the flames still burning, the three of us swam across the Crystal River, and Adeelee cast Spirit of the Forest on us as we headed back towards the Mist Vale.

# Chapter 21

*01/05/0001*

"Orc!" a voice shouted, and I felt an arrow whizz by my ear and land with a thud.

"Awww, fuck!" Aaron groaned, grasping at the thin shaft protruding from his chest. "10%! I'm going to die!"

"Wait! Hold your fire!" Adeelee shouted. "He's not an orc!"

"Hold!" the voice shouted again.

It was dark, and the torch that I held up didn't give great visibility, but I could see the faint outline of an elf guard climbing down from his post at the top of a tree.

Adeelee lifted her hand and cast Nature's Regrowth on Aaron as he wrenched the arrow from his chest, and I used my last bandage to patch him up.

"Princess!" the guard said. He looked at her and then back to Aaron. "What is this?"

"He's with us," she said.

"Why is he dressed like an orc?"

"He lost all of his belongings and looted some wear from the orc soldiers we fell."

The guard snarled. "I'd rather go naked than dress in garb like that."

"Hey, guy…" Aaron said, shaking his head. "Don't be jealous of my sexy furs."

The jaw of the elf guard dropped, and then his lips twisted in anger. "Are you sure you want to bring him into the Vale, my lady? He seems rather unsuitable for—"

"It's okay," Adeelee said calmly and turned towards Aaron and I. "Come on now."

As we started past, the guard grabbed at the wolf pelt on Aaron's head, yanked it off, and shoved it at him. "Take this thing off unless you want another arrow to chest!"

Aaron rolled his eyes and we continued towards the village.

At each step of the way, guards seemed to stand to alert and question us as to why we had a human dressed as an orc, and when we made it to the path leading to the palace, the two guards there seemed especially concerned.

"It's alright," Adeelee promised again and explained the situation for the tenth time.

We eventually made it inside the palace and were told by one of the guards that the King and Queen were enjoying dinner, insisting that we not spoil their appetite by bringing someone dressed like Aaron into the banquet hall. Adeelee ignored the advice and we continued further into the palace until we reached a pair of large, marble doors.

When we pushed the doors aside, the two royals were sitting alone at opposite ends of a table, and two other elves were walking about serving them food, drink and whatever else they wanted.

One of the servers dropped a platter the moment she saw us, spilling wine on the floor, and when Queen Faranni turned around, her eyes went wide and a vine shot up from the floor, bursting through the marble, and wrapped tightly around Aaron's body.

"Mother, no!" Adeelee shouted. "He's not an orc!"

The Queen's eyes darted back and forth between Adeelee and the wrapped bundle of furs. "What is he?"

"He's a Reborn."

"Another Reborn?"

"Yes, mother."

The Queen released her cocoon of vines, and Aaron feel the to the ground coughing, trying to catch his breath.

"Holy shit!" Aaron said. "I guess we went overboard with the elf-on-orc hatred programming."

The Queen stood from her chair and walked over to Adeelee, wrapping her arms around her daughter. "I'm glad you returned home safely, my dear." She unwrapped her arms and looked down at the damage in the floor left from the vines. "But look what you did to my floors!"

"I didn't think you'd act so swiftly, Mother. It's not like a single orc could make it past the palace guards."

"He could've had a high level of Sneak skill."

Adeelee shook her head and sighed.

"What about the camps at the Crystal River, and why is this man dressed this way?"

Aaron grabbed onto his furs and tugged. "Hello, can you guys see? It's fur fucking armor! It doesn't mean I'm an orc! For fuck's sake!"

The Queen's eyes went wide with anger, and I felt a slight rumbling under my feet. Aaron clearly didn't know what he was dealing with. I shoved an elbow into his back and pushed down hard on his shoulder. "Kneel, asshole."

I kneeled, and Aaron shoved my hand away as he kneeled as well.

The floor stopped rumbling, and the Queen huffed before saying, "You may rise."

"Invite the guests to the table, Faranni," the King said, watching the scene patiently from his chair.

The Queen gave Aaron an ominous glare before saying. "Come… Join us then."

The three of us joined the King and Queen at the table, and the two server elves began running around to fetch us all food and wine.

"The three camps along the Crystal River are no more," Adeelee explained. "We eradicated everyone inside and burned their shelters to the ground."

The King raised his goblet in the air. "Wonderful news, Adeelee."

"That should warn Ergoth against moving troops so close to the forest again," the Queen said. "And thank you for your assistance, Gunnar."

> *You have completed the quest: **Push Them Back!***

> *You have gained 2000 XP!*

"There was a warlock in one of the camps—a commander," Adeelee explained. "According to him, they had little interest in disturbing the forest. They were looking for a member of the Sparrows."

"A Sparrow?" the Queen asked. "Why in the world would they send that many soldiers just to find a Sparrow?"

"He claimed that Prince Azhug was murdered by a Sparrow and his Fellblade was stolen. They apparently chased him to the forest. I'm afraid that may not be the last we see of the orcs."

"If a rogue murderer ran into the forest to avoid capture, he'll probably leave now that the camps have been destroyed. The orcs will be a problem for the Freelanders, not for the elves. We've done enough for now."

"We could find this Sparrow and return the Fellblade to King Ergoth," Adeelee suggested.

Queen Faranni snorted and smirked. "Imagine that. Elves hunting people down in order to assist the orcs. I think you've been spending too much time away from the forest, Adeelee. You're no longer thinking clearly."

"If we could return the Fellblade to the orcs, it would encourage peace in the Freelands and the chances of the orcs making another dip into Addenfall is less likely."

"I'll hear no more of that hogwash," The Queen spat.

"She's right, my love," the King said. He cleared his throat when the Queen locked menacing eyes to his. "I mean, you're both right. If Ergoth is enraged, his anger will eventually spill into the forest. It would be blasphemous for the elves to assist the orcs, but we do know someone who might be able to smooth the situation over." He lifted his goblet to his mouth and made a half shrug as he tilted his head towards me.

"Gunnar," the Queen said. "I have yet to reward you for your assistance. Tell me, have you found a location to call home yet?"

"My home?" I asked. "I'm perfectly fine staying in my room here in the Vale."

The Queen smiled. "The Vale is home of the High Elves. You're welcome to pass through anytime and stay a night or two, but is not a home for humans… or Reborns."

"Well, then I haven't really thought about it…"

Aaron lifted a fork topped with vegetables to his lips and spoke with his mouth full. "Building a home is essential to character progression. You'll need somewhere to store your loot and rest—else you'll be limited to what you can carry and can only stay in camps and Inns."

"The King of Highcastle controls the Freelands, but anyone can build a home there without a tax," the Queen explained. "I am happy to reward you with 5,000 gold so you can afford to build your first home there."

"The Freelands is where the Scourge camps were?" I asked.

"That's right," Adeelee answered. "But the Freelands stretch for many miles. There's plenty of room for you to find a space to your liking. Or you could buy a home in one of the human villages, but that would cost you much more than what Mother is offering you."

"What about Addenfall? I feel comfortable in the forest."

"Addenfall is an ancient forest," the Queen explained, "and thus we don't allow humans to build there. The closest you can get is on the outskirts of Linden."

"What about Jax Horn?" I asked. "He stays in the forest of Addenfall."

The Queen swallowed hard. "Jax is a special circumstance. He is nearly as close to the forest as the elves."

"Gunnar here has bonded with a great panther, Mother," Adeelee said with a grin. "It may be that he's a Reborn, but I feel like he's not like other humans."

"At your level? You bonded with a great panther?" the Queen asked.

"Just a baby," I explained.

"That is certainly most impressive," the Queen said, a look of surprise on her face. "But I'm not sure it's reason enough to grant you building rights in one of our most sacred forests."

"What about Edgewood?" the King suddenly asked. "If he's comfortable in the forest, we could allow him to build there."

"Edgewood is crawling with dark elves. They would not be happy about a human taking up shelter there," the Queen said.

"You're the Queen... even the dark elves should respect your choices."

"*Should*," the Queen stressed.

"He's proven himself as a friend of the Vale," the King added. "He could act as a sort of ambassador between the two forests. We have no High Elves who want to live there."

The Queen looked deep in thought for a moment before turning to me. "Edgewood is a small forest on the on the opposite edge of the Freelands, not too far from Highcastle. You'll have easier access to the human villages there. If you'd like, I can deed you building rights there."

*Do you accept building rights in **Edgewood**?*

I turned to Aaron, expecting that he might have some insider information to share, but he just shrugged at me and made a clueless face as he stuffed more food in his mouth.

"I can change homes if I'd like, right?"

"If you don't like Edgewood, you can always build a new home somewhere in the Freelands."

I shrugged. "Okay then. I'll go with Edgewood."

"Very well," the Queen clucked. "When you're ready, I'll have a few elves skilled in carpentry accompany you to Edgewood to work on your home. Any expansions or upgrades you make to your home will be at your own expense."

I nodded.

*You are now permitted to build structures in* ***Edgewood!***

"Hey, I helped with that little quest today," Aaron said. "If it weren't for me, these guys might be dead."

"You almost got us killed," I muttered.

"Yeah, and then I saved your ass right when you were about to get roasted."

"Is that true?" the Queen asked.

"It's true," Adeelee recounted. "He helped to the best of his ability."

The Queen gritted her teeth and panned up and down Aaron's fur ensemble. "Very well. I'll commission a hut for you in Edgewood as well."

"That'll be nice if we survive," Aaron said sarcastically.

"Whatever do you mean?" The Queen asked.

I placed my hand on Aaron's arm, knowing that he would just spark a confusing conversation. "We've got business in Linden tomorrow. It's complicated."

The Queen seemed to dismiss Aaron's comment. "Well, then. It would be against my morals to ask you on a mission that would assist the orcs in any way, but I do hope you'll keep your eyes open while you're in Edgewood and do whatever is necessary to help maintain peace."

"I'll do what I can," I said with a nod.

We finished our mostly vegetarian meal, and the Queen granted Aaron permission to stay in a room near mine for the night. Adeelee walked us out of the palace and to the lower levels of the Vale.

"Thanks for everything today," Aaron mumbled as we stood in front of the door to his room. "I mean saving me from the orcs and all."

"Yeah, no problem," I replied. "I guess I should thank you for saving me from the shaman too."

Aaron shrugged. "But mostly thanks for agreeing to help me. It's bigger than us."

"If it's true, then I guess I don't have much of a choice."

Aaron held out a hand, and I shook it while we both exchanged smiles. I couldn't explain why, but I felt a little bit awkward. Not because Aaron was dressed like an Eskimo, but because he was human—a real human—and I felt the same social weirdness towards him that I had with other people on Earth.

"Goodnight guys," Aaron said before retreating inside his room.

Adeelee and I said 'goodnight' back to him and started towards my room.

"The things that you and Aaron talk about are so difficult for me to understand. Earth, game world, blockchain… These are terms I've never heard before."

"Hmmm…" I mumbled. I grabbed at my bag and opened it up for Adeelee to see. "The bag you gave me. It opens to another world, right? The Otherworld?"

"Yes, of course."

"Earth is another world, the same as Otherworld. We Reborns come from that world, but unlike the beasts or the items that we send back and forth there, we can't return to Earth."

"Can elves go there?"

I immediately started laughing, and the more I thought about it, the more uncontrollable my laughter became. I could just imagine High Elves spawning in the middle of a big city, pulling up to a drive-thru on the back of a tiger, trying to order elven pie. Or how humans would rush to get plastic surgery once they found out that pointy ears were the new 'in' look.

"What's so funny?"

"Nothing," I huffed, trying to calm my laughter. "Elves can't go to Earth."

"What about 'game world'?" Adeele asked.

"'Game world' is here in Eden's Gate," I explained. "But that's not a really accurate term. The more I stay here, the more I realize that this is a real world. The people on Earth, however, don't think that it's real, and that's what Aaron wants me to help him prove."

Adeelee took a deep breath and shook her head. "That's all so very complicated."

I chuckled. "Trust me. I know."

"Well, Gunnar Long from Earth," Adeelee said, "I'm very glad that you're here with us now." Her large green eyes sparkled, and her smile was perhaps the most sincere that it had been since I first saw her.

"I'm glad to be here," I replied, frozen by her beauty. "I think."

Adeelee blinked a couple times and then turned to walk away. "I'll find you and Aaron tomorrow morning to escort you to Linden."

"Goodnight," I said as she walked away.

"Goodnight, Reborn."

I stepped inside my room and closed the door. I was feeling exhausted after everything, but I had been missing someone a lot. Oddly enough, it wasn't Rachel or Adeelee.

"Sora," I whispered and pressed my hand against the floor, attempting to summon her for the first time.

I thought I saw a pulse ripple from my hands, but it wasn't nearly as intense as when Jax or Adeelee had summoned their beasts, and for a moment there was nothing but silence. I thought maybe I failed to summon or maybe it just didn't work indoors.

But then there was a tiny meow, a little louder and a little hoarser than what I remembered. Another meow, and Sora poked her head out from under my bed.

The moment she saw me, she jumped onto my leg and started to climb up my body, resting on my shoulder and licking at my ear. What was surprising was that she was significantly bigger than before I released her to the Otherword—at least 3 or 4 pounds. She was clearly still a cub, but there was a noticeable growth in her strength.

*Name:* Sora
*Race:* Great Beast
*Level:* 3
*Health/Mana/Stamina:* 30/15/30
*Status:* friendly

Sora licked viciously, meowed, and pawed at my head, now being more careful not to scratch me with her claws. Thank goodness... Her nails had grown significantly longer and more sharp.

"I missed you too," I said rubbing her thick fur. I kneeled down and motioned towards the bed. She seemed to understand what I was asking when she jumped off, and I began to take off my armor.

I lay in bed, playing with Sora for a couple hours as I pondered how much my life had changed. It was strange that I felt so comfortable around the NPCs in Eden's Gate, but when I met up with Aaron, I just felt the same awkwardness that I had with people back on Earth, despite him being a pretty decent guy.

Expectations, I guessed. I had always played games when I was back on Earth to escape from the real world, to be whoever I wanted to be, and Aaron Sizzle was a reminder of the real world. But I knew he wasn't going be the last Reborn that I'd encounter in Eden's Gate and there was nowhere else for me to hide. This was my real world now unless I somehow learned otherwise.

His claim that there would be a mass blackout on Earth to shut down my new world seemed far-fetched, but then again, I never thought I'd be dead and stuck inside a world where I was slaying orcs and dining with High Elves.

Nothing seemed beyond the realm of reality anymore.

# Chapter 22

## *01/06/0001*

I opened a food ration and tossed it to Sora as I equipped all my armor and weapons. She devoured the whole thing in less than a minute, and climbed up to my shoulder as I headed out the door.

I stopped by Rhys' shop and replaced my leather tunic—which was down to its last 1 durability—for a new chestpiece.

> **Lightweight Elven Leather Vest.** *+21 Armor. Durability: 10/10. Quality: Average. Rarity: Common. Weight: 1.3 kg*

I also picked up a couple bandages and some filler arrows to fill my quiver for the ones I had lost. All in all, I walked away 125 gold poorer, which left me with 450 gold pieces. I got a quote from him on my Siphon Spirit scroll, and he was willing to offer a whopping 800 gold for it, but I decided to hang on to it for a bit longer just in case.

I pulled up my stats and realized that I had forgotten to assign my attribute points and level points from my last level-up and quickly dumped two attribute points into dexterity and one point into intelligence. Since I had just leveled up my Fire Magic and I was already close to a natural level-up in swords, I placed my LP into Fire Magic. I made a conscious decision that it was my last

LP investment into Fire Magic unless I found some higher-level spells.

To my delight, I was already at 40% progress into level 7 from all the XP that I had gained from completing Queen Faranni's quest.

# GUNNAR LONG

| | |
|---|---|
| Race: | Human |
| Level: | 7 (Progress 40%) |
| Title: | None |
| Health/Mana/Stamina: | 145+/120/110 |
| Strength: | 17+ |
| Dexterity: | 19 |
| Intelligence: | 18 |
| Vitality: | 12+ |
| Wisdom: | 13 |
| Willpower: | 11 |
| Charisma: | 10 |
| AR Rating: | 41 |
| Resists: | |
| | 10% Fire Resistance |
| | 15% Water Resistance |
| Traits: | |
| | Elven Touch |
| Primary Skills: | |
| | First Aid Lvl 2: progress 0% |
| | Sneak Lvl 3: progress 0% |
| | Inspect Lvl 3: progress 0% |
| | Tinkering Lvl 1: progress 0% |
| | Summon Beast: Mastered |
| | Inscription Lvl 1: progress 0% |
| Combat Skills: | |
| | Dodge Lvl 2: progress 90% |
| | Small Blades Lvl 2: progress 0% |
| | Backstab Lvl 1: progress 0% |
| | Archery Lvl 3: progress 70% |
| | Block Lvl 1: progress 80% |
| | Swords Lvl 3: progress 80% |
| | Snipe Shot Lvl 1: progress 69% |
| | Dirty Fighting Lvl 1: progress 0% |
| Magic Skills: | |
| | Fire Magic Lvl 5: progress 0% |

As I was leaving Rhys' shop, Aaron came running out of his room, pulling his fur chestpiece over his head. "Hey! Are we ready to go?!" he asked.

"We have to wait for Adeelee. I'm sure she'll be around within a couple hours."

"A couple hours? Hell, we've got to leave."

"Relax," I said. "Without Adeelee it would take us forever to get there."

Sora arched her back and gave her best panther growl in Aaron's direction.

"Vicious pet you've got there."

I chuckled. "She's got spirit."

"And an unusual one too. I recall us programming humans to have a higher bonding ability towards domesticated animals like horses, camels and dogs. Most Reborns of your level wouldn't even be able to get close to a beast like that."

"I was in the right place at the right time." I looked up towards Rhys' shop. "You might want to buy a starter bow and some supplies before we head out. I'll show you to the runestone you can bind to when you're ready."

When Aaron entered the Rhys' shop, I heard him yell out, "Put the bow down. I'm not an orc! It's just fur," which made me laugh.

He spent a few minutes in the shop and when he exited, he had a small shortbow and a basic quiver of arrows strapped to his back. I walked him up the hill towards the runestone, and right when we reached the top, there was a deafening howl that pierced through the air.

I looked up to see where the sound was coming from and just about wet my pants when a 50-foot, yellow dragon swooped overhead, so close to us that the wind from its wings practically knocked us down.

I instinctively kneeled and pulled out my sword, and Sora climbed around to my back and held on for dear life. It was futile move to pull out my blade as there was almost no chance I'd be able to do anything if the monstrosity had actually attacked, but I held it tightly just in case.

My eyes locked on the massive beast as it soared through the sky and was only interrupted when another dragon appeared—this one red—flying towards the other, its wings causing loud rippling waves to resonate all around us.

"Holy shit!" Aaron said. "I never saw any dragons during testing."

The two dragons wailed at each other and began circling a slender, steep mountain in the distance with a narrow, rounded peak. It wasn't clear where they went from where we were standing, but eventually they disappeared behind the tip of the rocks.

"Dragon's Crest," Adeelee said from behind us.

Aaron and I turned to see Adeelee walking up the path we had followed.

"The dragons are rather passive for now. They steal cattle from time to time and only kill people who try to enter their homes."

"That's good to know," I said.

"But the tablets in Highcastle say that the day when the Reborns arrive, so too will a day when dragons breathe fire once again."

"That's odd," Aaron said. "Dragons... breathe fire again? The tablets that we designed talked about Reborns shaping the landscape, but I don't remember them talking about dragons. Dr. Winston obviously took several liberties that we weren't told about."

"Yeah, like locking us inside the game," I said sarcastically. I pulled up my settings menu and tried the log out button just for shits and giggles. I was pretty sure it wasn't going to work, but hey—you never know.

Nothing happened. Not even a click.

"Shall we pray before we leave?" Adeelee asked.

I nodded and sheathed my sword as Adeelee dropped before the runestone. She pressed her hands together and started mumbling something while Aaron walked up to the stone, touched it and bound himself there.

Adeelee finished praying, stood up and stretched her arms out. "Are you two ready?"

We nodded, and she immediately cast Spirit of the Forest on us all. We sprinted off for Linden.

I didn't put Sora away as we traveled through the forest and she seemed to enjoy the ride, digging her paws into my leather armor, eyes wide as the trees and greenery around us passed by in a blur. I figured it was a similar kind of training that her mother would have given her, preparing her for the day that she too traveled the forest at such speeds.

An hour later, we cleared the forest and reached Linden. It was right before noon, and there were many more people outside going about their daily duties than the first time that I arrived.

"Is there anything else I can help you with, Gunnar?" Adeelee asked. "If not, I will return to the Vale."

"I think we're okay from here."

Adeelee reached out and touched my neck. It was the first time that I could remember her skin touching mine, and the feel of her soft bare hand against me send shockwaves through my body. She was warm, and had a skin texture just like a human. She may have seemed real before, but the fact that she *felt* real put her on a totally different plane of realism.

"Good luck in your journey, and I hope to see you again, Gunnar Long," she said. She pulled her hand off me and turned to Aaron. "Good luck, orc man."

Aaron held his hands up and out to his side. His jaw went slack and his brow was creased. "I'm not an orc! What the hell?!"

Adeelee winked. "What? Never heard an elf tell a joke before?" Adeelee raised a hand, closed her eyes, and brown streams of energy fled from her fingertips and poured into Aaron and I. A square, textured icon appeared below my health bar.

> **Barkskin I**: *Your skin is harder to penetrate than the bark of a Redwood tree. +20 Armor. Spell duration: 2 hours. Source: Adeelee*

"Take care, my nizzles," Adeelee cooed before dashing back into Addenfall Forest.

"Damn…" Aaron said. "That's my kind of woman." He rubbed his fingers against his skin. "Knows how to take care of a man."

I touched my skin as well, and while it didn't feel any different, I had a deep-down sense that I was more durable than before, and the stats on my status screen showed the +20 armor in effect.

"By the way, Gunnar," Aaron added. "Put a couple points in charisma for God's sake."

"What for?"

"It's pretty clear that Adeelee has a thing for you. A few charisma points and you could be hittin' that."

"Hittin' that? I don't know how good I'd feel about sleeping with someone just because I put points in one of my stats."

"That's not how it works. You could have a charisma rating of 100, but if you're a douchebag, nobody is going to be interested in you. But you've already got this girl interested with your natural charm— you're blind if you can't tell—and a little boost in charisma would be just enough to put you in the 'fly zone'… if you get my drift."

"She's a NPC, and I've got a girlfriend…"

Aaron laughed. "And what will you do if you can't find your girlfriend or she isn't in the game anymore? You'll just stay alone forever, ignore all the other fine options around you?"

"Don't start being annoying again," I scoffed.

"I'm not being annoying. I'm being real."

I shook my head. "Rachel's got to be out there…"

"But what if she's not?"

I sighed and shook my head again. "Then I guess I'd move on. Or at least I'd try."

Aaron cleared his throat. "Charisma dude. Put some points in charisma... I 'beta tested' some ladies before launch. Oh, my god. You can't tell the difference."

I grinned and rolled my eyes. I just couldn't take the guy seriously.

I patted Sora on the head and then dismissed her before we headed for Eanos' shop. When we pushed through the door, the old man I remembered opened his arms wide and bellowed, "Welcome to Eanos' shop of magic! Have a look around!" His eyes met mine. "Ohhhh! Welcome, repeat customer!"

Not the usual Eanos...

There was another patron inside, looking at the magic rings that he had displayed under a glass case. He looked up when we entered but immediately turned back towards the rings.

"Just play it cool until the other guy leaves," I whispered in Aaron's ear.

We made a play of looking at scrolls and other items, and I noticed right away that many of the things I saw before had been marked up in price by 50% or more. When the other customer left, I asked Eanos, "Why are your prices so much higher than before?"

Eanos gave his brightest smile. "Business has been booming! You've got to adjust your prices to keep up with demand, right? My customers have more than tripled."

"Hmm... Well, I guess that's good."

"What brings you back Gunn... umm...was it Gunther?" Eanos asked.

"Gunnar."

"Right. Nice to see you again, Gunnar. What can I help you with?"

I was surprised by the shop keep's sudden friendliness and customer service attitude, but I couldn't tell if it was being faked or not. "I have a favor to ask you."

"A favor?" Eanos questioned.

"You told me you're skilled in arcane magic, right?"

Eanos nodded.

"We need a way to get teleported somewhere... Gramora."

"Oh..." Eanos said, raising his eyebrows. "I can't help you with that..." Eanos turned to his inventory. "But if you'd like to buy anything, be my guest!"

"Why can't you help us? You're not skilled enough?"

"I never said that," Eanos replied, dropping his smile. "But you can't just come walking into my shop asking me to teleport you to such and such places. Do I look like a travel agent?"

"I don't know how to explain this to you," I said, "but we have a time-sensitive situation on our hands. We need to get to Gramora to prevent Eden's Gate from shutting down. We really need your help."

Eanos waved a dismissive hand. "Take a boat across the Serpent Sea like everyone else."

"We don't have time for that," Aaron interjected.

"And who is this idiot dressed like an orc?"

"He's an idiot who's trying to save your life."

Eanos rolled his eyes and laughed. "I have no idea how to deal with nutcases like you. You two are the last people I need to save my life."

"Right now you're our only hope, Eanos."

"What part of 'no' don't you understand?" Eanos replied. "I don't spend my mana on people for free. I'm a businessman, not a charity."

"I can do you another favor," I suggested.

Eanos' eyes went wide and he lifted his chin high and to the side. "I don't recall you ever doing me any favors." He glared at me with eyes that told me to keep my mouth shut.

"We could do you *a favor...*" I corrected.

"I don't require any assistance at this time, but thank you for your generous offer."

I swallowed hard. "Maybe I'm asking the wrong question. Is there anything we can offer to get you to transport us to Gramora?"

Eanos crossed his eyes and sighed as he bobbed his head from side to side. After a few seconds of thought he said, "800 gold would cover the cost, I suppose."

"800 gold for something that costs you nothing?! That's outrageous," I blurted.

"Channeling a portal is a very taxing endeavor. I'm certain that I'll want to take a nap afterwards. It's also a spell that requires reagents to cast, which I don't have at the moment. So... 800 gold plus the required reagent."

"400 gold," I countered. After all, I only had 450 in my purse.

"Oh please..." Eanos moaned. "I'll make that amount by selling a single low level scroll."

I reached in my bag and reluctantly pulled out my Siphon Spirit scroll. I wasn't looking forward parting with it, but it was one of my last options. "I'll give you this scroll in exchange for a portal."

Eanos grabbed the scroll and laid it on his counter. He lifted a finger, and yellow sparkle swam out of the tip then fell onto the scroll. "Oh…" he said, raising his eyebrows. "Now, this is interesting."

"Deal?" I asked.

"400 gold plus the scroll and we have a deal."

"400 gold plus the scroll? I've already been offered 800 for the scroll!"

"I don't see anyone else in the room offering to buy your scroll or cast portals for you."

"You're a real dick, man!" Aaron spat.

Eanos scowled.

I flicked my fingertips at Eanos and sighed. "Fine, take the scroll, and I'll give you 400 gold." I already knew how stubborn the guy was, but that didn't erase the regret of not selling the scroll to Rhys.

"I'll still need the required reagent," Eanos said.

"What reagent is that?"

"Just one mandrake root is all the spell requires."

"Where do we get that?" I asked.

Eanos snapped his lips and placed his hands on his hips. "In the Freelands near the village of Thorpes, there's a grassy knoll where mandrake grows sporadically, but you'll need to be careful there because—"

"We don't have time to go back to the Freelands!" Aaron shouted.

I shook my head. "It would take us more than a day to travel there and back on our own. We've got to leave today."

The mage sighed and rolled his eyes. "Well, I suppose Gerard might have some. You could try over there if you must." He said as if it were the worst possible suggestion he could ever make in his life.

We left the arcane shop and headed for Gerard's general good store, and when I pushed the door open, I wasn't greeted by the same bubbly man that I had been greeted by before. Instead, Gerard was sleeping with his head on the counter, drool dripping out of his unshaven lips.

"Gerard?" I called.

The shopkeeper mumbled.

"Gerard?" I said again a little louder.

Gerard moaned and lifted his head off the counter, blinking his eyes several times. "Oh... A customer. Welcome..." he said groggily. "How can I help you?"

"We'd like to buy a reagent," I replied.

Gerard wiped the back of his hand across his eyes and blinked again. "Oh, I remember you. You want to buy *magic* reagents?"

"Yeah..." I looked around and noticed that his shop looked quite a bit more organized than it had before.

"Right over here..." he said, pointing to a glass case with several flowers and roots underneath.

I immediately noticed that strange, brown root with long, stringy extremities labeled as mandrake. "This one," I said, pointing. "The mandrake root."

Gerard yawned. "I can give you a bundle of it for 100 gold. I usually sell bundles for 200, but business has been extremely slow lately."

"I only need one," I replied.

"Only one?" Gerard asked. "I assure you that this is authentic mandrake, and 100 gold is quite the steal."

"I believe you," I said.

"So then a bundle?" he asked again.

"Only one…"

Gerard sighed. "Look, you're the first customer I've had in two days… At this rate, I won't be able to pay my building dues. I'll be forced to close my shop within a week or two."

"It's that bad?" I asked.

Gerard rattled his head and his eyes were glistening with sadness. "I don't know who, but someone must have traded me fake magic items. I had three customers complain that using their scrolls made their homes stink of foul! No one in Linden wants to buy from me anymore!"

I felt terrible knowing that I was responsible for Gerard's business going bad, but there was little I could do to fix things. "What would be the cost of one mandrake root?"

Gerard sighed again. "I'll sell you one for 10 gold. At least I'll be able to eat tonight."

I reached into my purse and pulled out 50 gold pieces. "Here. Take 50 gold for one. Consider it overpayment for the kindness you've shown me."

"Really?" Gerard said, his eyes going wide when I placed the gold in his hand. "Thank you!" He rounded the store counter and threw a pair of strong arms around me. "You're a kind man, indeed. We need more people like you here in Linden."

*Oh god... If he only knew what I did to him.* I made a mental note to come back and check in on the guy if I ever had another opportunity.

I left Gerard's shop with just enough gold to pay Eanos. When we walked back into the magic shop, I handed him the mandrake, the gold and gave him the evil eye as he counted it all out.

"You're a greedy bastard, Eanos," I said.

"Oh hush," he replied, still counting the coins. "Don't go and spoil our deal, now."

He pocketed the coins and walked to the back of his shop, pulling out a thick, hardcover book. "You're lucky that my runebook has an inscription for Gramora, but I can't guarantee it'll be anywhere near wherever you're trying to go."

"Go on and cast the damn spell, already," Aaron barked.

"Well, I'm not going to cast it here," he replied. "Imagine what my customers would think if they walked in here and there was a portal inside. It wouldn't be at all professional, I'll tell you that!"

We followed Eanos outside, where he finished locking up his shop and led us to a small wooded area a few hundred meters outside the edges of Linden.

"I suppose this is far enough that no children will see it and curiously wander inside," Eanos sneered. He placed the mandrake root on the ground and took a step back, waving his hand at us. "Stand several paces away now."

Aaron and I took a few steps back from where Eanos rested the root, and the mage opened his runebook, flipping through the pages. I could see from where I was standing that there were several designs on each page, similar to the ones on runestones.

I leaned over to Aaron's ear. "Runebooks have to do with inscription?" I asked.

Aaron nodded. "But only high-level scribes can mark runebooks."

Eanos settled on a particular page in the runebook and held out his hand towards the location where he placed the mandrake root. He closed his eyes, and the inscription inside the book started glowing a bright, white light, and a small, blue swirl of energy appeared a few feet above the mandrake root. As he continued channeling the spell, the blue energy continued to grow in size and the root sizzled and turned to ash.

It was about twenty seconds after he began casting, that the blue swirl of energy had grown into a portal the size of a small door. It was slightly opaque and looked like the tiny particles were dancing around on its surface.

Eanos snapped his book shut and swung his hand to his back, stumbling a bit but catching himself against a tree before he fell. "There's your damn portal," he huffed as if he were out of breath. "You've got 24 hours before the portal dissipates, so don't get lost unless you want to stay there."

"Got it…" I affirmed. "Thanks."

Eanos turned around and started limping his way back towards Linden. It looked like the guy really needed a cane. "And don't come back to my shop unless you want to buy something!" he shouted before he was out of earshot.

I looked at the portal and then over to Aaron. "Have you used these before?" I asked.

"No, actually… When the game was in development, I had access to the admin console. I could make myself appear wherever I wanted instantly."

"Well then, you're up first."

Aaron shrugged. "Well, let's just hope it doesn't hurt." He grinned and made a running jump straight into the center of swirling blue energy. There was a 'zinggg!' sound when his body was fully consumed.

"Why do I have the strange feeling I'm going to regret this?" I muttered to myself. I took two steps back, ran forward, and dove head first inside the portal.

# Chapter 23

### Day 6 (Earth)

"Japan just went offline," the Secretary of Defense announced.

Senator Gates smiled. "Everything is going a lot smoother than expected."

The President licked his lips and sat the cup of coffee he was drinking down on the conference room table. "That leaves Mexico and Canada, right, Bill?" The stress of the last two days weighed fine lines under his eyes, and several strands of his gray hair were sticking up from their usual slicked-back position.

"That's correct, Mr. President, sir. They will be going offline by midnight tonight as planned."

"Okay, good. Make sure that your team does another data scan to make sure there are no unauthorized signals being beamed to satellites that we don't know about. If this plan fails, there's no chance we'll get the cooperation of the world's nations again. We're making history here."

"Yes, sir," the Secretary said before turning and exiting the conference room.

"And you're for *certain*," the President stressed, lowering his eyes to Kendra, "that any VR units that are still out there won't be able to function once the CPU blockchain has been wiped out?"

Kendra nodded. "Theoretically, they would power on but won't be able to connect to anything, so a consciousness transfer wouldn't be possible."

The President turned to Senator Gates. "Even if we don't connect, I want to make sure every piece of that damn hardware is confiscated, so there's no risk of it getting hacked and connected to another game somewhere down the line."

"That's all lined up, sir. There's no question in my mind that we can get them all." The Senator cleared his voice. "But with all due respect, Mr. President, I'm not sure having Ms. Ramos here in our strategy room is in our best interest—considering she helped the lead programmer perform an illegal log in into a Nexicon VR."

"You read the suicide note," Kendra said.

"That he's going inside so that he can 'show us something' is a little vague. And the fact that you found the body and the note so soon after death is more than a little suspicious."

"Hey, I—" Kendra started but was quickly cut off.

"Settle down, both of you." The president pointed towards Senator Gates. "She's innocent until proven guilty, and she's our best point of contact at Nexicon now that both Dr. Winston and Aaron Sizemore are gone."

"And the fact that you're allowing *her* technology in here—"

"Senator Gates," the President said sternly. "This issue is no longer up for debate. The Secret Service has checked her computer, and it's clean. If–and that's a big if—there's something we can learn by connecting to

324

Eden's Gate, we at least have to give it a chance. We've all lost people close to us in this incident."

"So what if we get some chat messages?" Senator Gates asked. "Or if there's a video, how do we not know it's pre-recorded?"

"That's not all you'll get," Kendra explained. "If Aaron is able to open the port from inside the game, we'll get a live audio/video stream and be able to communicate back and forth. We'll be able to see into the world, so long as they keep the port open."

Senator Gates adjusted his position in his chair and smirked. "6 days and no communication. No screenshots, no video, no audio... Nothing to indicate that something is going on inside that death trap. I'm not holding my breath that we're going to suddenly be able to peek into Pandora's box less than a day before we're wiping it out."

"That's enough," the President said. "We'll have someone monitoring the feed until total blackout tomorrow. In the meantime, I need both of you to work together to make sure this all goes according to plan."

Kendra clenched her teeth as the President started rattling off more orders, hardly able to focus on the things he was saying. She looked down to the 'No Signal' that was splashed across her laptop's screen. *Come on Aaron*, she thought. *Don't let your death be for nothing.*

# Chapter 24

*01/06/0001*

I fell out of the other side of the teleporter, face-first into a thick puddle of mud, and I immediately heard thunderous footsteps pounding on the ground. The soft dirt around me was shaking.

"Run!!!" Aaron yelled.

I pulled my head up and wiped my face with the back up my hand, just as I saw a giant four-legged monster stomping its way towards me. One of its legs alone were four or five times the size of my body, and under its thick, hairless hide of skin, its muscles undulated. Four massive horns, jutted forward from its face, which complimented the horror of its endless rows of sword sized teeth.

*You have failed to inspect your target!*

I stood, slipping on the nasty swampland and dashed awkwardly towards Aaron. In every direction was mud and tall grass, but worst of all, in every direction I could see creatures looming: flying insects, mutant snakes, floating humanoids, and atrocities that looked like a mix between dinosaurs, reptiles, and men.

"What the fuck is this?!" I yelled as Aaron sidestepped a group of creatures that looked like airborne frogs with butterfly wings.

"Just run!" he yelled back.

We just keep running, not seeing any safe place to escape to, when I saw a human-like hand reach up out of

327

the mud and latch onto Aaron's ankle. Aaron tripped and fell face-forward in the mud as the hand pulled on him hard, apparently trying to drag him into the ground somehow.

"Oh shit!" Aaron yelled as he clawed at the mud, trying to grasp onto anything for traction but failing.

I pulled out my blade as I caught up to him and slashed at the base of the arm sticking out the mud. There was a loud squeal and the arm let go and retracted back under the surface.

"Get up!" I yelled and held out my hand to help Aaron stand.

"Watch your legs!" he yelled as he managed to get back to his feet.

More hands started sprouting out of the ground all around us trying to grab on to something above. I swung my sword around wildly, trying to ward them off.

"Over there!" Aaron shouted, pointing to a dry-looking, unoccupied hill in the distance.

"Go!" I yelled, swiping my sword at another clawing hand. We ran, lifting our knees high to our chest to avoid getting stuck in the mud or grabbed by one of the sprouting arms.

When we got near the base of the hill, it seemed like there were no other monsters close by that were in range of attack, but a pair of tall, upright creatures with long spears noticed us a from a distance and started racing at us. They were both naked, and between their legs was nothing but smooth scaly skin just like the rest of their body. Their frame bore resemblance to humans, but their fishy faces had pulsating gills on each side, and a fin was sticking out of the top of their head.

*Name:* Bloodthirsty Swamprunner
*Race:* humanoid
*Level:* 8
*Health/Mana/Stamina:* 120/0/120
*Status:* aggressive

As the Swamprunners ran towards us, I placed my hand on Aaron's shoulder to stop him from moving. "Stand your ground here! There's no other monsters attacking!" I lifted my sword and held it with both hands.

"Party up!" Aaron said.

> *You have been invited to join **Aaron's Party**.*
> *Do you accept? Yes/No*

I willed myself into Aaron's party just as the first Swamprunner closed in and darted the tip of its spear at my chest. I parried, slapping the spear out of the way with my sword, then swung upwards to slash the monster across its chest.

The Swamprunner screamed in pain, and I rolled forward towards its friend that was approaching behind him. "Keep the other one busy!" I yelled to Aaron, referring to the monster I just injured.

The second Swamprunner swung its spear at me, which I easily blocked with my sword, and I shot a Fireblast at its face and watched as it dropped the spear and screamed in agony. Swamprunner=Swamp=Water…. Clearly beings that lived near water would be weak against fire and vice-versa.

I drove my sword into the Swamprunner's chest as it clawed at the flames, ending its life immediately, then turned around and saw Aaron ducking and dodging the attacks of the other. It seemed like Aaron just couldn't get close enough with his dagger to land any strikes.

I shot a Fireblast at the other Swamprunner, and it dropped its weapon and howled. Another swipe of my sword across its back, and it fell lifeless to the ground.

*You have gained 400 XP!*

I walked to the base of the hill and sat down to catch my breath. Aaron's chest heaved as he sauntered over to join me.

"Gramora, huh?" I asked. "Fuck this place, man."

"When I placed the portal here, I didn't expect I'd have to come at level 3. I figured I'd be level 10 at least."

"You're level 3 already, huh?"

"Yeah, I gained a level back at the orc camp… when I killed the shaman."

"When you *helped* kill the shaman."

"Yeah, whatever."

I looked out across the swamp and saw monsters everywhere. The hill that we were on was pretty much surrounded. But I also felt a thick, heaviness in the air, and it was almost as if I could hear a low ringing sound.

"Do you feel magic or something?" I asked. "I can't tell if I'm imagining things."

"Yeah, I feel it. It's like a buzz."

Aaron stood up and climbed to the top of the hill. "Hell yeah. Jackpot," he said when he reached its peak. "Get over here."

I scaled my way up to Aaron, and he pointed down to a giant runestone that was jutting out of the base of the mound.

"We need that," he said.

Hoovering near the runestone was a creature that looked much like the Swamprunners, but instead of legs was a long tail curled to the back and large nipple-free breasts. It floated in the air as it moved, and tucked under one of its arms was a spellbook.

**Name:** *Swamprunner Sorceress*
**Race:** *humanoid*
**Level:** *8*
**Health/Mana/Stamina:** *80/100/80*
**Status:** *aggressive*

Far in the distance was a group of four other sorceresses, all huddled together.

"Get down," I said and lay in a prone position as I pulled my bow from my back

Aaron followed suit.

"I'm going to try to snipe her, but you should nock an arrow too, just in case I miss or it's not enough to kill her."

Aaron nodded, and I readied my Snipe Shot while Aaron pulled back an arrow. My vision zoomed on the area right between the Sorceress's large, bloodshot eyes, and I waited as my body stilled. *1... 2...*

"Shit!" Aaron let go, and I watched as his arrow flew from his hands, down towards the Sorceress. I relaxed my arm and my heart pumped in anticipation of the unknown, but his arrow missed by a mile, and made only the slightest sound when it landed in the mud. The sorceress turned towards the sound, but seemed generally unalarmed.

"Sorry," Aaron whispered. "It slipped from my hands."

"Be careful," I said as I readied my Snipe Shot again. It probably wasn't the best situation for him to start training archery against level 8 monsters, but it was what it was.

I let my Snipe Shot fly and it soared through the air and landed silently between the Swamprunner's eyes. The Sorceress collapsed down into the mud.

*You have reached level 2 in* **Snipe Shot**!

*You have gained 320 XP!*

Aaron darted up and started for the runestone, but I called for him to stop. "Let's loot the other two we killed first."

We returned to the two corpses, and other than a small purse and the weapons they were carrying, there wasn't much else to search, given that they were basically naked. I looted 15 gold from one and let Aaron have the spoils of the other. I inspected one of the spears and noticed there were no stat requirements.

> ***Warped Spear.*** *6-14 Attack Damage. Durability: 6/10. Quality: Poor. Rarity: Common. Weight: 2.1*

"You should equip this," I suggested. "That training dagger will be hard to use against anything with a reach."

Aaron agreed and started pulling the spear's tiny holster off one of the monsters and tying it onto his armor. "Not a big fan of polearms, but I guess using them will be simple enough."

"Yeah, just take the pointy end and poke it into something, preferably up someone's ass."

Aaron smiled. "Oh, so you're not always Mr. Serious Pants?"

I made a low chuckle. "Shouldn't you be more serious since... uh... the fate of our lives supposedly rests on us getting into this dungeon?"

Aaron slid the spear into the holster on his back. "More than five million lives, actually." He took a step forward and placed a hand on my shoulder. "But not having a laugh isn't going to get us there any faster." He smiled and started for the other side of the hill. "Come on. Let's bind up."

I followed Aaron to the runestone and touched the hard, gritty surface as I focused on making that location my starting point.

*You have **bound** to **this location**. Using a
Recall Home spell or death will return you to
this position.*

"So where's your dungeon?" I asked Aaron as he
lifted his hand off the stone.

"There," he said, pointing to a humongous weeping
willow far in the distance. "I chose Gramora because
that massive tree is visible from virtually anywhere
you're standing in the zone."

There was a thick cloud of fog that hovered over the
muddy ground, so it was difficult to make out everything
that was in the path leading to the tree, but even with the
smoke, I could tell that there would be quite a number of
monsters we'd have to fight in order to get there.

"So I guess we'll just slowly grind our way over
there and retreat to the hill if we get in trouble," I said.

"We could try, but this area is mixed with all sorts
of levels. I think it's better just to make a run for it."

"We don't have enough stamina to make it there in
full sprint."

"Surely we can find a resting spot or two
somewhere in between."

I shrugged. "Alright, your call…" I took a few steps
forward towards the fallen sorceress and started
examining the corpse. "Let me see what kind of loot this
gal has first."

*You've received: **25 Gold Pieces***

*You've received: **Emerald Ring.** Durability:
90/100. Quality: Exceptional. Rarity:
Common. Weight: 0.1 kg.*

*You've received:* **Tattered Spellbook**. *Durability: 4/10. Quality: Average. Rarity: Rare. Weight: 0.3 kg*

I pocketed the gold and the emerald ring, but then I opened the spellbook, most of the pages were covered with mud, ruined ink, or fell apart when I tried to open the page, but there were still two pages of the book that I could read. They looked similar to a scroll, but because I wasn't trained in their area of magic, I couldn't read anything other than the description.

**Water Jet:** *Release a powerful spray of water onto a target. Requires 15 Intelligence. Water Magic Level 2.*

**Divine Sight:** *Your eyes can see through the darkest of darks. Immunity to blinding spells and attacks. Requires 12 Intelligence. Divine Magic Level 1.*

I bagged the spellbook. "That sorceress gave a lot of XP and had some decent loot on her. We should take the rest of them out before we move forward."

"I say we just run right past them. Forget the loot, dude."

"They're casters," I replied. "We'll take damage from them for sure, and we're not sure what they're capable of. It's safer to try to kill them. Besides, they seem weak to my fire damage."

"Hmm," Aaron grunted. "Alright, but let's try to make it quick."

We positioned ourselves near the runestone and tried to strategize how to take them out. The basic plan we came up with was for me to fire a Snipe Shot at one, and then follow up with a quick Fire Arrow on another. In the meantime, Aaron would try to land as many basic arrow shots as possible and I'd switch to basic attacks after my first two moves. I couldn't afford to burn all my arrows up in flames.

I readied my Snipe Shot and prayed that Aaron didn't let another arrow slip out of his hands as he nocked an arrow back. As my body stilled, I watched as the four floating sorceresses drifted around somewhat aimlessly. It was odd that they seemed perfectly fine without any sort of interaction with each other, but then again, they were fish people. I had never seen any fish that cared for deep, intellectual discussion.

My arrow soared through the air and pierced through one of the sorceresses' skulls, and before the other sorceresses realized what was happening, I had already readied another arrow and let it fly towards a second, casting Fire Arrow on it after it left my hands. Aaron fired at the same time, and our arrows landed simultaneously, one sorceress being knocked back by my attack and screaming as the flames scorched her skin, while the other howled when Aaron's arrow pierced through her breast.

The burning sorceress continued to swat at flames as I sent an arrow in her direction while the other two sorceresses swam quickly in our direction. Another basic arrow from Aaron and I, and the second sorceress went down.

*You have reached level 4 in **Archery**!*

As the sorceresses grew closer, I reached out my hand to cast a Fireblast, but as the flames started pouring from my fingertips, one of the monsters made a high-pitched wail in our direction and my magic was quenched. My head swam when I tried to cast Fireblast or even tried to remember how. It was as if I had a mental block of some sort, and the idea of magic just made me dizzy.

That's when I noticed a small circle with three tiny dots under my stats bar. When I focused on the icon, I could see why I was suddenly dumbed down.

> *You have been **silenced** and cannot use magic or special abilities. Duration: 60 seconds.*

Aaron let loose another arrow just as the other sorceress raised its scaly arm, and a transparent bubble of magic formed around the two sorceresses' bodies. The arrow hit the shield and bounced off, falling into the mud.

"Oh shit!" Aaron spat, trying to swap his bow for his spear. "Burn them!"

"They silenced my magic! We've got to get in close!"

I pulled on the hilt of my sword, and before I could even take a step forward, one of the sorceresses swiped an arm across its chest, and a thick wave of muddy water shot up from the ground, smashing against Aaron and I, the pressure so intense that it knocked us to the ground.

I coughed through muddy lips as the wave subsided and picked myself off the slippery ground. The wave had knocked 15% from my health and 30% from Aaron, so I knew there wasn't time to think.

"What the hell!" Aaron said as he stumbled to his feet, his thick orc furs matted in nasty mud.

"Charge them!" I yelled, and dashed through the mud as quickly as I could.

The third sorceress, the one that I had burned earlier, had finally recovered from my fire and was closing in on its friends when it made the same motion to cast another wave spell.

"Dodge to your right!" I yelled, and made a quick roll to my left barely missing another wave of thick, powerful mud.

*You have reached level 3 in **Dodge**!*

"What!?" Aaron yelled, right before he was slammed in the face and knocked down again.

I leapt forward, and barely in the range of the first two sorceresses, I swung my sword in a wide motion and clipped both of them across the breast. They reared their heads back and screamed, then swiped at me with the sharp nails of their free hands.

My armor plus Adeelee's Barkskin buff seemed to protect me from most of their physical damage. Each blow only knocking my health down by about 3%, and when I swiped my sword back the other direction, I slashed their chests again, then dove the tip into one of their necks.

*You have reached level 4 in **Swords**!*

*You have gained 1 point of **Strength**!*

The sorceress' eyes went blank and fell to the ground, and just as I was about to turn to finish off the second one, I felt my body rising into the air.

I was caught in a large, transparent bubble that the scorched sorceress we'd forgotten about seemed to have cast on me. I swung my sword at the bubble, but it just but it bounced back at the magical field, and I continued to rise and rise.

Aaron dipped his spear into the side of the sorceress that I had cleaved and it reached back and swiped him. He pulled his pole back and slammed it in again, and then again, and finally the sorceress died. They were at a distinct disadvantage at close range, so long as none of their friends were in range to cast spells—spells like the one that I got caught in.

When the sorceress holding me in the bubble saw Aaron charging for her, she lowered her hand, and the bubble around me popped. I must have been at least 12 feet in the air at that point and I screamed as I fell backwards and down to the ground below. A waterlogged tree branch was jutting out of the ground, and while most of my body slapped into soft mud, the back of my head clipped the wood, causing my eyes to erupt with stars upon impact.

I squeezed my lids tight and blinked several times, attempting to clear my vision. I lay there stunned for several seconds. When I finally sat back up, my head was throbbing, and I saw that the fall had brought me down to 20% health. A few meters away, Aaron was ducking and dodging the sorceress' quick scratch attacks, trying to find an opening for his spear.

There was no barrier around the last fish-woman, and I noticed that my silence had finally worn off. I raised a palm and sent a Fireblast in her direction, knocking her back and burning her last bit of health up in flames.

> *Advancement! You have reached **level 8** and gained 3 attribute points. To assign your attribute points, open your status page. You can also increase any of your known skills by 1 level. Choose wisely, as your choices cannot be undone.*

> *You have gained 10 SP!*

Aaron's shoulders slumped and he took a few deep breaths before turning. His feet wearily trudged through the mud, and when he was finally beside me, he sat his ass down hard in the soft soil. His health was at 30%.

"That was close," he huffed.

"Way too close," I agreed. "And we're nowhere near that tree yet."

I pulled up my stats, so that I could assign my newly earned AP and LP. Given how low the monsters had managed to bring my health, now seemed like as good time as any to put an LP into First Aid and an AP into Vitality.

What was most concerning about the fight was my fall. The hard impact left me stunned for several seconds, and if there had been another enemy around after that, I would have certainly died. So I put a point into Willpower to help work towards curbing those kind of incidents.

I considered for a moment to throw an AP into Charisma like Aaron had suggested. I wasn't having too much difficulty fighting creatures of roughly my level, and it would be pretty cool to get back from a long mission in Gramora and have Adeelee—or any other babes for that matter—thirsty for some Gunnar attention. But then again I wouldn't even exist in the world if the consequences of not reaching the dungeon were true.

And I still needed to find Rachel.

I placed another point in Willpower. The panty melting, irresistible Gunnar Long would have to wait for another day.

"Let's loot these bitches and keep moving," Aaron said.

"You need to get some of your health back first." I reached inside my bag, searching for one of the two food rations I was carrying. We still had a long way to go for me to blow my health potions, so the increased regen from food would have to do.

There was a sudden, rapid patter of strong footsteps coming from behind us, and before I could even turn to see what was coming, large jaws with long, inwardly curved black teeth clamped down around Aaron's skull and pulled back with such speed and force that his head was ripped completely from his body.

Blood spewed into the air from Aaron's severed neck, and the monster tilted its body back and chomped it teeth, letting the head slip down its throat. The dark green-skinned thing looked like a giant velociraptor, but had a longer body and a slender, fish-like tail with fins jutting from the tops of its length. It's long, black talons looked like they could pierce steel.

I gripped my sword and scrambled backwards on the mud, but the thing just turned to me and leapt. I didn't even have time to swing, as its razor sharp fangs sank deep into the bone of my face, and I screamed bloody murder right before it ripped my lower jaw right from my skull, stopping me from making any additional sounds.

The pain was severe, even more than when I had been backstabbed in the woods. My health dropped to 0, and I watched for the last couple seconds of my life as the monster dropped my lower jaw on top of me and dipped its head down to rip a mouthful of flesh and entrails from my belly.

*YOU HAVE DIED*

*All of your current level's progression has been reset to 0% and any unused attribute and level points have been lost.*

*You will respawn at your last bound location in approximately 2:00:00*

*Take this time to reflect on your choices.*

# Chapter 25

*01/06/0001*

The darkness surrounding me began to disseminate, and I once again found myself in Gramora. I touched my jaw and gripped at my abdomen, making sure that I was really all there. My heart pounded as I relived the horrifying moment before death. "Holy shit..." I muttered.

"You died too?"

I turned to see Aaron sitting on the mud in his white boxer shorts, rubbing at his neck. I nodded. "Yeah, it... it... I watched it eat my fucking stomach, dude! How are you just sitting there so calmly? It ripped your head off!"

"I had a pretty swift death, I guess. I mean... I only felt pain for a second or two at most."

"Why?!" I asked him loudly.

"Why what?"

"Why did you guys program the world to have pain like that?!"

Aaron leaned back and looked up to the sky. "Have you ever eaten spicy food?"

"Yeah... but what does that have to do with anything?"

"Pain receptors. Without pain, there could be no spicy food."

"So you're telling me you guys wanted people to feel their organs getting chewed out because you wanted them to be able to eat spicy food?"

"Not me. Dr. Winston." Aaron leaned back and smiled. "What if I told you that your girlfriend is dead? Both in the game and in the outside world? How would you feel?"

I creased my brow. "Why would you say that?"

"Pain," Aaron explained. "That feeling you'd experience is pain. The way that Dr. Winston put it is, 'Without pain, you cannot feel. Without pain, normal becomes pain and pleasure becomes normal.'"

"What? Say that again?"

"There was no way to turn pain off and keep people feeling human. If pain was turned off, people suddenly didn't care. 'No pain' games work fine when you're conscious on the other side of the game, because you're still feeling pain somewhere. But if you're only conscious in one world and have zero pain, then you become less human than a NPC."

"I guess that makes sense, but still..." I shook my head and shuddered as I remembered the sound of razor sharp teeth crunching into my bone.

"Besides," Aaron said as he picked himself off the ground and wiped a swathe of mud off his shorts. "Without pain, people would 'Leeeeeroy Jennnnnkins' their way into a high-level shit just for the hell of it."

"Which is kind of what we're doing now." I pushed myself to my feet and noticed that my Elven Bag of

Unburdening had made it with me but all its contents were gone.

"Not for the hell of it," he reminded me. Aaron lifted his finger and pointed to the spot where we died. "I still see our stuff over there. Let's move before more nasties show up."

I nodded and we jogged to where our gear was lying.

"What happened to our bodies?" I asked as we started equipping our weapons and armor.

"The bodies of Reborns stay in the world until they respawn. After that, they vanish and all their stuff falls to the ground. Good thing a humanoid didn't kill us. They would've run off with whatever they could carry." He looked up as he saw me stuffing potions and bandages back in my bag.

"That bag is a Spirit Item?"

"Yeah," I said. "I got it from the High Elves after a quest."

He shook his head from side to side. "Level 8 and already have a bound bag? You're a lucky bastard, you know that?"

I lifted my Elven Leather Vest and the lower front of it was shredded. The durability was on its last couple points and the amount of protection was almost cut in half.

> **Ragged Lightweight Elven Leather Vest.**
> +12 Armor. Durability: 2/10. Quality: Average. Rarity: Common. Weight: 1.3 kg

"If I'm lucky, today isn't proving it."

Aaron ran his hand around a large patch of tall grass. "Looks like it ate my wolf cap along with my head."

"Oh, it definitely did... It definitely did."

My Barkskin buff was gone, and after putting on my poor excuse for a chestpiece, I pulled up my stats to see what other damage had been done.

## GUNNAR LONG

| | |
|---|---|
| Race: | Human |
| Level: | 8 (Progress 0%) |
| Title: | None |
| Health/Mana/Stamina: | 145+/120/120 |
| Strength: | 18+ |
| Dexterity: | 19 |
| Intelligence: | 18 |
| Vitality: | 13+ |
| Wisdom: | 13 |
| Willpower: | 13 |
| Charisma: | 10 |
| AR Rating: | 32 |
| Resists: | |
| | 10% Fire Resistance |
| | 15% Water Resistance |
| Traits: | |
| | Elven Touch |
| Primary Skills: | |
| | First Aid Lvl 3: progress 0% |
| | Sneak Lvl 3: progress 0% |
| | Inspect Lvl 3: progress 0% |
| | Tinkering Lvl 1: progress 0% |
| | Summon Beast: Mastered |
| | Inscription Lvl 1: progress 0% |
| Combat Skills: | |
| | Dodge Lvl 3: progress 0% |
| | Small Blades Lvl 2: progress 0% |
| | Backstab Lvl 1: progress 0% |
| | Archery Lvl 4: progress 0% |
| | Block Lvl 1: progress 0% |
| | Swords Lvl 4: progress 0% |
| | Snipe Shot Lvl 2: progress 0% |
| | Dirty Fighting Lvl 1: progress 0% |
| Magic Skills: | |
| | Fire Magic Lvl 5: progress 0% |

Thank goodness I assigned my points before death, but I definitely lost a little progress in some stats. I remember being particularly close to leveling Block, but now I was back to square one in that skill.

"Stop fucking with your stats dude. We've gotta move."

I closed my stats. He was right. I surveyed the area around us, and it mostly looked the same. There was the small area ahead of the of the runestone that we had cleared, but there were still monsters in every direction.

> *You have been invited to join **Aaron's Party**.*
> *Do you accept? Yes/No*

I accepted his invitation.

"Run for it?" Aaron asked.

I shrugged. "I guess we can give it a try."

Aaron stuck his knee out as if he were about to run a race. "Alright. On the count of three."

I checked to make sure my things were tightly secure and got in a starting stance as well.

"1...2...3..."

Aaron and I kicked off through the mud, but we only made it a few paces before I yelled at him to stop.

"What is it?" he asked holding his hands out to the side.

"The sorceresses' loot is still here."

I kneeled and picked up a spellbook out of the cold, dead sorceress' hand. Every page had been burned to the point that they were unreadable. There were two more that were either burned or ruined by mud, but the last spellbook had two legible pages inside.

> ***Ice Prism:*** *Freeze and damage an enemy in a prism of ice for 3 seconds. Requires 24 Intelligence. Water Magic Level 5.*

> **Destabilizing Thoughts:** *Fill your target's mind with unsettling thoughts, causing damage over time for 3 seconds. Requires 16 Intelligence. Dark Magic Level 3.*

Too bad I couldn't understand them. The same spellbook also had a thin piece of folded parchment that fell out when I opened it. Inside of the parchment was the picture of a runestone with an unusual, red symbol drawn on its face.

> *You've Received:* **Schematic: Runestone of Minor Fire Damage**. *Adds additional on-hit fire damage. Requires 10 Intelligence. Requires Inscription Lvl 1. Requires: Red Inscription Powder. Durability: 7/10. Quality: Average. Rarity: Rare. Weight: 0.1 kg*

I tossed the tattered spellbook and schematic in my bag.

"This one has a magic ring," Aaron said, pulling a gold band off one of the sorceress' fingers.

"Hand it to me, and I'll identify it."

Aaron tossed me the ring.

> *You've received:* **Invoker's Band**. *Durability: 9/10. Quality: Average. Rarity: Rare. Weight: 0.1 kg. +5 Intelligence*

"Plus five intelligence," I said and tossed the band back to him. "Nice find."

"Keep it. I don't have any magic skills yet."

"You sure?" I asked as Aaron handed me back the ring.

"Yeah, dude. It should give you a little bit of a damage boost."

I tried slipping the ring onto my finger, but it felt like there was a magnetic force preventing it from going on.

> *You are limited to one magic ring on each hand!*
>
> *You are limited to one magic ring on each hand!*
>
> *You are limited to one magic ring on each hand!*

Hmph, I thought. I guess it would be overpowered if I could slip as many stat boosting rings on my fingers as I wanted. "Here," I said as I pulled my Ring of Sturdiness off my finger and handed it to Aaron. "This one will be useful to you. I'm at my ring limit." The +15 HP that I got from the ring would be missed, but I figured it would help keep Aaron alive, and the +5 intelligence from the new ring would probably be more useful for taking out enemies with my fire magic.

"Thanks," Aaron said.

There was a low rumble that reverberated on the ground, and I could see a puddle of mud nearby shake. Something big was moving close to us.

"We should probably go..." I suggested.

Aaron nodded and got back in his sprinting position. "No stopping 'til we reach a safe clearing, alright?"

I nodded.

"1...2...3..."

Aaron and I ran as fast as we could for the tree, and within 10 seconds, we were in range of another group of Bloodthirsty Swamprunners. They ran after us, but we had a very slight speed advantage, so while they didn't give up chase right away, they couldn't close in on us either.

I heard screeches, and as I looked behind us, I could see arms darting up from the ground, looking to grab onto something at the areas where we had stepped. "Don't slow down," I said. "Those arms are back."

The fog grew thicker as we continued to run, and we ended up stumbling into a thick swarm of small, buzzing mosquitoes. We swatted as we continued to run, assuming that we'd eventually clear the swarm, but the cloud of the tiny insects seemed endless.

They buzzed in my ears, and clung to my arm, and the ones that made it onto my face and neck bit me, knocking down 1 HP with each bite.

"Dude!" Aaron spat with heavy breath, his health bar being depleted 1 HP at a time as well. "This is ridiculous!"

I held out my hand and cast Fire Curtain, in an attempt to do anything, and a long wall of fire formed ahead of us. The insects that got caught in the curtain died instantly and the ones that hadn't been caught, began to disperse far away, trying to avoid the flames.

*You have gained 3 XP!*
*You have gained 3 XP!*
*You have gained 3 XP!*
*You have gained 3 XP!*
*You have gained 3 XP!*
*You have gained 3 XP!*

"Run close to the fire!" I yelled, and when we closed in on the flames the mosquitoes that were latching onto us let go and buzzed away.

I glanced at my stamina bar as we pulled out of the cloud of mosquitoes and fog, and it was already cut down by one third. We reached a small clearing, but far to the left I could see another group of Swamprunner Sorceresses, and far to the right was a massive frog that looked like it could eat either of us alive.

"Rest!" I said, and Aaron and I slowed. We stopped for a second to catch our breath, but I could hear the sound of the Bloodthirsty Swamprunner's feet pattering somewhere behind us. "Never mind." I rolled my eyes in frustration. "Let's go."

We pushed on, and ahead of us I could see a large, long, muddy pond surrounded by alligators. A large, fallen log lay stretched across the center of the pond, and on the left side there were more Swamprunner Sorceresses, and on the other side was tall grass and bamboo—we had no way of telling what lurked inside of there.

When we paused to assess the situation, I could hear the patter of the Swamprunners still coming up behind us.

**Name:** *swamp gator*
**Race:** *animal*
**Level:** *5*
**Health/Mana/Stamina:** *60/0/40*
**Status:** *unknown*

"Over the log?" I suggested. "The gators are only level 5."

Aaron nodded and reached for his spear.

I grabbed my sword and stepped closer to the gators, letting off a Fireblast to the gator closest to the log. It let out a growl and shook its head viciously before it stopped moving and smoke rose out of its dead body.

*You have gained 100 XP!*

That alligators nearby looked alarmed, turned around, and we immediately had 10 alligators or more charging at us.

"Oh shit!" Aaron said.

I raised my hand and cast Fire Curtain in front of the charging gators, and 4 of them died, while another couple of them got scalded by the flames. The two Fire Curtains that I had cast and the Fireblast put a huge dent in my mana, and I had roughly enough for another couple Fireblasts.

Aaron stepped forward and dove his spear into the tip of one of the gator's head, and I swung my sword, slicing open the tip of one of the gator's nose. Another gator lashed out and clenched onto my leg with amazing speed, and I yelled as I switched my attention, slamming the tip of my sword into its head. The gator died, just as I looked up and saw Aaron dashing away from a corpse and going for his second kill. His spear's reach advantage made the gators a perfect target for him.

> You are **bleeding** and require medical attention. Bleeding is a damage-over-time effect.

I slashed at the injured gator, killing it as well when I heard movement coming from behind. I turned and saw the Bloodthirsty Swamprunners had already caught up to us.

"Run!" I yelled

Aaron yanked his spear out of the one of gator's head and when he saw the Swamprunners, he bolted for the log.

Aaron reached the log first, and I was right behind him. A few angry gators clanked their teeth behind us but didn't dare trying climbing onto the log. It was thick, the log, but we both held out our hands as we crossed to keep balance, moving at roughly half our usual run speed.

The Swamprunners didn't seem to mind though. They hopped on the logs, using their spears to balance as they started to cross right behind us.

One the other side of the pond were three more gators, and Aaron jumped off and immediately went into attack. He drove his spear into one just as another clamped onto his leg. I fired a Fireblast at the third and whipped my sword around for a deep thrust into the one that was biting down on Aaron. It released its grip and died.

I looked behind us and the Swamprunners were two-thirds of the way down the log.

"Keep running!" I yelled and grabbed at Aaron's arm.

Aaron took a step forward and stumbled to the ground, grabbing at his leg. "I can't!" he said breathlessly.

"Suck it up! I'll bandage you when we're in a safe spot."

"No, I can't," he said again. "It's not the wound. I'm out of stamina."

I glanced up our status bars and saw that Aaron's stamina was down to 0, and I barely had 20 points left. With just a little bit of stamina remaining, and my mana running low, there was little chance we were going to survive the Swamprunner's attacks.

"You can go... save yourself," Aaron groaned. "I'll try to get back."

I could've kept running, hoping to find a hiding spot with last my last bit of Stamina. Maybe I could've looted Aaron's body and met him back at the runestone. I certainly didn't want to experience the pain of death again. That's what I would've done if I had been playing any other game...run. I had always been a solo player before Eden's Gate, and I didn't like to be held down by other player's weaknesses.

But something inside me just couldn't just leave him there without at least trying to save him. Maybe it was the fact that I knew the pain that he would go through in death, or maybe it was the fact that Jax and

Adeelee had been there for me when I needed them. Hell, even Aaron jumped in and risked his life to save me at the orc camps.

Maybe it was the fact that they weren't just other players; they were my friends. It wasn't something that I was used to saying about other people, but yeah... Aaron was my friend. Jax and Adeelee were my friends.

It didn't feel right to leave my friend to die alone.

I lifted my sword, gripped it with both hands, and strafed in front of Aaron as the Swamprunners stepped off the log and began to line up in front of us. I counted five on the ground and many more pattering their webby feet on the log as they raced to join them.

> *You are **bleeding** and require medical attention. Bleeding is a damage-over-time effect.*

My health was at 70%.

One of the Swamprunners smiled as best as it could with its fishy face and hissed as all five of the ones on the ground rushed towards us.

I fired off a Fireblast, knocking one of them back, and made note that while I didn't have enough mana to fire another, with my mana regenning, I'd have enough for one more in a few seconds. It was all futile, but I was going to take down as many of them as I could before we died. It would give us a better chance of recovering our loot after death.

One of the Swamprunners thrust its spear at me, and I dodged, right before an arrow struck it in the side of the head, killing it immediately. A whizz of arrows filled the air, and another struck one of the monsters that was about to hop on Aaron. Three at a time, arrows flew in the sky, connecting with the bodies of the Swamprunners and alligators nearby. A thick bolt flew into another.

"Ayyyye! Gunnar, matey!" a hard, raspy voice rang out, and through the thick fog, I saw a tangled, red beard appear.

"Kronos?!"

The stout dwarf was sitting on top of plump ram with long horns and a matted white pelt. In his hand was an oversized wooden crossbow, and covering his body was thick, steel plate armor. Right behind him was Jax, sitting on top of Fenris, lobbing off arrows, three at a time from his bow.

Aaron was starting to get up when Kronos raised his crossbow and pointed it at me. "Stand away mate! There's an orc behind ye!"

"Nooo! He's not an—"

Kronos' bolt sped past me and slammed into Aaron's skull with a thud. Aaron's eyes rolled into the back of his head, and his body flopped to the mud as his health fell to zero.

"He's not an orc…" I muttered.

Kronos swung his crossbow around, smacking a Swamprunner across the face, then loaded up another bolt and killed it at point blank range. He hopped off his ram and raised a glowing hand towards me before fastening his crossbow and reaching for the sword he had strapped to his back. It looked like the same sword I had recovered from Nambunga's Cave.

White energy surrounded me, and my health immediately jumped to 100%.

He swung his sword effortlessly at another Swamprunner, barely paying any attention to it as he continued moving towards me, his eyes focused on the furry body behind me. "Not an orc?" he asked. "Then why the hell is he dress'n like that?!"

"It's a long story."

More Swamprunners continued crossing the log and Jax fired an endless stream of arrows, knocking most off the log and into the pond before they could touch down. I reached my hand out and shot a Fireblast into the face of one of the Swamprunners that was about to catch Kronos in the back. Kronos whipped around and severed its head as it screamed from the burns.

Jax lowered his bow and hopped off Fenris as the chaos subsided. "That's all of them," he said.

"What are you guys doing here?" I asked.

> You are **bleeding** and require medical attention. Bleeding is a damage-over-time effect.

I flinched and grabbed at my leg.

"Let's have a look, why don't we?" Kronos kneeled and placed a hand over my alligator bite. A white pulse exited his hand, and my bleeding icon went away.

"I ran into Adeelee on my way to have a drink at the inn in Linden," Jax explained. "She told me about your plan to find a mage to transport you to Gramora. A bit crazy to come here at your level."

"And when I got word from Jax, here, that there might be a portal to Gramora, I jumped on the opportunity," Kronos added. "My town, Stonefort is just a couple zones away. The portal saved me a good week or more of traveling across the Serpent Sea."

Jax continued: "I knew that Eanos was the probably the only guy in Linden who could cast a portal and his lazy ass wouldn't go too far from town to place it. After Kronos and I had a drink, it only took us a few minutes of scouring the outskirts before we found your portal. Fenris caught your scent as soon as we stepped through."

"So you're going to Stonefort too?" I asked.

"No, but I'd figure that I'd make sure Kronos made it to the edge of Gramora safely."

"Oh mate," Kronos said with a laugh. "You know I can handle me own just fine."

Jax smiled. "I guess I wanted to see if a low-level Reborn could survive Gramora as well. Or maybe I still have a soft spot for you, I'm not sure." His tone was kinder than the last time I saw him. Perhaps he had forgiven me about the sword incident.

"Maybe we should've let him die," Kronos said. "I'd like to see a Reborn come back to life."

"Aaron is a Reborn also," I said. "You'll see him when he appears at the runestone we ran from in about 2 hours."

"Another Reborn?" Kronos cried. "And 2 hours?! Eeeeesh!"

There was a loud bubbling sound that came from the pond that we had crossed, and we all turned to see what was happening. Another gurgle filled the air, and then another, right before a large messy mass of green poked its head out of the water. It came up so that its eyes were visible first and paused a moment before bringing its full torso out of the water.

It was huge, a good ten feet tall I imagined, and while it had a torso, arms and legs like a human, it was completely covered in a tangle of seaweed, grass, and vines. It was hunched over with one of its arms visibly longer than the other and its head almost looked like it was wearing a hood with the amount of vegetation that was hanging down from it.

"You-kill-in-my-home..." its sloppy, gurgled voice sputtered, and it slowly started trudging its way out of the pond.

"Stand back, Fenris!" Jax shouted and the wolf stepped several paces away. Jax slowly backed up as well, holding a tight grip on his bow.

"Oh, ho!" Kronos cooed. "Now, I really get to put me brother's sword to use!" He nodded towards his ram, and it turned and ran off into the distance as he lifted his sword and smiled. "I think we might need your help with this one, young Gunnar."

> *You have been invited to join **Kronos' Party**.*
> *Do you accept? Yes/No*

I willed myself to join Kronos' party, and both his and Jax's health bars appeared.

Kronos raised his sword in the air with both hands and touched the hilt against his head. A blast of bright light flashed out, and I suddenly felt more powerful. He touched his hand against the sword again, and another blast of light shot out.

An icon of an orange arrow pointing upwards and another of a white shield with a cross on it appeared below my stats bars.

> **Divine Vigor**: *Your stamina regenerates 100% faster. Spell duration: 3 minutes. Source: Kronos*

> **Divine Resistance:** *You gain 50% resistance against all non-divine magical attacks. Spell duration: 3 minutes. Source: Kronos*

The monster swung its long, viney arm at Kronos just as he was finishing casting his spells, and the dwarf dropped to a prone position just in time to avoid the blow.

Jax started shooting arrows as fast as he could, but when they landed they seemed to have little effect other than irritating the giant, green thing. "Use your magic, Gunnar! He's probably weak to fire!"

I launched a Fireblast at the monster's face as it pounded its fist down in a hammer motion, trying its best to smash a dodging Kronos below. Kronos rolled out of the way, and the monster reared back and let out a gurgling roar when my fire connected.

"More of that!" Kronos shouted and dashed for one of the monster's legs, hacking his sword against its tree-like calves.

I tried to Inspect the monster and was surprised when I got the results.

**Name:** *Swamp Lord*
**Race:** *monster*
**Level:** *25*
**Health/Mana/Stamina:** *400/190/200*
**Status:** *aggressive*

I wasn't sure if I had a lucky dice roll or maybe I was able to see the monster's stats because I was in a group with two obviously higher levels than me, but at level 25, the Swamp Lord was the highest level creature I had seen—or at least had been able to identify.

Jax stopped lobbing arrows at the monster's body and reached into his pouch, pulling out a round vial of black liquid. He reached his arm back and tossed the vial at the monster like a soldier launching a grenade, and when it connected the monster's body, it burst with a loud explosion, sending bits of seaweed, vines, and other organic matter flying in every direction.

I shot another Fireblast at its face right after Jax.

The monster grasped frantically at the fire on its face and the deep, black crater that was left in its chest from Jax's potion and roared. "Arrrrrrgh!"

The green from its longer arm snaked forward, forming a large, viney hammer in front of it, and the Swamp Lord lifted it high in the air and pounded it hard on the ground.

The rumble of the blow knocked all three off us off our feet, and I took 10% damage to my health from the fall. The Swamp Lord swung its hammer again, this time connecting with the fallen Kronos who was still struggling back to his feet.

"Kronos!" Jax yelled.

I glanced at Krono's health bar and could see that he only had 50% of his health taken from the blow, but another hit like that would probably kill him. I shot another Fireblast at the monster as Kronos pulled himself out of the impression made by the Swamp Lord's hammer.

*You have gained 1 point of Wisdom!*

"Ow, me noggin's ringin'!" Kronos said as he scurried away. He raised his palm upwards, and a ball of light surrounded him. He was suddenly back up to 80% health. The dwarf had some amazing healing powers.

I switched to my bow and started launching arrows to avoid draining my mana dry, and the Swamp Lord turned to me. Its eyes glowed, and I lost my footing as a large circle of earth below me turned to soft quicksand-like mud.

"What the hell!" I screamed and grasped for anything, throwing my bow to the hard earth nearby to avoid it sinking in the mud.

Jax looked in my direction and scrambled to the edge of the muddy circle I was sinking in and reached out a hand. "Try to swim here, fast!"

"Alright mates," Kronos spat. "Looks like I need to end this before it gets too ugly!"

"Yeah!" Jax yelled sarcastically as he inched forward trying to get close enough to grab me without falling in himself. "I think that's a good idea!"

I was waist-deep in mud when Kronos lifted his sword and cast something. Light burst out of his blade and the steel continued to glow brightly as he jumped forward, swinging hard at the Swamp Lord's leg, cutting through it like a knife cutting through butter.

The Swamp Lord howled and fell on its stump, swinging an arm in Kronos' direction.

The dwarf held up his sword to block, and when monster's arm made contact, the sword sliced through the limb, leaving it attached, but dangling listlessly by a couple vines.

Jax managed to grab my hand, and pulled me over to solid ground, where I began to climb my way out of the sinking mud. I hadn't even made it all the way out before I turned and angrily sent another Fireblast hurtling at the Swamp Lord's face.

"Now!" Jax yelled and turned to Fenris.

The wolf sprinted forwarded and jumped up, grabbing the monster's partially severed arm with its teeth. It pulled back and darted its head, trying to topple the monster to the ground.

The monster gurgled through its scorched lips and put its remaining arm down on the ground to support itself from falling over completely. Kronos ran to the arm immediately, jumped, and landed a quick foot on the monster's bent elbow. He jumped high again, arching his sword in a downwards, whirling motion as he fell, cutting through half of the Swamp Lord's head in the process. The massive body tumbled to the ground with a thud.

*You have gained 1350 XP!*

"Well, that was fun!" Kronos said with a smile. The glow in his sword faded away and he returned it to his back.

Fenris strolled up the to the body and sniffed curiously. He raised head back and barked a couple of times.

"Found something, boy?" Jax asked. He walked up to where Fenris was sniffing and kneeled down. "Oh… looks like this swamp baddie was packing some goodies. Jax lifted a slimy slab of green from the side of the monster and tugged at something inside until a wet, white pouch fell out of it. "Damn," he said as he opened it to inspect the contents. "500 gold, two inscription powders, a blank runestone, a few rare herbs, a mana potion, and a pair of magic plate gloves."

Jax handed Kronos 125 gold and 250 to me. "You should give half of it to your friend. A bit of an apology for his death."

I nodded. "Are you guys scribes? If not, I could use the runestone and inscription powders."

"What level are you?" Jax asked.

"Just level 1, but I plan on training it."

Jax rolled his eyes then handed the two powders and the runestone.

> *You've received:* **Blank Runestone.** *Durability: 10/10. Quality: Average. Rarity: Rare. Weight: 0.1 kg. A mysterious stone with lots of potential.*

> *You've received:* **Red Inscription Powder.**
> *Durability: 5/5. Quality: Average. Rarity:*
> *Uncommon. Weight: 0.1 kg. Used for*
> *Inscription.*

> *You've received:* **Green Inscription Powder.**
> *Durability: 5/5. Quality: Average. Rarity:*
> *Uncommon. Weight: 0.1 kg. Used for*
> *Inscription.*

"There's only one of us wearing heavy armor!" Kronos tutted.

"I can identify the gloves for you," I said.

"Oh, you have a wand on you, do ya?" Kronos asked.

"No, I can identify by touch."

"What now?! Only high level elves can do that."

"A gift from the Queen," Jax explained as he handed me the gloves.

> *You've received:* **Indestructible Pillager's**
> **Gauntlets**. *+50 Armor. Durability:*
> *1000/1000. Quality: Exceptional. Rarity:*
> *Legendary. Weight: 0.3 kg. +5 Strength.*
> *+20% Chance to Critically Hit. +50%*
> *Critical Damage*

I read the stats off to Kronos and his eyes lit up like a Christmas Tree. "Oh, ho! I've hit the jackpot today!" I handed him the gauntlets and he couldn't get his old ones off fast enough. He put them on his hands and smiled. "They go well with my set! The dwarves in Stonefort will be green with envy."

Jax grinned. "I'll keep the herbs and the potion."

I took the chance to inspect Kronos and Jax. I could tell that they were much higher level than me, especially with how easily they handled the level 25 monster.

| KRONOS ROCKFOOT | |
|---|---|
| Race: | Dwarf |
| Level: | 23 |
| Title: | Adventurer |
| Health/Mana/Stamina: | 200/170/160 |
| Strength: | 37 |
| Dexterity: | 22 |
| Intelligence: | 26 |
| Vitality: | 33 |
| Wisdom: | 17 |
| Willpower: | 45 |
| Charisma: | 16 |

| JAX HORN | |
|---|---|
| Race: | Human |
| Level: | 19 |
| Title: | Forester |
| Health/Mana/Stamina: | 170/110/190 |
| Strength: | 23 |
| Dexterity: | 29 |
| Intelligence: | 20 |
| Vitality: | 25 |
| Wisdom: | 10 |
| Willpower: | 27 |
| Charisma: | 25 |

"We were headed for a dungeon inside the weeping willow. If you guys have time, it would awesome if you helped us crawl through it." I couldn't believe I was saying that even when I was saying it. I had never been the type to admit when I needed help with something. I was independent and liked handling things on my own...

But the longer I spent inside of Eden's Gate, the more I realize why Rachel thought it was so important that I have friends.

Kronos glance up to the sky. "Ohh... Sorry mate. There's not much light left in the sky, and the nasty bits like to lurk around here late at night. I'll need to get out of Gramora before that happens."

"Jax?" I asked.

Jax turned to his companion, and Kronos said, "Up to you, my friend. I'll have no problem making it out of Gramora on my own."

Jax huffed. "How much time on your portal?"

"Eanos said it would expire in 24 hours, so tomorrow morning."

"Alright... I'll go check it out with you. But I'll only go as far as it's safe. If things get too sticky, you're on your own." Jax looked up and surveyed our surroundings. "Kronos, if you have time before you leave, might you help us clear a path from the runestone to the tree?"

Kronos smirked and reached for his sword again. "I guess I have a wee bit of time for some more mashing."

# Chapter 26

*01/06/0001*

"Thank you my friend," Jax said when we made it back to the runestone, reaching a hand out towards Kronos.

"Anytime, matey!" Kronos replied, shaking it vigorously.

We must have killed 50 or so more monsters to clear a path to the dungeon, but Kronos and Jax did most of the work, dispatching the good majority of them with a single swipe or arrow to the head. Luck was on our side as we didn't run into any more higher level creeps like the Swamp Lord or whatever the thing was the had killed me and Aaron.

I managed to gain another level from all the XP, 10 HP, and finally made it to level 2 in block. Jax and Kronos bagged most of the loot to sell off, but I scavenged another 100 gold, and a couple of health potions. Through it all, my armor had taken a beating.

"I'm not an orc! I'm not an orc! I'm not an orc!" I turned to see a sparkly, translucent image of Aaron curled up in a fetal position, eyes closed, gradually filling out into his body.

"They really are Reborns…" Kronos muttered as he watched Aaron come into view. Both he and Jax looked mesmerized.

Aaron opened his eyes and screamed as soon as he saw Kronos. "Don't kill me! Please! I swear I'm not an orc!"

"It's okay, man," I said. "They're not going to kill you."

Aaron scurried up to his feet and darted his eyes around. "We've lost a lot of time. We've got to make another run for the dungeon."

Jax tossed a large sack at Aaron's feet. "All your gear is inside."

"They helped clear a path to the tree. We can make it there without any issues now." I handed Aaron 125 gold. "And here's your share from some sort of boss monster we killed."

"Use it to buy yourself some decent-people clothes when you're back in town!" Kronos cried.

Jax and I both started laughing.

Aaron scratched his head and gave an embarrassed smile. "I will… and thank you for the help."

"And better yet, Jax and Fenris is coming with us," I added.

Aaron looked back and forth from the dwarf to the hunter, not sure who was who.

I introduced the three of them and gave Aaron a 15-second history of how I met Jax and Kronos before Kronos indicated that he needed to leave. He closed his eyes and pounded both of his fists to the ground, summoning his ram.

"I came across a divine spell in a spellbook before you guys showed up," I said.

"Oh… What spell?" Kronos asked.

"Divine Sight."

"Oh...! That's a rare spell, but I'm afraid I already know that one."

"Actually, I was hoping you could teach me Divine Magic before you leave."

Kronos chuckled. "Well, you're lucky that I just hit the minimum level to teach someone divine. I suppose it wouldn't hurt to try. Come over here, young Gunnar."

I walked over to Kronos and had to kneel so that my head was in reaching distance.

He put his thick, stubby palm over me and cleared his throat. "How does that saying go? Oh yeah… With my Divinity, I release your Divinity! Become one with the Divine!

There was click inside of me, and it felt like energy was being released in my body. It was a bit different than when I learned fire magic, but it was a power surge nonetheless.

> *Advancement! You have learned the skill:* **Divine Magic***. Now you can literally count your blessings! Divine Magic is linked the base stat Intelligence. Increase your Intelligence to increase your ability to perform Divine Magic.*

"Thank you," I said.

"Hey, can I get some of that too?" Aaron asked. "I wouldn't mind learning some magic…"

"You have a divine spell to learn also?" Kronos asked.

"No, not yet. But I might as well open up the branch for when I do. Divine would be the perfect fit for me."

"Without a scroll or spell, I don't see any rea—"

"Hey, dude. You put a crossbow bolt in my forehead. It would be a nice way for me to forget the little 'accident'."

Kronos snarled and squeezed his fist, but then his face softened. "Alright, come over here then... And sorry for the thunkin' to your head."

Aaron kneeled and Kronos repeated the same process on him, releasing his divine magic abilities. After that, we all shook Kronos' hand and he trotted off on his ram.

I pulled up my stats, and since I had made so much progress in my Swords and Archery leveling, I decided to throw my unused LP into Dodge. I dropped one AP into Intelligence for a little extra magic damage, one in Vitality for durability, and one into Dexterity to help round out my archery and sword fighting skills.

# GUNNAR LONG

| | |
|---|---|
| Race: | Human |
| Level: | 9 (Progress 20%) |
| Title: | None |
| Health/Mana/Stamina: | 140/120/120 |
| Strength: | 18+ |
| Dexterity: | 20 |
| Intelligence: | 24+ |
| Vitality: | 14+ |
| Wisdom: | 14 |
| Willpower: | 13 |
| Charisma: | 10 |
| AR Rating: | 27 |
| Resists: | |

10% Fire Resistance
15% Water Resistance

Traits:

Elven Touch

Primary Skills:

First Aid Lvl 3: progress 0%
Sneak Lvl 3: progress 10%
Inspect Lvl 3: progress 0%
Tinkering Lvl 1: progress 0%
Summon Beast: Mastered
Inscription Lvl 1: progress 0%

Combat Skills:

Dodge Lvl 4: progress 0%
Small Blades Lvl 2: progress 0%
Backstab Lvl 1: progress 0%
Archery Lvl 4: progress 60%
Block Lvl 2: progress 5%
Swords Lvl 4: progress 75%
Snipe Shot Lvl 2: progress 0%
Dirty Fighting Lvl 1: progress 0%

Magic Skills:

Fire Magic Lvl 5: progress 75%
Divine Magic Lvl 1: progress 0%

There was a loud reptilian growl somewhere in the distance.

"We've got to move fast. We're almost out of light," Jax said.

Aaron pulled on the last bit of his armor, and we all jogged towards the weeping willow in the center of the swamp.

Just approaching the tree was foreboding. Though it was three or four stories tall, its large branches stretched out in every direction and its stringy flora hung so low that it touched the ground in some places. In a way, it gave a feeling like it was alive, and I don't mean the way that plants are alive, but more like it could sense our presence and was going to rise out of the ground and attack at any second. Given the kind of creatures I had already encountered in the swamp, I wouldn't have been surprised.

At the base of its massive trunk, a rusty metal door had been built in its side, and Aaron wasted no time yanking on the handle as soon as we were upon it. A cool, musty breeze shot out as soon as he did. Inside the door, I could see large steps gradually leading down in a spiral pattern, but beyond that was pitch black.

It would be a tight squeeze for Fenris to fit inside, but he'd probably be able to make it.

I pulled out the tattered spellbook with the Divine Sight spell inside, and when I flipped to the page, the words practically flew off the paper when I started to read.

> *Advancement! You have learned the spell:*
> ***Divine Sight.***

I attempted to cast the spell on myself first, and when I raised my palm and closed my eyes, a cool, almost shocking energy jumped out of me. It wasn't nearly the same warm, almost violent feeling that I got when I performed fire magic.

All around me, everything became crystal clear, and when I looked down the stairs that led to the dungeon, it was like I was staring at a well-lit room.

One-fourth of my mana was eaten by the spell, and an icon of a bright, yellow eye appeared below my stat bars.

> **Divine Sight:** *Your eyes can see through the darkest of darks, and you have immunity to blinding spells and attacks. Duration: 20 minutes.*

I turned and tried to cast the spell on Jax and then again on Aaron. Light circled their eyes for a moment then faded, and they both confirmed that they could see the same as me.

"I'll go first… There's no high-level monsters in here, so it should be easy from here on out."

Jax and I nodded, and Aaron started leading us down the stairs. I was behind him, followed by Jax and lastly Fenris."

The stairs looped again and again, leading us further and further underground. After the tenth circle, Fenris barked a few times.

"What is it, buddy?" Jax asked.

He barked a couple more times.

"Fenris says he senses danger ahead," Jax explained. "You sure there's nothing but low levels in here?"

"Wait," I said to Jax. "He *told* you that there's danger ahead? As-in the wolf can talk to you?"

"I thought you knew," Jax replied, creasing his brow. "After you're bonded to a pet for long enough you can understand each other's speech more than simple gestures."

"Wow…"

"He must have picked up on the rats and snakes that are down in this area," Aaron said, not impressed by the human to animal speech, apparently.

When we were only a few spirals away from reaching the floor, we could see Aaron was wrong. Etched across the walls and sticking to the lower spirals were spider webs. Some of them were free of inhabitants, but many of them had nasty looking black spiders with pointy legs the size of crowbars and bodies the size of basketballs, red stripes down the center of their back.

*Name: Cave Weaver*
*Race: Insect*
*Level: 4*
*Health/Mana/Stamina: 25/0/25*
*Status: unknown*

At the bottom of the cave were a few even bigger spiders with abdomens the size of beach balls and legs twice the size as the ones hanging on the sides. The larger ones each stood guard over a cluster of fat, cream-colored eggs.

**Name:** *Cave Spinner*
**Race:** *insect*
**Level:** *9*
**Health/Mana/Stamina:** *100/20/150*
**Status:** *unknown*

Did I mention that I hate spiders? When I was back on Earth, any encounter with a spider generally resulted in the war of worlds and near panic. If there wasn't something around that I could spray it with from a distance, then I'd resort to throwing any inanimate object at it until I killed it or it at least got far, far, away from my personal space.

And that was for spiders the size of pennies. These things were monsters.

"What the hell?" Aaron said. "These all weren't in here before…"

"One must have wandered in and bred," Jax said.

My heart was racing as we passed the weavers. Occasionally, I would see one make a subtle adjustment to their legs, but none of them attacked. I took another step, and the side of my face connected with a sticky web that I hadn't seen, probably because my eyes were glued to the spiders surrounding us.

"Fuck!" I spat and lashed out, slapping wildly at my own face. "Fuck, I can't do this!" I turned and pushed past Jax, trying to go back up the stairs and distance myself from the spiders as much as possible.

"Hey, wait!" Aaron shouted.

"Nope. I can do monsters but I can't do spiders. A virtual game, sure, but this shit is too real."

As I tried to push past Fenris—whose body was taking up pretty much the entire step he was standing on—I tried hugging the very edge of the steps, cautious to avoid the spiderwebs on the other side. That's when I accidently stepped on Fenris' tail, which caused him yelp low and pull his tail away, the force causing me to slip and fall backwards and down to the floor below.

I screamed as I fell back, my life flashing before my eyes as I imagined getting devoured by my greatest fear, landing on a soft bundle of eggs on the floor below. My head jolting back in the fall, and my health dropped by 20%.

"Gunnar!" Aaron yelled.

My eyes were wide with fear as the Cave Spinner protecting the eggs jumped on me immediately, and the other two nearby let out a high-pitched screech. I held my hands up, pushing away as the spider snapped at me with nasty, wet fangs, and my stomach turned at its beady, arachnid eyes.

I shot an immediate Fireblast right between those eyes.

The blast knocked the spider away, and I reflexively willed a Fire Curtain in a circle around me. I wasn't even sure if I could cast a curtain in a circle, but it damn sure worked, and the spiders on the floor continued screeching as they were blocked from accessing their prey… me.

I looked up and saw that the spiders' screams had apparently awakened the weavers, and Jax was shooting arrows at spiders that were making their way off their webs and towards them. Aaron was driving his spear into anything that came near while Fenris was swatting them away with his paw.

I stood there in the middle of my fire on the edge of a panic attack. I wanted to crawl into a hole. Maggots were nasty, sure. Skeletons, goblins, swamp monsters and orcs were dangerous, sure. But spiders were just something else entirely.

I was trapped in a fucking nightmare.

Jax glanced down at me. "Don't just stand there, Gunnar!" he said as he launched another arrow. "We've got to kill these things."

I closed my eyes and swallowed hard as I tried to calm myself. *Stay calm*, I said to myself. *Stay calm.*

My Fire Curtain started to fade, and the moment I could see the eyes of another Cave Spinner, I immediately cast another Fire Curtain around me.

"Da fuck are you doing?!" Aaron yelled. "Blow your mana killing them, not on hiding!"

"Fenris, go!" Jax yelled, and in the corner of my eyes, I saw Fenris leap onto the floor and could hear the screech of spiders and the crunching sound of Fenris' jaw clamping into something crispy. Jax pulled out his sword and ran down the last couple spiral of stairs as my second Fire Curtain began to fade.

He dove his sword into one of the spinners and Fenris jumped onto another, making short order of the last of the eight-legged creatures on the floor. Aaron dove his spear into a final weaver and then ran down to where the rest of us were.

"What the hell was that?" Aaron asked.

I breathed heavily and tried to stop my hands from trembling. "I'm sorry... I just can't stand spiders. Something about them triggers me."

"Something about them is going to get us all eaten alive if you keep pulling stunts like that!" Aaron barked.

Off to the side, I could see Fenris lapping up the innards of one of the Cave Spinners and Jax was using his sword to slash patches of thick spider webs that were holding down the eggs, stuffing it in his bag.

"This is amazing!" Jax said. "Spider's Silk is hard to find... I need it for at least 3 recipes. If I had only brought some empty vials so I could collect some venom as well."

It was hard for me to understand how spiders had such a profound effect on me, but didn't seem to bother Jax and Aaron at all.

I pushed myself to my feet as I started to get my bearings. "Rats and snakes?" I asked.

Aaron shrugged. "Eden's Gate changes organically. A level of a zone or even a whole dungeon can be taken over by a totally different group of creatures as they move around. I'm just surprised that this one changed so soon." Aaron turned to one of the Cave Spinner carcasses. "Judging by how big these guys are, they must have eaten most of the low-level creatures that were inside."

"Alright, well how far 'til we reach your hidden portal?"

"If I remember right, this dungeon goes on for five levels, but the portal is at the end of level three."

"Let's hurry," I said. "I want to get out of here as soon as possible."

Jax threw another patch of Spider's Silk in his bag and stood up. "Ready."

The circular room that we were standing in had only one path forward, and we set forth down the hallway. The walls throughout the dungeon were a dark gray of uneven stones without markings, and in the hallway, there were several sealed tombstones set in crevices near the floor. Jax tried to push a couple of them open, but they were sealed—by magic or something else.

Thankfully, there was only one other spider that was in the hallway—a Cave Weaver—which Jax dispatched from afar with a Snipe Shot, but when we got close to the next chamber, Fenris started barking again.

"More up ahead," Jax said. "Be alert."

Jax took the lead and, waving his blade in front of him, cut away random spiderwebs that were blocking our path, and once we were at the arch of the next chamber, he hugged his body against each side of the hall, trying to get as much of a survey of what was inside as possible.

"Looks like there's Cave Weavers covering the walls nearest to us, and there's a single Cave Spinner sitting inside right in the center of the room."

"Aw fuck," I said. I thought I wasn't going to panic anymore, but my fear of spiders was uncontrollable.

"Look," Jax said. "The Cave Weavers didn't attack until you fell on the nest of eggs and upset the Spinners, and though the bigger ones seem aggressive, I don't think they'll attack until we're in a certain proximity to the eggs. If you can hold your shit together, we might be able to walk by these guys without a fight."

"I don't know," I said. "Maybe we should just kill them."

"Listen to Jax," Aaron said. "It'll save us a lot of time if we can avoid a fight with another group of spiders."

I gritted my teeth and swallowed. "Alright, I'll try."

"Keep your guard up but don't attack, Fenris," Jax said to the wolf. Fenris reared his head back, which I assume meant that he understood.

Jax and Fenris stepped slowly into the chamber, followed by Aaron. I timidly brought up the rear, following along as our group hugged the cave wall, walking within inches of the Cave Weavers and their webs.

Thick cobwebs formed ropes on the floor and led to the center of the circular room where a Cave Spinner sat, guarding a batch of eggs like the ones we saw in the first room. Right behind the eggs and the Cave Spinner was a large hole where the cobwebs fell and disappeared to wherever the hole led—I imaged to the $2^{nd}$ level of the dungeon.

The Cave Spinner turned its body and licked its fangs as we moved across the room, looking like at any moment it was going to pounce. It didn't leave its eggs, however, as we continued to circle along the outer edge, closer and closer to the other hemisphere of the room where there were no spiders or webs.

My brow was sweating as a Cave Weaver lifted its legs and rubbed them together right beside my face. The sound of its bristly limbs felt like nails across a chalkboard, and I was certain that if I had been even a little older than I was, I would've needed an adult diaper to keep myself from losing control.

"Almost there," Aaron whispered calmly. "Keep it together, man."

Jax reached the bare portion of the stone floor first, and when Fenris stepped off of the webbing, he lifted his legs and started to shake them individually as if he were getting an invisible icky off his paws. I practically darted to the other side of the room when there were just a few steps left, and I bent over and put my hands on my knees as if I had just run a marathon.

A loud, female laugh echoed from below us and bounced off the walls, causing the webs that the weavers were hanging on to shake. All three of us jumped at the foreboding sound, and Jax readied his sword as if he were about to fight.

The Cave Spinner guarding the eggs reared on its hind legs then scurried down the hole in the center of the room at a frightening speed.

"What the hell was that?" I asked.

"I don't know..." Aaron said. "But there's definitely something else lurking in here."

"We'll find out soon enough. Let's move," Jax said.

There was a small hallway in front of us which led to another room, thankfully free of any cobwebs or spiders. As we walked further down the hall, I could see that the room was virtually empty, save for a small hole just slightly bigger than a human, and behind the hole was a half-human, half-fish skeleton that appeared to have once been some variation of a swamprunner. In its hand was long spear with a sparkling tip and draped on its skull was a ringmail coif. Off to its side was a sparkling red gem, a dusty scroll and a small mess of coins.

Feeling comfortable that we were further away from the spiders, I stepped into the room and started for the coins. There was a click noise that sounded when my foot landed on a loose stone, and I felt it sink a little under my foot.

Two darts shot out from each side of the room, one landing in my shoulder and the other landing in my neck, wiping out 30% of my health.

> *You have been **poisoned** and require medical attention. Poison is a weakening and damage-over-time affect.*

"Ow!" I yanked the tiny darts out of my skin and dropped them to the floor.

"Damnit!" Jax grunted. "I haven't been in a dungeon for a while. Forgetting the basics."

Jax placed his hand on the floor and scanned the room while I pulled out my cure potion and guzzled it. The poison alert went away, and I suffered no further damage.

"I don't sense any other traps," Jax said.

"Thanks…" I muttered.

I grabbed the skeleton's gear first.

> *You've received: **Swamp Defender's Spear**. 10-15 Attack Damage. Durability: 7/10.*

> *Quality: Great. Rarity: Rare. Weight: 2.1. +3 Dexterity.*

> *You've received:* **Rusty Chainmail Coif.** *+6 Armor. Durability: 4/10. Quality: Poor. Rarity: Common. Weight: 0.9 kg* **Price: 15 Gold**

I read the stats off and handed them to Aaron. "I think you'll want these…"

"Oh yeah…" He cooed. "One step closer to not looking like an orc." He slid the coif on his head and dropped his old spear. He tested the new spear by twirling it and thrusting it forward a few times.

I counted 30 gold on the ground which I split three ways between us.

> *You've received:* **Ruby.** *Durability: 100/100. Quality: Exceptional. Rarity: Common. Weight: 0.1 kg.*

> **You've received: Scroll: Boiling Blood I.** *Your inner flame boils your blood, increasing your movement, attack speed, and physical attack damage by 35% for 15 seconds. Your willpower is increased by 200% during this time. Can only be activated when you're at 50% health or less. Requires 20 Intelligence. Fire Magic Level 6. Durability: 7/10. Quality: Average. Rarity: Epic. Weight: 0.1 kg*

I tossed the ruby to Jax and read of the details of the scroll to both of my party members.

"Epic find, dude," Aaron said as I bagged the scroll. My fire magic was only at 80% progress in level 5, so I couldn't use the item yet, but I was really looking forward to putting it to the test.

Jax leaned over to the hole in the ground and indicated a metal ladder that led down. "Well, Fenris isn't going to fit down this," he said. He walked over to his wolf and kneeled, grabbing his head and rubbing violently while the wolf licked all over his face. "We'll see each other again soon, buddy. Go get some rest."

The wolf howled and dashed back towards the room of the spiders, disappearing before he aggravated anything.

I kicked the humanoid skeleton over and its bones toppled to the ground. "Let's hope whatever got this guy doesn't offer us the same fate."

I cast another round of Divine Sight on all three of us, careful that we didn't run out of light, and Jax started down the hole first.

# Chapter 27

### *Day 6 (Earth)*

The Secretary of Defense opened the door to the control room. "Total blackout, sir. We're not detecting any unauthorized networks running."

The President smiled. "Thank you, Bill." He turned his head to Kendra. "And your blockchain software is still running without issues?"

Kendra pressed a button on her computer. "I can still see the blockchain running."

"We've had Canada and Mexico offline for four hours now," Senator Gates said. "It would be a benefit to the American people if we just pulled everything offline right after midnight."

"But you told the public tomorrow," Kendra said. "No one will be expecting a blackout tonight."

"We did tell everyone tomorrow," the President agreed.

"But we didn't tell them what time tomorrow. If we took the core down overnight, we could probably have a good chunk of infrastructure back online by the time everyone gets to work tomorrow," the Senator explained. "It would save the country billions of dollars."

The President arched his hands in front of his face and twiddled his fingers together. He was lost in thought for a moment before he turned to Kendra. "Is there any reason why that wouldn't work?"

Kendra swallowed, almost choking on the lump in her throat. "I mean, technically we could go offline at any time, but we should still allow the originally planned amount of time for Aaron to open the data port."

"If he was going to open anything, he would've done it already." The Senator slammed his hand down hard on the table.

"And... and..." Kendra stuttered trying to come up with any other excuse, "what of the people who aren't expecting it so early?"

"Oh, that's hogwash," the Senator countered. "There'll be less people affected by launching it in the middle of the night, and that's a fact."

Kendra sighed and turned to the President with pleading eyes.

The President tapped his fingers together a few moments as he considered his options, then leaned back in his chair. "Senator Gates is right. Let's go ahead and get this fiasco over with. We've disrupted enough lives already, and I'm anxious to put this all in the past." He placed a hand on the table and looked up at the Secretary of Defense. "Get all the officers we have stationed on the phone, and let's plan to have this thing shut down after midnight."

"Yes, Mr. President." The Secretary turned and walked out of the door for the 20th time that day.

Kendra's heart sank. There wasn't much time left— a few hours at most, depending on how fast they were able coordinate the shutdown. Her computer still read 'no signal' and as every second passed, she feared that was the way it was going to stay.

# Chapter 28

*01/06/0001*

There was another female's laugh when we dropped down the 2nd level of the dungeon. The laugh was so sinister sounding that it sent chills up my spine.

Ahead of us was a large, square room that had mysterious table in the center with a torch burning a strange, blue light. The rest of the room was empty.

Jax placed his hand on the ground and scanned the surroundings. "This room is trapped too," he muttered.

"Where?" Aaron asked.

Jax pointed towards an area near the table.

Aaron and I didn't see anything.

"It's a single, thin silk. Look," Jax said and drew an arrow. "Get ready to hurry back up the ladder if we need to."

He let the arrow fly, and when it struck the line of webbing, the silk glistened and broke. The sound of steel grinding against stone bounced off the walls, and four massive pendulums with axe blades on each end swung down from the ceiling and continued to swing back and forth.

"There's our trap," Jax said.

"Someone's put in work here." Aaron slapped me on the shoulder. "That would've been worse than the little dart you got."

"No kidding," I said.

Jax studied the pendulums for a moment and said. "One at a time…"

The pendulums swung in unsynchronized timing, and as they passed, they let out a loud 'whoosh' as they passed. I had no doubt that contact with them would kill any of us, including Jax.

Jax went first, waiting for the first pendulum to swing by, and stepped ahead of it just enough that he cleared it but wasn't in range of the next one. When the second pendulum swung, he dashed forward into the larger clearing near the table. The last two pendulums swung so that the blades intercepted each other near the ground at almost the same time, so Jax dashed ahead at full speed to clear them both at the same time. We couldn't see him at the other end after he cleared, so we could only assume he made it okay.

I went next, following the same pattern that Jax made to cross the first two pendulums, but when I made it to the table, I paused. The strange torch was sitting on top of a platform that was raised off the ground no more than a millimeter, but in that tiny crevice, I could see a piece of parchment poking out of the edge. I tugged at the end to pull it out.

> *You've Received:* **Schematic: Runestone of Arcane Resistance**. *Adds arcane magic resistance. Requires 15 Intelligence. Requires Inscription Lvl 2. Requires: Blue Inscription Powder. Durability: 8/10. Quality: Average. Rarity: Rare. Weight: 0.1 kg*

That reminded me that I still had a schematic in my bag along with its requirements that I needed to craft. I bagged the new schematic, and after watching the timing of the pendulums, I dashed ahead and met Jax at the other side.

Aaron made it through a little more sloppily, barely missing each pendulum by an inch, but thankfully he made it through unscathed.

There was another narrow hallway that we passed through that led to another large, square room and inside the room was nothing but six fish-humanoid skeletal remains that were resting in a sitting position on either side of the room. The furthest two skeletons were gripping onto bows, and the closest four were holding onto curved swords and round wooden shields.

Jax kneeled down and surveyed the room. "I'm not detecting any traps."

"Well, then let's loot up and move on," Aaron said and skipped towards the closest skeleton.

There was another female laugh that echoed throughout the dungeon, and before Aaron could make it to the skeleton to loot it, its bones began to shake. He stepped back, and all the skeletons began to rattle wildly.

We all readied our weapons as the skeletons suddenly sprung to life and stood to their feet. They trembled as they started moving towards us, but in the most unusual way: their heads looked limp and their bodies looked loose and limber. Their feet skipped across the ground.

*Name:* Skeletal Puppet Archer
*Race:* undead
*Level:* 11
*Health/Mana/Stamina:* 100/0/200
*Status:* aggressive

*Name:* Skeletal Puppet Warrior
*Race:* undead
*Level:* 11
*Health/Mana/Stamina:* 120/0/180
*Status:* aggressive

The fact that they moved strangely didn't affect how dangerous they were. One of the bow wielders sent an arrow whizzing right past my head before any of any of us could figure out was going on.

"Attack!" Jax yelled.

I slung a Fireblast at one of the warriors, which was powerful enough to knock it back and to the ground, then pivoted and slashed my sword at another one of the warriors. It blocked my sword with its shield and then swung back, which I blocked with my sword. Still, its blow was powerful, and the reverb from his strike cost me 10% of my health.

"This isn't good!" Jax cried as he fired off a string of arrows that landed without damage into one of the warrior's shields. Another arrow whizzed by my head and struck Jax in the shoulder. He yelped and grabbed at the arrow, yanking it out immediately, then fastened his bow and pulled out his sword.

I shot a Fireblast at the skeleton I was fighting, knocking it back, but then I felt cold steel course down my back as another skeleton made its move on me. I groaned, and my eyes went wide, but before I turned to face the other skeleton, I saw that Aaron was about to get cleaved and fired a Fireblast at his attacker, knocking it back and saving his life.

I turned as quickly as I could and a curved blade was rushing to my face. I had just enough time to raise my sword to block it, but another 10% was knock off my health. Add that with the damage that I had taken to my back, and I was at 60% health. The wound must have not been deep as no bleeding indicator popped up.

The skeleton lifted its sword and swung down again, but I rolled forward, out of the way, and whirled my sword at one of its legs, knocking it to the ground.

"Back into the hallway!" Aaron yelled. "There's too many of them!"

I stood to my feet, and we all ran back into the hallway towards the swinging pendulums. When I turned, I could see the skeletons that we had dropped simply standing back up and coming towards us.

"What the hell?" Aaron asked. "They don't seem to take damage…"

"My arrows didn't affect them at all…"

The skeleton's marched forward in twos, and the small hallway blocked any opportunity for the archers to hit us with arrows. Jax and I stood at the other end, and Aaron stood behind us, ready to push his poker forward in any hole that he saw an opening.

The warriors swung their swords at Jax and I, and we blocked, parried and knocked the skeletons back, but they just kept coming no matter how many times we knocked them down. I fired a Fireblast at one of them, and that's when I noticed the light of the fire glisten off a tiny string that was attached to one of the skeletons.

I looked up and all across the ceiling were webs, and tiny, near-invisible strands of spider silk were strung down, attached the skeleton's bodies. It felt like a bit of a 'derp' moment, as I should have figured it out the moment I saw the name of the monsters and the unusual way they moved.

I parried one of the skeleton's attacks and swung my sword above its head, clipping the strings that were attached to its body, and immediately the skeleton fell.

"They have strings!" I yelled. "Stop fighting them and clip their strings."

Jax kicked out at a skeleton, causing it to buckle then swung across its head, and it fell. Again and again we did this until each of the skeletons were severed at the cord, and all that was left was a heap of bones and threads of useless spider's silk dangling from the ceiling.

When all was said and done, we all sat on the floor near the bones to allow our wounds to heal. Jax bandaged his wounds and pulled out a food ration. I pulled out two food rations as well and tossed one to Aaron.

"This was supposed to be easy," I said.

"It should have been..." Aaron said. "I guess one of the appeals of the world is that it's unpredictable. Even NPCs can throw you for a loop."

"NPCs?" Jax asked. "What is that?"

Aaron and I laughed.

"Don't worry about it, man," Aaron said. "It's Reborn language."

Jax scrunched his brow. He clearly wasn't pleased with the answer.

While I waited for my health to refill, I pulled out my blank runestone and the red inscription powder. I placed the schematic for the Runestone of Minor Fire damage nearby and began to chisel out the design. My creation didn't look too bad compared to what was on the parchment, but I was a bit off in some spots.

I poured the red inscription powdered on the stone and it glowed then snapped.

> You've received: **Runestone of Minor Fire Damage**. +1 fire damage on hit. Durability: 10/10. Quality: Poor. Rarity: Rare. Weight: 0.1 kg

Another not-so-impressive craft attempt, but just the one success brought my progress in inscription up to 30%

I offered the runestone to Jax, but he didn't have any items with open slots, and I was already sure Aaron didn't have any slots, so I placed the runestone up to the remaining open slot on Mythanthar's Blade and it was sucked right in. The sword didn't feel much different with the added rune, but it was more comfortable in my hands without an open groove on the hilt.

Once we were all healed up, we searched the skeletal bodies, but pretty much everything that they had was trash. The swords were rusted out, and their bows were warped short bows. Nothing that was better than our current equipment. We passed on picking anything up and moved forward.

There was a set of steps that led downward at the other end of the room, and at the bottom of the steps was a closed, steel door.

# Chapter 29

*01/06/0001*

When we swung open the door, the stench of death filled the air. Inside the room, I could see cobwebs lining nearly the entire room, and immediately my skin began to crawl. Hanging from the ceiling were several cocoons of what looked to be humanoid bodies and a few other cocoons that just looked like heavy sacks.

"What the hell is this?" I asked low.

"I don't know, but it doesn't look pretty," Jax said. He kneeled and placed his hands against the ground as he surveyed. "No traps that I can see."

The room was wide and long, the biggest room we had encountered so far, and the number of bodies hanging from the ceiling had to have numbered the hundreds. At first it seemed like the room was uncontested, but as we neared the far door, two enemies were standing guard, both holding long halberds in their hands. They didn't seem to notice us yet.

*Name: Arachnid Guard*
*Race: monster*
*Level: 19*
*Health/Mana/Stamina: 210/0/190*
*Status: unknown*

The two monsters had cream colored torsos of nude, human women, both with short black hair and scaled to the size of humans, but below their abdomens were long, black bodies that curved to the back, and attached to that body were eight massive legs. Some sort of half-human, half spider abomination.

I immediately felt unsettled, but the fact that they had human torsos—and nice boobs I must add—made them a bit less intimidating to me for some reason. "Level 19?" I whispered.

"Are you sure you guys want to do this?" Jax asked. "I can probably take one of them on my own, but two of them will be a challenge at your levels."

"We don't have a choice," Aaron said. "The portal is in the next chamber. We *have* to get through. I'm only level 5, but I'll dish out as much damage as I can."

"You're level 5?" I asked, surprised that he was just now mentioning his progress.

"Yeah… almost level 6. I've been fighting monsters much higher level than me with you, so I've been getting good experience. I'm not going to say "DING!" every time I level if that's what you're expecting."

I shook my head at the clown and raised an eyebrow. "Okay, well what's the plan?"

"We'll need to take one out at a time, so focus all fire on one." Jax turned to Aaron. "What's your archery level?"

"2…"

"Okay, then you can't learn Snipe Shot yet. Gunnar and I will try to Snipe Shot one of them, and you just prepare for them to close in."

Aaron nodded.

Jax and I readied our arrows and focused on the monster that was guarding the right-hand side of the door. We both paused, and I made my sure my body was completely still as my vision zoomed in to the area right at the base of arachnid's throat.

"1…" Jax whispered, "2…3."

We both let our arrows fly and looked up in anticipation of two critical shots, but instead, the moment our arrows were close to the guard, a translucent blue shield surrounded the creature, and our arrows simply bounced off and fell to the floor.

"Oh, bloody hell…" Jax mumbled.

The two guards look up, hissed and scurried towards us so fast that I almost didn't have time to ready my sword.

Both hybrids swung their halberds at Jax and I nearly at the same time, and when I tried to block the swing, my sword was knocked to my side from the force. The monster whipped her halberd back in the other direction, and the sharp point of the razor-sharp blade, ripped through my abdomen in the area where my chestpiece had been shredded. 30% of my health was knocked away from that single attack.

> *You are **bleeding** and require medical attention. Bleeding is a damage-over-time effect.*

Aaron jumped in and dove his spear into the side of the spider-being, and it screeched, raising its hand with a blow across the side of Aaron's face.

Just that one blow took 50% of Aaron's heath and sent Aaron sliding against the ground.

The hybrid raised its halberd again, ready to slam it down on me, and I shot a Fireblast between her breasts, trying to stop her attack. But again, an almost-clear blue shield surrounded her, and my Fireblast had no effect.

I rolled to the side, barely missing a blow that might have ended my life, and slashed my sword against one of its legs, knocking off a chunk of hard, black material. I saw a momentary spark where I landed the blow, a small amount of fire from my runestone coming into play. The hybrid reared back and started shaking the wounded leg erratically.

"They're completely immune to ranged attacks!" I yelled. "Even my magic doesn't work!"

Jax's sword clanked against other hybrid's halberd, and he ducked, dodged and jumped as he fought solo. I saw him land a solid blow against the monster's torso, but he was chipping away at her very slowly at best.

I hurried towards Aaron as he picked himself off the ground. "Are you okay?" I asked.

"Behind you!" I turned again and the halberd was coming for my face. I ducked, and when I raised my head back up to counter attack, the hybrid leaned forward and opened its mouth wide.

Strings of thick, sticky spider's silk shot from somewhere deep within her throat and landed on me hard, knocking me to the ground and locking me there.

The webs stuck to my body, my arms and the ground, making even the slightest movement difficult.

"Run!" I yelled to Aaron.

Aaron held out his spear as the hybrid turned his attention to him, and I knew that there was little chance would survive for more than a few seconds.

"Run!" I yelled again. "It'll kill you!"

"If I run, it'll kill you!"

> *You are **bleeding** and require medical attention. Bleeding is a damage-over-time effect.*

My health dropped to 50%.

"Fuck," I spat as the hybrid's creepy feet tapped forward, ready to pounce on Aaron. I yanked hard against the web and tried to tilt the sword that I still clenched in my hand, but nothing was working. There was only one thing left for me to try.

I concentrated on casting a Fire Curtain right on top of the monster, and when the flames rose from the ground, the spider-thing screeched and dropped its halberd, swiping away at the flames.

> *You have reached level 6 in **Fire Magic**!*

Aaron ran to me while the Spider was distracted and used his spear to cut away the webs that were holding me down. "That works!"

"It seems they can block ranged attacks, but area-of-effect attacks are still effective." I yanked myself up from the last strands of webbing and watched as the spider continued to struggle with the fire.

Jax was across the room, still battling solo with the other hybrid. He dodged a nasty halberd strike and rolled backwards, pulling out a vial of dark potion, and tossed it at the monster. It exploded on impact and the spider was stunned.

Jax turned his head to us and dropped to one knee. "I'm almost out of stamina!"

Aaron and I ran across the room, and I channeled another Fire Curtain on top of the spider that Jax was fighting and it had the same effect as it had on the first hybrid. It screamed and began tossing itself around erratically, trying to remove itself from the flames.

I stepped forward and slashed at one of its legs, severing it, then slammed the tip of my sword deep into its torso.

*You have reached level 5 in **Swords**!*

It screamed and swung a hand at me, knocking another 10% off my health.

Aaron charged forward with his spear and struck the same monster in the chest, and finally, the beast fell over, curling its legs into a ball.

*You have gained 950 XP!*

"One more," Aaron said.

> *You are **bleeding** and require medical attention. Bleeding is a damage-over-time effect.*

The pain made me cringe, and I was down to 35% health.

Jax started to rise back to his feet, his stamina bar recovering much faster than ours, given his higher vitality level.

The other hybrid had since shaken off its flames and turned back towards us and screeched before raising its arm in the air and clattering its teeth together wildly.

All around the Arachnid Guard, Cave Weavers began to form—about 10 of them first appearing like a hologram, and then filling out into real spider flesh.

"Make that a LOT more!" Aaron yelled. "Fuck!"

Jax bumped my shoulder and held a health potion out at me. "Take this… You won't last long without it."

I shook my head and reached into my bag. "No, I have another idea…"

We had all sustained substantial damage and were running low on stamina, so the chances of killing the guard with weavers attacking from every direction was low, and even if we did, at least one of us would likely die in the process. But I had just hit level 6 in fire magic which meant that Boiling Blood was on the table. With me well below 50% health, it seemed like it was worth a try.

I pulled out the scroll and started reading as the spiders clattered towards us, my hands trembling at the thought of getting pounced. But the words flew off page, and it took only a second for me to memorize the spell.

*Advancement! You have learned the spell:*
**Boiling Blood.**

I focused on the spell and heat filled me instantly. Something like a bubbling sounds rumbled in my ears. I felt powerful, unafraid, and…. angry. A light, reddish hue surrounded my body, and the spiders in front of me suddenly seemed like nothing but mere insects that needed to be squashed under my toes.

"Stand back," I said to my companions.

A weaver jumped towards me and I easily dodged out of the way, and slashed at it, killing it in the process. Before it had even fallen to the ground, I was already dashing to the next weaver, killing it with a fast strike, then dashing to the Arachnid guard, severing one of its legs.

The guard screeched and swung its halberd, but I was far too fast at that point and had already leapt to another weaver, slicing its body in two. The 35% speed boost of Boiling Blood didn't seem like much on paper, but with it activated, everyone else's attacks seemed like they were in slow motion, and every time something jumped at me, I was gone before they had a chance.

Aaron stood back wide-eyed, and Jax had pulled out his bow and was clipping down some of the remaining weavers when I returned my attention to the guard, severing a leg, then dashing aside and severing another.

The Arachnid Guard fell to its side and was immobile when I severed its fourth leg, and in a last-ditch effort, it attempted to spray me with another patch of sticky web—easily dodged.

> *You are **bleeding** and require medical attention. Bleeding is a damage-over-time effect.*

With my increase in willpower from Boiling Blood, I didn't even notice the pain.

Below my stat bars, I could see the icon of a blinking flame starting to fade, and I knew my time with the spell was almost up. I swung at another weaver and jumped on the back of the arachnid, driving my sword deep into the monster's back. A mix and red blood and green guts came shooting out of the thing and it screeched wildly, knowing its life was almost over.

Aaron yelled like a Viking and ran forward with his spear at full force, driving the tip right between the arachnid's breast.

The bastard was *such* a last-hit stealer.

The hybrid's legs curled and the hard-fought battle was over.

> *You have gained 1350 XP!*
>
> *Advancement! You have reached **level 10** and gained 3 attribute points. To assign your attribute points, open your status page. You can also increase any of your known skills by 1 level. Choose wisely, as your choices cannot be undone.*
>
> *You have gained 10 MP!*

My health, mana and stamina all shot to full capacity, and the bleeding stopped. Jax and Aaron's stat bars also filled to 100%, so they must have leveled as well from the encounter.

"Dude, that ability is so overpowered," Aaron said. "And your eyes looked crazy as hell—red even!" He bit down on his bottom lip and raised his hand in a high-five which I returned. Aaron turned towards Jax and offered another high-five.

Jax creased his brow and raised his hand mockingly. "What is this all about?"

Aaron sighed. "It's kind of like a handshake, but more like saying 'good job' to your friends!"

"Ahhh," Jax said and held his hand out more openly. Aaron slapped Jax's hand and Jax looked down at his palm awkwardly.

"Let's loot these things and get going," Aaron huffed. "I don't know how much more time we have."

Another female laugh filled the chamber, this time sounding much, much closer. It made the hairs on my skin stand on end.

"This place is creepy as fuck!" I spat.

"The portal is in the next room. We'll be out of here soon enough."

The two hybrids weren't carrying anything but their halberds and they were both identical.

> *You've received:* **Shimmering Halberd of Bloodletting**. *10-35 Attack Damage. Requires 20 Strength. Durability: 8/10. Quality: Average. Rarity: Rare. Weight: 5.7kg. +5 Strength. +10% Critical Chance. +50% Chance to Cause Bleeding.*

Aaron couldn't use them given their strength requirement, but because of the great stats, I placed both in my unburdening bag and watched them get sucked into the Otherworld. I planned to give one to Aaron when we got out of the dungeon, and I'd take the other to be dismantled or sold.

We watched as Jax opened the mouth of one of the hybrids and stuck his hand deep down its throat. It was gruesome to watch, but he didn't seem bothered by the fact that he was elbow deep in the strange creature's internals. When he pulled his hand out, a slimy, gray sack came sliding out with it.

"Arachnid Sack," he said. "Not too useful for Alchemy, but I can sell it for a lot to a vendor."

It seemed the things I witnessed in Eden's Gate just kept getting weirder and weirder.

Where the hybrids were standing guard, was a tall, iron door, and Aaron stepped up to it and tugged viciously. The door scraped against the stone of the floor as it swung open, and what I saw when it was fully open made me want to drive my sword into my skull so I could respawn at the runestone.

Giant spider eggs filled the room and tattered webs hung from the ceiling. There was only one creature that I could see inside, however, and that was a massive hybrid spider the size of a monster truck. Its eight enormous legs clung to a huge web that was etched at the far side of the room, and the web bounced up and down erratically as the monster went about weaving more into its web.

Unlike the guards which didn't trigger my arachnophobia to its maximum degree, the boss hybrid

409

didn't have flesh like a human and a nice set of tits to throw me off. Instead, its human-like torso was decrepit, and its flesh looked more like a corpse that had been resting under stagnant water for weeks. Its hair was matted, and while its face looked somewhat human, four massive fangs pinched together on each side of its mouth.

Frankly, it was the scariest thing I had ever seen, and I had to take a step back and catch my breath to keep from panicking.

"What the hell is that?" Aaron asked.

I turned back to have another look.

> *You have failed to inspect your target!*

> *You have failed to inspect your target!*

> *You have failed to inspect your target!*

"I can't get any information about it."

"I can't inspect it either," Jax said. "It must be a pretty high level. I do have a spell that might work though." Jax placed two fingers up to his nose and closed his eyes. A tiny sparkle rose into the sky and started floating towards the creature in silence. Eventually, the sparkle reached the creature and disappeared.

After his spell, I was able to see the creature's details.

**Name:** *Arachnid Queen Puppetmaster*
**Race:** *monster*
**Level:** *29*
**Health/Mana/Stamina:** *500/200/350*
**Status:** *unknown*

"Level 29…" I muttered. "That's higher than the Swamp Lord."

The spider turned around, raised its hands, and strings shot from its fingers and up to the ceiling. It laughed violently and moved its arms around as if it were playing with something from afar.

"It must have been what was controlling the skeletons on level two," Aaron said.

"Sorry guys, but this is the end of the road," Jax said. "We've got to turn back."

"We can't," Aaron said. He pointed towards a discolored rock to the right of the web that was a slightly lighter colored gray than the rest of the room. "That rock isn't really a rock. It's the hidden portal. We have to get there."

Jax sighed. "We can't get there. Did you not see how much trouble we had with two level 19s? That level 29 will eat us alive… literally."

Aaron shook his head. "We can't turn back." He turned to me. "This is what we came for. We have to get to that portal or everything is done. You, me, this whole world is finished."

"I understand," I said. "I really don't want to fuck with another spider, but we've got to try."

Jax shook his head. "I'm sorry, but this is as far as I can go. The creature there would sense us inside and attack before any of us got close to the portal. There's no way we would be fast enough, and sneaking is unlikely to work. Unfortunately, I'm not a Reborn. I won't get a second chance."

I nodded to Jax. "I understand. I don't think we can ask you to go any further. But is there anything you can suggest we do help our chances?"

Jax looked at the giant spider as it bounced up and down on its web. "Against that? No… Maybe if Kronos were here we've have a chance, but I suspect you'll both be respawning at that runestone soon enough." Jax kneeled and placed his hands on the floor. "I don't sense any traps inside the room if that helps."

Jax stood and I reached out to shake his hand. "Thank you for coming with us this far. We couldn't have made it without you."

"It's been fun," Jax said with a grin, and he pulled the slimy spider sack out of his bag. "And I got some decent loot too."

"Thanks," Aaron said and gave him a handshake too.

Jax turned and started back towards the entrance of the dungeon.

"I guess we're on our own now. How are we going to do this?" I asked.

"Leeroy Jenkins it?" Aaron questioned.

"Oh, hell no. That won't work."

"Well, we can't fucking kill it. That's for sure. Should we try to sneak?"

"My Sneak skill is at level 3... That won't work." My skin crawled as I watched the monster lift its creepy legs up and down off the web. "I don't even want to get close to that thing."

"You want to try Fireblast it and train it down the hall?"

"No, it has 200 mana. It probably can summon more spiders like the guards. If it does that we'll miss any shot we have at this."

"Well then, what's your idea?"

I gulped. I had an idea, but I didn't like it too much. "Stab me with your spear."

"What?"

"Stab me with your spear," I repeated.

"Yeah, I got that part. Why the hell would you want me to stab you?"

"When I cast Boiling Blood, my fear disappears. And with the huge increase in movement speed, it might be enough that I can dodge its attacks for a bit. If I can keep it distracted long enough, that should buy you time to jump into the portal."

"And then what?"

"And then I'll probably die. The likelihood of that thing not hitting me or casting a spell on me is pretty low once I get its attention."

"What? I don't want you to—"

"Look," I interrupted. "You said that this world depends on it, right? I don't want to be eaten by that thing, but the pain will be a small price to pay if you can make it to the portal and make things right."

Aaron dipped his head. He nodded slightly and sighed. "Are you sure?"

"No, not really, but fuck it. Just stab me and let's get this over with."

Aaron sucked in his bottom lip and bit down. I could tell that the idea was hard for him to cope with. He pulled his spear back and said, "Thank you, Gunnar," before slamming it hard into my leg.

"Ohhhhh shit!" I screamed as I grabbed at wound. "Why my leg?!"

"I don't want to hit any vital organs and get an accidental critical strike." He pulled the spear back and rammed it again in my shoulder."

"Ohhh fuck!" I screamed. My health was down by 30%.

He pulled the spear back and slammed it back into the exact same shoulder.

> *You are **bleeding** and require medical attention. Bleeding is a damage-over-time effect.*

"Ahhh!" I cried.

"Shhh," Aaron said. "You might attract the spider if you make too much noise."

I winced. "Why do I have the feeling you're getting enjoyment out of this?"

"Trust me I'm not."

My health was down by 40% before Aaron grabbed my head and lifted a hard, flying knee to my jaw, knocking me down and putting me below the 50% mark.

I groaned as I grabbed my wounds and picked myself back off the floor. "I'll get payback for that one day."

"If we make it through this, I'll let you." Aaron grinned.

"I'm bleeding, so I'm going to have to make this quick."

Aaron holstered his spear and nodded.

I pulled my sword out of its sheath and held it out in front of me.

"What's with the blade?" he asked.

"If I'm going to die, I might as well make it feel a little pain before it takes me out." I smiled heinously and ran inside the room.

My hands started to tremble as I got closer to the massive spider, but I cast Boiling Blood on myself before my anxiety got too extreme. My body raged with heat, and suddenly I didn't fear the spider at all, nor had a fear of death, despite knowing that death was imminent.

I shot a Fireblast at the spider Queen, and it hissed and turned to me, jaws clamping in an almost delightful manner that prey had entered its nest. It jumped off its web and scrambled towards me with an alarming speed, then jumped again like a cat pouncing on its prey.

I dodged the pounce, but it did require effort. I was faster than the beast with my Boiling Blood active, but not by the same margin as the monsters I fought in the previous room.

"Over here, asshole!" I yelled, making sure its attention stayed on me as I watched Aaron out of the corner of my eye, running for the portal.

The Queen shot a ball of webbing out of its mouth, and again I dashed to the side.

I ran in a half circle as the spider lifted each of its legs and slammed them down at me, trying its best to crush my body, and then I rolled towards its underside and heard a "Zrrrrp" sound. When I looked up, Aaron was gone... He fucking made it.

I glanced to the Boiling Blood icon under my stat bars and saw that it was already near fading. I knew it would be dead soon, but I at least wanted to get a couple more strikes off before I ended up curled in a cocoon and hung from the floor like the rest of the monster's victims.

I swung out my sword to the inner side of one of its massive legs, knocking off a small piece of its crispy outer shell.

To my surprise, the Queen screamed and reared its legs back, and I dashed from underneath it as it fell back down with a resounding thump. The beast grabbed at its head with its arms and shook around furiously as it continued to cry and scream at the top of its lungs. It looked like it was in serious pain, and I was perplexed at what was happening until I looked down at a message that I hadn't noticed the moment I made my strike.

> *You have applied* **Torment** *to Arachnid Queen Puppetmaster!*

*Fucking hell, Mythanthar!* I thought to myself. I turned and scrambled for the portal as fast as my legs would allow while the Queen continued crying out in agony.

Halfway through down the room, my Boiling Blood faded away and my feet slowed to a normal run, but I still felt like I had a +10% in run speed as I knew what was waiting behind me.

I heard the monster recovering from my on-hit effect, and I turned my head briefly to see it climb to its feet and scuttle towards me.

My heart was beating, and I kept telling myself over and over to stay calm and put everything I had into my legs.

Four more steps, three more steps, two more steps… I glanced behind me one final time and saw the pincers of the spider moving towards me, and I jumped, diving head first into the gray, discolored stone.

*Zrrrrp!*

# Chapter 30

## 01/06/0001

My body slammed onto the hard wood of a floor, and I slid forward, landing onto something tough and pointy. Beer spilled all over my head and into my eyes.

> You are **bleeding** and require medical attention. Bleeding is a damage-over-time effect.

"Fuckkkk!" I groaned.

"Gunnar?! You made it?! How?"

I rubbed my eyes, clearing it of the beer and saw that I was in a large wine cellar with beer kegs and bottles lining every inch of the walls. Aaron was standing there with a bottle in his hands.

My health was down to 25%, and I reached into my bag for a potion and bandage as I spoke. "I got a lucky on-hit effect on the spider Queen. I barely made it into the portal."

Aaron smiled. "I can't believe it…"

"Me either… If I had been a second slower, I'd be dead." I wrapped a bandage around my shoulder and leg then downed a health potion.

Aaron pulled another wine bottle off one of the racks and used the tip of his spear to pry it open. He tilted his head back and started chugging. "Have a drink to celebrate," he said, pulling another bottle off the rack and holding it out towards me.

"I'll just have some beer," I said and ducked my head under the beer that was still falling out of the broken keg. The foamy liquid tasted like heaven, and I needed it; it had been the longest day of my life.

*Spiders. Ugh...*

I lifted myself back up and shook my head when I had my fill, and Aaron tossed his wine bottle to the ground.

"Let's go find my boss." Aaron turned and climbed a tiny, wooden ladder that lead to a trap door. He pushed it open, climb up and into the castle. I followed right behind.

The floors and walls of the castle were mostly a beautiful brushed stone, but as we marched down the hallways, I noticed that many of the rooms had wood and marble features. Sculptures were everywhere, and paintings I recognized from Earth hung on the walls: The Mona Lisa, The Son of Man, Saturn Devouring His Son. I guess in Eden's Gate, Rupert Winston could have anything he wanted.

"Are we safe here?" I asked. "This is the Mastalands, right? Permadeath?"

"We're in the Mastalands, yeah. But I don't think Dr. Winston would hurt us. Be on guard in any case."

We approached a set of tall double doors, and one of them was open. I could hear the slight sound of someone humming from inside. Upon the sound reaching our ears, Aaron started into a jog.

"Hey..." I muttered and picked up the pace to keep after him.

Aaron slapped his hand against the open door and stopped at the entrance. "Dr. Winston…" he said in a desperate tone.

The humming stopped, and there was demonic hiss that answered Aaron's call.

Inside the room was Dr. Winston's Library with a view overlooking a dark, foreboding landscape. Books lined the walls, and the room looked just like I remembered from the broadcast on my first day of the game. Dr. Winston sat behind a large, wooden desk, covered in a brown robe, holding a pen over a piece of paper as if he had been writing something before he was disturbed.

Beside him was an astonishing, well-endowed woman wearing nothing but a dark red thong and dark leather boots that rose to her knees. It complemented her pink-hued skin, and her beauty rivaled that of some of the elves I had seen in the Vale. Well, except for the large demon wings that were extending from her back—that was a little weird.

The succubus held its mouth wide, revealing sharp fangs that looked like it was thirsty for our blood. I placed my hand on the hilt of my sword, not sure what to expect.

"Aaron?!" Dr. Winston said. "You… logged into Eden's Gate? Already?"

"Yeah, and there's not a lot of time. We have to talk," Aaron said.

"What? Wait. How did you get here?" He scanned Aaron up and down. "You're level six. There's no way you could have gotten past the monsters in this zone."

"I placed a hidden portal to here in a dungeon inside Gramora." Aaron shook his head. "But that's beyond the point now. Please, can you listen?"

Dr. Winston narrowed his eyes and dropped his pen. "I'm listening…"

Aaron looked up at the succubus. "Maybe without this this umm… whatever-it-is ready to violate us?"

Dr. Winston nodded his head at the succubus and she walked seductively past us and out of the room. An odd, intoxicating smell followed her and my mouth watered as she disappeared down the hall. *Deadly…*

"Don't worry," Dr. Winston said. "She can't harm you. This place is in the Mastalands, but the inside of the castle is the only place where characters cannot attack each other in any way. I made it that way in case someone sought me out."

"Why didn't you tell me what you were going to do at the keynote?!" Aaron demanded as he stormed into the room and placed his hands on Dr. Winston's desk.

Dr. Winston leaned back in his chair. "How could I tell you, Aaron? What would you have done? I trusted you, but this was too big. I had to keep much about the world a secret, including my plan at the keynote."

"You have no idea what you've done…"

"I know exactly what I've done, and I'm glad that you made the decision to join me here. Now you can have a wonderful, eternal life in a much better world."

I stepped further into the room and interrupted their debate. "Why did you block us from logging off?"

Dr. Winston looked to me and then to Aaron. "And who is this?"

"This is Gunnar Long—a player. He helped me get here." Aaron said.

Dr. Winston reached a friendly hand out to me. "Pleasure to meet you, Gunnar."

Aaron shook his hand and slammed his palm on the desk. "No! Stop! Listen! Outside… I mean on Earth right now people are trying their damnedest to shut Eden's Gate down."

Dr. Winston laughed. "They can't do that. The CPU Blockchain will make sure this world persists forever."

"No," Aaron said again. "You're a genius, Rupert, and you thought of virtually everything before you did what you did, but the one thing you underestimated was just how far people would go bring this place offline."

"And why would they do that?" Dr. Winston shrugged. "I've created a world where the crippled can walk again, where the chronically ill can live out fruitful, healthy lives. I've created an opportunity for humanity beyond what was previously possible."

"But you cut the Earth off too soon," Aaron explained. "No one believes that people are really living in here. You believe. I believe. But that's because we've experienced it. The people who are non-gamers can't get their head around it."

"Well that's too bad for them then. If they can't wrap their heads around it, I guess they'll miss their chance, but they'll never be able to shut this world down. That would take a literal global blackout, and there's no way—"

"That's exactly what they're in the process of doing right now," Aaron said.

Dr. Winston laughed again. "Impossible." He shook his head. "The Nexicon software is on far too many devices. They couldn't shut it all down... There would be far too many moving parts."

"Right now on Earth," Aaron spoke slowly, "90% of the world is probably undergoing a blackout if their plans went as intended. There'll be a near global blackout in less than half a day."

Dr. Winston shook his head again and gave a cocky smirk, but I could sense a little bit of doubt in his eyes. "It won't happen... It just won't work."

"But what if it did work?" Aaron asked. "If they shut the CPU blockchain down, we're gone. Everyone in Eden's Gate is gone forever. This world that you worked so hard to build would have been for nothing!"

Rupert swallowed hard and locked eyes with Aaron. "And what would you have me do? I can't reverse what's been done."

Aaron placed a finger on the desk. "I need you to open the communication port with Earth. Kendra should be standing by waiting for us to connect."

"I'll do no such thing!" Dr. Winston scoffed. "The whole idea of Eden's Gate is the have an isolated, real world. This is not a game!"

"Then prove it to them! Open it and prove to them that we're alive in here and that it's not just a game." Aaron's chest heaved as he stared daggers into his boss. "No one ever believed you could create something as magnificent as this, so don't underestimate other people's ability to do the impossible. My life depends on this world now as well."

Dr. Winston took a deep breath and there was a long silence.

"Please," Aaron pleaded.

"Very well," Dr. Winston said. He reached into a tiny drawer of his desk and pulled out something resembling a thin laptop that looked completely out of place in Eden's Gate. He flipped open the lid and started pressing keys as the screen lit up.

# Chapter 31

## Day 7 (Earth)

"New York is down," the Secretary of Defense exclaimed. "Most of the New England states are down."

"Good," the President replied.

"How much longer 'til we're offline here?" Senator Gates asked.

"No more than 30 minutes and we'll have global darkness," the Secretary explained.

The President gave a head nod, and his Secretary left the room.

*Beep…. Beep.*

Kendra's heart thumped when she heard her laptop and rubbed her finger over her touchpad to turn her screensaver off.

*Establishing Connection with Eden's Gate…*

"Wait!" she shouted. "I'm getting a connection!"

Her computer beeped two more times and then flashed before Dr. Winston, Aaron, and an unknown appeared on her screen.

"Hello, Kendra," Dr. Winston said with a smile.

"Rupert!" Kendra mashed a few buttons to send the image on her computer to the projector that was on the wall. She turned her laptop to the President and stood to move behind him along with Senator Gates. "I'm with the President."

"Well, hello Mr. President," Rupert said.

The President face was flat and confused. "Hello, Dr. Winston."

"I hear you have a plan to shut Eden's Gate down," The doctor said.

"Dr. Winston," the President said firmly, "what you've done is inexcusable, and I only wish that you were here on Earth so that you could face punishment for your actions."

"Mr. President, I have done nothing but created a new world and allowed millions of people to join me in this lovely place. I assure you that anyone in Eden's Gate now will be better off than on Earth."

"This is ridiculous!" Senator Gates exclaimed. "How do we know this is really Dr. Winston? This could be some sort of scam from Kendra here."

"I'm real... Everyone in here is real," Dr. Winston said. "Just as real as you sitting there. Our consciousness is just present on another plane of existence that operates under different rules."

"Hi Aaron!" Kendra said with a smile.

"Hello, Kendra. And good job." Aaron winked and raised a fist.

Dr. Winston cleared his throat. "I implore you to stop whatever it is you're doing to shut down Eden's Gate. If it worked—and that's a big if—you would be destroying millions of lives in the process."

"Lives?" Senator Gates barked. "The only lives are here on Earth! I don't know what kind of setup this is, but there is no real life inside of a computer!"

Dr. Winston chuckled and turned to the unknown man. "What don't you tell them about yourself? Tell them if you think this is real or not."

The young man in the tattered leather armor swallowed. "My name is Gunnar Long. I live... I mean I lived on 116 Sycamore St. Apartment 12 in Los Angeles, California. I worked at BestFoods before I came here, and I am definitely alive and existing inside of this game."

"Fake..." Senator Gates claimed.

The President rubbed his chin. "So more than five million people are supposedly in your world and you only have *one* guy there that doesn't work for Nexicon?"

Dr. Winston smirked. "Oh, I can show you more." He tapped on his computer a few times and selected a random player to broadcast back to Earth.

The image on Kendra's screen switched to the view of a mid-50s man walking around a green, grassy hill, picking herbs that were growing out of the soil. He whistled while he worked, not seeming to have a care in the world. A female voice called out from somewhere, "Dinner is ready! Get your ass home soon!" The man looked up and smiled.

The Dr. switched the image back to his library. "People are living their lives out here."

"That could have been anybody... a computer-generated person," Senator Gates said. "Doesn't mean a thing."

Rupert sighed. "Well, do any of you know someone who has logged in? I can give you an image of their life now."

Senator Gates leaned forward and glanced at the President and Kendra before turning back to the screen. "My niece's name is Terry Gibbins. She's one of the ones who died when she logged into your stupid game."

Dr. Winston typed the name into his computer and immediately found a Terry Gibbins. He switched the view over to her.

Terry—an early 20s lady dressed in basic cloth attire—was sitting in an inn with a few other humans, laughing and drinking beer. Festive music filled the air. She raised her mug up to one of the men that she was sitting with and their cups clanged. She took a chug out of her mug, raised out of her seat, and started dancing with a wide smile on her face.

The image flipped back to Dr. Winston's castle.

"Was that the right girl?" Dr. Winston asked.

The Senator's eyes softened and his jaw was slack as he gave a slight nod of his head. "It looked like her, but I've never seen her like that," he muttered. He bowed his head low and went into thought. "She can't possibly be that happy."

"She's alive Senator. Let Eden's Gate be," Dr. Winston said. "It's up to you how you want to handle new people entering the game, but I'm sure you can see how real we are here. Why would you want to destroy us; destroy Terry?"

Senator Gates looked up to the president but he didn't speak.

"What we're doing here is wrong, Senator," Kendra said. "We need to put an end to this shutdown now." She turned her head towards the president. "Mr. President?"

The Secretary of Defense poked his head into the room, holding a phone up to his ear. "10 minutes and we'll be at global," he said. He eyed everyone in the room, noticing that the tone had changed and clicked off his phone. "Is everything okay?"

The room sat in silence.

"A few days ago, I was right there with you on Earth," Aaron spoke. "And now I'm here, no different than before."

The President clenched his jaw and then looked up to the Secretary of Defense. "End the blackout now, and start bringing everything back online."

There was an audible sigh from Kendra. "Yes! Thank you…"

Senator Gates sat silent, lost in his own confusion.

"But we haven't finished the operation, sir," the Secretary replied.

"I want you to issue press releases in the morning saying that the operation was successful and that Eden's Gate is offline," the President ordered. "Continue with the recall and destruction of the VR units, and don't stop until we have them all."

"But we—" the Secretary started.

"That's an order, Bill. I want the public to think that Eden's Gate is no more, but we're going to leave it running for now. We've received sufficient evidence that leads me to believe that people are actually living inside the game… or at least something is going on that we don't understand."

The Secretary's eyes dropped, and his face twisted as he tried to process the President's words. He nodded and turned to exit the room.

"Dr. Winston," the President said. "If we're leaving your world up, I'd like to maintain an open line of communication."

Dr. Winston shook his head. "I'm afraid I can't do that, Mr. President. Eden's Gate needs to operate outside of any Earthly influence."

"For peace of mind, doctor," the President urged. "I'm compromising for you, so you compromise with me. A monthly meeting would be sufficient."

Rupert snarled. He didn't like compromises, but he didn't want to deal with more attempts to shut down his creation. "Every 6 months, I'll open the communication port and we can have a discussion."

The President shifted uncomfortably in his chair. "Fine... So long as your world isn't causing any yet-to-be-seen harm, we'll reconvene in 6 months."

Dr. Winston nodded. "Thank you, Mr. President. Thank you, Kendra."

The screen flashed and the 'No Signal' message reappeared.

# Chapter 32

## *01/07/0001*

Dr. Winston slapped his hands together and exhaled. "Well, that's taken care of now. Thank you, Aaron." He smiled as he scanned up and down his friend's attire. "I guess you must have killed a few orcs on your way here?"

"More than just orcs," Aaron replied.

"Well, I never would've taken you as the heroic type."

Aaron chuckled and slapped a hard hand down on my shoulder. "I'm hardly a hero. If it weren't for Gunnar here, I would've never made it."

Dr. Winston smiled. "Thank you, Gunnar."

"I have a request," I said sharply.

"Oh?" Dr. Winston asked with a raised eyebrow. "What's that?"

"My girlfriend logged into the world with me, and I'd like to find her. I was hoping you could tell me where she is."

"I see…" Dr. Winston eyes lowered and he looked thoughtful as he considered my plea. "I'm trying my best to avoid playing 'God' of Eden's Gate. I want everything to happen naturally here just like a real

433

world. But... because of your assistance, I suppose I can make an exception." He turned back to his computer. "What's your girlfriend's name?"

I stepped forward and my heart started to race a little. Finally, I was going to be pointed in the right direction. "Rachel Rollins," I said.

"Rachel... Rollins..." the doctor said as he keyed the name into his computer. He sighed and turned back towards me. "I'm not showing anyone in the system by that name. Could she have selected a different character name after logging in?"

I thought hard about any other names that may have used. "She used the name Puff Muffin in Battle League and her forum name was Rachel604907."

"Well, you can't use numbers in your Eden's Gate username." Dr. Winston typed in 'Puff Muffin' and searched for it as well. "And sorry, no Puff Muffin either," he said shaking his head. "Maybe she logged out of the world before the keynote event. I'm sorry, Gunnar..."

"Just Rachel?" I asked.

Dr. Winston tapped the keys once more. "I'm showing over four hundred entries with some variation of Rachel as a first or last name."

My heart sank. I lifted a knuckle to my chin and shook my head defeatedly. Aaron placed a hand on my shoulder.

The doctor sighed. "Gunnar Long is your real name, right?"

"Yeah..." I muttered. "I used my real name."

"Well, then if she's somewhere out there in this world, you've still got a chance to find her."

I looked up attentively. "How?"

"Make a name for yourself, Gunnar." The doctor smirked. "Build a city, conquer a town, slay a king, or become a hero. There's no internet or television in Eden's Gate, but songs of greatness can travel to every corner of the world. If she hears your song, then she'll surely come to you."

That wasn't the answer I was expecting. I was actually beginning to feel a little angry at the situation.

"Why did you prevent us from logging off?" I asked. "What if I want I to go back to Earth? What if I hate it here?"

"Is that how you feel?" the doctor asked.

I bit my inner lip but I didn't speak. It wasn't how I felt, but I didn't like my life to be in someone else's hands. I didn't like the fact that I couldn't find Rachel due to someone else's actions.

"If you were back on Earth, and I offered you a chance to play the brand new, ultra-high-tech, cutting-edge, portable Nexicon gaming device, would you want to play?"

My eyes narrowed. Why was he changing the topic? "Yeah, of course I would want to play."

"And now that you're here in Eden's Gate? If I pulled a gaming device out of my desk drawer and handed it to you, would you want to play?"

"No…" I muttered low.

"Exactly," the doctor cooed. "Back on Earth, people are constantly trying to escape, constantly trying to get away from their mundane and plastic lives. Many of them feel trapped. But here? You can *live*… Your life is how you make it." The doctor stood and placed both his hands on my shoulders. "Go out there and live, Gunnar." He looked towards Aaron. "Both of you."

I nodded slightly as I took in his words. Even if I couldn't find Rachel, the last several days I spent in Eden's Gate had been the most exhilarating of my life. I had met interesting people, made great friends, and every day had been an adventure. I finally felt like more than just some lame stock boy at a grocery store.

"Well, then," Dr. Winston said, stepping back from me. "Where did you place that portal, Aaron?"

"In the wine cellar." Aaron tilted his head guiltily. "We had a few drinks... It had been a long day."

Dr. Winston chuckled. "It's quite alright."

"We can't go back through that portal," I said. "The level 29 spider is still there."

"Oh, don't worry about going back through the portal," Dr. Winston said. "I'm going to have that thing closed-up immediately. I need my privacy and can't have random people just teleporting inside my home." He threw a stink eye at Aaron. "I'll port you both back to the city of your choice."

I looked over to Aaron. "Linden?"

Aaron nodded in agreement.

# Chapter 33

*01/07/0001*

The leaves crackled under the hooves of our caravan as we traveled through Edgewood forest. Aaron, Jax and I each sat on three mighty horses that the elves of the Vale had commissioned us, and in front of us was one of the Queen's workers, his horse pulling a small wagon with some initial building supplies and surveying tools.

Sora sat curled up in front of me. She had grown three times the size she was since I last saw her, and having her on my shoulders for extended amounts of time was impossible. She was getting heavy, and her claws could pierce my armor.

"This looks like a good spot," I said as we entered a fair sized, flat open clearing. "We wouldn't have to cut down many trees here."

"Maybe none at all," Jax commented.

"What do you think?" I asked Aaron. "Deep enough in the forest that we wouldn't be visible from the Freelands, but not so far that we could leave the forest each day without it being a burden."

"Works for me," Aaron said.

"Let's stop here!" I yelled to the elf. "We'll build in this location."

437

The elf stopped and nodded, hopping off his horse and tying it to a nearby tree. Me and my two companions followed suit and tied our horses off as well.

After Dr. Winston teleported Aaron and I back to Linden, we found Jax strolling into the town center right at the same time. He looked exhausted as we gave him a brief rundown of how we returned to town without getting killed by the monstrous spider, and he shared how he'd had an amazing time running from the pissed off weavers that were apparently a lot more agitated when he made his way back out of the dungeon.

The next morning, we all headed for the Vale, where we let Queen Faranni know that we were ready to build our homes. Within minutes, the Queen had our caravan ready, and Jax decided to accompany us as he had yet to visit the forest of Edgewood. Adeelee wasn't around at the time—off on one adventure or another.

The elf unlatched his wagon and drove two stakes in the ground at the spot we indicated to place our homes. He hopped back on his horse and gave us a nod. "I'll return with builders and more supplies. It shouldn't take us more than a few days to have your homes completed." When it was clear that we understood, he rode off back towards the Vale.

The four of us walked casually through Edgewood, Aaron and I getting a feel for the place that we'd be planting roots and Jax surveying the area for game. I grudgingly allowed Sora to perch herself on my shoulders, despite all the added weight.

Thin, white-barked trees stood tall all through Edgewood, layered with a few dark trees with larger, wider trunks. The forest was young alright—much different than the ancient mammoths of Addenfall or the jungle overgrowth in the Vale. It was beautiful though; rustic flowers were littered between the trees and the sound of songbirds filled the air in every direction.

"What are you planning to do now that Eden's Gate isn't on the verge of being wiped out?" I asked Aaron.

Aaron shrugged. "I think I'll take up crafting. Carpentry, armorsmithing... something along those lines. Get some hunting skills under my belt like Jax here. Maybe find me a hot wife to keep me warm at night." He smiled wide. "And what about you? What do you plan to do?"

I took a deep breath and looked out to the depths of the forest. "Well, the doctor said that I should make a name for myself, right?"

Aaron nodded.

"Then I won't stop until everyone in this world knows my name. I'll climb Dragon's Crest, and I'll find me a castle like Dr. Winston's..." I turned around towards the stakes that the elves drove into the ground. "Or maybe I'll just build one." I smirked at the thought. "Gunnar Long... Lord of Edgewood. I could put this place on the map, ya know?"

"Ambitious..." Aaron said. "You might want to start with a guild first."

"A guild?"

"And I could be your first member." Aaron smiled, lifted two fingers to his chin and rubbed. "The guild crafter, 'The Sizzler'. That would be pretty cool."

"Hmm..." I said with a chuckle. "I like the sound of that."

I pulled up my stats and threw the LP from my last level into Sneak. My sneaking skills were a little weak considering how often I used it, so I figured it need a boost.

"And there's a certain elf girl back in the Vale that I'll be paying a few visits to." I dumped all three of my AP into Charisma.

"Hell yeah!" Aaron said. He reached a fist out towards me, and we fist bumped.

Jax kneeled and grabbed a handful of dry leaves. "Something big was through here recently." He stood back up and continued ahead of us slower, his eyes full of caution. "Be on alert," he said low.

"So what should we name this guild?" Aaron asked quietly. "How about the—"

Jax suddenly fell awkwardly on his back, cutting off our conversation. He slid a few inches on the ground and his feet lifted into the air. He hung aimlessly by one of his ankles, snared by a tight, black rope. A necklace and several gold coins fell out of his pocket, chinking on the ground below.

We immediately ran to help him, but before we had made it two steps, two small, steel arrows whizzed right in front of us, slamming into the closest tree.

"Don't move any further," a calm voice said.

Aaron and I held up our hands and turned to see an elf ambling towards us. Sora let out her best roar. It was an actual roar now, but she was still too small for it to scare anyone.

The elf looked much like the High Elves of Mist Vale but his skin was almost devoid of color. He wasn't really 'dark', but it looked like something had sucked all the saturation out of him, giving his skin a light, grayish color. He was wearing a stiff, polished black armor that was obviously not metal, but quite a bit more rigid than leather. His fist was pointed towards us, and attached the top of the strange gauntlet that was covering his arm was a device with a gleaming arrow ready to be unleashed.

"Edgewood is not a part of the Freelands, humans."

"Kneel," I whispered to Aaron.

"What?" he asked. "He'll kill us."

"Kneel," I said again and slapped Aaron on his chest. I dropped to my knee and bowed my head. Aaron followed suit.

The elf chuckled low. "You may rise."

Aaron and I both stood, and I glanced up to see Jax swinging back and forth clumsily, trying to get his foot unleashed. It was a bit comical given how poised he usually was.

"We mean you no harm," I said to the elf then nodded towards Aaron. "This is our home now." I pointed up to the hanging Jax. "He's just tagging along for today."

"Humans are not permitted to live in Edgewood," he spat. He stepped forward and waved his gauntlet at us. "And you travel through here at your own peril."

"We have permission to build here from Queen Faranni," I explained.

"Hah!" the elf huffed.

"I have the building rights here." I reached for my pocket to get the parchment that Queen Faranni had given me that morning that stated that I had unlimited rights of building and passage in Edgewood.

The elf jabbed his gauntlet towards me. "Slowly…"

I moved slower as I slipped the paper out of my pocket and held it out towards the elf. He grabbed the paper and opened it with his one free hand. As he read it, he glanced up to me and back down at the paper several times. Eventually, he stepped back and lowered his gauntlet.

"This is unusual," he said as he handed the paper back to me. "But I respect our Queen's wishes." He cleared his throat and unenthusiastically said, "Welcome to Edgewood Forest."

"Thank you," Aaron and I both said in unison.

I pointed up towards Jax, who was flailing around like a troubled caterpillar. "Can we cut our friend down?"

The elf smirked, lifted his gauntlet, and shot an arrow at the rope that was attached the tree. He had impossible aim, severing the rope with a single volley and causing Jax to fall to the ground with a loud thump.

Aaron and I ran over to Jax to make sure that he was okay, and he groaned and held on to his back as we helped him to his feet. I dropped to the ground and began to pick up his fallen gold coins, and when I reached for the necklace that fell out his pocket, I froze.

At the end of the necklace was a black medallion with a Sparrow carved onto its face.

Jax bent over and quickly swiped the necklace off the ground. He jammed it into his pocket and smiled at me as I handed him back his coins.

Jax... was a Sparrow? A million questions ran through my mind. Was he the guy who killed me that night when I ran off with the sword? He had a motive, I suppose. But if so, why had he continued to help me... even going as far as joining me on a dungeon crawl?

"I appreciate that you show respect to elves... even those of us with darker skin. And I find it rather odd that this panther isn't clawing your eyes out." The dark elf held out his hand for a handshake. "My name is Donovan Sylvari. I can't guarantee the other inhabitants of Edgewood will be as welcoming as I."

I shook the elf's hand, his words barely being processed by my brain as I continue to struggle with the idea that Jax was a Sparrow. "Gunnar," I said back.

"Aaron."

"Jax Horn."

I wouldn't confront Jax then. Not while I was in a strange forest in front of a dangerous, dark elf. Jax seemed oblivious to the fact that I knew about the Sparrows as he smiled and gripped the newcomer's hand. I needed to keep my mouth shut and gather information as I waited for the right time.

I took a deep breath and turned to Aaron. In a short period, he had become something like a best friend of mine—something I had never had back on Earth. And even if Jax was a Sparrow, it was hard for me to think of him as anything other than a friend. Both of them taught me the importance of friendship—the one thing that I promised Rachel I'd work on before I placed the Nexicon visor on my head that day.

Promise fulfilled? I hoped.

Whether Rachel was in the game or not and whether Jax was a Sparrow, I was ready to continue my progression in Eden's Gate. I would find that castle—or build one. I'd level up and carve my name in the world until people around the world sung songs about me. I'd make new friends. Lots of them, hopefully. Start a guild even.

If Rachel was out there, maybe we'd find each other. *One day...* I thought. Until then I planned to live my new life and make Eden's Gate my bitch... starting with Edgewood Forest.

I smiled wide. "It's a pleasure to meet you, Donovan Sylvari."

# GUNNAR LONG

| | |
|---|---|
| Race: | Human |
| Level: | 10 (Progress 0%) |
| Title: | None |
| Health/Mana/Stamina: | 140/130/120 |
| Strength: | 18+ |
| Dexterity: | 20 |
| Intelligence: | 24+ |
| Vitality: | 14+ |
| Wisdom: | 14 |
| Willpower: | 13 |
| Charisma: | 13 |
| AR Rating: | 25 |
| Resists: | |

10% Fire Resistance
15% Water Resistance

Traits:

Elven Touch

Primary Skills:

First Aid Lvl 3: progress 30%
Sneak Lvl 4: progress 0%
Inspect Lvl 3: progress 30%
Tinkering Lvl 1: progress 0%
Summon Beast: Mastered
Inscription Lvl 1: progress 30%

Combat Skills:

Dodge Lvl 4: progress 20%
Small Blades Lvl 2: progress 0%
Backstab Lvl 1: progress 0%
Archery Lvl 4: progress 65%
Block Lvl 2: progress 25%
Swords Lvl 5: progress 25%
Snipe Shot Lvl 2: progress 20%
Dirty Fighting Lvl 1: progress 0%

Magic Skills:

Fire Magic Lvl 6: progress 5%
Divine Magic Lvl 1: progress 50%

# Author's Notes

Thank you so much. I can't express how much I appreciate the fact that you not only picked up my story but also stuck through it all the way through the end.

I consider myself a gamer just as much as an author. I was a gamer long before I even started my first day in school. My first experience with RPGs was a gem called Shining in The Darkness for the Sega Genesis. The first time "Sorcerer 1 casts level 1 BOLT" fell across my screen, my life changed forever.

My first foray in the MMORPGS was Ultima Online, which again was a life-changing event. There's something special about everyone's first MMO experience, and I'll never forget mine. I was the leader of a PvP guild on the Atlantic Server, and the highlight of my day was logging in and spending time with my online friends who often felt closer to me than my friends in real-life. [You can expect lots of PvP in future books! Oh yes!]

I went on to play every notable MMO from EverQuest, to Ascheron's Call to Dark age of Camelot to World of Warcraft. I could continue with the list... Age of Conan... Elder Scrolls Online... but my long, long list of games would stretch on for an eternity.

Eventually, I found myself leaving every MMO at some point or another. It wasn't because I wasn't having fun, but because my playtime often felt laced with guilt, and I'd find myself asking, "Why am I wasting so many hours playing this?" Well, the answer was clear— because it was fucking fun! But my more responsible consciousness always won out and told me to get off my ass and be productive.

I've been a fiction writer for years now, and before that I was an avid reader, so you can't imagine how stoked I was when I discovered LitRPG. It's like I can have a gaming experience without spending hours upon hours of my life grinding MOBs and have a more personal storyline in the process. It's something that a non-gamer can enjoy but a gamer can relish. Without a doubt, this was the most fun I've had putting pen to paper.

While LitRPG is still new, I've noticed that many of the stories have Mary Sue characters who can do no harm, make perfect choices or are nearly invincible in comparison with the other characters in the world, so I knew I was taking a chance when I created Eden's Gate. I didn't want to make Gunner the idealized hero who always makes the right moral choices that I—or readers—would root for him to make, nor did I want to make him a super-villain. Instead I wanted Gunner to be a "shade of gray" like most people would be (even if they don't want to admit it) if they were faced with similar situations.

Eden's Gate isn't just a story about a guy who's gaining levels and trying to find his girlfriend but a story of Gunner's personal journey from someone who's flawed, awkward and a little standoffish due the difficulties that he's faced in the real world, to a guy who realizes the value of friends and family through the help of his new home.

So yes, I know it stings a little when Gunnar does things like running off with Kronos' sword, but remember Jax wasn't the perfect hero either. He let his friend go back down in the cave alone to die, not yet knowing that Gunnar was a Reborn, and he gave no indication of sharing any of the small fortune that he was going to get for the sword. He might have even killed Gunner. Did he? He's a Sparrow. Or is he? We still don't know Jax's true motives, and I'm not about to spoil it for you. You'll have to read Book 2! *Evil Laugh*

Basically, Gunnar and some of the other characters made—and will make—some bad choices, but every mistake is a chance for them to grow. I enjoy the overpowered, virtuous, Mary Sue story from time to time, but I'm not good at writing those. I like to explore that "shade of gray" that I mentioned earlier and see my characters come out a little different from where they started, and I can't wait to see how Gunner and the rest of the crew turn out in the end.

Again, thanks so much for reading the first book of Eden's Gate, and if LitRPG readers enjoy it, I'll continue writing more in the genre. Please, if you liked my book leave me a review on Amazon. It would be super appreciated and the best support that you could give me as an author. I'll write my next book whether you review it or not, but a great review would be some awesome encouragement to get me to write faster!

-Edward

If you want to know as soon as the next book in the Eden's Gate saga is available join my mail list and check me out here:

http://www.edwardbrody.com

https://www.facebook.com/authoredwardbrody

http://amazon.com/author/edwardbrody

You can also email me at any time.
edward@edwardbrody.com

27282311R00267

Printed in Great Britain
by Amazon